n of the World

•Ironpass

•Northwarden

•Highcastle

OLD

THE BLACKWOOD

•Dolth

Euper•

Rodez

Ran

•Romney

•Tiburn

Bas-Tyra

Sadara

•Silden

Cheam

Rillanon

ac's Cross

dor

•Timons

THE
KINGDOM
OF
ROLDEM

ny's Vale

he
ey
nge

THE KINGDOM SEA

GREEN REACHES

Deep Taunton•

Mallow Haven

The Peaks of Tranquillity

Pointer's Head•

OF GREAT KESH

Rise of a Merchant Prince

Rise of a
Merchant Prince

Volume II of the Serpentwar Saga

Raymond E. Feist

William Morrow and Company, Inc. • *New York*

Library of Congress Cataloging-in-Publication Data

Feist, Raymond E.
    Rise of a merchant prince / Raymond E. Feist.
        p.   cm.—(Serpentwar saga; v. 2)
    ISBN 0-688-12409-7
    I. Title.   II. Series: Feist, Raymond E. Serpentwar saga; v. 2.
    PS3556.E446R5   1995
    813'.54—dc20   95-34380
                                                                            CIP

Printed in the United States of America

First Edition

1 2 3 4 5 6 7 8 9 10

BOOK DESIGN BY CINDY DUNNE

*This book is dedicated to
Diane and David Clark,
good friends*

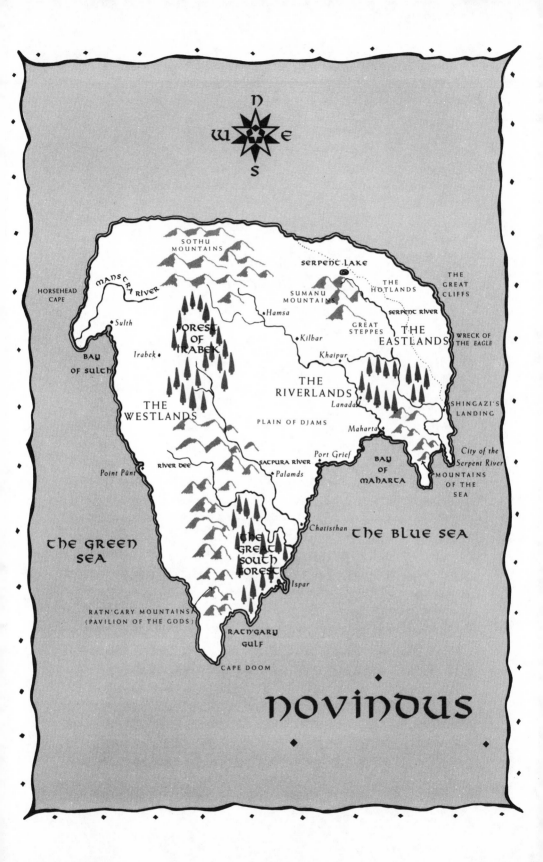

Cast of Characters

AGLARANNA—Elf Queen in Elvandar, wife of Tomas, mother of
 Calin and Calis

ALFRED—corporal from Darkmoor

AVERY, ABIGAIL—daughter of Roo and Karli

AVERY, DUNCAN—cousin of Roo

AVERY, HELMUT—son of Roo and Karli

AVERY, RUPERT "ROO"—young merchant of Krondor, son of Tom
 Avery

AVERY, TOM—teamster, Roo's father

AZIZ—sergeant at Shamata

BETSY—serving girl at the Inn of the Seven Flowers

BOLDAR BLOOD—mercenary hired by Miranda in the Hall of Worlds

BORRIC—King of the Isles, twin brother of Prince Erland, brother of
 Prince Nicholas, father of Prince Patrick

CALIN—elf heir to the throne of Elvandar, half brother of Calis, son of
 Aglaranna and King Aidan

CALIS—"The Eagle of Krondor," special agent of the Prince of
 Krondor, Duke of the Court, son of Aglaranna and Tomas, half
 brother of Calin

CARLINE—Dowager Duchess of Salador, aunt of the King

CHALMES—ruling magician at Stardock

CROWLEY, BRANDON—trader at Barret's Coffee House

DE LOUNGVILLE, ROBERT "BOBBY"—sergeant major of Calis's
 Crimson Eagles

DE SAVONA, LUIS—former soldier, assistant to Roo

DUNSTAN, BRIAN—the Sagacious Man, leader of the Mockers, used to be known as Lysle Rigger

ELLIEN—town girl in Ravensburg

ERLAND—brother of the King and Prince Nicholas, uncle of Prince Patrick

ESTERBROOK, JACOB—wealthy merchant of Krondor, father of Sylvia

ESTERBROOK, SYLVIA—Jacob's daughter

FADAWAH—general leading the Emerald Queen's army

FREIDA—Erik's mother

GALAIN—elf in Elvandar

GAMINA—adopted daughter of Pug, sister of William, wife of James, mother of Arutha

GAPI—general in the Emerald Queen's army

GASTON—wagon dealer in Ravensburg

GORDON—corporal at Krondor

GRAVES, KATHERINE "KITTY"—girl thief in Krondor

GREYLOCK, OWEN—captain in the Prince's service

GRINDLE, HELMUT—merchant, father of Karli, partner of Roo

GRINDLE, KARLI—daughter of Helmut, later wife of Roo Avery, mother of Abigail and Helmut

GUNTHER—Nathan's apprentice

GWEN—town girl in Ravensburg

HOEN, JOHN—manager of Barret's

HUME, STANLEY—trader at Barret's

JACOBY, FREDERICK—founder of Jacoby and Sons, traders

JACOBY, HELEN—wife of Randolph

JACOBY, RANDOLPH—son of Frederick, brother of Timothy, husband of Helen

JACOBY, TIMOTHY—son of Frederick, brother of Randolph

JAMES—Duke of Krondor, father of Arutha, grandfather of James and Dash

JAMESON, ARUTHA—Lord Vencar, Baron of the Prince's Court, son of Duke James

JAMESON, DASHEL "DASH"—younger son of Arutha, grandson of James

JAMESON, JAMES "JIMMY"—elder son of Arutha, grandson of James

JAMILA—madam at the White Wing

JASON—waiter at Barret's, later accountant for Avery and Son and the Bitter Sea Company

JEFFREY—wagon driver for Jacoby and Sons

KALIED—ruling magician at Stardock

KURT—bullying waiter at Barret's

LENDER, SEBASTIAN—litigator/solicitor at Barret's Coffee House

McKELLER—head waiter at Barret's

MILO—innkeeper in Ravensburg, father of Rosalyn

MIRANDA—magician and ally of Calis and Pug

NAKOR THE ISALANI—gambler, magic user, friend of Calis

PATRICK—Prince of Krondor, son of Prince Erland, nephew of the King and Prince Nicholas

PUG—magician, Duke of Stardock, cousin of the King, father of Gamina

RIVERS, ALISTAIR—innkeeper of the Happy Jumper

ROSALYN—Milo's daughter, wife of Rudolph, mother of Gerd

RUDOLPH—baker in Ravensburgh

SHATI, JADOW—corporal in Calis's company

TANNERSON, SAM—thief in Krondor

TOMAS—Warleader of Elvandar, husband of Aglaranna, father of Calis

VINCI, JOHN—merchant in Sarth

VON DARKMOOR, ERIK—soldier in Calis's Crimson Eagles

VON DARKMOOR, MANFRED—Baron of Darkmoor, half brother of Erik

VON DARKMOOR, MATHILDA—Baroness of Darkmoor, mother of Manfred

WILLIAM—Knight-Marshal of Krondor, Pug's son, Gamina's adopted brother, uncle of Jimmy and Dash

BOOK II

Roo's Tale

Wealth, howsoever got, in England makes
Lords of mechanics, gentlemen of rakes;
Antiquity and birth are needless here;
'Tis Impudence and money makes a peer.

—Daniel Defoe
THE TRUE-BORN ENGLISHMAN, PT. I

Prologue

Demonia

THE SOUL SCREAMED.

The demon turned, and as its gaping maw was set in a permanent grin, the only hint of its increased delight was a slight widening of its eyes, black orbs resembling those of a shark: flat and lifeless. It studied the jar it held for a moment, its only possession.

This soul was especially active and the demon had been fortunate to find it and keep it. Placing the jar under its chin, the demon closed its eyes and felt the energy flow into it from the jar. The creature's emotional makeup knew nothing that could be called happiness, only lessened states of fear or anger, but the surge of feeling within was as close to happiness as the creature could know. Each time the soul within the jar struggled, the energy created filled the little demon's mind with new ideas.

As if suddenly concerned its toy would be taken from it by one of its more powerful brethren, the demon glanced around. The hall was one of many in the grand palace of Cibul, capital of the now destroyed Saaur race.

Then the demon remembered: destroyed save those who had fled through a magic gate. It felt its anger return, and then the emotion quickly fled. As a minor demon, it was not intelligent, only cunning, and it didn't fully understand why the escape of a small part of this nearly obliterated race was important. But it was, for the Demon Lords were even now gathered upon the plains to the east of the city of Cibul, inspecting the site of the now closed rift through which the Saaur survivors had fled.

The Lords of the Fifth Circle had attempted once to open the portal, managing to keep it open long enough to slip a tiny demon through, before it collapsed upon itself, sealing the rift between the two realms and stranding the tiny demon on the other side of the rift. There was much consultation among the greater demons on reopening that rift and gaining entrance to this new realm.

The demon wandered the halls, oblivious to the ravages around it. Tapestries that had taken a generation to weave were torn from the walls and trodden upon, soiled by dirt and blood. The demon cracked a Saaur rib bone underfoot and absently kicked it aside. At last it came to its secret room, the one it had claimed as its own while the Host of the Fifth Circle resided on this cold planet. Leaving the demon realm was a terrible experience, thought the young demon. This had been the demon's first journey to this realm, and it wasn't sure it cared much for the pain of transition.

The feasting had been glorious; never had it known such a wealth of food, even though it was limited to scraps from the feasting pits, thrown out by the mightiest of the host as they fed. But scraps or not, the demon had devoured much and had grown. And that was creating problems for itself.

It sat down, attempting to find a comfortable position as its body changed. The feasting had continued for nearly a year and many of the lesser demons had grown. This particular demon had grown faster than most, though it still hadn't matured enough to have developed significant intelligence or a sexual identity.

Looking down at the plaything, the demon laughed, a silent gaping of jaws and sucking of wind. The mortal eye could not behold the thing within the jar. The demon, who didn't have a name yet, had been most fortunate to snare this particular soul. A great demon captain, almost a lord, had fallen to mighty magic even as the great Tugor had crushed and eaten the leader of the Saaur. One of the Saaur magic users, a powerful one, had destroyed the demon captain, but at the cost of his own life. The little demon might not be intelligent, but it was quick, and without hesitation it had seized the fleeing soul force of the dead magic user.

The demon inspected the device again, the soul jar, and poked at it. The magic soul within rewarded it by thrashing, if something without a body could be said to thrash.

The demon shifted its weight. It knew it was getting more powerful, but the nearly nonstop feeding was at an end. The last of the Saaur were dead and devoured, and now the demon host was depending on lesser animals for food, animals with negligent soul force. There were some client races, who would breed children, some of which would go to the feasting pits, but that meant slow growth in this realm. Its body would continue to mature, but not significantly until the next realm had been entered.

Cold, the demon thought as it glanced around the large room, ignorant of its original use: a bedroom for one of the Saaur leader's many wives. The native realm was one of wild energies and pulsing heat, where the demons of the Fifth Circle grew like wild things, devouring one another, until strong enough to escape and serve the Demon King and his lords and captains. This demon had but vague recollections of its own beginning, remembering only anger and fear, and an occasional moment of pleasure as it devoured something.

The demon settled down on the floor. With a changing body, it couldn't seem to find a comfortable position. Its back itched, and with certainty it knew wings would grow there soon, tiny at first, then growing larger as it rose in power. The demon was clever enough to know it would have to fight to gain rank, so it had better rest. It had been lucky so far, as the critical periods in its growth had come during the war on this world, and most of the host were too occupied with devouring the inhabitants of this world to contest in their own ranks.

Others were now fighting, and the losers would add strength to the winners as they were devoured; any demon without enough rank was a fair target for another save when a lord or captain demanded obedience. It was simply the way of this race, and each who fell was considered unworthy of a second thought. This demon considered that there must be a better way to gain more strength than an open challenge and outright attack. But it couldn't think of what it could be.

Glancing around what had once been a regal and richly appointed dwelling, the demon closed its eyes, but not before glancing one last time at the soul jar. Feeding might cease awhile, and with it physical growth, but it had learned during the war that physical growth, while impressive, wasn't as important as knowing things. The contents of the soul jar were a being rich in knowledge, and this little demon meant to have that knowledge. The demon placed the jar against its forehead and mentally prodded the soul, causing more thrashing, and the energy that resulted flowed into the demon. Powerful, like a drug to a mortal, the sensation was among the most glorious known to demonkind. The demon felt something new in its experience: satisfaction. Soon it would be smarter, know things, and then it would be able to use more than animal cunning to gain rank and a position of power.

And when the Demon Lords finally discovered a way to open fully the gate that had been sealed behind the fleeing Saaur, then the Demon Host of the Fifth Circle would follow and then there would be ample opportunity to feed upon the Saaur and upon whatever other intelligent, soul-bearing creatures lived upon the world of Midkemia.

One

Return

A SHIP SWEPT INTO THE HARBOR.

Black and dangerous, it moved like a dark hunter bearing down on its prey. Three tall masts, majestic under full sail, propelled the warship into the harbor of a great city as other ships gave way. Although she looked like a great pirate vessel from the distant Sunset Islands, her foremast flew the Royal Ensign, and all who saw the ship knew that the King's brother was returning home.

High aloft that ship, a young man worked quickly, reefing the mizzen topsail. Roo paused a moment as he tied the final reef point, and looked across the harbor at the City of Krondor.

The Prince's city spread out along the docks, rose on hills to the south, and spread out of sight to the north. The panorama was impressive as the ship sped in from the sea. The young man—eighteen years of age at the next Midsummer's festival— had thought on numerous occasions over the past year and more that he would never see the city again. Yet here he was, finishing up his watch atop the mizzen mast of the *Freeport Ranger*, a ship under the command of Admiral Nicholas, brother to the King of the Kingdom of the Isles and uncle to the Prince of Krondor.

Krondor was the second most important city in the Kingdom of the Isles, the capital of the Western Realm and seat of power for the Prince of Krondor, heir to the throne of the Isles. Roo could see the multitude of small buildings scattered across the hills surrounding the harbor, the vista dominated by the Prince's palace, which sat atop a steep hill hard against the water. The majesty of the palace was in stark contrast to the rude buildings that lined the waterfront close by, warehouses and chandlers' shops, sail- and rope-makers, carpenters and sailor's inns. Second only to the Poor Quarter as a haven for thugs and thieves, the waterfront was thrown by the proximity of the palace into an even more seedy aspect.

Yet Roo was pleased to see Krondor, for now he was a free man. He glanced one last time at his work, ensuring that the sail was properly reefed, and moved quickly along the footrope with a sure balance learned while crossing treacherous seas for nearly two years.

Roo considered the oddity of facing his third spring in a row without a winter. The topsy-turvy seasons of the land on the other side of the world had contrived to provide Roo and his boyhood friend, Erik, with such a situation, and Roo found the notion both amusing and oddly disquieting.

He shinnied down a sheet, reaching the top of the mizzenmast ratline. Roo didn't particularly like top work, but as one of the smaller and more nimble men in the crew, he was often told to go aloft and unfurl or reef the royals and topgallants. He scampered down the ratline and landed lightly on the deck.

Erik von Darkmoor, Roo's only friend as a boy, finished his task of tying off a yard brace to a cleat, then hurried to the rail as they sped past other ships in the harbor. A full two heads taller and twice the bulk of his friend, Erik made with Roo as unlikely a pair as any two boys could have been. While Erik was stronger than any boy in their hometown of Ravensburg, Roo was among the smallest. While Erik would never be called handsome, he wore an open and friendly expression that others found likable; Roo had no illusions about his own appearance. He was homely by any standards, with a pinched face, eyes that were narrowed and darting around as if constantly looking for threats, and a nearly permanent expression that could only be called furtive. But on those rare occasions when he smiled, or laughed, a warmth was revealed that made him far from unattractive. It was that roguish humor and willingness to brave trouble that had attracted Erik to Roo when they were children.

Erik pointed and Roo nodded at those ships moving away from

their own as the *Freeport Ranger* was given right of way to the royal docks below the palace. One of the older sailors laughed and Roo turned to ask, "What?"

"Prince Nicky's going to irritate the Harbormaster again." Erik, his hair almost bleached white by the sun, looked at the sailor, who had blue eyes that stood out in stark contrast to his sunburned face. "What do you mean?"

The sailor pointed. "There's the Harbormaster's launch." Roo looked to where the man pointed. "He's not slowing to pick up a pilot!"

The sailor laughed. "The Admiral is his teacher's student. Old Admiral Trask used to do the same thing, but he'd at least allow the pilot up on deck so he could personally irritate him by refusing to take a tow into the dock. Admiral Nicky's the King's brother, so he doesn't even bother with that formality."

Roo and Erik glanced upward and saw that old sailors were standing by waiting to reef in the last sails on the Admiral's command. Roo then looked to the poop deck and saw Nicholas, formerly Prince of Krondor and presently Admiral of the King's Fleet in the West, give the signal. Instantly the old hands pulled up the heavy canvas and tied off. Within seconds Roo and the others on the deck could feel the ship's speed begin to fall off as they neared the royal docks located below the royal palace of the Prince.

The *Ranger*'s motion continued to drop off, but to Roo it felt as if they were still moving into the docks too fast. The old sailor spoke as if reading his mind. "We're pushing a lot of water into the quay, and that'll push back as we come alongside the docks, slowing us down to almost a full stop, though she'll make the cleats groan a bit." He made ready to throw a line to those waiting on the dock ahead. "Lend a hand!"

Roo and Erik each grabbed another line and waited for the command. When Nicholas shouted, "Cast away!" Roo threw to a man on the dockside, who caught the rope expertly and quickly made it fast to a large iron cleat. As the old sailor said, when the line went taut the iron cleats seemed to groan as the wooden docks were flexed, but the bow wake returned from the stone quay and the huge ship seemed to settle in with a single rocking motion, as if it sighed in relief that it was good to be home.

Erik turned to Roo. "Wonder what the Harbormaster will say to the Admiral."

Roo glanced aft as the Admiral made his way to the main deck, and considered the question. The first time Roo had seen the man had been at Erik's and Roo's trial for the murder of Erik's half brother, Stefan. The second time he had seen him had been when the survivors of the mercenary company to which Roo and Erik belonged had been rescued from a fishing smack outside the harbor of the city of Maharta. Having served under the Admiral on the voyage homeward, Roo's opinion was "He'll probably say nothing, go home, and get drunk."

Erik laughed. He also knew that Nicholas was a man of calm authority, who could embarrass a subordinate to the point of tears with a stare and no words spoken, a trait he shared with Calis, the Captain of Roo and Erik's company, the Crimson Eagles.

Of the original company, numbering in the hundreds, fewer than fifty men survived—the six who had fled with Calis and some stragglers who had found their way to the City of the Serpent River before the *Freeport Ranger* had departed for Krondor. Nicholas's other ship, *Trenchard's Revenge*, had remained in the harbor at the City of the Serpent River for an extra month, in case more men from Calis's troop found their way there. Any who were not there when she weighed anchor would be considered to be dead.

The gangplank was run out, and Roo and Erik watched as Nicholas and Calis were the first to disembark. On the dock waited Patrick, Prince of Krondor, his uncle Prince Erland—nephew and brother respectively to Nicholas—and other members of the royal court of Krondor.

Erik said, "Not much of a show, is it?"

Roo could only nod. A lot of men had died to bring back the information Nicholas carried to his nephew, the Prince. And from what Roo knew, it was scant information at best. He turned his attention to the royal family.

Nicholas, formerly Prince of Krondor until his nephew had come from the capital of the Kingdom of the Isles to assume the office, looked nothing like his brother. Erland's hair was mostly grey, but there was enough red remaining to reveal its original hue. Nicholas, likewise going grey, was a man of dark hair and intense features. Patrick, the new Prince of Krondor, was somewhere between his two uncles in appearance, darker of skin than both, but his hair was a middle brown in color. He seemed to have something of Erland's powerful build and Nicholas's intensity.

"No," said Roo, "you're right; not much by way of ceremony."

Erik nodded. "Then again, by now they all know there's not much glory in any of this. The Prince and his uncle are probably both anxious to hear what news Calis and Nicholas have."

Roo sighed agreement. "None of it good. It's all bloody business and it's going to get worse."

A friendly slap to the back caused both Roo and Erik to turn. Robert de Loungville stood behind the two young men, grinning in a way that up until recently made both men expect the worst, but this time they knew he was merely showing the more affable side of his nature. He kept his receding hair cropped close to his skull, and he needed a shave. "Where to, lads?"

Roo jingled a purse of gold tucked into his tunic. "I think a good glass of ale, the tender touch of a bad woman, and then I'll worry about tomorrow, tomorrow."

Erik shrugged. "I've been thinking, and I want to take up your offer, Sergeant."

"Good," said de Loungville, sergeant of Calis's company. He had offered Erik a place in the army, but in a special command being formed by Calis, Prince Nicholas's mysterious and not-quite-human ally. "Come by Lord James's office at midday tomorrow. I'll leave word at the palace gate you're to be admitted."

Roo studied the men on the dock. "Our Prince is an impressive-looking man."

Erik said, "I know what you mean. He and his father both look the sort who have been in some serious places."

De Loungville said, "Never let their rank fool you, lads. Erland and our King, and their sons after them, spent their time along the northern borders fighting goblins and the Brotherhood of the Dark Path." He used the common name for the moredhel, the dark elves who lived on the far side of the mountains known as the Teeth of the World. "I heard that the King got into some serious business down in Kesh once, a run-in with slavers or some such thing. Whatever it was, he came out of it with a good opinion of the common man, for a king.

"We haven't had a court-bred king since King Rodric, before

old King Lyam took the throne, and that was before I was born. These are tough men who've spent some time soldiering, and it'll take a few more generations before any in this family becomes soft. The Captain will see to that." There was something in his voice that hinted at strong emotions; Roo glanced at the sergeant and tried to glean what it was, but de Loungville's expression had returned to a broad grin.

"What are you thinking?" asked Erik of Roo, his best friend since childhood.

Roo said, "Just how funny families can be." He pointed to the group on the dock, listening carefully to Nicholas.

Erik said, "Notice our Captain."

Roo nodded. He knew Erik meant Calis. The elflike man stood off to one side, with just enough distance between himself and the others to be apart, yet close enough to answer questions when asked.

Robert de Loungville said, "He's been my friend for twenty years. He found me serving with Daniel Troville, Lord Highcastle, and dragged me away from the border wars to go to the strangest places a man can imagine. I've been with him longer than any man in his company, eaten cold rations with him, slept beside him, watched men die in his arms, even had him carry me for two days after the fall of Hamsa, but I can't say I know the man."

Erik asked, "Is it true he's part elf?"

De Loungville rubbed his chin. "I can't say I know the truth of that. He told me his father came from Crydee originally; a kitchen boy, he claims. He doesn't talk about his past much. Mostly he plans for the future, and takes barracks rats like you two and turns them into soldiers. But it's worthwhile. I wasn't much more than a barracks rat myself when he found me. Worked up from that to my grand station today." He said the last with an even broader grin, as if he were nothing more than a common sergeant and that remark a joke, but both Erik and Roo had been told he carried high court rank in addition to his military rank. "So I never asked too many personal questions. He's very much what you might call a 'right now' sort of fellow." De Loungville's voice lowered, as if Calis might somehow overhear from down on the dock, and his expression turned serious. "He does have those pointy ears. Still, I never heard of any such being—half-man, half-elf—yet he can do things no other man I know can do." He grinned again as he said, "But he's saved all our hides more times than I can count, so who's to care what his line is? Your station at birth means nothing. A man can't change that. What's important is how you live." He slapped both young men on the shoulder. "You were worthless dogmeat when I found you, fit only for starving crows, but look at you now!"

Erik and Roo exchanged looks, then laughed. Both were wearing the same clothing they had worn when escaping the destruction of the city of Maharta, oft patched, stained beyond cleaning, reducing both men to the appearance of common street thugs.

Roo said, "We're two men in need of some fresh clothing. Save Erik's boots, we look the part of ragpickers."

Erik glanced down and said, "And these need mending." The boots were all he had left from the Baron of Darkmoor's legacy, a grudging admission to Erik of his paternity, along with not denying Erik the right to call himself "von Darkmoor." The boots were riding boots, but Erik had walked enough to wear the heels down to nearly nothing, and the leather was weather-beaten and cracked.

Sho Pi, an Isalani from the Empire of Great Kesh, came up on deck from below, carrying his own travel bag. Behind him came Nakor, also an Isalani, and the man Sho Pi had decided was destined to be his "master." He appeared old, but moved with a spry step and quickness that both Erik and Roo knew well. He had instructed them in hand-to-hand combat, and Roo and Erik knew that the odd little man, as well as Sho Pi, was as dangerous unarmed as most men were with weapons. Roo was convinced he had never seen Nakor move as fast as possible, and wasn't sure he would welcome such a demonstration. Roo was a gifted student of the open-handed school of fighting practiced in the Isalani provinces of Kesh, only surpassed by Sho Pi and Nakor in Calis's company, but he knew either man could easily defeat him with a quick killing blow.

"I am not going to have you trailing around behind me, boy!" insisted the bandy-legged Nakor, yelling over his shoulder. "I haven't been to a city in nearly twenty years that wasn't being burned to the ground or overrun by soldiers or otherwise unpleasant in some fashion, and I intend to enjoy myself awhile. Then I'm going back to Sorcerer's Isle."

Sho Pi, a head taller than Nakor, and in possession of a full head of dark hair, otherwise looked like a much younger version of the wiry little man. He said, "Whatever you say, Master."

"Don't call me master," insisted Nakor, putting his own travel bag over his shoulder. Moving to the rail, he said, "Erik, Roo! Where are you going?"

"To get a drink, a whore, and new clothing, in that order," said Roo.

"Then I'm going home to see my mother and friends," said Erik.

"What about you?" asked Roo.

"I'm going with you," Nakor said, hoisting his bag, "until the 'going home' part. Then I shall hire a boat to take me to Sorcerer's Isle." He looked straight down the gangway, ignoring the younger countryman, a step behind.

Erik glanced at Sho Pi and said, "We've got to go below and get our kits. Then we'll join you on the dock."

Roo was a step ahead of his friend as they hurried below, bade farewell to the sailors who had become friends, and found Jadow Shati, another of their company of "desperate men," just finishing gathering up his few possessions.

"What are you going to do?" asked Roo as he quickly grabbed his small kit.

"A drink, I'm thinking."

"Join us," said Erik.

"I think I will, as soon as I tell Mr. Robert de Loungville, the little swine, that I'm taking up his offer of becoming his corporal."

Erik blinked. "Corporal? He offered me the position."

Before the two men could begin arguing, Roo said, "From what he said, he's going to need more than one."

The two large men exchanged glances, then both laughed. Jadow's face settled into a grin, teeth dramatically white against his ebony skin, an expression so happy that it always made Roo smile in response. Like the other desperate men, Jadow had been a killer and lifelong criminal, but in the brotherhood of Calis's company he had found men for whom he was willing to die and who would die for him.

Roo hated to admit it, as one who flattered himself for being completely selfish, but he loved the survivors of that company almost as much as he loved Erik. Rough men all, dangerous by any standards, they had passed through a bloody trial together, and each knew he could depend on the others.

Roo thought about those lost on the journey: Biggo, the large, laughing thug with a strange streak of piety running through him; Jerome Handy, a giant of a man with a violent temper who could tell a tale like an actor and make shadow play on the wall that came alive; Billy Goodwin, an otherwise gentle youth with a violent temper, who had been cut down in a pointless accident before ever understanding anything of life; and Luis de Savona, the Rodezian cutthroat whose wit was as sharp as his dagger, who knew both court intrigue and dark-alley brawls; a man of temper and strange loyalties. Roo tied his bundle and turned to see both Erik and Jadow watching him.

"What is it?"

"You were lost there a moment," said Erik.

"I was thinking about Biggo and the others . . ."

Erik nodded. "I understand."

"Maybe some of them will show up when *Trenchard's Revenge* gets here," ventured Jadow.

Roo said, "That would be fine." Slinging his pack over his shoulder, he added, "But Billy and Biggo won't."

Erik nodded. He and Roo had watched Biggo die in Maharta, and Erik had seen Billy fall from his horse, cracking his head on a rock.

The three men were silent as they climbed back on deck and hurried down the gangway to find Robert de Loungville chatting with Nakor and Sho Pi.

"Hey now, you vile runt of a man!" said Jadow without ceremony to the man who for nearly three years had controlled his life.

De Loungville turned. "Who are you talking to like that, you Valeman scum!"

"You, Bobby de Loungville, Sergeant *sir*!" snapped back Jadow, but Erik could easily see the mocking humor in both men's expressions. Battle had made him very aware of his companions' every mood, and he knew they were having fun with each other. "And who are you calling 'scum'? We men of the Vale are the best fighting men in the world, don't you know, and we are usually wiping our boots to clean them of something that resembles you."

He sniffed loudly, bending forward as if to make sure de Loungville was the source of the offending odor. "Yes, very much like you."

De Loungville grabbed one of Jadow's cheeks and pinched it as a mother does a child's, saying, "You're so lovely I should kiss you." Playfully slapping him on the face, he said, "But not today."

To the group, de Loungville said, "Where are you off to?"

"Drinks!" said Nakor with a grin.

De Loungville rolled his eyes heavenward. "Well, don't kill anyone." He asked Jadow, "You coming back?"

Jadow grinned. "I don't know why, but yes."

His own smile vanishing, de Loungville said, "You know exactly why."

Instantly all humor fled. Each man had seen exactly what the others had, and all knew that a terrible enemy gathered across the sea, and that no matter how much had been accomplished in recent months, the struggle had only just started. A decade or more might pass before the final confrontation with the armies gathered under the banner of the Emerald Queen, but eventually every man living in the Kingdom would either stand and fight or die.

After a moment's silence, de Loungville waved them down the street. "Get away with you. Don't have too much fun." As the men walked off, he called after, "Erik, you and Jadow be back here tomorrow to get your papers. On the day after, you're deserters! And you know we hang deserters!"

"That man," said Jadow as they moved down the street in search of an inn. "Always with them threats. He has an unnatural love of hanging, don't you know?"

Roo laughed and the rest joined in, and the mood lightened as an inn seemed to appear by magic on the corner before them.

Roo awoke, his head pounding and his mouth dry. The inside of his eyes felt as if someone had put sand behind the lids, and his breath smelled as if something had crawled into his mouth and died. He moved and Erik let out a groan, so he moved the other way, only to find Jadow groaning and pushing him away.

With no other choice, he sat up and instantly wished he had remained asleep. He forced himself to keep whatever was in his stomach from coming up and at last managed to focus his eyes.

"Oh, wonderful," he said, and instantly regretted talking. His own voice made his head hurt.

They were in a cell. And unless Roo was mistaken, he knew exactly what cell. It was a long cell, open along one side to a hall, with floor-to-ceiling bars and a door with a heavy iron lock plate. Slightly above head height opposite the bars, a long window, less than two feet in height, ran the length of the cell. He knew the cell was below ground level, as the window was only a foot or so above ground, giving a peculiar angle so those inside the cell could see the scaffold dominating the courtyard beyond. He was now in the death cell beneath the Prince of Krondor's palace.

He pushed Erik and his friend groaned as if tortured. Roo shook him insistently and at last Erik came awake. "What?" he said as he tried to focus his attention on his friend's face. "Where are we?"

"Back in the death cell."

Erik looked instantly sober. He glanced around and saw Nakor curled up in the corner, snoring, while Sho Pi lay a short distance away.

They shook the others awake and took stock. Several of them were splattered with dried blood, and they all nursed an assortment of bruises, scrapes, and cuts. "What happened?" croaked Roo, his voice sounding as if he'd eaten sand.

Jadow said, "Those Quegan sailors, remember?"

Sho Pi and Nakor, who seemed, of the company, the least worse for wear, exchanged glances, and Nakor said, "One of them tried to remove a young woman from your lap, Roo."

Roo nodded, then wished he hadn't. "I remember now."

Jadow said, "I hit someone with a chair. . . ."

Nakor said, "Maybe we killed those Quegans."

Erik tried to stay on his feet by leaning against the wall, his knees shaking from his hangover, and said, "It would be just the sort of black joke the gods make that after all we have been through, we end up back here waiting for the gallows again."

Roo felt vaguely guilty, as he always did when he had drunk too much the night before. He was a slight man, so trying to keep up drink for drink with men the size of Jadow and Erik was foolish, even though Erik didn't have much of a head for drink. "If I killed someone, you'd think I'd remember," Roo observed.

"Well, what are we doing back here in the death cell, man?" asked Jadow from where he sat in the corner, obviously disturbed at their circumstances. "I didn't sail around the world and back again so Bobby de Loungville could finally hang me."

As they were attempting to gather their wits, the door to the hall was yanked open, clanging into the wall hard enough to make every man visibly wince. De Loungville walked into view and shouted, "On your feet, you swine!"

Without thought, everyone except Nakor leaped to his feet, and each man groaned an instant later. Jadow Shati turned his head and vomited into the chamber pot, then spat. The others stood on unsteady feet, Erik having to grip the bars of the cell to keep himself upright.

With a grin, de Loungville said, "What a lovely bunch you are."

Nakor asked, "What are we doing back here, Sergeant?"

De Loungville moved to the cell door and pulled it open, showing it hadn't been locked, and said, "We couldn't think of anywhere else to put you conveniently. Did you know it took the better part of a full watch of the city guard *and* a squad of the palace guards to arrest you?" He beamed like a proud father. "Quite a brawl. And you had the good sense not to kill anyone, though you did damage quite a few."

With a wave, de Loungville indicated they should follow him. "Prince Patrick and his uncles felt it was better to keep you lot close by for the rest of the night," he said as he led them from the cell.

Roo glanced around and remembered the last time he had seen these passages, as he was being led to the mock hanging that had set his feet upon a path he never could have imagined before leaving his birthplace. The first journey he had made along here was almost lost on him, so far had his mind retreated into terror then. Now he could barely focus because of the abuses of the night before.

He and Erik had fled their lifelong home in Ravensburg after killing Erik's half brother Stefan, then Baron of Darkmoor. Had they stayed and faced trial, they might have convinced a judge it was self-defense, but their flight counted heavily against them and they had been sentenced to die.

They reached the steps that led up toward the yard where the gallows stood, but this time they passed them by. De Loungville, the man who had held their lives in his hand from the moment they had fallen to the hard wooden floor of the gallows until they had departed ship the day before, said, "You're a scruffy bunch, so I think we should clean you up a bit before your audience."

"Audience?" asked Erik, still showing signs of damage from the night before. One of the strongest men Roo had ever known—uncontestedly the strongest boy in Ravensburg—Erik had pitched a guardsman through a window just before another broke a wine jar over his head. Roo couldn't tell if he had taken more damage from the blow or from the large amounts of wine he had been drinking before the fight started; Erik had never been much of a drinker.

"Some important men would like a word with you. It wouldn't do to have you in court looking as you do. Now," he said, pushing open a door, "strip off!"

Hot tubs of soapy water waited and the men did as they were bidden. Two years of following de Loungville's orders without question had formed a habit too hard to break, and soon the five men were sitting in tubs, letting palace pages sponge them down.

Pitchers of cold water were provided and the men all drank their fill. Between the very hot bath and the large amounts of cold water he drank, Roo began to feel again that life might be worth living.

When clean, they discovered their clothing had been removed. De Loungville pointed to two black tunics with a familiar mark upon the breast. Erik picked one up and said, "The Crimson Eagle."

De Loungville said, "Nicholas thought it fitting and Calis didn't object. It's the banner of our new army, Erik. You and Jadow are my first two corporals, so put those on." To the others he said, "There's some clean clothing over there."

Nakor and Sho Pi both looked odd in the clean tunic and trousers instead of the usual robes they affected, but Roo found his own appearance improved dramatically. The tunic might be a little large for his diminutive frame, but it was certainly the finest weave he had ever worn, and the trousers fit perfectly. He was still barefoot, but months at sea had toughened his feet to the point he didn't think twice about it.

Erik retained his worn boots, but Jadow, like the others, went barefoot.

After they dressed, the men followed de Loungville into a familiar hall; here the men of Calis's desperate company had stood trial before the Prince of Krondor—at the time, Nicholas. The hall hadn't changed much, Roo thought, but he realized that his mind had been so numb from terror the last time he had been there he had barely noticed his surroundings.

Ancient banners hung from every ceiling beam, casting the hall into shadow as they cut the light from windows high in the vaulted ceiling. Torches burned in sconces along the wall to provide illumination, for despite the large windows in the far wall, the hall was immense enough the light did not reach far enough. Roo considered he would have the banners removed, were he the Prince.

Along the walls stood courtiers and pages ready to do the royal bidding at a moment's notice, and a formally attired Master of Ceremony struck the floor with an iron-shod staff of office, announcing Robert de Loungville, Baron of the Court and Special Agent of the Prince. Roo shook his head slightly in amusement, for de Loungville was the company's sergeant, and to think of him as a court baron was too alien a task.

Members of the court watched as the squad came to stand before the throne. Roo calculated as best he could the worth of the gold used to decorate the candle holders along the near wall, and decided the Prince could better use his wealth by replacing them with brass—highly decorative, but far less costly, freeing up wealth to invest in the proper enterprise. Then he wondered if he might be allowed to speak to the Prince on just such a subject.

Thinking of the Prince returned Roo's attention to the man who had once pronounced the death sentence upon him. Nicholas, now his nephew's Admiral of the Western Fleet, stood to one side of the throne beside his successor, Prince Patrick. To the other side stood Calis and the man Roo knew to be James, Duke of Krondor, speaking to the man they had seen on the docks, Patrick's uncle Prince Erland. And sitting upon the throne was his twin. Roo suddenly flushed when he realized they were being presented to the King!

"Your Majesty, Highnesses," said de Loungville with a courtly bow, "I have the honor to present five men who acquitted themselves with bravery and honor."

"Only five survived?" asked King Borric. He and his brother

were both large men, but there was an edge to the King, a toughness beyond his brother's own powerful appearance. Roo couldn't
rightly judge the why of such things, but he instinctively considered the King a more dangerous opponent than Prince Erland.

"There are others," said de Loungville. "Some will be presented this afternoon at court—soldiers from your various garri-
sons. But these are the only ones to survive from among the
condemned."

Nakor said, "That we know of."

De Loungville turned with a look of irritation on his face at the
breach of protocol, but Borric only grinned. "Nakor, is that you in
that getup?"

Returning the King's smile, Nakor moved forward. "It's me,
Majesty. I went, too, and came back. Greylock is with the other
ship, and any others who survived and made their way to the City
of the Serpent River will be with him."

De Loungville bit back anything he was going to say to Nakor.
It was obvious that he and the King knew each other. Nakor nodded toward Erland, who also smiled at the sight of the little Isalani.

To the four prisoners the King said, "You are all pardoned, your
crimes and your sentences are vacated." Glancing at Erik and Jadow, he said, "We see you've taken service."

Erik merely nodded, while Jadow stammered, "Ye-yes, Majesty."

Looking at Sho Pi and Roo, the King said, "You have not."

Sho Pi bowed his head. "I will follow my master, Majesty."

Nakor said, "Stop calling me master!" He turned toward the
King. "The boy thinks me some sort of sage and insists upon
traipsing around after me."

Prince Erland said, "I wonder why. It wouldn't be because he
saw you pulling your 'mystic sage' scam, would it, Nakor?"

"Or is it the 'wandering priest' dodge?" asked the King.

Nakor grinned as he rubbed his chin. "Actually, I haven't tried
those in a while." Then his expression darkened. "And I never
should have told you two about them when we rode back from
Kesh."

The King said, "Well, take him along with you, then. You could
probably do with an extra set of hands on the road."

Nakor said, "On the road? I'm returning to Sorcerer's Isle."

The King said, "Not for a while. We need you to go to Stardock on the Crown's behalf, to speak with the leaders of the Academy."

Nakor's expression darkened. "You know I'm quits with Stardock, Borric, and you have a good idea why, I have no doubt."

If the King objected to being addressed so informally, he didn't show it as he said, "We know, but you also have seen firsthand what we're up against, and you've been to Novindus twice. We need you to persuade the magicians at Stardock what stands against us. We will need their help."

"Find Pug. They'll listen to him," said Nakor.

"If we could find him, we would," said the King. He leaned back in the deep well of the throne and sighed. "He's been leaving messages here and there, but we've not managed to get him to come speak with us in person."

"Try harder," answered Nakor.

Borric smiled. "You, friend, are the best we've got. So, unless you want us to let every gambling hall in the Kingdom get word about how you can handle cards and dice, you'll do this one little favor for an old friend."

Nakor made a disgusted expression and waved his hand as if dismissing the King's remark. "Bah! I liked you better when you were just the Madman." He held his sour look for a moment while Borric and Erland exchanged amused glances.

Turning his attention to Roo, the King said, "And what of you, Rupert Avery? Can we not enlist your aid as well?"

The King's direct address caused Roo to forget momentarily how to speak; then he swallowed hard and said, "Sorry, Majesty. I promised myself if I lived long enough, I'd come back and get rich. That's what I propose to do. I'm going to be a man of commerce, and I can't do that in the army."

The King nodded. "Commerce? We suppose it's a better trade than many you could choose." He avoided any further remarks about Roo's past. "Still, you've seen what few men outside our service have seen. We count upon your discretion, and if our meaning isn't clear, we *expect* your discretion."

Roo smiled. "I understand, Majesty. And I will promise this much when the time comes, I'll help in whatever way I can. If those snakes come here, I'll fight." Then with a twinkle and a smile he added, "Besides, the day may come when I can be of more use to you than just another sword."

"Perhaps, Rupert Avery," said King Borric. "You certainly do not lack for ambition." He waved over Lord James and said, "If it doesn't compromise our dignity, see if we can be of a little help in getting Mr. Avery's career under way. Perhaps a letter of introduction or some such." He then waved over a squire who carried five bags, which were distributed one to each of the men. "A thank-you from your King."

Roo hefted the bag and knew inside there was gold and even could estimate the worth from the weight. He quickly calculated he was already a year ahead of schedule in his plan to become wealthy. Then he noticed the others were bowing and moving away, so he quickly made an awkward bow to the King and hurried after the others.

Outside the hall, de Loungville said, "Well then, now you're free men again." To Jadow and Erik he said, "Stay out of trouble and be back here on the first day of next month." To Nakor and Sho Pi he said, "The King's messages will be ready tomorrow. See Duke James's secretary, and he'll give you travel warrants and money."

He turned to Roo and said, "You're a rodent, Avery, but I've come to love that pinched-off little face of yours. If you change your mind, I can use another experienced soldier."

Roo shook his head. "Thanks, Sergeant, but I've got to find a merchant with a homely daughter and start making my fortune."

To the assembled men, de Loungville said, "If you must enjoy the pleasures of the flesh before returning home, go to the Sign of the White Wing, over near the Merchants' Gate. It's a brothel of high standard, so don't track mud inside. Tell the lady who meets you that I sent you. She may never forgive me, but she owes me a favor. See you don't cause a riot there, because I can't bail you out two nights running." Looking from face to face, he said, "All things considered, you did well, lads."

No one spoke until Erik said, "Thank you, Sergeant."

To Jadow and Erik, de Loungville said, "Stop by the Knight-Marshal's office on your way out and get your warrants. You're the Prince's men, and from this day forward you answer only to Patrick, Calis, and me."

Erik said, "Where?"

"Down this hall and turn right, second door on the left. Now get out of here," said de Loungville, "before I change my mind and have you arrested again for being such a bunch of ruffians." He sent Roo down the hall with a playful slap to the side of the head, then turned and set out on his own affairs.

The five men walked down the hall and Nakor said, "I'm hungry."

"You're always hungry, man," said Jadow with a laugh. "My head is still reminding me that I was not wise last night. My stomach hasn't forgiven me either." Then he paused, and added, "But I might do with a bite to eat, after all that."

Erik laughed. "I'm hungry, too."

"Then let us find an inn—" said Nakor.

"A quiet inn," Roo interjected.

"—a quiet inn," continued Nakor, "and eat."

"Then what, Master?" asked Sho Pi.

Nakor grimaced, but said only, "Then we go to the Sign of the White Wing, boy." He shook his head. Pointing to Sho Pi, he said to the others, "This one has much to learn."

The Sign of the White Wing was nothing like what Roo expected. Then he considered he really hadn't known what to expect. He had trafficked with whores before, but that had been on the line of march, with camp followers who would tumble a man beside to his comrades and be off to the next as soon as he could count out her pay.

But this was a different world. The five slightly inebriated men had had to ask several times to find their way. After a few failed attempts, they finally discovered a modest building near the edge of the Merchants' Quarter. The sign out front had been almost impossible to make out, being little more than a simple metal wing painted white, unlike the more boldly painted large ones marking more traditional trades.

The door had been opened by a servant who admitted the five without a word, indicating they should wait in a tiny anteroom, without furnishing of any sort, only decorated by some nondescript tapestries that hung on the two side walls. Opposite the entrance stood another door, of simple painted wood. When it opened, a well-dressed if somewhat matronly woman had stepped through.

"Yes?" she had asked.

The men glanced at one another, and it was Nakor who had at last answered. "We were told to come here."

"By whom?" she then asked, looking somewhat unconvinced.

"Robert de Loungville," said Erik softly, as if afraid to raise his voice.

Instantly the woman's features had transformed themselves from dubious to joyful. "Bobby de Loungville! By the gods, if you're friends of Bobby's, you're welcome here."

She then clapped her hands once and the door she had slipped through opened wide, revealing a short entryway occupied by two large armed guards. As they stepped aside, Roo thought it clear they had been standing by to ensure the safety of the woman.

"I'm Jamila, your hostess, and here," she said, reaching another door, which she pulled wide, "we enter the House of the White Wing."

The five men gaped. Even Nakor, who had seen riches in the court of the Empress of Great Kesh, stood in stunned awe. The room wasn't that opulent; far from it. In fact it was the lack of gaudy displays of wealth that made the setting so impressive. Everything about the room was subtle and tasteful, though Roo would have been hard put to say what made it seem so. Chairs and divans were placed around the room so that those inside would be within sight of one another, yet there was a clear sense of each area being apart from the others. This was made abundantly clear by the fact of a wealthy-looking man sprawling upon one divan, sipping wine from a goblet while two lovely young women attended him. One sat upon the floor, allowing him to caress her shoulders and neck, while the other hovered over him, offering him sweetmeats from a gilded tray.

As if by magic, girls appeared through several curtains. All were modestly dressed, like the two attending the man already in the room, wearing loose-fitting gowns of light material. That they were covered from neck to ankle did nothing to hide the curves of their bodies as they moved to greet their guests.

Each man found a pair of girls leading him toward one of the chairs or divans, allowing him to choose how he wished to relax, sitting or lying down. Before he knew it, Roo had been led to a divan and gently pushed down on it, had his feet raised and placed on the divan, had a goblet of wine handed to him; one of the girls began firmly kneading the muscles in his shoulders before he spoke.

The woman called Jamila said, "When you're ready, the girls can show you to your rooms."

Jadow, circling the waist of one of the young girls with one powerful arm, pulled her toward him, planted a loud kiss upon her cheek, and said, "Men and gods, I've died and gone to paradise!"

This brought a round of laughter, and Roo settled back, letting the light touch of the girls' hands relax him in a way he'd not experienced in years.

Two

Homecoming

ROO YAWNED.

The body next to him stirred under white sheets and he realized where he was. He smiled, remembering the night before, and ran his hand under the sheet and across the back of the young woman next to him. He didn't think of her as a whore; the term was fit for the women who followed soldiers around camp, or who leaned over the balconies in the Poor Quarter of Krondor shouting ribald suggestions and insults at the workers and sailors below, but these *ladies*, he decided, were unlike anything he had imagined as a boy.

They were flirtatious, seemed well educated, were impeccable in their manners, and, as Roo had discovered the night before, creative and enthusiastic. The young woman next to him had taught Roo more things about pleasing a woman and himself in one night than he had learned from every woman he had been with in his young life. And they smelled wonderful, like flowers and spices. He found himself becoming aroused and with a grin continued to caress the body next to him.

The girl awoke, and if she had any problem with being awakened thus, she masked it with incredible skill; she actually seemed pleased to discover Roo lying next to her.

"Good morning," she said with a wide smile. Running her fingers along his stomach, she said, "What a nice way to wake up."

As he gathered the girl into his arms, Roo considered himself fortunate. He had no illusions about his looks; he was easily the homeliest boy from Ravensburg, but he had managed to bed two of the local girls in town before he and Erik had been forced to flee. He knew, given enough time, he could charm most anyone, though he rarely tried. But now he was alive, with gold in his belt, and a woman willing to make him feel handsome. It was the start of a wonderful day.

Later he bid the girl good-bye, realizing that he couldn't remember if her name was Mary or Marie. He found Erik already dressed and waiting in the antechamber, speaking with a particularly pretty young blonde.

Erik looked up. "Ready to leave?"

Roo nodded. "The others?"

"We'll see them when we get back from Ravensburg, or at least I will." He rose and was still holding on to the girl's hand.

There was something about his manner that struck Roo as odd, and as they left the brothel, he remarked, "You seemed smitten with that pretty girl."

Erik blushed. "Nothing of the kind. She's . . ."

After a silent moment, Roo supplied, "A whore?"

The city was busy at that hour of the morning, and they were forced to wend their way through the press. Erik said, "I guess. Something more like a lady, I think."

Roo shrugged, the gesture lost on Erik. "They get paid well, that's for certain." He was now considering the diminishment of his purse as he weighed the cost versus the reward. He decided he needed to husband his capital a bit more carefully. There were far less expensive whores to be found.

"Where to next?" asked Roo.

"I need to talk to Sebastian Lender."

Roo brightened. Barret's Coffee House was one of the places he wished to visit, and having a social call to make upon one of the solicitors who plied their business there was an eminently acceptable reason.

They headed to the area of the city known locally as the Merchants' Quarter, even though it held only a slightly higher percentage of businesses than elsewhere in the city. What marked the Merchants' Quarter was a high number of very costly homes, many erected behind or above the stores that generated their wealth, the highest concentration of influential men who were not nobility.

The craftsmen had their guilds—the thieves, too: the Mockers—and the nobility had their rank from birth, but men who pursued their fortune through commerce and trade had only their wits. While a few of them had banded together to create trade associations from time to time, most were independent businessmen without allies but with many competitors.

So those who survived and became successful had few peers with whom to share their pride of accomplishment, few fellows with whom to boast of their good fortune and perspicacity. A few, like a merchant Roo had met named Helmut Grindle, kept their appearance modest, as if to call attention to themselves might bring ruin. But others chose to shout their success to the world by building huge town houses, rivaling those owned by the nobility, throughout the city. And over the years the nature of the Merchants' Quarter had changed.

As more and more rich merchants purchased property in the area, the cost of land rose so high that now few businesses *in* the Merchants' Quarter were owned by those who lived there; the price of housing was too dear. There were a few modest storefront enterprises, established by the fathers or grandfathers of those tending them now, that continued to provide conventional goods and services to those in the area—a bakery on one street, a cobbler on another—but they were quickly being replaced by shops specializing in luxurious items for these very wealthy merchants: jewelers, tailors of the finest clothing, and traders in rare goods. And those who lived in the Merchants' Quarter were now almost exclusively these very wealthy businessmen, those with far-flung financial empires elsewhere in the province or in distant cities. In time the last of the modest merchants would sell their property, as the offers to buy became too good to refuse, and relocate to more distant quarters in the foulburg, that expanding portion of the city beyond the old wall.

Barret's Coffee House stood at the corner of a street now known as Arutha's Way, in honor of the late Prince of Krondor, father to the King—but still called by most locals Sandy Beach Walk—and Miller's Road, a route that had once led from a mill no longer extant to a farmer's gate long torn down. Barret's was a tall building, three stories, with two open doors at the corner, one on each street. Standing in each door was a waiter: a man with a white tunic, black trousers, black boots, and a blue-and-white-striped apron.

The three other street corners were occupied by a tavern, a ship's broker, and, diagonally across the street from Barret's, an abandoned home. It had once been splendid, perhaps one of the finest in Krondor, but misfortune had cost its owner dearly from all appearances. It had been neglected long before it was abandoned, and its past glory was now faded by peeling paint, boarded-up windows, missing tiles from the roof, and dirt everywhere.

Roo glanced at that building. "Maybe someday I'll buy that house and fix it up."

Erik smiled. "I don't doubt it, Roo."

Roo and Erik walked past the waiter standing at the door on Miller's Road, and entered. The two outside doors opened on a simple receiving area, offering several well-upholstered chairs, but otherwise closed off from the main floor of the coffee house by a wooden railing. There was one opening in the railing blocked by a man attired in a manner similar to the two waiters at the door. The main difference was that his apron was black.

A tall man, he looked eye to eye at Erik, then down at Roo as he said, "Yes?"

Erik said, "We've come to see Sebastian Lender."

The man nodded. "Follow me, please." He turned and walked onto the main floor of the coffee house.

Roo and Erik followed and were led through a large area of small tables, several occupied by men drinking coffee, while waiters hurried from table to table. To the left as they reached the center of the room a broad flight of stairs led up to a balcony rather than a true second floor, leaving the center of the room open to the high vaulted ceiling. Looking up, Roo saw there was no third floor, but rather a double set of high windows above the second-floor balcony. Barret's was a very open, well-lit building as a result. They reached another waist-high railing, which cut off the rear third of the room, and there the waiter said, "Please wait here."

The waiter moved a small section of the rail that was on hinges, and stepped through and toward a table at the far side of the house. Roo motioned upward and Erik's eyes went to where he pointed.

Above them, on the second-floor landing, men sat at tables. Roo said, "The brokers."

"How do you know?"

"I've heard a thing or two," said Roo.

Erik laughed and shook his head. Most likely he had heard it from Helmut Grindle, the trader they had traveled with for a while when coming to Krondor. Roo and Grindle had spoken of many things commercial, and while Erik had found some of the conversation diverting, as often as not it put him to sleep.

A moment later, a dignified-looking man wearing an unadorned but expensive tunic with an overvest and cravat approached. He studied the two young men before him for a moment, then said, "My word! Young von Darkmoor and Mr. Avery, if I'm not mistaken."

Roo nodded as Erik said, "Yes, Mr. Lender. We gained our pardon."

"Most unusual," said Lender. He motioned for the waiter to open the railing for him to step through. "Only members are permitted behind this second railing." He indicated with a wave of his hand that Roo and Erik should sit at an empty table a few feet away.

He motioned for the waiter and said, "Three coffees." Looking at Roo and Erik, he asked, "Have you broken fast today?" When they answered in the negative, he said to the waiter, "Some rolls, jams and honey, and a platter of cheese and sausage."

As the waiter hurried off, Lender said, "As you are pardoned, you obviously do not need my services as a solicitor, so perhaps you need them as a litigator?"

Erik said, "Not really. I came to pay you your fee."

Lender began to object, but Erik said, "I know you refused to take gold before, but despite your having lost the pleading, we are here and alive, so I think you're entitled to your fee." He produced his money pouch and put it upon the table. It clinked with the heavy sound of gold coins.

Lender said, "You've prospered, young gentlemen."

"It's a payment for services from the Prince," said Roo.

Shrugging, Lender opened the purse, counted out fifteen golden sovereigns, then closed the purse, pushing it back toward Erik. He pocketed the coins.

"Is that enough?" asked Erik.

"Had I won, I would have charged you fifty," said Lender as the coffee arrived.

Roo had never cared for coffee, so he sipped at it, expecting to put aside the cup and ignore it. But to his surprise, instead of the bitter brew he had tasted before, this was a rich complex taste. "This is good!" he blurted.

Erik laughed and tried his, then said, "It is."

"Keshian," said Lender. "Far superior to what is grown in the Kingdom. More flavor, less bitterness." He waved his hand around the room. "Barret's is the first establishment in Krondor to specialize exclusively in fine coffees, and as a sign of his wisdom, the founder placed his first shop here in the heart of the Merchant's Quarter, rather than trying to sell to the nobility."

Roo instantly came alert; stories of success appealed to him. "Why is that?" he asked.

"Because the nobility are difficult to approach, expect extreme discounts, and rarely pay in a timely fashion."

Roo laughed. "I've heard that from the wine merchants at home."

Lender continued. "Mr. Barret knew that the local businessmen often needed a place away from their homes or offices where they could discuss business over a meal, without the distractions of an inn's taproom."

Erik again nodded, having spent a fair part of his life in the taproom of the inn where he had worked as a child.

"So was born Barret's Coffee House, which prospered from the first week it was opened. Originally a more modest enterprise, it has existed for nearly seventy-five years, in this location for close to sixty."

"What about the brokers, and syndicates, and . . . you?" asked Roo.

Lender smiled as a tray of hot rolls, breakfast meats, cheeses, and fruits, along with pots of jam, honey, and butter, was brought to the table.

Suddenly hungry, Roo took a roll and slathered butter and honey on it while Lender answered him. "Some of those without offices of their own used to conduct business all day long and, to keep Barret happy, would buy coffee, tea, and food in a steady stream.

Seeing this a pleasant alternative to hours of empty tables between meals, Mr. Barret ensured certain tables would remain reserved for those businessmen.

"They formed the first syndicates and brokerage alliances. And they needed representation"—he put his hand upon his chest and bowed slightly—"hence litigators and solicitors became habitués of the establishment. When things became crowded, the son of the founder moved to this inn, tore out the third floor, and created the exclusive members' area above, and things have continued that way since." He motioned at the second rail. "Some members were forced to use this end of the ground floor, hence the newer railing. Now one must purchase a location in the hall for one's syndicate or brokerage, or risk not having a table at which to sit when arriving to conduct business."

Glancing around, he added, "You now are in the heart of one of the most important trading centers in the Kingdom, certainly the most important in the Western Realm, and rivaled only by those in Rillanon, Kesh, and Queg."

"How does one become a broker?" asked Roo.

"First you need money," answered the litigator, not in the least put off by the youngster seeking instruction. "A great deal of money. This is why there are so many syndicates, because of the great cost of underwriting many of the projects that are conceived of here at Barret's or brought to us from the outside."

"How does one start?" asked Roo. "I mean, I have some money, but I'm not sure if I want to invest it here or try my own hand."

"No partnership will admit an investor without good cause," said Lender. He sipped his coffee, then continued. "Over the years a complex set of rules has evolved. Noblemen often come to Barret's seeking either to invest wealth or to borrow it, and as a result, the interests of those here who are commoners need to be closely protected. So, to join a syndicate, one needs a great deal of money—though not as much as to become an independent broker—and one also needs a sponsor."

"What's that?" asked Roo.

"One who is already a member of Barret's or who has close ties to one of the members who can vouch for you. If you have the capital, then you need the introduction."

"Can't you do that?" asked Roo, obviously eager.

"No," said Lender with a slightly sad smile. "For all my influence and position, here I am but a guest. My office has been here for nearly twenty-five years, but only because I work on behalf of nearly thirty different brokers and syndicates, and I have never placed a copper piece of my own capital at risk through any offering."

"What's an offering?" asked Erik.

Lender put up his hand. "There are more questions than time, young von Darkmoor." He signaled to one of the ever-present waiters. "In my property box you'll find a long blue velvet bag. Please bring it here." To Erik and Roo he said, "I enjoy the break from the routine, but time doesn't permit a leisurely discourse on the business at Barret's."

Roo said, "I plan on being a broker."

"Do you?" said Lender, and his face lit up with delight. His expression wasn't mocking, but he seemed to find the pronouncement entertaining. "What is this venture, then, that you spoke of?"

Roo leaned back. "It's a plan I have that would take too long to speak of, I'm sorry to say."

Lender laughed while Erik blushed at his friend's bold freshness. "Well said," answered Lender.

"Besides," added Roo, "I think discretion is in order."

"Often that is the case," agreed Lender as the waiter returned with the requested item. Lender took the velvet bag and opened it, removing a dagger. It was a deftly fashioned thing, with a sheath of ivory set with a small ruby and bound at the top and tip with gold. He handed it to Erik. "It was the other part of your legacy from your father."

Erik took the dagger and pulled the blade from the sheath. "Impressive," he said. "I may not be as well practiced with weapons at the forge as I am with horseshoes, but this is fine work."

"From Rodez, I believe," said Lender.

"Best steel in the Kingdom," agreed Erik. The blade was embossed with the von Darkmoor family crest, finely cut into the steel, and yet it was well balanced, both decorative and deadly. The hilt was carved bone, perhaps from the antler of an elk or moose, and capped with gold to match the sheath.

Lender pushed back his chair. "Young sirs, I must be back to my business, but please feel free to linger awhile and refresh yourselves. If you ever have need of a solicitor or a litigator, you know where to find me." He waved vaguely at the place from which he had appeared and added, "Good-bye. It was good seeing you well."

Erik rose, as did Roo, and they bade their host farewell, then looked at each other. As old friends do, they shared a single thought between them, and Roo said, "Home."

They moved through the crowded common room of Barret's, a place both strange and exciting to Roo, and exited. At the door, Erik turned to one of the waiters and asked, "Where can a man buy a good horse?"

"Cheaply!" injected Roo.

The waiter didn't hesitate. "At the Merchants' Gate," he said, pointing along Arutha's Way, "you'll find several dealers. Most are thieves, but there's a man named Morgan there who can be trusted. Tell him Jason at Barret's sent you and he'll treat you fairly."

Roo studied the young man's face. Brown hair and light freckles marked him and Roo said, "I'll remember you if he doesn't."

The young man frowned, ever so slightly, but said only, "He's honest, sir."

"What about new clothing?" ask Erik.

Jason said, "The tailor at New Gate Road and Broad Street is a cousin of mine, sir. Tell him I sent you and he'll see you right for a reasonable sum."

Roo didn't look convinced, but Erik said thanks and led his friend away. They remained silent as they wended their way through the crowded city streets. It took them the better part of an hour to reach the tailor's and an hour to select clothing for travel that fit. Erik choose a riding cloak to cover his uniform tunic, and Roo purchased an inexpensive tunic and trousers, a cloak, and a slouch hat. Erik also found a cobbler who provided him with a pair of boots to wear while those left him by his father were mended. Roo had gotten used to going barefoot while aboard ship, but purchased a pair of boots for riding.

Soon after they were at the Merchants' Gate and spent another hour haggling for a pair of horses, but the waiter had been truthful with them and Morgan was an honest trader. Erik picked out two sturdy geldings, a bay for himself and a grey for Roo. Leading the horses away with rope halters, they found a saddler a half-block away and quickly had the horses tacked up and ready to ride.

Roo settled into the saddle and said, "I don't care how much I do it, I'll never get to like riding."

Erik laughed. "You've become a better than average horseman, Roo, despite your objections. And this time you can ride without much worry about having to fight while on that creature's back."

Roo's expression darkened.

Erik said, "What?"

"What's this 'much' business?"

Erik laughed even louder. "There are no guarantees in this life, my friend." So saying, he put heels to sides, and the horse moved out briskly toward the Merchants' Gate and the road eastward. "On to Ravensburg!" he shouted.

Roo could only laugh at his friend's merriment, and he followed suit, discovering that this horse was inclined to argue with every command. Taking a firm hand, and knowing that the sooner the battle was fought the sooner it was won, Roo slammed his heels hard against the horse's sides and drove him after Erik's mount. Quickly they were outside the city wall, on their way home.

Rain pelted them, its insistent beat a physical assault. Night was rapidly approaching and the only traffic on the road was local businessmen and farmers hurrying home. A resigned wagon driver barely looked over at Roo and Erik passing as he urged his slowly plodding horses to continue through the mud. The King's Highway might be the artery that carried the lifeblood of commerce from one border to the other, but when the rains came to the Barony of Darkmoor, the blood didn't flow, it oozed.

Erik shouted, "Lights."

Roo looked out from under the sodden brim of his once handsome slouch hat. "Wilhelmsburg?"

"I think," said Erik. "We'll be home by tomorrow afternoon."

"I don't suppose I could convince you to sleep in some stranger's barn, could I?" said Roo, having spent more money on this journey than he had planned.

"No," answered Erik without humor. "I'm for a dry bed and a hot meal."

That image overcame Roo's reluctance to spend another coin,

and he followed his friend toward the lights of the town. They found a modest inn, with a sign of a plowshare swinging in the wind, and rode through the side gate to the stable. Erik shouted, and a lackey came out, bundled against the weather, to take the horses. He listened politely to Erik's instructions and nodded, and Erik assumed he would be wise to return after supper to see the boy cared for the animals as he ordered.

They hurried into the taproom and, once inside, shook off the water from their cloaks.

"Evening, sirs," said a young girl, pleasant-looking, with brown hair and eyes. "Will you be needing rooms for the night?"

"Yes," said Roo, obviously displeased at the cost, but now that warmth was returning to his bones glad they were not returning to the weather outside.

"Fit to be blowing up a rare storm tonight," said the innkeeper as he came and took their cloaks and hats. "Will you be dining?" He handed the cloaks and hats to the girl, who took them somewhere warm to hang and dry.

"Yes," said Erik. "What wine have you?"

"Fit for a lord," said the man with a smile.

"Any from Ravensburg?" asked Erik as he made his way to an empty table.

Save for a solitary man with a sword in the far corner and two merchants obviously taking their ease before the fireplace, the inn was deserted. The innkeeper followed them, "We do, sir. It's the next town over, then one more, and on to Ravensburg."

"So we are in Wilhelmsburg," said Roo.

"Yes," answered the innkeeper. "Are you familiar with the area?"

"We're from Ravensburg," answered Erik. "It's just been a while since we've been there and in the darkness we weren't sure which town this was."

"Bring us some wine, please," asked Roo, "then supper."

The meal was filling, if not memorable, and the wine better than expected; it clearly had a style and finish familiar to both Roo and Erik. It was the common wine of Ravensburg, but compared to what they had been drinking the last year and more, this seemed a bottle fit for the King's table. Both young men fell into a quiet mood, anticipating the homecoming the next day.

For Roo it was nothing much to do with his past; his immediate family was his father, Tom Avery, a drunken teamster whose only legacy to Roo had been beatings and teaching him to drive a team of horses. Roo was much more interested in seeking out some minor wine merchants he knew and arranging what he hoped would be the start of his rise to riches.

For Erik it was coming home to his mother and the shattered dream of his youth: a blacksmith's forge and a family. He had served old Tyndal the smith for years before Tyndal's death, then a year and more with Nathan, who had been the closest thing to a father he had known. But life took its own course, and nothing seemed to be as he had hoped it would, when he was a child in Ravensburg.

"What are you thinking?" asked Roo. "You've been quiet a long time."

"You haven't exactly been bending my ear," replied Erik, a smile on his face. "Just about home and what it was like before."

He didn't have to say before what. Roo knew: before a struggle with Erik's half brother Stefan ended up with Roo's dagger driven into Stefan's chest as Erik held him. After that they had fled Ravensburg and had not seen friend or family since.

Roo said, "I wonder if anyone told them we live?"

Erik laughed. "If they didn't, our arrival tomorrow will be something of a surprise."

The door opened and the howl of the wind caused the two young men to turn. Four soldiers in the garb of the barony entered, cursing the night's foul weather.

"Innkeeper!" shouted the corporal as he removed his sopping great cloak. "Hot food and mulled wine!" He glanced around the room, then his gaze returned to Roo and Erik. His eyes widened.

"Von Darkmoor!" he blurted. The other three soldiers fanned out, not quite sure why their corporal had called out their Baron's name, but clearly alerted to trouble by his tone.

Erik and Roo stood, and the two merchants moved away from their chairs before the fireplace, hugging the wall. The only other person in the room, the swordsman, looked on with interest, but didn't move.

The corporal had his sword out, and as Roo made to draw his own, Erik motioned for him to return it to its scabbard. "We're not looking for trouble, Corporal."

The corporal said, "We heard you'd been hung. I don't know how you and your scrawny friend escaped, but we'll soon put that right. Seize them."

Roo said, "Wait a minute—"

The men moved quickly, but Erik and Roo were both quicker, and the first two soldiers who laid hands upon them found themselves on the floor, their heads ringing from swift blows. The two merchants spied a pathway past the trouble and beat a hasty exit from the room, running outside into the rain without their hats or coats. The man at the table laughed. "Well done!" he shouted.

The corporal leveled his sword and thrust, but Erik slipped aside and had him by the wrist before he could react. One of the strongest men Roo had ever seen, Erik also had been trained in bare-handed combat, and his iron grip wrung the corporal's sword from his fingers as he gasped in pain.

Roo simply thrust with his hand, palm out, fingers extended, and delivered a sharp blow with the heel of his hand upward to the chin of the other standing soldier, who went down in a stunned heap.

"Wait a minute!" commanded Erik in the voice he had developed as Robert de Loungville's corporal on their return from Novindus. The other two soldiers, who were slowly standing, hesitated, and Erik shouted his command: "Hold, damn you!"

He released the corporal's wrist while kicking aside his sword so he couldn't reach for it easily, then showed that his hands were empty of weapons. "I have a paper." He reached slowly inside his tunic, removed the document given him the day before by an officer in the office of the Knight-Marshal of Krondor, and handed it to the corporal.

The man took it and glanced it over. "Got the seal of Krondor at the bottom," he grudgingly admitted, while still sitting on the floor. Then his eyes lowered as he said, "Can't read."

The swordsman stood and with a relaxed air moved to Erik's side. "If I may help, Corporal," he said, extending his hand.

The corporal handed back the document and the man read aloud: "Know you by my hand and seal that Erik Von Darkmoor is sworn to my service and . . ." His eyes glanced to the bottom of the document. "It's a lot of mumbo jumbo, Corporal. The short of it is you just tried to arrest one of Prince Nicholas's personal guards. A corporal, like yourself, it says."

"A fact?" asked the corporal, his eyes widened.

"Yes, not only is the document signed by the Duke of Krondor's own Knight-Marshal, the Prince himself signed it."

"True?" was the corporal's next remark as he slowly rose to his feet.

"True," answered the stranger. "And from the way he took your sword from you, I think there's a reason he's in the Prince's personal service."

The corporal rubbed his wrist. "Well, perhaps." His eyes narrowed. "But we heard nothing about this, and last time Erik's name was mentioned it was when we heard he was to be hung for killing the young Baron."

Erik sighed. "The Prince pardoned us."

"So you say," said the corporal. "But I think me and the boys will hurry back to Darkmoor and see what Lord Manfred has to say about this."

He picked up his sword and signaled to his men to depart. One of them shook his head in disgust at forgoing a hot meal and the other threw Erik and Roo a black look as he helped the one Roo had stunned back to his feet.

That man, still trying to focus his eyes, said, "We're leaving? Did we eat? Is it morning?"

The other said, "Shut up, Bluey. A bit of that cutting rain will sort you out, quick like."

The soldiers left the inn and Erik turned to the stranger. "Thanks."

The man shrugged. "If I hadn't read it, the innkeeper or someone else would."

Erik said, "I'm Erik von Darkmoor."

The man took his hand. "Duncan Avery."

Roo's eyes widened. "Cousin Duncan?"

The eyes of the man who had named himself Avery narrowed as he studied Roo. After a long moment he said, "Rupert?"

Suddenly they were laughing, and the man Rupert called cousin gave him a quick hug. "I haven't seen you since you were a tadpole, youngster." He stepped back and a wry smile graced his features.

Erik glanced back and forth and couldn't see even the most remote resemblance. While Roo was short, wiry, and signally unattractive, Duncan Avery was tall, slender, with broad shoulders, and handsome. Moreover, he dressed like a dandy, save for his sword, which was well used and well cared for. He sported a slender mustache, but otherwise was clean-shaven, and his hair hung to his shoulders, where it was cut evenly and curled under.

Pulling out a chair, Duncan signaled the serving girl to bring his plate and mug over, and sat.

Erik said, "I didn't know you had a cousin, Roo."

Roo's eyes narrowed. "Of course you did."

Erik waved away his previous comment. "I mean, I know you have a number of them in Salador and elsewhere in the east, but you've never mentioned this gentleman before."

Duncan thanked the girl and winked at her, causing her to retire with a giggle as he said, "I'm crushed, Rupert. What does your friend mean, you've never spoken of me?"

Roo sat back, shaking his head. "It's not like we were close, Duncan. I saw you, what? Three times in my life?"

Duncan laughed. "Something like that. Tried my hand at the teamsters trade when I was a boy," he said to Erik. "Got as far as riding with Roo's pa from Ravensburg to Malac's Cross, where I quit. Roo was no more than five then." His face turned somber. "Only time I got to meet his ma."

"When was the last time we saw each other?" asked Roo.

Duncan rubbed his chin. "Can't say I remember, save there was that lovely girl at the fountain: slender waist, ample hips and bosom, accommodating attitude . . . who was she?"

"Gwen," supplied Roo. "And that must have been four or five years ago." Roo pointed a fork at Duncan. "You were her first." Then he grinned. "Many of the local lads owe you some thanks; you imparted a . . . certain enthusiasm in Gwen that we came to appreciate."

Erik laughed. "I'm not one of them," he said.

Roo said, "Maybe the only boy in Ravensburg who didn't."

"How are you related?" Erik asked Duncan.

Duncan said, "My father is cousin to Roo's father, Erik, and neither of those worthy gentlemen has much use for me." To Roo he said, "How is your pa?"

Roo shrugged. "Been a couple of years, really. We're on our way to Ravensburg now. Where are you headed?"

"I'm for the east, seeking my fortune as usual. I tried my hand doing mercenary duty down in the Vale of Dreams, but the work's too dangerous, the women too dangerous"—both Erik and Roo laughed at that— "and the money scarce. So I'm for the eastern courts, where a man's wits stand him as well as his sword."

Roo said, "I might have some use for that wit."

"What's the plan?" asked Duncan, suddenly interested.

"Nothing dodgy. Some honest business, but I think I can use someone who knows his way around polite company."

Duncan shrugged. "Well, I'll ride with you to Ravensburg and we can talk along the way. Besides, you've got my curiosity piqued."

"Why?" asked Erik.

"The way you two moved . . . it was a sight. When I last saw Rupert he was a scrawny kid barely able to keep himself upright while he pissed, but now he looked downright lethal when he knocked out that soldier. Where did you learn to handle yourselves that way?"

Roo and Erik exchanged glances. Neither needed to be reminded of the network of spies already established in the Kingdom by the agents of the Emerald Queen. Distant cousin or not, Roo had no illusions about the man's honesty. "Here and there," said Roo.

"That's some Isalani open-handed fighting, or I'm a cow's newborn," said Duncan.

"Where'd you see it before?" asked Erik.

"As I said, I just returned from down in the Vale. You see a few Isalani there as well as some other Keshian-born who know the tricks." He leaned forward, and his voice lowered. "I hear you can crack a man's skull with your hand if you know how to do it."

Erik said, "That's easy. Just make sure you've got a smith's hammer in the hand when you hit him."

Duncan stared at Erik a moment, then burst into laughter. "Good one, lad," he said as he dug into his meal. "I think I'm going to like you."

They continued to chat as they ate, and after, Erik went to check on the horses. When he returned, the three men retired for the night to the common sleeping area upstairs, so they might get an early start in the morning.

*   *   *

The village seemed at once unchanged and smaller. Roo said, "Nothing's different." They rode at a walk, having taken the bend at the road that put them within sight of Ravensburg. They had been passing familiar farms for the last hour, both vineyards and fields of oat, wheat, and corn. But in the distance they now at last were in sight of the small buildings at the edge of the town.

Erik remained silent, but Duncan said, "Doesn't look any different to me and it's been years."

Riding past familiar landmarks, Roo thought that he was wrong. Everything had changed, or at least he had changed and therefore how he saw things had changed. Reaching the Inn of the Pintail, Erik said, "Few things in Ravensburg ever change, but we have," echoing Roo's thoughts of a few moments before.

Duncan said, "That's always true, I guess." Erik had taken a liking to the affable man, and Roo was pleased, for he liked his cousin as well, though he barely trusted him; he was an Avery, and Roo knew what that meant. There had been a distant uncle, John, who had made a terrible reputation for himself as a pirate, long before Roo had been born, and more than half those uncles and cousins who had died since Roo's birth had been hanged or killed during a robbery attempt. Still, there were a few Averys who had turned a hand toward honest labor, and Roo thought that gave him a chance of getting rich without having to resort to murder or robbery.

As they dismounted, a boy ran from the stable and said, "Care for your horses, gentlemen?"

Erik said, "Who are you?"

"Gunther," said the boy. "I'm the smith's apprentice, sir."

Erik tossed the reins to the boy. "Is your master about?" asked Erik.

"He's taking his midday meal in the kitchen, sir. Should I fetch him for you?"

Erik said, "Never mind, I can find the way." The boy took the horses and led them away.

Roo said, "Your replacement?"

"So it seems," said Erik shaking his head. "He can't be more than twelve or so."

"You were younger when you started helping Tyndal around the forge," reminded Roo.

Roo followed Erik as he moved to the rear door, the one that led directly into the kitchen. Erik pushed open the door and stepped through.

Freida, Erik's mother, sat at the kitchen table talking to Nathan the smith. She looked up as Erik came through the doorway. Her eyes widened and her color drained away. She half stood; then her eyes rolled up into her head and she swooned, caught by the smith before she fell to the floor.

"Damn me," said Nathan. "It's you. It really is."

Erik hurried around the table and took his mother's hand. "Get some water," he instructed Roo.

Roo got a pitcher and filled it from the pump at the sink and brought a clean kitchen rag, which he wet and placed upon Erik's mother's brow.

Erik looked across his mother's still form at the man with whom she had been eating and saw the smith regarding him with amazement in his eyes, which were brimming with tears. "You're alive," he said. "We didn't know."

Erik swore. "I'm an idiot."

Roo took off his travel cloak and sat down, motioning to Duncan to do the same. "Rosalyn!" he shouted. "We need wine!"

Nathan shook his head. "Rosalyn's not here. I'll get us a bottle." As he stood, he said, "There's a lot to be talked of, it seems."

A moment later he returned, with Milo the innkeeper a step behind. The innkeeper said, "My Gods! Erik! Roo! You're alive!"

Erik and Roo both exchanged a glance, then Roo said, "Well, it was a secret, wasn't it?"

Nathan said, "Are you hunted?"

Roo burst out laughing. "No, Master Smith. We are free men, by the King's own hand. And prosperous ones, as well." He jingled his purse significantly.

Nathan pulled the cork of the wine bottle he carried and poured a round of drinks while Freida regained consciousness. She blinked and said, "Erik?"

"Here, Mother."

She threw her arms around his neck and started to cry. "We were told you were tried and convicted."

"We were," said Erik softly. "But we gained our pardon and were set free."

"Why did you not send word?" she asked, a slight note of reproach in her voice. She touched his face as if uncertain of his substance.

"We couldn't," said Erik. "We were in the Prince's service and"—he glanced around the room—"we were not permitted to let anyone know. But that's all in the past."

She shook her head slightly in amazement. She touched his cheek, then kissed it. Resting her head on his shoulder she said, "My prayers are answered."

Nathan said, "She prayed, lad." He wiped away a tear. "We all prayed for you."

Roo saw that Erik's own emotions were starting to rise, but Erik forced them down, never having been one to show his feelings openly. Roo took a deep breath, suddenly feeling self-conscious over the moisture gathering in his own eyes.

Erik asked, "What of you? How are you?"

Freida sat back and took Nathan's hand. "There have been changes."

Erik glanced from his mother to the smith. "You two?"

Nathan smiled, "We wed last summer." Then his expression darkened. "You've no objections, I take it?"

Erik let out a whoop and leaned across the table and seized his stepfather in a bear hug, nearly knocking the wine over; only Roo's quick reflexes saved it. "Objections! You're the best man I know, Nathan, and if I could have named my father, it would have been you." Sitting back he looked at his mother with an unashamed tear rolling down his cheek, then he took her in another bear hug and said, "I am so happy for you, Mother."

Freida blushed like a bride. "He came to me and was so sweet when you fled. He saw to my hurt every day, Erik." She touched Nathan's cheek with more tenderness than Erik could ever remembering her showing anyone, including himself. "He made me care again."

Slapping his hand on the table, Erik said, "We celebrate!" To Milo he said, "I want your best bottle and a meal tonight to embarrass the Empress of Kesh!"

"Done!" said Milo, his own eyes glistening with emotion. "And I'll only charge you cost."

Roo laughed. "You haven't changed, Master Innkeeper."

"Where's Rosalyn?" said Erik.

Milo and Nathan exchanged glances and Nathan said, "She's with her family, Erik."

Erik glanced around, not understanding. "Family? You're her father—"

Roo reached over and took his friend's arm. "She's with her husband, Erik." He looked at Milo. "Is that what Nathan's saying, Milo?"

Milo nodded. "Aye, and I'm a grandfather, too."

Erik sat back. His emotions were in turmoil. "She's had a baby?"

Milo looked at Erik. "That's a fact."

Erik said, "Who's the father?"

Milo glanced around the room and said, "She married young Rudolph, the baker's apprentice; you know him?" Erik nodded. "He's now a journeyman and will set up his own ovens soon. She's living with his family, over by the square."

Erik rose. "I know the house. I want to see her."

Freida said, "Go slowly, son. She also thinks you're dead."

Leaning over to kiss his mother again, he said, "I know. I'll try not to scare her to death. I want her to come tonight." Then he added, "With Rudolph."

Roo said, "I'll go with you."

Freida squeezed his hand. "Don't be long, else I'll think this all a dream."

Erik laughed. "Hardly. Roo's cousin Duncan will charm you with tales wondrous and improbable."

The cousins smiled. Nathan looked at the handsome Duncan and said, "He'll not be charming her too much, I'm thinking."

Erik laughed. "We'll be back soon."

Roo and Erik hurried from the kitchen, through the empty common room of the inn, and out the front door. They hastened down the street that led to the town's square and hardly noticed those few townspeople who stopped to stare in open amazement at the familiar figures of Rupert Avery and Erik von Darkmoor hurrying along. One man dropped a crock of wine as his eyes widened at the sight of the reputedly dead men striding past. One or two others tried to say something, but Roo and Erik were away before they could give voice to the greeting.

Reaching the town square, they turned and made their way to the bakery where Rudolph worked and lived. At the front door

Roo saw Erik hesitate. Roo knew Erik's feelings for Rosalyn were never simple. She was like a sister to him, but at the same time there was something more. Roo and the others around town knew that Rosalyn was in love with Erik, even if he had been too thick to know. At least, he had been aware just before his departure from Ravensburg that her feelings for him were more than sisterly. He had talked about it with Roo more than once. And Roo knew that Erik still didn't really understand how he felt about her.

Suddenly embarrassed by his own hesitation, Erik entered the bakery. Rudolph stood behind the counter, and when he looked up he said, "Can I help—" His eyes widened as he said, "Erik? Roo?"

Erik offered a friendly smile. "Hello, Rudolph." He extended his hand as he crossed the small space between door and counter. Roo followed.

Rudolph had never been what either Roo or Erik would count a friend, though in a town as small as Ravensburg all the children of similar age know one another. "I thought you dead," he half whispered, as if afraid to be overheard.

"That seems to have been the general opinion," Roo said. "But we were freed by the King."

"By the King?" asked Rudolph, clearly impressed, as he took Erik's hand and gave it a perfunctory shake. Then he shook with Roo.

"Yes," said Erik. "And I'm back." When Rudolph's expression darkened, he quickly added, "For a few days. I'm the Prince of Krondor's man now." He pointed to the crest on his tunic. "I must be back there before the end of the month."

Rudolph relaxed. "Well then, it's good to see you." He looked Erik up and down. "I expect you've come to see Rosalyn?"

"She was a sister to me," said Erik.

Rudolph nodded. "In the back. Follow me."

Erik and Roo walked to the end of the counter, where Randolph lifted the hinged top, and stepped through. They followed Rudolph through the large bakery, past now-cooling ovens that would be heated again after nightfall, as the bakers plied their tasks all night long, so there would be hot bread for sale at first light. Large tables, now cleaned, waited for the bakers, and vats that would hold dough after supper were empty. Rows of clean baking pans waited to be filled, and in the corner two apprentice bakers slept in anticipation of the night's work ahead.

Rudolph moved to another door and they exited the bakery and crossed a small alley, to a room in a residence that Roo knew belonged to Rudolph's employer. Rudolph said, "Wait here," and entered.

A few moments later, Rosalyn appeared at the door, a child upon her left hip. She gripped the doorjamb tightly, while Rudolph stood behind her, offering her support. "Erik?" she half whispered. "Roo?"

Erik smiled, and Rosalyn stepped forward and put her right arm around his neck, hugging him fiercely. He held her gently, trying to be aware of the squirming baby, and then he realized she was crying.

"Here, now," he said softly pushing her away. "None of that. I'm fine. I did the Prince of Krondor a service and was pardoned for my crime."

"Why didn't you send word?" she whispered harshly.

Roo was surprised by the anger in her voice toward Erik, but Erik glanced at Rudolph, who nodded at the question.

"We couldn't," said Erik. He pointed to the crest on his tunic and said, "I'm the Prince's man now, sworn to his service, and I was under oath not to speak of my freedom since"—he didn't want to bring up the rape and the trial in Krondor—"I left. But now I'm here."

Rosalyn's child started to squirm and complain and she turned to calm the child. "Shush, Gerd."

"Gerd?" said Erik.

"It was my father's name," said Rudolph.

Erik nodded as he looked at the little boy. Then his eyes widened and Roo saw his knees go weak. Roo grabbed Erik's arm as he gripped the doorjamb.

"What?" asked Roo, then he looked again at the little boy. Realization hit him. Rudolph was a stocky, short man, with reddish brown hair. There was nothing of him in this child's face. But from the expression that showed there, and the size of the child, he knew instantly what had occurred while he and Erik had been gone.

Softly Roo asked what Erik seemed unable to say: "Stefan's?"

Rosalyn nodded. Without taking her eyes from her foster brother's face she said, "Gerd's your nephew, Erik."

Three

Bargains

THE BABY CRIED.

Roo laughed as Erik quickly handed him back to Rosalyn. He had offered to hold the boy, but the squirming youngster had had Erik looking overwhelmed in less than a minute.

The mood in the room was guarded, a mix of happiness and apprehension. While everyone was pleased to see Roo and Erik alive and well, those in the taproom of the Inn of the Pintail knew that word of Erik's return would quickly reach his half brother. The Prince of Krondor might have pardoned Roo and Erik for their crime against Erik's half brother Stefan, but the surviving brother, Manfred, might not. And Stefan's mother certainly would not. There was a long leap between the letter of the law and its practice when vengeful nobles were involved, everyone knew.

Milo and Nathan motioned Roo aside and Nathan said, "Are you planning on staying long?"

Roo glanced to where Erik sat studying his nephew, fascinated by the little life before him. "Erik mostly wanted to see his mother and you," he said to them. "I've got some business. We'll be gone in a week or so."

Nathan whispered. "Better sooner than later, Roo."

Roo nodded. "I know. Mathilda von Darkmoor."

Milo put his finger alongside his nose and nodded once, indicating Roo was correct in his surmise.

Roo said, "But Freida threatened Mathilda's boys' inheritance. You're telling everyone that the baby's Rudolph's, aren't you?"

"Yes," said Nathan.

"But it's as plain as the nose on your face who his sire is, Roo," said Milo, looking fondly across the room at his grandson. "There are no secrets in this town. By now the Baron surely knows the baby exists."

Roo shrugged. "Maybe, but I overheard Manfred talking to Erik—"

"When?" demanded Nathan, his voice an anxious whisper.

"In the death cell. The night before we were to be hung. He came and told Erik there was no hard feelings; he said Stefan was a swine."

Nathan shook his head. "One thing to say that to a man you count dead the next day, another to a rival to the title of Baron."

Roo said, "I don't think that's a problem. Manfred said there were other bastards, not just Erik. Seems the old Baron loved the ladies."

Milo nodded. "That's truth. I hear there's a lad over in Wolfsheim who looks a lot like Erik."

"Well," said Nathan, "see if you can't get Erik away as soon as possible. We'll do what we can to protect little Gerd, but if Erik's presence calls undue attention to the baby . . ."

"I'll see what I can do," said Roo. "I have business, and the sooner I get it done, the sooner we'll leave."

"Anything we can do to help?" asked the smith.

A calculating looked entered Roo's eyes. "Well, now that you mention it, I could use a reliable wagon—but one that's not too dear, you understand."

Milo's eyes rolled heavenward, and Nathan laughed at the obvious ploy. "Gaston's still the only place you're likely to find a wagon," said the smith.

Erik glanced over to where his friend stood talking to the smith and the innkeeper, the three of them smiling while Nathan laughed at something Roo said, and shook his head with a smile of affection. Roo saw the gesture and returned it, as if to say, "Yes, it's good to be home."

Roo was out at first light, only slightly hung-over, making his way to the outskirts of town.

"Gaston!" he cried as he came into sight of his destination. The building was little more than a run-down barn, made over to a sort of storage building, with a small shed attached to the front. A sign hung over it, crudely painted hammers, crossed as if they were a noble's swords.

As Roo reached the door to the shop, a head stuck out and a narrow-faced man of indeterminate years regarded him. "Avery?" he exclaimed, half-pleased, half-irritated by his manner. "Thought you hung," he observed.

Roo stuck out his hand, "Wasn't," he replied.

"Kind of obvious," returned the man named Gaston. He spoke with a slight accent, one common to those living in the smaller backwater towns in the province of Bas-Tyra, but he had lived in Darkmoor since before Roo had been born. He shook Roo's hand and said, "What you need?"

Roo said, "Got a wagon?"

"One out back for sale. She not much to look at; need a little work, but she sound."

They walked around the building, a combination carpentry shed, tannery, and tinker's shop. Gaston was master of no trade, but adept at fixing all manner of things, and the only source of repair for those without sufficient funds to pay the local smiths and carpenters. If a poor farmer had a scythe that needed to last one more harvest, he brought it to Gaston, not the forge where Erik used to apprentice to old Tyndal and then Nathan. Roo had heard Erik comment that Gaston might not be a fine smith, but he was solid on the basics. And Roo's father had always taken his wagons to Gaston for repair.

They moved to a low fence, composed mostly from scraps of wood Gaston had found here and there, and Gaston opened the rickety gate. It swung open on stiff, loud hinges, and Roo entered the yard where Gaston stowed most of his property. Roo halted a moment and shook his head. He had been in the yard countless times; nevertheless he was amazed whenever he saw the colossal collection of refuse Gaston lay claim to: scraps of metal, a shed full of cloth, and a huge covered stack of wood, all organized in a fashion known only to Gaston, but one which Roo knew was flawless. If Gaston had what you needed, he knew where it lay, and could put his hands on it in moments.

"Saw your papa."

"Where's he now?" asked Roo, not entirely interested.

"Sleepin' off a drunk. He came back from a run down to Salador. Six or seven wagons, I don't remember, but they got there in good order and were paid a bonus, then he picked up a cargo and came back full, so he blew off a bit last night."

Gaston hiked his thumb over his shoulder to a bundle of rags under one of two wagons nestled against the lee side of the barn. Roo went over and found the bundle was snoring. He recognized one of the two wagons as his father's. It was as familiar to Roo as his own pallet had been at home. And truth to tell, he had slept in it about as often. When his father got into one of his drunken rages, Roo had often hidden under the canvas tie-down and slept the night there, rather than risk a pointless beating.

"Too drunk to walk three streets home?" said Roo, kneeling and pulling back the topmost rag. The stench that struck him as he did made him wish he hadn't. Not only hadn't his father bathed in some time, his breath hit Roo full on as he snored in obvious stupor.

"Gak!" Roo moved back a couple of steps.

Gaston scratched his chin and said, "We had a few, truth to tell. Tom was buying, so I weren't going to leave him lying there in the street. I bring him over here; I wasn't going to take him all the way home, by damn."

Roo shook his head. "Not likely." He regarded the snoring face of his father. The old man seemed smaller somehow. Roo wondered at that, but knew that he would seem large enough if he was awakened before he bestirred himself.

Then Roo laughed. He wasn't a boy any longer and his father hadn't towered over him in years. Roo wondered, if his father tried to strike him again, would he cower as a child would before an enraged parent, or would he act without thought and break his father's jaw?

Not willing to put that to the test, he said, "We'll let him sleep. He probably didn't miss me when I was gone, so I doubt he'll be glad to see me now."

Gaston said, "You shouldn't go saying that, Roo. He was right enough upset you were going to be hung. Said it more than once. Thought thirty years' hard labor was fair, he said."

Roo shook his head and changed the subject. "The wagon?"

"She be over there," said Gaston, pointing to the one that sat next to Roo's father's. It was a serviceable wagon, though in need of some repair and a lot of paint.

Roo quickly inspected it, ensuring the axles and wheels were sound. He said, "We need to replace some of the fittings on the tongue, but it'll do. How much?"

Gaston and Roo began haggling and after a minute a deal was struck. It was slightly more than Roo wished to pay, but a fair price, and the wagon was exactly what he was looking for. He paid the money and said, "Horses?"

"Martin still be cheapest for sound animals," answered Gaston. "Your papa got an extra team these days. Won them in a dice game last month."

A calculating look crossed Roo's face and he said, "Thanks. That's good to know." Glancing at the snoring figure of his father, he said, "If he wakes before I return, keep him here. I need to talk to him before I leave town."

Roo started for the gate and Gaston said, "Where are you off to now?"

"Growers' and Vintners' Hall. I have to buy some wine."

He left the yard and made his way down the street as the town began to stir into the day's activities. Workers were already at their shops, and now those women heading out to purchase goods and food for their families were also about. Roo nodded in greeting at a few familiar faces, but mostly he was lost in thought about the next step in his plan for wealth.

As he reached the town square, opposite the Growers' and Vintners' Hall, a clatter of hooves upon cobbles heralded the approach of riders, and from the sound, Roo knew they were coming fast. A moment later the squad appeared around the corner of the very hall for which Roo was bound, five riders at a canter. Pedestrians scampered out of the way as the five men in the colors of the Baron of Darkmoor hurried by. Roo marked the leader, the same corporal they had encountered in Wilhelmsburg, and he knew instantly where they would eventually stop: Milo's inn. Roo hesitated and decided against heading directly there. He had business to conduct and, besides, he was pretty sure this would be a matter between Erik and his half brother Manfred. If the Baron needed to speak with Roo Avery, he could come looking for him after he finally found Erik. Roo entered the hall.

* * *

Erik stood admiring the forge. Nathan and his apprentice Gunther were showing off the changes they had made since Erik had left. They were minor, but Erik made a point of admiring the boy's work. It was clear he doted on Nathan and had developed much the same attitude that Erik had toward the smith, that of a boy for a foster-father. Nathan's own children had been killed in an almost forgotten war and he took special pains to care for his apprentices.

"You look fit," said Nathan. "You like the army?"

Erik said, "There's much about it I don't like, but . . . yes, I think I like the order, the sense of knowing what is expected of you."

Nathan motioned with his head for Gunther to find some task to attend to, leaving them alone. "And the killing?"

Erik shrugged. "Not much. There are times when it's like hacking wood for the fire. Something you must do. Other times I'm too scared to think. But mostly it's . . . I don't know . . . ugly."

Nathan nodded. "I've worked with a lot of soldiers in my day, Erik. Be cautious of those who enjoy the butchery. They serve when the fighting's hard, but they're like guard dogs; better to keep them on a short leash most of the time."

Erik looked at Nathan and their eyes locked. Then Erik smiled. "I promise I'll never get to liking it."

"Then you'll do," said Nathan, returning Erik's grin. "Though you'd have been a fine smith, no doubt."

"Smithing is something I still enjoy. Maybe you'll let me turn a hand to some—"

Roo approached. "Nathan! Erik!"

Erik said, "How is this mysterious business deal of yours going?"

"Just about finished," answered Roo with a grin. "A couple of things more and I'll be ready to go." He made a face. "Besides, there are soldiers wandering around town looking for you."

The sound of riders entering the inn's courtyard cut short Erik's reply. They left the forge and rounded the barn, entering the courtyard just as the Baron's five guardsmen were getting ready to dismount.

Erik recognized the leader, the corporal they had encountered two days before. "You," he said, pointing to Roo and Erik. "The Baron wants a word with you two."

Roo rolled his eyes heavenward, patting his tunic pocket to ensure he still carried his royal pardon. "Can't this wait?"

"No! But I'll give you a choice: ride your own horse or I'll be happy to drag you behind him."

Roo said, "I'll get my horse."

A few minutes later, Roo and Erik were mounted and rode past the squad. The corporal said, "Wait a minute! Where do you think you're going?"

They slowed to let the corporal overtake him, then Erik said, "You came cantering in, yet your horses are barely winded and none of them are sweating. So you rode less than a mile to fetch us. Manfred's camped in the old sheep meadow at the edge of town."

The corporal looked astonished, but before he could speak, Erik put heels to his horse's barrel and was off at a canter, Roo a second behind. The squad followed suit, and soon the seven of them were hurrying through the town.

A few minutes later they passed through the buildings at the east edge of town, and as Erik had predicted, they found Manfred's field tent erected in the old sheep meadow where the King's Highway intersected the road south.

Erik dismounted and tossed the reins to a guardsman standing near the entrance of the tent. As the five riders came up alongside, Erik regarded the corporal. "What's your name?" asked Erik.

"Alfred," said the corporal. "Why?"

Erik smiled. "I just wanted to know. Watch the horse." Roo and Erik moved to the tent and one of the soldiers there drew aside the flap.

Sitting inside was Erik's half brother Manfred. "I must confess, I never thought I'd see you two again," said the Baron, indicating they should sit, "considering the circumstances of our last meeting."

"At the time, I thought the same," answered Erik.

Roo studied the half brothers. Manfred looked nothing like Erik. Erik was the mocking likeness of their father, the very fact of which had driven Manfred's mother to demand Erik's death over the murder of Stefan, her elder son. Manfred was his mother's son. He was dark, intense, and handsome in a nervous way. He wore a neatly trimmed beard, a new affectation, and Roo thought it a little silly, though he kept that opinion to himself.

"My lord the Duke of Salador, who as you may know is the King's cousin, has ordered me to send a squad of men to Krondor, for special duty. No details of why or for how long are forthcoming. Do you know something about this?"

Erik nodded. "Something."

"Will you tell me?"

"I cannot."

"Cannot or will not?"

"Both," said Erik. "I am the Prince's man and obey his injunctions against speaking before I'm bidden."

"Well, if you have no objections, I'd like them to return to Krondor with you and your friend."

Erik sat back. "An escort?"

Manfred smiled, and in that one expression there was a hint of the man who sired them both. "In a manner of speaking. As you are the Prince's man in this, I'll place them under your command. Being the dutiful soldier you are, I have no doubt you'll hurry to bring them safely to our most noble Prince as quickly as possible."

Erik leaned forward. "If I could tell you, Manfred, I would. You will never know how much it meant to me for you to come see me in jail as you did; it was very kind of you. It made a difference. But when you finally do know why the Prince is commanding this levy, you'll understand why I may not speak it now, and that it is of the utmost importance."

Manfred sighed. "Well, very good. I trust you'll not be lingering in Ravensburg, either of you?"

Erik raised an eyebrow. "I'm bound to be back at Krondor within the month, but Roo is a free man and may choose to stay."

Manfred smiled. "He may choose what he wishes, but if your friend is wise, he'll quickly leave." He looked at Roo. "My mother has not forgiven either of you, and while I will not seek to do either of you injury, I cannot protect you from her agents. If you wish to live to an old age, you better do it elsewhere." He leaned over toward Erik, lowering his voice, and lost his smile. "You gain a significant protection by wearing that new tunic, Erik. Even here in sleepy Darkmoor we know of the Eagle of Krondor; you're the Prince's Man's man. But your friend Rupert has no patronage and few friends. It's better for everyone if you take him with you."

"I'm getting a cargo together and will be leaving in a couple of days with my cousin," said Roo.

Manfred rose. "See that you do. It would be well for you both not to be in town when my mother learns you are alive and back within her reach." Glancing at the two men, he said, "Even in Krondor, watch your backs."

"What about the child?" asked Erik.

Manfred said, "Mother still doesn't know of his existence, and I would like to see it kept that way for as long as possible." He looked troubled. "It's a bit of a different story here than it was with you, Erik. The boy is Stefan's baby, not her philandering husband's; it's her own grandson. But he's a bastard, and as I have yet to wed . . ."

"Understood."

"Your presence in Ravensburg might push her to side against the child: have you considered that?"

Erik shrugged. "Not in that fashion. Truth to tell, Manfred, I've not been much of a thinker the last two years. Too much to do. Not enough time to ponder."

Manfred shook his head and said, "You've changed. You were the town lad when we met, and now . . . you're a harder man, Erik."

Erik studied his brother's face. "I think we both are."

Manfred rose and said, "I'm 'out hunting,' so I'd better have something to show Mother when I return this evening to the castle. Be about your business and expect the levy to appear tomorrow at that inn you called home."

Erik followed the Baron outside. "One of these days I hope we can meet under more favorable circumstances."

Manfred laughed and again the resemblance showed itself. "I doubt it. Our fortunes and fates are very different, brother. As long as you live and I have no children, Mother sees you as a threat to her line. It's that simple."

Dryly Roo said, "Then get married and have some."

Manfred said, "Would that it were that simple. I serve at the King's pleasure and my Duke of Salador's whim. They have yet to indicate to me which noble daughter would prove suitable wife material." He sighed slightly, but Erik noticed. "And, truth to tell, I haven't pressed them to decide. I find the company of women . . . difficult."

"Is there someone?" said Erik, suddenly sensing that his half brother, mostly a stranger to him, barely held some sorrow in check.

Manfred's manner turned neutral. "Nothing of which I choose to speak."

Erik had nothing more to say and his brother didn't offer his hand. Erik saluted and started back to where his horse waited. Roo headed toward the tent flap. With a quick move, Erik turned back toward his brother. "That corporal, Alfred."

"What of him?"

"Send him with the levy."

Manfred shook his head and smiled slightly. "You have an account with him?"

"Of sorts," said Erik.

Manfred shrugged. "There's not much to recommend the man. He's a brawler. He'll never make sergeant because of it."

"You have a need for brawlers," said Erik. "Once they're broken of brawling, they're the kind of men we need."

"You can have him." Turning back into the tent, Manfred vanished.

Roo and Erik returned to their horses and mounted. Erik looked down at Alfred and said, "Fare you well, Corporal."

"We'll meet again, bastard," said Alfred with a baleful stare.

"Oh, count on it." Erik returned the dark look.

Roo added, with an evil smile, "Sooner than you think."

With heels to their mounts, Roo and Erik left the soldiers behind and returned to Ravensburg.

"And I'm telling you that if you put any more on that wagon, you're going to break an axle!" shouted Tom Avery.

Roo stood nose to nose with his father, who was only slightly taller than his son, and after a moment said, "You're right."

Tom blinked, then nodded once, curtly, saying, "Of course I'm right."

The two wagons sat in the yard behind Gaston's shop, loaded with small barrels of wine. Duncan inspected each tie-down carefully, for the third or fourth time, and looked dubious about the prospect of so many barrels of wine remaining secure.

Roo had spent the day conducting business, spending every coin he had as well as what Erik had given him in purchasing a modest-quality wine that, he hoped, would realize him a significant profit once it reached Krondor.

While not an expert on wine, Roo was a child of Ravensburg and knew more about it than most merchants in Krondor. He knew that the high cost of wine in the Prince's city was due to the cost of shipping it bottled. Only the most common bulk wine came otherwise, shipped in large barrels. But the smaller barrels of modest-quality wine, used in the taprooms in the area, were never shipped much farther away than a neighboring village, because the wine commanded little profit in an area where high-quality wine was taken for granted. While still not as fine as the great wines served to the nobility, this wine would stand out in Krondor's common inns. Roo had shrewdly purchased wines he knew to be a cut or two above the quality of what he had drunk in the Prince's city. Roo calculated that if he could get the inns and taverns frequented by the businessmen of the Merchants' Quarter to buy his wine, he could realize as much as a threefold profit on this venture, including the cost of wagons and horses.

Duncan said, "You sure you know how to drive this thing?"

Tom wheeled to face his nephew and said, "Roo's a first-rate teamster, as you'd have been had you not run off after that girl—"

Duncan smiled in remembrance. "Alice," he supplied. "That didn't last long. Besides"—he put his hand upon the pommel of his sword—"this is how I earned my living for the last fifteen years."

"Well, we'll need it," said Tom, rubbing his chin. It was the spot Roo had hit him when the old man had come awake and started to bully his son. Three times he had tried to lay hands on the boy and three times had found himself in the dust, looking up at his son. The last time Roo had punctuated his lack of patience for this conflict with a stiff right jab to the old man's face. After that, Tom Avery looked on his son with a newfound respect. Turning to Roo, he said, "You sure you know your way along this road you told me of?"

Roo nodded. It was a backcountry road, little more than a trail in places, where he and Erik had encountered Helmut Grindle, a trader from Krondor. Roo had learned there was a way from Ravensburg to Krondor that was passable without having to pay toll on the King's Highway. Erik had papers from the Prince, which had saved them any charges on the way to Ravensburg, but Erik and his company of levies from Darkmoor had left that morning for Krondor, and they would be in the Prince's city a week before the slow-moving wagons would arrive.

Roo knew that the wagons were loaded to capacity, and that any trouble would leave half his cargo stuck in the backwoods between Darkmoor and the coast. But if his plan worked, he'd have enough capital for something more audacious, and he was sure he could make enough on this one journey to get his career fairly launched.

"Well," said Roo, "no reason to linger. The sooner started, the sooner finished." He said nothing of Manfred's warning about his mother's vengeance. He didn't trust Duncan enough to count on his staying close by should he learn that a noble might be sending agents after Roo. His father, he knew, could be trusted to drive his wagon: say what you might about Tom Avery, he was steadfast in his work when sober. But in a fight he would be useless, no matter what bluster and boasting he indulged himself in when drunk. "Ride with me," Roo said to Duncan. "I'll reacquaint you with driving a team."

Duncan rolled his eyes heavenward but climbed aboard. He had sold his horse for a small price, which earned him a share in Roo's venture, and now was a minority owner of one wagon, four horses, and a great deal of wine. Roo's father had insisted only on his usual fees, not a coin more or less, which silently pleased Roo. He enjoyed his father's treating him as he would any other trader.

Gaston waved farewell as they rolled through the gate out of his yard and turned down the cobbles of Ravensburg. The wagons creaked and groaned under the weight and the horses snorted at being asked to work, but they were under way, and Roo felt a keen sense of anticipation.

"Try not to get yourself killed," called out Gaston as the gate shut.

Roo ducked behind the wagon as another arrow sped through the space he had just occupied; the first had struck inches from his head. He yelled a warning to his father and Duncan as he scrambled under the wagon, drawing his sword and trying to ascertain from where the arrow had come. A third shaft emerged from the evening gloom and he marked where he judged it had originated. He signaled to Duncan that he was going to back between the wagons and move in a circle around the ambushers. Duncan signaled he understood and motioned around the campsite, indicating he should be wary of other attackers.

They had been on the road for almost a week, having left the King's Highway just west of Ravensburg and making their way across open country to the small westward trail road Roo and Erik had used when fleeing the area two years earlier.

The travel had been uneventful and the wagons were proving sturdy and the horses sound, which had contributed to Roo's increasing optimism as the days passed. If his father had judged him daft for picking a large, unwieldy cargo, he kept his opinion to himself. He was an old teamster and had driven stranger cargo than dozens of small wine casks before.

They camped each night at sundown, letting the horses graze along a picket, supplementing the grass with a small amount of grain, mixed with honey and nuts, which kept them fit and energetic. Each day Roo used what knowledge of horses he possessed to check their soundness, and more than once he had silently wished for Erik's presence, as he would find anything that Roo might miss. But Roo had been astonished to discover that his father knew as much as Erik, at least on the subject of draft animals, and each day the old man inspected right alongside his son, and each day he judged the animals fit to continue the journey.

Now Roo crab-crawled on elbows and knees, turning as he moved between the wagons, and when he had the wagons between himself and the source of the arrow fire, he stood and ran into the woods. Only two years of combat and intense training saved his life, for another bandit had moved opposite the first and tried to impale Roo on his sword point. The only thing he accomplished was to die silently; Roo hardly broke stride as he ran him through, dodging sideways into the dark woods in case there was another bandit close by.

Silence greeted him as he paused to consider his next move. He slowed his breathing and looked around. The sun had set less than an hour before and the sky to the west might still hold some glow, but under the thick trees it could have been midnight. Roo listened. A moment later he heard another arrow flight, and he moved.

Circling as quietly as he could through the darkness, he ran swiftly to the place where he thought the bowman might be hiding. At this point he was convinced he was being besieged by a pair of poor bandits, trying to pick off the two guards so they could plunder whatever cargo ventured along the small road far from the King's justice.

Roo waited. After a few more moments of silence, he heard someone stirring in the brush ahead of him and he acted. As quick as a cat on a mouse, he was through the brush and on top of the other bandit. The struggle was quickly over. The man attempted to drop his bow and pull a knife when he sensed Roo's approach from behind.

The man died before the knife was out of his belt.

"It's over," said Roo.

A moment later, Duncan and Tom appeared, wraithlike in the gloom. "Just two of them?" asked Duncan.

"If there's another, he's halfway to Krondor," said Tom. He had obviously fallen hard, as he was dirty from boot to the top of his head on his left side, and he had a bruise on his left cheek. He held his right arm across his chest, holding tight to his left biceps, and flexed the fingers of his left hand.

"What's the matter?" asked Roo.

"Fell damn hard on this arm, I guess," answered his father. "It's all tingly and numb." He seemed short of breath as he spoke. Blowing out a long note, he added, "Some time of it, that was. Not ashamed to admit I was scared for a bit."

Duncan knelt and rolled over the bandit. "This one looks like a ragpicker," he said.

"Few honest traders and only a few more dishonest ones brave this route," said Tom. "Never been a rich outlaw I heard of, and certainly not around here." He shook his hand as if trying to wake up a sleeping limb.

Duncan came away with a purse. "He might not have been rich, but he wasn't coinless, either." He opened the purse and found a few copper coins and a single stone. Walking back into the light of the campfire, he knelt to inspect the gem. "Nothing fancy, but it'll fetch a coin or two."

Roo said, "Better see if the other one is dead."

He found the first man he had encountered lying facedown in the mud, and when he rolled him over, discovered a boy's face on the corpse. Shaking his head in disgust, Roo quickly found the boy without even the rude leather pouch the other bandit had possessed.

He returned to the wagons as Duncan put down the bow he had taken from the first bandit. "Pretty poor," he said, tossing it aside. "Ran out of arrows." Roo sat down with an audible sigh.

"What do you think they'd be doing with all this wine?" asked Duncan.

"Probably drink a bit," said Tom. "But it was the horses and whatever coin we carry, and the swords you have and anything else they could sell."

Duncan said, "We bury them?"

Roo shook his head. "They'd not have done the same for us. Besides, we've no shovel. And I'm not about to dig their graves with my hands." He sighed. "If they'd been proper bandits, we'd have been feeding the crows tomorrow instead of them. Better keep alert."

Duncan said, "Well then, I'm turning in."

Tom and Roo sat before the fire. Because of his age, Roo and Duncan allowed Tom the first watch. The man with the second had it roughest, having to awake for a few hours in the dark, then turn in again. Roo also knew that dawn was the most dangerous time for attack, as guards were the sleepiest and least alert and anyone contemplating a serious assault would wait for just before sunrise. Chances were near-certain if Tom had morning watch, should trouble come he'd be sound asleep when he died.

Tom said, "Had a stone like that one Duncan's got, once."

Roo said nothing. His father rarely talked to him, a habit that had developed in childhood. Rupert had traveled with his father many times as a boy, learning the teamster's trade, but on the longest of those journeys, from Ravensburg to Salador and back, he'd rarely had more than ten words for the boy. When at home, Tom drank to excess, and when working, remained sober but stoic.

"I got it for your mother," said Tom quietly.

Roo was riveted. If Tom was a quiet man when sober, he was always silent about Roo's mother, sober or drunk. Roo knew what he did about his mother from others in the village, for she had died in childbirth.

"She was a tiny thing," said Tom. Roo knew his diminutive status was a legacy from his mother. Erik's mother had mentioned that more than once. "But strong," said Tom.

Roo found that surprising. "She had a tough grit to her," continued Tom, his eyes shining in the firelight. "You look like her, you know." He held his right arm across his chest, clutching his left arm, which he massaged absently. He peered into the fire as if seeking something in the dancing flame.

Roo nodded, afraid to speak. Since he had struck his father, knocking him to the ground, the old man had treated him with a deference Roo had never experienced before. Tom sighed. "She wanted you, boy. The healing priest told her it would be chancy, with her being so tiny." He wiped his right hand over his face, then looked at his own hands, large, oft scarred, and calloused. "I was afraid to touch her, you know, with her being so small and me having no gentleness in me. I was afraid I'd break her. But she was tougher than she looked."

Roo swallowed, suddenly finding it hard to speak. He finally whispered, "You never speak of her."

Tom nodded. "I had so little joy in this life, boy. And she was every bit of it. I met her at a festival, and she looked like this shy bird of a thing, standing on the edge of the crowd at the feast of Midsummer. I had just come up from Salador, driving a wagon for my uncle, Duncan's grandfather. I was half-drunk and full of myself, and then she was right there before me, bold as bright brass, and she says, 'Dance with me.' " He sighed. "And I did."

He was silent awhile. He hugged himself, and his breath seemed labored, and he had to swallow hard to speak. "She had that same look you do, not fetching with her thin face and uneven teeth, until she smiled—then she lit up and was beautiful. I got her that stone I was speaking of for our wedding. Had it set in a ring for her."

"Like a noble," said Roo, forcing his voice to a lighter tone.

"Like the Queen herself," Tom answered with a shallow laugh. He swallowed hard. "She said I was mad and should sell it for a new wagon, but I insisted she keep it."

"You never told me," said Roo softly.

Tom shrugged and was silent. He took a deep breath, then said, "You're a man now. Showed me that when I woke to find you standing over me at Gaston's. Never thought you'd amount to much, but you're a shrewd one, and if you can beat the King's own hangman and learn to handle yourself so I can't bully you, why, I figure you'll turn out all right down the road." Tom smiled slightly and said, "You're like her that way; you're tougher than you look."

Roo sat in silence a minute, not knowing what to say, then after a bit he said, "Why don't you turn in, Father. I have some thinking to do."

Tom nodded. "I think I will. Got a pain in my neck." He moved his left shoulder as if to loosen tight muscles. "Must have really twisted it hitting the ground when those lads started shooting arrows at us. Hurts from my wrist to my jaw." He wiped perspiration from his brow. "Broke a bit of sweat, too." He sucked in a large breath and blew it out, as if just standing had been exertion. "Getting too old for this. When you get rich, you remember your old father, hear me, Roo?"

Roo started to smile and say something when his father's eyes rolled up into his head and he fell forward, facedown into the fire. Roo yelled, "Duncan!" and with a single move yanked his father out of the flames.

Duncan was over in an instant and saw the waxy pallor of Tom's face, the white eyes, and smoldering burns on his cheek and neck. He knelt next to Roo, then said, "He's dead."

Roo remained motionless as he silently regarded the man who had been his father, and who had died still a stranger to him.

Four

Setback

ROO SIGNALED.

Duncan reined in the second wagon, coming to a halt behind the first. Roo turned, stood, and shouted, "Krondor!"

They had been traveling this way since burying Tom, in a grave Roo had dug with his bare hands, covering him with stones to keep scavengers away. Duncan had become a fair driver. He had remembered a few things taught to him by Tom when he was a boy, and Roo had increased his skill until he no longer had to spend every minute worrying about the second wagon and its cargo.

Roo was still troubled by his father's death. He couldn't escape the feeling that he had glimpsed something in his father when he had been speaking about Roo's mother. Roo knew there was a great deal about his own history he didn't understand. His father had always been an aloof man when sober and abusive when drunk, and in part Roo now understood why: each time Tom looked at his son he saw a reminder of the wife he had loved beyond measure, taken from him at Roo's birth.

But there had been more, and Roo now had dozens of questions, none of which his father would ever answer. He vowed to return to Ravensburg and try to find those few people in the town Tom might have called friend, to ask them those questions. Perhaps he might travel to Salador to visit with Duncan's branch of the family. But he wanted answers. Suddenly Roo had been made aware that he really didn't know who he was. Pushing aside that thought, he insisted to himself it wasn't as important who one is as who one becomes, and he was determined to become a rich, respected man.

Duncan tied off the reins and jumped down from his wagon, walking to where Roo stood. Roo had come to like his cousin, though there was still the rogue in his manner, and Duncan didn't bring out any strong sense of trust, the way Roo trusted Erik or the other men he had served with under Calis. But he liked the man and thought he might be useful, for he had enough experience with nobility to tutor Roo in manners and fashion.

Duncan climbed up on the first wagon and looked at the distant city. "We're going in tonight?" he asked.

Roo glanced at the setting sun and said, "I don't think so. I'd have to find a stable yard to house this wine until we could move out in the morning. We're still more than an hour from the gate now. Let's make a camp and we'll head in at first light, try to sell some of this before the inns get too busy."

They made camp and ate a cold meal before a small fire, while the horses, tied in a long picket, grazed along the roadside. Roo had given them the last of the grain and they were making satisfied noises. "What are you going to do with the wagons?" asked Duncan.

"Sell them, I think." Roo wasn't sure if he wanted to depend on other shippers, but he didn't think his time was best spent actually driving the wagons back and forth between Ravensburg and Krondor. "Or maybe hire a driver and send you back for another load after we sell off this lot."

Duncan shrugged. "Not much by way of excitement, unless you count those two hapless boy bandits."

Roo said, "One of those 'boy bandits' almost put an arrow through my head"—he tapped the side of his skull—"if you remember."

"There is that." Duncan sighed. "I mean by way of women and drink."

"We'll have some of that tomorrow night." Roo glanced around. "Turn in—I'll take the first watch."

Duncan yawned. "I won't argue."

Roo sat by the fire as his cousin grabbed a blanket and crawled under one of the wagons to protect himself from the dew that would form during the night. This close to the ocean it wasn't a possibility, it was a certainty, and waking up wet wasn't either man's idea of a pleasant way to start the day.

Roo considered what he would do first in the morning, and made up several speeches, rehearsing each and discarding this phrase or that as he tried to determine which sales pitch would work best. He had never been a focused thinker in his youth, but so much was riding on his doing well that he became lost in his thinking, and didn't realize how much time had passed until he noticed the fire burning down. He considered waking Duncan, but decided instead to reconsider some of his sales pitch, and just stuck some more wood in the fire.

He was still practicing his pitch when the lightening sky finally took his attention from the now merely glowing embers of the fire and he shook himself out of his half-daze, half-dreaming, and he realized that he had not truly slept all night. But he was too filled with excitement and too ready to rush forward into his new life and he figured Duncan wouldn't object to the extra rest. He rose, and found his knees stiff from sitting in the damp, cool night air without moving for hours. His hair was damp, and dew shone upon his cloak as he shook it out.

"Duncan!" he yelled, rousing his cousin. "We've got wine to sell!"

The wagons clattered over the cobbles of Krondor's streets. Roo indicated Duncan should pull up behind him, over to one side, allowing some room for traffic to pass on the narrow side street. He had picked out his first stop, a modest inn named the Happy Jumper near the edge of the Merchants' Quarter. The sign was of a pair of children turning a rope for a third who was suspended in midair over it.

Roo pushed open the door and found a quiet common room, with a large man behind the bar cleaning glasses. "Sir?" the bar-man asked.

"Are you the proprietor?" asked Roo.

"Alistair Rivers at your disposal. How may I be of service?" He was a portly man, but under the fat Roo detected strength—most innkeepers had to have some means of enforcing order. His manner was polite, but distant, until he knew the nature of Roo's business.

"Rupert Avery," said Roo, sticking out his hand. "Wine merchant in from Ravensburg."

The man shook his hand in a perfunctory manner and said, "You need rooms?"

"No, I have wine to sell."

The man's expression showed a decided lack of enthusiasm. "I have all the wine I need, thank you."

Roo said, "But of what quality and character?"

The man looked down his nose at Roo and said, "Make your pitch."

"I was born in Ravensburg, sir," began Roo. And then he launched into a brief comparison of the bounties of that small town's wine craft and what was commonly drunk in Krondor's more modest establishments.

At the end of his pitch he said, "The service to Krondor has either been bulk wine for the common man or impossibly priced wine for the nobles, but nothing for the merchant catering to a quality clientele, until now. I can provide wine of superior quality at bulk prices, because I don't transport the bottles!"

The man was silent a minute. "You have a sample?" he asked at last.

"Outside," said Roo and he hurried out to fetch down a sample cask he had filled before leaving Ravensburg. Returning inside he found a pair of glasses on the bar. He pulled the cork, and as he filled the two glasses with a taste, he said, "It's a bit shocked, having rolled in this very morning off the road, but give it a week or two to rest before you serve it, and you'll have more business than any other inn in the area."

The man looked unconvinced, but he tasted. He rolled the wine around his palate, then spit it into a bucket, while Roo did the same. Alistair was quiet again, then said, "It's not bad. A little jumbled, as you said from the road, but there's some structure there and abundant fruit. Most of my customers won't know it from the usual plonk, but I do have a few businessmen who frequent my establishment who might find this diverting. I might be interested in a half-dozen barrels. What is your price?"

Roo paused, and quoted a price he knew to be three times what he would accept, and only 15 percent below what the finest noble wines from Ravensburg would fetch. Alistair blinked, then said,

"Why not burn my inn to the ground and have done with it? You'll ruin me far quicker." He offered a price that was a few coppers less per barrel than what Roo had paid in Ravensburg. Then they began haggling in earnest.

They were waiting for Roo when he came out of the third inn an hour after midday. His first two negotiations had proven profitable, earning him more than he had anticipated. He had gotten about 10 percent higher a price from Alistair Rivers than he had hoped for, which had made him bargain harder at the Inn of Many Stars. His final price had been within coppers of what he had sold wine to Alistair for, so he knew what he was likely to get at the Dog and Fox Tavern. He had concluded his negotiations in quick order, and as he came out of the Dog and Fox he said, "Duncan! We need to unload five barrels!"

Then he halted. Duncan moved his head slightly to indicate the man sitting close to him on the wagon, who had a dagger point in Duncan's ribs, though you had to look to notice it. To passersby it appeared he was merely having a quiet conversation with the driver of the wagon.

Another man stepped up and said, "You the owner of these wagons?"

Roo nodded once as he studied the man. He was rangy to the point of gauntness, but there was quickness and danger in his movements. Roo saw no weapons in the man's hands, but guessed there was more than one of them secreted on him, within easy reach. His narrow face was covered by a two- or three-day growth of beard, and grey-shot, raggedly cut black hair hung loosely about his forehead and neck.

"We was noticing you driving around and making deliveries. Wondered if you were new to Krondor?"

Roo glanced from the man's face to the man next to Duncan, then looked around to see if the two were alone. A couple of others lingered in close proximity to the wagons, men who could aid their companions in moments, without calling attention to themselves until needed. Roo said, "Been here before, but just rolled into the city this morning."

"Ah!" said the man, his voice surprisingly deep for one so thin. "Well then, you'd not be knowing about the local licenses and duties, would you?"

Roo's gaze narrowed. "We declared our cargo at the gate to the Prince's magistrate, and nothing was said about licenses and duties."

"Well, these aren't the Prince's licenses and duties, in a manner of speaking." The man lowered his voice so he would not be overheard. "There are ways to do business in the city and there are other ways, if you catch my drift. We represent interests that would seek to keep you from encountering difficulties in Krondor, if you follow me."

Roo leaned against the back of the wagon, attempting to look casual, while judging how fast he could kill this man if needs be and what chance Duncan stood of disarming the man who held a dagger on him. Of the first he was confident; he could kill this man before his companions could take two steps in his aid, but Duncan didn't have Roo's combat training, and while a competent swordsman, he would probably die. Roo said, "I'm very stupid today. Pretend I don't know anything and educate me."

The man said, "Well, there are those of us in Krondor who like to make sure the daily commerce of the city goes undisturbed, if you see what I mean. We don't care much for unseemly price wars and large fluctuations between supply and demand. Toward that end, we make sure that everything coming into the city has a reasonable profit, so that no one has too much an advantage, don't you see? Keeps things civilized. We also keep thugs from roughing up merchants and destroying property, as well as make sure that a man can sleep in his bed at night without fear of having his throat cut, don't you see? Now, to that end, we expect a compensation for our work."

Roo said, "I see. How much?"

"For your cargo, it would be twenty golden sovereigns"—Roo's eyes widened—"for each wagon."

That was easily close to one half his expected profit on this cargo alone. His outrage couldn't be kept below the surface. "Are you mad? Twenty sovereigns!" He took a quick step back and said, "I think not!"

The man took a step after Roo, which he had anticipated, saying, "If you want your friend there to stay health—"

Suddenly Roo had his sword out and at the man's throat before he could move away. The man was quick and tried to move back, but Roo followed, keeping the point of his sword touching skin. "Ah, ah!" said Roo. "Don't move too quickly; I might slip and then you'd get blood over everything. If your friend doesn't get his dagger out of my cousin's ribs or if either one of those two men across the street makes the wrong move, you're sucking wind through a new hole."

"Hold on!" shouted the man. Then, glancing sideways without moving his head, he shouted, "Bert! Get down!"

The man next to Duncan got down without question, while the man whom Roo held at sword's point said, "You're making a big mistake."

"If I am, it's not the first," said Roo.

"Cross the Sagacious Man and it's the last," said the would-be extortionist.

"Sagacious Man?" said Roo. "Who would that be?"

"Someone important in this city," answered the thin man. "We'll mark this a misunderstanding, and you ask about. But when we come back tomorrow, I'll expect better manners from you."

He motioned for his two distant companions to leave and they quickly darted into the midday crush of people. Other pedestrians had stopped to watch the display of one man holding another at sword's point, and it was obvious the thin man didn't care for the scrutiny. A merchant looked out from his shop and started shouting for a city constable.

Glancing at Roo the man said, "If I'm handed over to the city watch, you're in even bigger trouble than you might be already." He licked his lips nervously. A shrill whistle sounded a block away, and Roo dropped his sword's point and the man ducked away, vanishing into the crowd.

"What was that?" asked Duncan.

"Shakedown."

Duncan said, "Mockers."

"Mockers?"

"Guild of Thieves," supplied Duncan as he patted his ribs to make sure they were still intact.

"I expect. He mentioned someone named the Sagacious Man."

"That's the Mockers, without a doubt. You can't do business in a city like Krondor without having to pay off someone."

Roo climbed aboard his own wagon and said, "Damn me if I will."

If Duncan had an answer, Roo didn't hear it as he untied the rope holding down the barrels and lowered the drop gate. A shout and men running down the street caused Roo to glance past the wagon to where members of the City Watch, wearing blue tunics and carrying large billy clubs, paused to see the merchant pointing at Roo.

Roo swore under his breath. The constable approached and said, "That gentleman tells me you was dueling in the street."

Roo tossed a rope to Duncan. "Dueling? Me? Sorry, but he's mistaken. I'm just unloading wine for this inn." He turned his chin toward the inn, as Duncan came down to help get the barrels off the top of the wagon.

"Well then," said the constable, obviously unwilling to go searching for trouble when it was so abundant in Krondor, "just see it stays that way." He motioned for his partner and they returned the way they came.

Duncan said, "Some things never change. Unless I miss my bet, those two will be back in whatever pastry shop they were in when the whistle blew."

Roo laughed. They lowered the five barrels to the street, and Roo convinced the innkeeper to send a worker to help Duncan carry them inside, so Roo could protect the wagons while the wine was delivered. After the remaining cargo was secured, they took reins and moved on to the next tavern.

At sundown, they had sold close to a third of the wine Roo had purchased in Ravensburg. More, they had recouped almost all the gold Roo had spent. Roo calculated that he stood to triple his money if business the next day or so was as brisk as it had been so far.

"Where do we spend the night?" asked Duncan. "And when do we eat? I'm starving."

Roo said, "Let us find an inn with a good-sized yard so we can guard this wine against our friends."

Duncan nodded, knowing full well whom Roo meant. They were in an area of the city unknown to Duncan, who had been to Krondor a number of times over the years, and from the wares displayed in the shop windows as they passed, not a terribly prosperous one. Roo said, "Let's go around the block and head back the way we came. I think we're leaving prosperity behind if we continue on this way."

Duncan nodded and watched as Roo headed his team out into the traffic of the road. The street was full of travelers as those finished with the day's work headed home, or to a local tavern or shop. Some shops were being shuttered, while others were lighting lanterns, indicating their proprietors were staying open past dark for those customers who could only shop in the evening.

They moved slowly through the press and Roo turned right into another street, and Duncan followed. It took them almost an hour to find an inn with a stable area big enough to accommodate their wagons behind locked gates. Roo made arrangements with the stable boy, took his sample cask, and led Duncan inside.

The inn was known as the Seven Flowers, and it was a modest establishment, catering to merchants and workers equally. Roo found a table near the bar and indicated Duncan should take a seat. He spied an interesting-looking bar maid, a little long in the face but with an ample spread of bosom and hip, and he said, "When you have a minute, if you'd bring us both a tankard of ale and dinner." He indicated the table where Duncan sat. The woman looked at the handsome Duncan and her smile betrayed her interest. Roo found his eyes fixed upon the woman's bosom where it strained against the fabric of her dress and said, "And if you're free at the end of the evening, join us." He tried his best to look charming, and the remark got him a neutral expression and a noncommittal noise. "Where's the owner?" asked Roo.

She indicated a heavyset man at the far end of the bar, and Roo made his way through a half-dozen customers and started his pitch. After providing samples of his wine and arguing price, Roo arrived at a price with the owner of the inn, including a night's lodging and food, and returned to the table.

The food was average but ample and after weeks on the trail tasted wonderful. The ale was also average, but cold and plentiful. After the meal, when business had thinned, Duncan started working his charms on the serving girl, a woman of middle years named Jean. Another barmaid, a thin young woman named Betsy, joined them and somehow ended up sitting in Roo's lap. Either Duncan was terribly funny in his storytelling or the ale gave everyone a more forgiving sense of humor. A couple of times the innkeeper had had to come over and order his barmaids back to work, but as the evening wore on, the two women had found their way back to Roo and Duncan's company.

The pairing was obvious: Duncan had captured the attention of both women, but Jean, the more attractive of the two, had staked her claim early on, while Betsy was content to spend her time with Roo's hand fondling her. Roo didn't know if the girl really liked him or expected recompense, but he didn't care. The soft heat of flesh under cloth had him aroused, and after a while he said, "Let's go upstairs."

The girl said nothing but rose and took his hand and led him upstairs. In his drunken state he didn't remember hearing Duncan and Jean entering the room with them, but soon he was lost in the feel, smell, taste, and heat of being with a woman.

He was vaguely aware of Duncan and Jean on the pallet next to the one he shared with Betsy, but he ignored them. He had been with whores in camp less than a hand's breadth from other soldiers, so he thought nothing of it.

He got out of his clothing and got Betsy out of hers in quick order, and was lost in passion when a shout came from outside followed by the sound of cracking wood. He almost didn't notice it at first, but another crack followed, and suddenly, before thought was his, he was on his feet, pulling his sword from the scabbard, yelling, "Duncan!".

Naked, Roo raced down the stairs and into the common room. Deserted and dark, the room was an obstacle course as Roo tried to get to the inn's courtyard door without laming himself on a chair or table. Duncan's oaths from behind told Roo he wasn't alone in his drunken difficulties.

Roo found the door, pulled it open, and hurried toward the stable where his horses were being cared for and his wagons were housed. His feet encountered wetness as his nose greeted him with a familiar aroma: wine.

He entered the dark barn cautiously, his intoxication gone with the rush of battle readiness. Duncan overtook him and Roo gripped his cousin by the arm, signaling in the dark to move to the side of the barn aisle. Something was wrong and Roo couldn't put his finger on what that was until he saw the first horse. The animal lay on the ground, blood pooling from its neck. Quickly he took an inventory and found all four of his horses had been killed, their necks cut in exactly the right place to bleed them as fast as possible.

"Oh, damn!" said Duncan, and Roo hurried to find the stableboy lying in his own blood.

They dashed to the wagons and found that every barrel had been stove in or had the bung pulled, so that wine flooded the courtyard. The cracking of wood that Roo had heard had been someone using a large hammer on the spokes of the wheels, so that the wagons were now useless without expensive repair.

The innkeeper came hurrying across the courtyard when he saw the two naked men holding their swords.

"What's afoot?" he asked, halting, as if afraid to approach these two strange apparitions any more closely. From his nightshirt it was clear he had turned in.

"Someone's killed your stableboy and my horses, and ruined my wagons and cargo," said Roo.

Abruptly a scream cut the night and Roo was running past the innkeeper before Duncan could react. Roo almost flew through the door to the inn, banging against a table, and took the stairs two at a time. He reached the room he and Duncan shared and took a half-step in, his sword leveled.

He faltered as Duncan came running up the stairs. Duncan looked over the shoulder of his shorter cousin and again he said, "Damn."

Jean and Betsy lay nude upon the two palettes, their vacant gaze telling both men they were dead before the men could see the dark spreading stains flowing from where their throats had been cut. Whoever had come through the window had taken the two women from behind, killing them quickly and pulling them back on the mats. Roo was suddenly aware he was standing in something sticky and warm and realized the women had probably come to the door after the men had raced out, only to die before they realized someone had entered the room from the window.

Then Roo realized his clothing was strewn around the room. He quickly searched, and as the innkeeper arrived, Roo looked at Duncan and said, "They took the gold."

Duncan seemed almost to go limp as he leaned against the door jam. "Damn," he said for a third time.

*   *   *

The constable of the City Watch was obviously anxious to be done with his investigation. He looked at the dead horses and the dead stableboy, and went into the inn to inspect the dead barmaids, and then asked Roo and Duncan a few questions. It was also obvious that he knew the Mockers were involved and this would be reported in as an "unsolved crime." Unless someone was caught in the act, finding criminals and proving guilt was a rare event in a city the size of the capital of the Western Realm. As the constable left he instructed them to report anything they discovered that might help solve the crime to the office of the City Watch, at the palace.

The innkeeper was devastated by the death of his three employees and voiced his fear that he was somehow slated to join them. He ordered Roo and Duncan out of his inn at first light and then barricaded himself in his room.

As the dawn came, Roo and Duncan walked out of the courtyard of the Inn of the Seven Flowers. The early morning press of business hadn't begun, but already workers were moving toward their places of employment. As they entered the street, Duncan asked, "What now?"

Roo said, "I don't know—" He inhaled as he spied a familiar figure across the street. Lounging against the wall of the building opposite them was the thin man from the day before. Roo crossed the street, almost knocking down a hurrying workman, and as he reached the man, he heard him say, "Quietly now, stranger, else my friends will have to shoot you."

Duncan overtook Roo in time to hear the remark and spun around, looking for the bowman. On the rooftop above, a bowman had an arrow drawn hard against his cheek, aimed in their direction. The thin man said, "I expect you now understand just the sort of troubles we can protect you from, don't you?"

"If I thought I stood a chance of not getting my cousin shot in the bargain," said Roo, his anger barely held in check, "I'd cut your liver out right now."

"Like to see you try," said the thin man. "You caught me by surprise yesterday, but it would never happen again." He then smiled, and there was nothing friendly in the expression. "Besides, there's nothing personal in this, lad. It's only business. Next time

you seek to do business in Krondor, let those who can help you
. . . help you."

"Why did you kill the boy and the girls?" asked Roo.

"Kill? Me? I don't know what you're talking about," said the
man. "Ask anyone and they'll tell you that Sam Tannerson was
playing pokiir at Mama Jamila's in the Poor Quarter all night long.
Did someone go and get themselves killed?" He made a signal
and moved away, saying, "When you're ready to try doing business
again, ask around. Sam Tannerson isn't hard to find. And he's
always willing to help." He quickly moved off into the press of
traffic and vanished from sight.

After a moment Roo asked again, "Why did they kill the girls
and the stableboy?"

Duncan said, "My guess is that if you're too stubborn to pay
them, they're making sure everyone else knows the price of doing
business with you."

Roo said, "I've only felt more helpless once in my life, and that
was when they were about to hang me."

Duncan had heard the story of how Roo and his friend Erik had
been reprieved from the gallows after a mock hanging. "Well, you
may not be dead, as they say, but what will we do?"

Roo said, "Start over. What else is there to do?" Then he added,
"But first we head for the palace, and the office of the City
Watch."

"What for?"

"To tell them we know the name of the man who was behind
this, Sam Tannerson."

"Do you think that's his real name?"

"Probably not," said Roo as he turned in the direction of the
palace. "But it's the one he uses, and it will do."

Duncan shrugged. "I don't know what good it'll do, but as I
have no better idea, why not?" He fell in beside his cousin and
they began walking toward the Prince of Krondor's palace.

Erik looked out over the yard where the levies hurried through
their drills. He remembered with some guilty pleasure the near fit
Alfred, the corporal from Darkmoor, had thrown when informed
he was now reduced to the rank of private in the Prince's new
army. The third time Erik had deposited him on his ear on the

parade ground had convinced him to shut up and do as he was told. Erik suspected he would turn out to be a better than average soldier if he could learn to control his temper.

"What do you think?" asked Robert de Loungville from behind.

Without turning to look, Erik said, "I'd know better what to think if I knew what exactly you, the Duke, the Prince, and everyone else you meet with every night have in mind."

"You've been down there. You know what's coming," said de Loungville without emotion.

"I think we've got a few men here who might do well enough," answered Erik. "These are all seasoned soldiers, but some of them are worthless."

"Why?" asked Robert.

Erik turned and looked at the man to whom he reported. "Some of them are barracks rats, fit for nothing much more than light garrison duty and three meals a day. I guess their lords decided it was cheaper to let us feed them. Others are too . . ." He struggled for a concept. "I don't know, it's like a horse that's been trained to do one thing, then you want to train him to do another. You've first got to break him of the old habits."

Robert nodded. "Go on."

"Some of these men just can't think on their feet. If you're in a battle and giving orders, they're going to be fine, but if they're on their own . . ." Erik shrugged.

Robert said, "Muster all the castle rats and those too set in their ways to think for themselves after the midday meal. We're going to send them back to their lords and masters. I want the ones who can think on their feet assembled an hour after the first bunch leaves the castle. I need to get this first bunch trained before we do some serious recruiting."

"Serious recruiting?"

"Never mind. I'll tell you about it when the time's right."

Erik saluted and was about to leave when a guardsman hurried out of the castle, saluted, and said, "Sergeant, the Knight-Marshal wants you and the corporal down at the City Watch office at once."

De Loungville grinned. "What do you think? Want to bet it's one of our own?"

Erik shrugged. "No bet."

Erik followed him through the maze of corridors in the Prince's palace. The original keep, built centuries before to protect the harbor below from Quegan raiders and pirates, had been added to over the years until a large sprawling series of interconnecting buildings with outer walls rested hard against the harbor side and covered the entire hill upon which the old keep was the summit.

Erik was starting to find his way around and feeling a little more comfortable, but there were still things he didn't understand about what was taking place here in Krondor. He had barely seen Bobby since returning to the city. He and Jadow had been given better than a hundred men each to oversee, with Bobby's orders simply being "Put them through their paces and keep an eye on them." Erik wasn't exactly sure what that meant, but he and the other corporal had contrived some vigorous training exercises based on the ones they themselves had endured when first coming into de Loungville's service. After a week of this, Erik now had a pretty good idea who would fit in with the sort of army Calis was fashioning, and who wouldn't.

Calis hadn't been seen since Erik returned, and when he had asked about their Captain's whereabouts, de Loungville shrugged and said he was off on some errand or another. That made Erik uneasy, as did the fact that Erik's place in the scheme of things was unclear to him. The regular guard in the palace either avoided him or treated him with unusual deference for a corporal. He had guard sergeants address him as "sir," and yet when he asked questions, he got brusque, even rude answers. It was clear there was some resentment on the part of the existing garrison over the creation of this new army of Calis's.

As they reached the office of the Watch Commander, Erik found his hand reaching for his sword without thought at the sight of Roo backing out of the Watch Commander's office with his own sword drawn.

A shout from within could be heard: "He'll not harm you! Put that sword away!" He recognized the voice as belonging to William, Knight-Marshal of Krondor.

Roo's appearance was one of a man totally unconvinced, yet Erik couldn't see what was causing his friend such alarm. He almost fell, he was so startled by what he saw next. Coming out of the Watch Commander's office was a green-scaled serpent with large red eyes in an alligatorlike head on a long sinuous neck. Then

Erik saw the thing's body and saw it had wings. It was a small dragon!

Before Erik could do anything, Robert said, "Relax." He stepped forward and said, "Fantus! You old thief!" He knelt next to the creature and put his arm around its neck, giving it a hug as if it were a favorite hound. Bobby told Erik and Roo, "This thing is a sort of pet to our Lord William, so don't be upsetting the King's cousin by trying to kill it, will you?"

Suddenly, from inside the office, Erik heard William's laugh and then his voice: "He said he'd like to see them try."

Bobby playfully rubbed behind the creature's eye ridges and said, "Still a tough old boot, aren't you?"

Erik took Robert at his word that this was a pet, albeit the most fantastic pet anyone had ever imagined. The creature looked him up and down and suddenly Erik was convinced there was intelligence behind those eyes.

Erik stepped around to where Roo remained hard against the wall and looked past the creature into the office. Inside, the Watch Commander stood, while Knight-Marshal William remained to one side of the desk. Lord William was a short man, barely as tall as Bobby, but he looked fit for his age, somewhere in his fifties. He was reputed to be among the shrewdest military minds in the Kingdom. It was said that in the last years of Prince Arutha's tenure he spent nearly every day talking with the old Prince, learning everything he could. Arutha's deeds had been part history, part legend, but he was accounted one of the finest generals in the annals of the Kingdom.

William said to Robert, "Lord James will be along in a minute," and added to Roo and Erik, "Would one of you please fetch some water. Your friend has fainted."

Erik looked down, saw Duncan's feet sticking through the doorway, and realized he must have been the first to step through the office and encounter the small dragon.

Erik said, "I'll go," and was off. To himself he said, "Just when I was thinking things couldn't get much stranger."

Five

Newcomer

ROO YAWNED.

The discussion had been under way for hours. His mind wandered, so that when he was asked a question, he had to say, "Excuse me, my lord? I'm sorry, I didn't hear what you said."

Lord James, Duke of Krondor, said, "Robert, I think our young friend here is in need of refreshment. Take him and his cousin down to the mess while William and I confer."

They had been holding a discussion in the Watch Commander's office since Roo had arrived, and until Lord James had mentioned refreshments and the mess, Roo hadn't given much thought to the fact he and Duncan had not broken their fast. De Loungville motioned for Roo and Duncan to follow him.

Outside the office, as they moved down the hall, Roo asked, "Sergeant, what's going on? I had almost no hope I'd ever see my money again, but I want that bastard Sam Tannerson's guts on a stick for what he's done."

Robert grinned back over his shoulder. "You're still a vicious little rodent, aren't you, Avery? I admire that in a man."

As they moved through the castle, Robert said, "It's not so simple as mustering the watch, going out, hauling in this Tannerson, and hanging him."

"No witnesses," offered Duncan.

"Right. And there's the issue of why there were these killings."

"Why were there?" asked Roo. "Destroying my wine would have been clear enough warning."

Robert motioned for them to pass through a door into the soldier's mess as he said, "Well, that's what the Duke and the Knight-Marshal are asking themselves this very minute, I'm betting."

Roo saw Erik and Jadow standing at one end of the mess while a bunch of soldiers in grey tunics and trousers sat eating. He waved and Erik came over. "Sergeant?" he asked, to see if there were orders.

"Tell Jadow to keep an eye on those recruits, and join us."

Erik did as he was ordered, and when he was seated with the others, castle serving boys hurried over with food and ale. Robert dug in and said, "I think we're going to have a bit of fun tonight."

Roo said, "Fun?"

"Well, if I can judge the Duke," said de Loungville, "I think he's going to come to the conclusion that there's been just a little too much killing going on of late, and it's time to do something about it."

"Do what?" asked Duncan. "The Mockers have been in control of parts of this city since . . . since before I was born, I know that much."

Robert said, "True, but then, there's never been a Duke of Krondor like Lord James, that's also a fact." He smiled and bit into a cold joint of mutton. Speaking around the mouthful, he said, "Better stoke up your fires, lads. I think we're going to have a long night ahead of us."

Roo asked, "Us?"

Robert said, "You'll want to come along, Avery. It's your gold we're trying to recover, isn't it? Besides, what else have you got to do that's better?"

Roo sighed. "Right now, nothing."

"We'll give you a bunk for the afternoon so you can get your beauty rest," said de Loungville. "I think we're going to be up most of the night."

Roo shrugged. "If there's a slim chance to get my gold back, I'll take it. It's about what I started with, so I'll be even—not counting my time." He looked at Erik. "That bit of gold you gave me was part of it, too."

Erik shrugged. "You don't invest thinking any venture's a sure thing. I knew that."

"I'll get it back for you somehow," Roo promised. He turned

his attention to the men at the far end of the hall. "Those your new band of 'desperate men,' Sergeant?"

De Loungville smiled. "Not desperate enough, but then we haven't really gotten started with them. Right now we're just weeding out those who don't have what it takes, right, Erik?"

"Right, Sergeant," Erik agreed. "But I'm still not quite sure what the three of us are supposed to be doing."

"We'll figure it out," said Robert in a noncommittal tone. "With luck, *Trenchard's Revenge* should be coming into port any day now, and maybe some more of our boys will be aboard."

Duncan raised an eyebrow in question, but no one volunteered any details to him.

Roo said, "Where's the Captain?"

Robert shrugged. "He took off with Nakor, for Stardock. He should be back in a few more weeks."

"I wonder what he's up to," mused Roo.

Robert de Loungville's expression changed to one that Roo knew well, and Roo instantly regretted his words. Everyone at the table, save Duncan, was privy to secrets known only to a few, and such lapses would put Roo into more trouble than he wished should he again speak out of turn.

Erik glanced at Roo and years of friendship communicated all Roo needed to see to understand that Erik also wished Roo to remain silent.

Roo cleared his throat. "I think I could use that nap if we're going out tonight."

Robert nodded and Erik smiled, and Duncan seemed not to notice any of the exchange, and table talk turned to the mundane.

Calis looked over the rail and said, "See that?"

Nakor squinted against the late afternoon sun. "Keshian patrol."

Calis and his companions were on a river boat, hugging the coast of the Sea of Dreams, a few miles away from Port Shamata. Calis said, "They're quite a long way on the wrong side of the border if we can see them from here."

Nakor shrugged. "Kingdom, Kesh, always fighting over this area. Good farmland, rich trade routes, but no one ever gets crops in and no one drives caravans through the Vale of Dreams because of the border raiders. So it lingers, like an old man too sick to live but not ready to die." He looked at his companion. "Tell the garrison commander at Shamata and he'll send a patrol out to chase the Keshians south!" he added with a grin.

Calis shook his head. "I'm sure someone will eventually mention it to him." He smiled a wry smile. "I don't think I need say anything to him. If I do, he might feel the need to impress the Prince of Krondor's special envoy by starting a war for my amusement."

Calis's eyes stayed fixed on the horizon long after the Keshian patrol vanished from view. Port Shamata was visible in the distance to the southeast, but they wouldn't be there for another hour, given the light wind of midday.

"What do you see out there, Calis?" asked Nakor, his voice hinting at concern. "You've been moody since we got back."

Calis didn't need to explain many things to Nakor, who probably understood more about the Pantathian serpent priests and their evil magic than any man living. He had certainly seen some of the worst manifestations of it. But Calis knew that right now Nakor wasn't speaking of anything that had to do with Calis's concerns over the distant threat to the Kingdom. It was a more personal issue that weighed on Calis's mind.

"Just thinking of someone."

Nakor grinned, and looked over his shoulder at Sho Pi, the former monk of Dala, who at Nakor's insistence now slept upon a bale of cotton. "Who is she?"

"You've heard me speak of her. Miranda."

"Miranda?" asked Nakor. "Heard of her from several men. A woman of mystery by all reports."

Calis nodded. "She is a strange woman."

"But attractive," added Nakor, "also by all reports."

"That too. There's so much I don't know about her, yet I trust her."

"And you miss her."

Calis shrugged. "My nature is not common—"

"Unique," supplied Nakor.

"—and issues of companionship are confusing to me," finished Calis.

"Understandable," said Nakor. "I've been married twice. First when I was young to . . . you know to whom."

Calis nodded. The woman Nakor knew as Jorna had evolved into the Lady Clovis, an agent of the Pantathians they had faced more than twenty years previously the first time Nakor and Calis had ventured south to Novindus. Now she was the Emerald Queen, the living embodiment of Alma-Lodaka, the Valheru who had created the Pantathians, and the figurehead of the army building across the sea that would someday invade the Kingdom.

"The second woman was nice. Her name was Sharmia. She got old and died. I still get confused when dealing with women I find attractive, and I'm six times your age." Nakor shrugged. "If you must fall in love, Calis, fall in love with someone who will live a long time."

"I'm not sure what love is, Nakor," said Calis with an even more rueful smile. "My parents are something unique in history and there's no small magic in their marriage."

Nakor nodded. Calis's father, Tomas, had been a human child, transformed by ancient magic into something not quite human, not quite Dragon Lord—as humans called the Valheru—and that ancient heritage had been part of what had drawn Calis's mother, Aglaranna, the Elf Queen in Elvandar, into a union with Tomas.

Calis continued. "While I've had my share of dalliances no woman has held my attention—"

"Until Miranda," finished Nakor. Calis nodded. Nakor said, "Perhaps it's the mystery. Or the fact that she's not around very much." Nakor pointed to Calis, "Have you and she . . ."

Calis laughed. "Of course. That's not a small reason I feel drawn toward her."

Nakor winced. "I wonder if there is any man alive who doesn't think he's in love between the sheets at least once."

"What do you mean?" asked Calis.

Nakor said, "I forget that while you're past fifty years of age, you're still considered young by your maternal race's standards."

"A child," said Calis. "Still learning how to conduct myself as a proper eledhel should." He used the name his mother's people used for themselves, the race humans called elves.

Nakor shook his head. "Sometimes I think those priests who take vows of chastity understand what a drain it is to be constantly thinking about who you're going to bed with."

"My mother's people are not a bit like that," said Calis. "They feel something grow between one of them and their destined mate and at some point they just . . . know."

Calis again looked out at the shore as the boat began to head in toward the inlet that led to Port Shamata. "I think that's why I'm drawn to my human heritage, Nakor. The stately progress of the seasons in Elvandar has a sameness that I find only slightly reassuring. The chaos that is human society . . . it sings to me more than the magic glades of my home."

Nakor shrugged. "Who's to say what is right? You are unlike any other, but like every other man or woman born on this world, no matter what your heritage at birth, ultimately you must decide who you are to be. When you're finished with this 'childhood' of yours, you may decide it's time to live for a while with your mother's people. Just remember this much from an old man who really isn't very good at learning things from other people: every person you encounter, whom you interact with, is there to teach you something. Sometimes it may be years before you realize what each had to show you." He shrugged and turned his attention to the scene before him.

As the boat headed in to the reed-lined shore, smaller boats could be seen wending their way along the coast, fowlers hunting ducks and other water birds and fishermen dragging their nets. The riverboat moved quietly along, and Nakor and Calis were silent for the remainder of the voyage.

Sho Pi awoke as the sounds of the town grew in volume, and by the time the boat rested at the docks, he was standing beside his "master" and Calis. As he was the Prince's envoy, Calis had the right of rank in departing, but he moved away from the gangway and allowed the other passengers to depart first.

When they at last left the boat, Calis studied the shoreline and the town of Port Shamata. The city of Shamata was separated from the port by almost eighty miles of farmland and orchards. Originally a garrison to defend the southern border of the Kingdom against Great Kesh, Shamata had turned into the Kingdom's largest city in the south. A squad of soldiers waited for Calis on the docks, and instead of heading down toward the city of Shamata, they would follow the shore of the Sea of Dreams until they reached the river that flowed down from the Great Star Lake. They would follow the river to the lake and then to Stardock town, which sat on the south shore of the lake, opposite the magicians' community on Stardock island.

Along the docks the usual assortment of beggars, confidence men, workmen, and hawkers moved, for the arrival of a boat from the coast meant opportunities, legal and otherwise. Nakor grinned as he said to Sho Pi, "Watch your purse."

"I don't have one, Master."

Nakor had finally despaired of ever getting the young man to stop calling him master, so he just ignored it now.

Calis laughed and said, "It's an expression."

They left the boat and were greeted at the foot of the gangway by a sergeant in the tabard of the garrison of Shamata. Like the border barons of the north, the garrison commander at Shamata answered directly to the Crown, so there was little court formality observed in the Vale of Dreams. Pleased to be free of any need to pay a social call on local nobles, Calis accepted the man's salute and said, "Your name?"

"Sergeant Aziz, m'lord."

"My rank is captain," said Calis. "We need three horses and an escort to the Great Star Lake."

"The pigeons arrived days ago, Captain," answered the sergeant. "We have a subgarrison here at the port, with ample horses and enough troops to provide for your needs. My Captain sends an invitation to dine with him this evening, Captain."

Calis glanced at the sky. "I think not. We can ride at least four hours and my mission is urgent. Send your Captain my regrets at the same time you send for mounts and provisions." Casting around, he pointed to a disreputable-looking inn across the street from the docks. "You will find us there."

"At once," said the sergeant, and he gave orders to a soldier nearby, who saluted and spurred his mount away.

"It should be no longer than an hour, Captain. Your escort, horses, and provisions should be here quickly."

"Good," said Calis, motioning for Sho Pi and Nakor to follow him into the dockside inn.

A genial setting, the inn was neither the worst any of them had seen nor the best. It was what one would expect from an inn located so close to the docks: fitting for a leisurely wait, but not somewhere one would choose to frequent if better accommodations were available or affordable. Calis ordered a round of ale and they waited for the return of their escort.

Halfway through their second drink, Nakor's attention was diverted by a sound from without. An inarticulate cry and a series of monkeylike hootings followed quickly by the sounds of a crowd laughing and jeering. He rose and looked through the closest window. "I can't see anything. Let's go outside."

"Let's not," said Calis, but Nakor had already vanished through the doorway. Sho Pi shrugged and followed his master out of the inn.

Calis stood and followed, deciding it was better to see what trouble Nakor could find before he got too deep into it.

Outside, a crowd had gathered around a man who hunkered down on his haunches as he gnawed on a mutton bone. He was easily the filthiest man Calis had ever seen. It looked—and smelled—as if the man hadn't bathed in years. Spending time in the fields made one indifferent to the level of fastidiousness required in the Prince's court, but even among common dockworkers and poor travelers, this man was a walking cesspool.

His hair was black, with touches of grey, and rank with oil and dirt. Shoulder-length, it was matted with debris and old food. His face was nearly black from dirt above an equally filthy beard, and the skin, where it showed through, was sunburned. He wore a robe so torn and ragged it seemed to have more holes than material; whatever color the robe had been was a memory, for now the shreds were stained and smeared.

Years of indifferent eating had left the man famine-thin, and there were sores on his arms and legs.

"Do the dance!" shouted one of the workers.

The crouching man growled like a beast, but when the call was repeated a few more times, he put down his nearly bare mutton bone and held out his hand. "Please," he said, with a surprisingly plaintive tone, almost as if a child were begging. The word came out "Plizzz."

Someone in the crowd shouted, "Dance first!"

The ragged beggar stood and suddenly executed a furious mad twirling. Calis stopped behind Nakor, who stood watching the beggar closely. Something about the movements seemed vaguely familiar to Calis, as if hidden in the mad twirling was familiar movement. "What is this?" he said.

Nakor spoke without looking back. "Something fascinating."

The man finished dancing and stood there, swaying with weakness, and held his hand out. Someone in the crowd threw him a half-eaten piece of bread, which landed at the beggar's feet. He instantly crouched and swept it up.

A supervisor shouted, "Here now, get back to work," and most of the dockworkers moved away. A few others remained a moment to watch the beggar; then they started to wander off.

Calis turned to a man he took to be a local and asked, "Who is he?"

"Some crazy man," said the stranger. "He showed up a few months ago and lives where he can. He dances for food."

"Where did he come from?" asked Nakor.

"No one knows," said the townsman, moving along.

Nakor went over to where the ragged man crouched and knelt down before him, studying his face. The man growled like an animal and half turned away to protect his meatless bone and crust of bread.

Nakor reached into his carry sack and pulled out an orange. He stuck his thumb in and pulled off the peel, then handed a section to the beggar. The beggar looked at the fruit a moment, then snatched it from Nakor's hand. He tried to stuff the entire orange into his mouth at once, creating a wash of orange juice that flowed down his beard.

Sho Pi and Calis came to stand behind Nakor and Calis said, "What is this?"

"I don't know," answered Nakor. He stood up. "But we need to take this man with us."

"Why?" asked Calis.

Nakor looked down at the grunting beggar. "I don't know. There's something familiar about him."

"What? You know him?" asked Calis.

Nakor scratched his chin. "He doesn't look familiar, but given all that dirt, who can say. No, I don't think I know him. But I think he may be important."

"How?"

Nakor grinned. "I don't know. Call it a hunch."

Calis looked dubious, but over the years Nakor's hunches had proven to be important, often critical, so he only nodded. The sound of riders approaching signaled the arrival of their own mounts and escort. Calis said, "You'll have to figure out how to convince him to get on a horse, though."

Nakor stood, scratching his head. "Now, that would be a trick."

Calis said, "And before anything else, we're going to have to give him a bath."

Nakor's grinned widened. "That will be an even better trick."

Calis returned the grin. "Then you figure out how to do it. If I must, I'll have the guards throw him into the sea."

Nakor turned and stood considering the options before him as the riders reached Calis.

They gathered at a modest inn in the Merchants' Quarter, a few streets over from the Poor Quarter of Krondor. The inn was under the control of the Prince of Krondor, though few who frequented it knew that fact. A back room was being used for a meeting, conducted by Robert de Loungville.

"Duncan, you and William here"—he indicated a man that Roo had never laid eyes on before—"will find your way to a small booth near the corner of Candlemaker Road and Dulanic Street. The man selling scarves and headcloths is a snitch for the Mockers. Make sure he doesn't say anything to anyone. Knock him senseless if you must."

Roo glanced at Erik, who shrugged. A dozen men who were strangers crowded into the small room with de Loungville and those who'd had lunch with him earlier in the day. It was now an hour past supper, and most of the shops were either closed for the day or doing their evening business. Erik and Roo were to travel with Jadow and de Loungville to a shop and wait across the street. Robert had impressed on them that if he gave the word they were to get into that shop as quickly as humanly possible. He said it twice, so Roo knew de Loungville viewed that as a critical part of the night's mission.

"You, you, and you," said Robert, pointing to three teams assigned to neutralize Mocker lookouts. "Out the back door."

He was silent for a few minutes, then pointed to Duncan and the man named William. "Go now, out the front."

They left, and over the course of the next ten minutes the rest of the agents were dispatched. When the four remaining men were alone, Roo said, "Who were those other men?"

"Let's say the Prince needs a lot of eyes and ears in his city," said de Loungville.

"Secret police," said Jadow.

"Something like that," said de Loungville. "Avery, you're the quickest man here; stay close to me. Erik, you and Jadow are too big to escape notice for long, so stay where I put you and don't move. Once we leave this inn, no talking. Any questions?"

There were none, and de Loungville led them out of the back of the inn. They hurried through the streets, attempting to look like nothing more than four citizens on some errand or another, urgent perhaps, but unremarkable.

They passed a booth at a corner where the Poor Quarter began and saw Duncan and the man named William engaged in deep debate with the vendor. Roo noticed that Duncan stood in such a way that his holding a sword point to the other man's ribs was difficult to ascertain, while William was ready to intercept any who might come too close to the booth.

They turned down a short street to another avenue paralleling the first, and turned the corner. With a wave of his hand, de Loungville motioned for Jadow and Erik to secrete themselves within a deep and relatively dark doorway, while he quickly moved across the street with Roo. Using hand signals, he indicated Roo should stand against the wall between a doorway and a window. De Loungville took up a position at the corner of the building, between the door and an alleyway that ran next to the building. From within the building, Roo heard the sounds of what he took to be a merchant moving portions of his inventory around. He resisted the impulse to peek into the window and tried to look like a man simply lounging for a minute, while he kept his eyes darting around, looking for signs of trouble.

A figure swept out of the darkness, bundled in a great cloak. Vaguely, behind him, figures seemed to melt away into the darkness and Roo sensed more than saw others taking up nearby positions.

The robed man moved purposefully past Roo and took the three steps up to the door of the establishment. Roo glimpsed him as he passed and Roo's eyes widened. The man entered the shop, closing the door behind. Roo heard a voice say, "Can I help—"

"Hello," interrupted a familiar voice.

A long silence was followed by the first voice saying, "James?"

"It's been a while," answered Lord James, Duke of Krondor. "What? Forty years?"

"More." There was a long silence, then the man said, "I assume your men are outside."

"Sufficient to make sure this conversation is uninterrupted and ends when I say it ends."

Again there was a silence, and the sound of two men moving around. What sounded like chairs being pulled across the floor ended with James saying, "Thank you."

"I don't suppose it would do any good claiming I've long since gone straight and am nothing more than a simple merchant."

"Claim all you want, Brian," said James. "Thirty years ago, when I had heard a merchant named Lysle Rigger had shown up in Krondor, I asked Prince Arutha to set agents on you like hounds on a trail. Even when I was ruling in Rillanon these last twenty years, I've had regular reports on you."

"Rigger. I haven't used that name in years. I haven't used that name since—where was it we met?"

"We met in Lyton," said James.

"Yes, now I remember," came the reply. "I used it only a few times since then."

"No matter." James sighed audibly. "It took the Prince's men a few years to make sure they had all your bolt-holes covered and your runners identified, but once they did, it was easy enough for me to keep track of you."

"You've better men than we thought. We're always on the look-out for agents of the Crown."

James said, "That's because until tonight we were content to simply watch. Remember, I used to be a Mocker. There are still a few around who remember Jimmy the Hand."

"Now what?"

"Well, you're going to have to change your name again, and do something about your appearance. If you don't, the beggars and thieves will decide it's time for a new leader."

There was a chuckle and Roo strained to hear every word. "You know, it all goes back to that business with the Crawler. If he hadn't tried to take over the guild in the first place, we'd have had a far more orderly change than we had when the Virtuous Man took over. That was a mess."

"So I hear," said James. "But that's neither here nor there. What brings me to you tonight, Lysle, or Brian if you prefer, is this: lately, you've lost control over the guild. Too many happy little cutthroats are running around my city killing my law-abiding, tax-paying citizens. A little theft and larceny are normal for a city like Krondor, but last night one of your butchers killed a stableboy, two barmaids, and four horses as a 'warning' to a young wine merchant that he needed to pay protection."

"That is excessive," agreed the man named Brian.

"So was the protection price," said James.

"Who is the man? I'll deal with him."

"No, I'll deal with him. If you want to keep your own head out of a noose, or more important, if you don't want your own people choosing a replacement for you before your body's cool, listen carefully.

"For some years to come I'm going to need Krondor especially quiet and free of trouble. In fact, I'm going to need it very prosperous and rich. The reasons I'm going to need things this way are none of your concern, but trust me when I say that in the long run it will benefit you and your ragged band of outlaws as much as anyone else in the city. Toward that end I'm going to find Sam Tannerson and his comrades and publicly hang them. You will find me a believable witness who saw him leaving the Inn of the Seven Flowers holding a bloody knife. Get me an earnest-faced little street urchin. A girl would be best. Someone who will have the judge convinced that Tannerson and his pals are barely worth the rope to hang them with.

"Then you'll tell your merry band of thieves that things are getting too hot for such goings-on and the next one of your bright lads to go getting creative ideas on setting examples won't live long enough to be hung. And I mean it, Brian: if one of your murderers steps out of line, you'd better string him up before I do, or I'll close you down for good and all."

"It's been tried before," came the answer. "The Mockers are still in business."

There was a long silence before James said, "I still remember the way to Mother's. If I shout out before you can reach that dagger you have secreted in your boot you'll be dead, and within an hour your Nightmaster will be under arrest and your Daymaster will be roused out of his bed and taken into custody. I'll have Mother's surrounded and closed down before sunrise. I'll have every thief who's known to my agents picked up, and while I won't get them all, or even half, I'll get enough of them. There will still be thieves and beggars in Krondor, Brian, but there will be no more Mockers."

"Then why haven't you shut us down?"

"It's been to my advantage just to keep you under observation. But, as I said, *now* I need certain things. As I'm sitting in his shop and chatting with him this instant, we both understand I know who the current successor to the Upright Man is; if I kill you, I might have to spend years finding out who the next leader of the Guild of Thieves is after you."

There was a moment of silence; then James said, "It's ironic, but the reason I knew you were back in the city all those years ago is because we look so damn alike."

A long sigh answered that. "I've often wondered about that. Do you think we're related?"

"I have a theory," came the answer, but no details followed. "Just do us both a favor and keep your animals on a short tether. A few robberies of modest gain, a shakedown here and there. Boost some goods off the dock and cheat the customs agents now and again out of their duties. I may even have a few jobs for you that will guarantee you and your ragged brotherhood a profit—commissions of sorts—but this wholesale crime spree is over and the killings must stop today; if I have to go to war I will. Is that clear?"

"I'm still not convinced, but I'll think on it."

James laughed, and to Roo it was a bitter laugh. "Think on it? Not hardly. You agree this moment or you don't leave here alive."

"Not much of a choice" was the hot reply. The man's voice showed his temper was held in check, but not by much.

Roo glanced about. The conversation had lasted only a few minutes, but it felt as if he'd been eavesdropping for hours. Things seemed shockingly normal on the street, though he knew at least a score of the Prince's men were within a hundred feet of where he and de Loungville stood.

"You have to understand," said James, "that when I say I need a quiet and prosperous city, it isn't my desire to make money for a bunch of merchants and provide an improved tax situation for my sovereign—desirable ends, in and of themselves—but the safety of my city depends on it, and I will say no more, save I will happily crush you, if I must. Do we have an understanding?"

"We do," said the merchant. There was a note of anger mixed in with the resignation.

"Then let me give you some good news," came James's voice, accompanied by the sound of a chair being pushed back. "For ten minutes after I leave, the door to one of your bolt-holes—the one that starts in the basement below and leads to the sewers—will be left uncovered. While I know exactly who you are, I am the only one. Flee to your next identity, and after you've cooled down and given some thought to what I've said, send me a message. If you understand, leak word on the street that the Sagacious Man has fled and the Upright Man has returned—tell your Daymaster and Nightmaster that it's to lead the authorities to think they've successfully driven you off. If I don't hear that message from you by this time tomorrow night, I will know that either you've been betrayed by your own people or you haven't taken my warning seriously. Either way the Mockers had best prepare for war."

There was a pregnant silence, and James finally said, "Good. I know if I were you I'd have thought for a brief second about going for that dagger, but I also judged you would decide against it. No one who is stupid rises to rule the Mockers."

"It was a close call."

"You wouldn't have lived; trust me. Now, as I was saying, you have ten minutes to flee. Go to Mother's and establish whatever new identity you need; those agents of mine who know you by sight do not know who you really are. They know you only as a merchant I wanted watched. Some no doubt think you to be an agent of Great Kesh or some other political foe. Those who know you by reputation and deed have no idea what you look like. I'm enough of a Mocker at heart to give you that much.

"But I will always be able to find you. Never for a minute doubt that, Lysle—for that's how I always think of you."

"I don't doubt that for a moment, Jimmy the Hand. One thing."

"What?"

"Were all the things they said about you true?"

There was a ironic laugh. "Not half of the truth, Lysle. Not a half of it. I was a better thief than I thought I was, and not half as good as I claimed, but I've done things no other Mocker has ever attempted, let alone succeeded at."

"Gods, that's the truth," came the grudging reply. "No man can argue that; never been another thief who's risen to the rank of bloody damn Duke and single most powerful man in the Kingdom next to the King."

"Now, where's Tannerson?"

"You'll probably find him hiding out in a whorehouse called Sabella's—"

Across the porch from Roo, de Loungville turned and hissed into the darkness, and then said quietly, "Sabella's!" A figure Roo hadn't seen there a moment before scurried off into the darkness.

"I know where that is. Have a witness for me first thing in the morning."

"She's dead, you know. If she rats out Tannerson and the others I have to put the death mark on her; you know Mockers' law."

"Get me a young one," said James. "If she's pretty and smart, I'll find a home for her in a distant city; maybe even save her from a whorehouse and put her with a noble family as a companion for their children. You never know. But she'd better be young enough she's not too set in her criminal ways." A pause, then, "After all, I was fourteen when I met Arutha, and I haven't forgotten a thing."

"That's the gods' truth, Jimmy, that's the truth," said Lysle.

Suddenly the door opened and Lord James, still covered from head to knee in a great cloak, swept down the steps. He paused for a brief moment next to Robert and said, "You heard?"

"I heard. Word's been passed" was all de Loungville said, and then the Duke of Krondor vanished into the night. In the gloom down the street, Roo could see others fall in around him, and in a moment the street appeared to be empty again.

Roo glanced at de Loungville, who held up his hand, signaling they should wait. The next ten minutes dragged by; then suddenly de Loungville put two fingers to his mouth and blew a shrill whistle. From a side street a squad of soldiers ran up, while Jadow and Erik dashed from across the street. To the soldiers de Loungville said, "You! Into that building and arrest anyone you find there.

Confiscate every document you find and let no one in or out of this building after you seal it." To Roo, Jadow, and Erik he said, "Come with me."

Roo said, "Sabella's?"

"Yes. And if we're lucky, your friend Tannerson will resist arrest."

Jadow said, "Man, don't he sound happy at that prospect?"

De Loungville said, "Haven't had a good excuse to kill anyone in too long a time, Jadow."

In silence, they hurried deep into the Poor Quarter.

Roo followed close behind de Loungville and they reached the street where Sabella's occupied the first third of the block.

De Loungville whispered to a man at the corner, "Are the men in place?"

"Waiting for you," came the reply. "Thought I saw something up there on the roof a few minutes back, but it might have been a cat. Things are pretty quiet."

De Loungville nodded, half seen in the gloom, then said, "Let's go!"

They entered the whorehouse as if it were an enemy camp. Jadow struck a bouncer a head-ringing blow that brought the man to his knees before he could stop them entering the room, and as he knelt on the floor, Erik caught him with another blow that rendered him unconscious.

Roo ran past de Loungville and a couple of women too startled by the eruption of violence to do more than sit in open-mouthed astonishment. He reached the stairs, where a large woman of middle years had just turned to see what the disturbance at the front door was. She found Roo's dagger at her chin. "Tannerson?" he said in a quiet voice dripping threat.

She went pale but whispered, "Top of the stairs, first door on the right."

Roo said, "If you're lying, you're dead."

The woman looked and saw Jadow and Erik coming toward her, and for the first time registered the size and lethal aspect of the two men bearing down on her. "No, I mean first door on the left!"

Roo was off and de Loungville a step behind. He turned and signaled for Erik and Jadow to hold the bottom of the stairs.

He then turned back to see Roo reach the top of the stairs. Roo hesitated, motioned for de Loungville to kick the door, then ducked low.

De Loungville kicked the door and Roo was through in a crouch, his sword at the ready. He needn't have bothered. Lying in bed was Sam Tannerson, his vacant eyes staring upward at the ceiling as blood dripped from a gash across his throat.

"What?" said de Loungville as he saw the tableau before him.

Roo hurried to the open window and looked out. Someone had exited the room minutes before they had arrived, from the look of things. Roo turned and started to laugh.

"What's so funny?" asked Erik as he reached the top of the stairs and looked in.

Roo pointed to the corpse on the bed. "Some whore killed Tannerson, and I bet it was so she could steal my gold."

De Loungville poked around in the man's garments and said, "No purse or coins."

Roo said, "Damn! So now some whore has all my gold."

De Loungville looked at the corpse. "Maybe. But we had better leave and talk about this somewhere else."

Roo nodded once, put up his sword, and followed de Loungville out of the room.

The girl watched as across the street the men who had attempted to capture Tannerson left the inn, dragging out those men who had been playing pokiir downstairs. Other men prowling the streets nearby were checking to see if they were being observed. She was certain they hadn't seen her leave Tannerson's room. She glanced at her hands, half expecting to see them shake, but instead they were firm upon the eaves of the roof where she crouched, sheltered in the darkness from the sight of those below. She had never killed before, but no one had murdered her sister before either. The cold rage that had fueled this revenge had not diminished with Tannerson's death, as she thought it would. There was no sense of closure, no sense of putting paid to the account. She still seethed inside and nothing would bring her sister back to her.

Curiosity pushed aside other concerns and she wondered who those men had been. She had been less than five minutes out of the bedroom when she had heard the voices raised in anger across the street. She had left her work clothes secreted in a bag behind a chimney on the roof of the house opposite the whorehouse Tannerson used as a headquarters, against her need to get out of bloody clothing after the job was done. When she had decided to avenge Betsy, she had vowed that either Tannerson or she would lie dead on the floor of that bedroom tonight.

Getting into Sabella's hadn't proven difficult; bribing the whore to tell Tannerson someone special waited for him in the room had been easy enough, as well. The girl's native stupidity had not caused her to think any farther than her full purse of gold without Sabella taking a cut. Now she'd keep quiet out of fear.

For the first few moments of her flight, fear had nearly overwhelmed the girl. For the first five minutes after reaching the roof, she had just sat, too numb to move. Tannerson's blood had covered her from chin to waist, and she had finally gotten her fouled clothing off. Then she had heard the movement of men down the streets below and fear kept her from attempting to leave. As she waited, fatigue pushed in on her, and she half dozed—for a minute or an hour, she wasn't clear—and then the raid had brought her alert. Now fatigue was pushed aside by fear; if those men who had entered Sabella's had been sent by the Nightmaster, she could have been seen or identified. Being hunted by the Prince's police was one thing; being hunted by the Mockers was another. Her only hope in the second instance would be to flee the city and get as far away as possible, up to LaMut or down into the Empire of Kesh.

She crept along the roof until she came to where she had left her rope. Tossing aside the small bag that had contained her regular trousers, shirt, vest, dagger, and boots—and now contained a bloody knife and a blood-soaked shirt and trousers—she glanced over the eaves.

Two men of the rear guard hurried past in the darkness below and she moved to another corner of the roof, where she saw others moving in the same general direction as those who had just left the whorehouse. The girl sat back on her heels, considering. None of the men she had glimpsed looked remotely familiar to her, and she should have recognized at least one of them if they were Mockers. Whoever had come into Sabella's were the Prince's men, no doubt, for no one else in the city would be able to mount such a raid, especially not with men who seemed to appear and disappear out of the darkness like the best in the Guild of Thieves. It had to be the Duke of Krondor's special agents, his secret police.

But what had they wanted with Tannerson and his band of thugs? wondered the girl. She was not worldly, but she was clever, intelligent, and curious. She gauged her distance to the next roof, backed up, and made a nimble leap to the roof opposite and continued along the "Thieves' Highway" after the men below. After a block she was falling behind and quickly found a drainpipe she could clamber down.

At this hour the streets were dark and nearly empty, so she had to keep to the shadows, lest she attract attention. Twice she spied rear sentries who were placed to prevent anyone's following, so she waited and slipped after them when they at last moved out.

It was an hour before dawn when she lost sight of the last man she had trailed, but she was near certain where the raiders had been bound: the Prince's palace.

They had used a circuitous route and they had taken pains to avoid being followed, but she had kept her wits and hadn't rushed, and now she could see they were moving directly for the palace.

She paused and looked around. The streets were completely deserted as far as she could tell, but there was an uneasiness in the pit of her stomach that made her suddenly wish she hadn't been so curious. Fatigue was again threatening to overwhelm her, and she was due to report to the Daymaster in less than two hours. She feared going to sleep, for if she did she was certain she wouldn't awake in time. Missing one day's picking pockets in the market wouldn't usually earn her more than a harsh word or a cuffing around, but not the morning after Tannerson's murder. She must do nothing to call undue attention to herself.

Tannerson had been a brute and a man of few friends, but he'd had many allies and had established himself as something of a minor power among that faction of the Mockers known as bashers, those given to strong-arm tactics—armed robbery, extortion, and protection, as opposed to the beggars and those who used more subtle forms of larceny. The Sagacious Man and his lieutenants, the Daymaster and the Nightmaster, had been reluctant to curb Tannerson and others like him who produced, and say what you might about the swine, he had produced. His small-scale reign of terror over the merchants near the docks and Poor Quarter had more than doubled the protection money coming into the guild over the previous year.

But if she could show up with an account of men moving through the streets to the palace, she might divert any suspicion from herself and ensure that the Sagacious Man was more concerned with the actions of the Prince's secret police than with those of a single girl pickpocket. She might even plant the idea that it was the Prince's men who had cut Tannerson's throat.

The girl's reverie, half from exhaustion, half from emotions spent in killing her sister's murderer, had dulled her wits. She was barely aware someone else was nearby when she turned and tried to flee.

A man's hand seized her wrist and held her in a grip like iron as she drew her dagger to defend herself. Another hand froze her movement as she looked up into the man's blue eyes. He was the strongest man she had ever encountered, for no matter how she squirmed she was unable to free herself. And he was quick; when she tried to kick him in the groin, he turned enough that her kicks fell harmlessly on thighs that were as hard as oaks.

Other men approached, and in the early morning gloom the girl could make out a ring of dangerous-looking men closing around her. A short, unattractive man with a balding head looked her up and down and said, "What do we have here?" He pried the dagger from her immobile hand.

Another man, whose features she couldn't make out, said, "This is the one who was following us."

Robert de Loungville said, "Who are you, girl?"

The large man who held her said, "I think there's blood on her hands."

A shuttered lantern was uncovered and suddenly the girl could make out the faces of the men who surrounded her. The one who held her was little more than a boy himself, roughly the same age as she. He might have arms on him as big as her thighs, but his face was still soft and boyish, though there was something in his eyes that made her wary.

The short man, who seemed to be in charge, looked down and said, "Sharp eyes, Erik. She tried to wipe them off, but didn't have water to bathe." Turning to a man in the outer rank of those who surrounded her, he said, "Return to Sabella's and check the rooftops and alleys around there; I think you'll find the weapon and whatever she was wearing when she killed Tannerson. She couldn't have dumped them into the harbor and had time to catch up with us."

Another man, even shorter than the leader, young like the powerful youth but thin, even scrawny, pushed forward and thrust his face an inch from the girl's.

"What have you done with my gold!" demanded Roo.

The girl spit in his face for an answer, and de Loungville had to hold him back from striking her in reply. "It's getting light and this is too public a place," said the sergeant, his voice held to a harsh whisper. "Bring her along to the palace, Erik. We'll question her there."

The girl decided it was time to cease being passive and screamed at the top of her lungs, hoping to startle the powerful youth into releasing his grip enough so she could yank free. All that happened was a meaty hand clamped down over her mouth and the short leader said, "Open your yap again, girl, and I'll have him club you to silence. I have no need to be tender with you."

She knew he was not making an idle threat. But as a shutter opened in a room above and as two street boys peeked out of a nearby alley, the girl knew she had achieved her goal. Before she reached the palace, word would reach the Daymaster that the thief called Kitty had been picked up by agents of the Prince, and at least she would have an acceptable excuse for not reporting to muster at Mother's this morning. She'd have a most reasonable excuse for the Daymaster when she got back to Mother's.

As the young man called Erik half carried, half led her through the predawn streets, the girl amended her last thought: if she ever got back to Mother's to explain.

When they reached the palace, the mood among the men who escorted the prisoner lightened, except for Roo, who had demanded to know about his gold. He fumed and kept a suspicious eye upon the girl.

They entered the palace through a small gate, moving past two alert guards who said nothing. Down a long hallway, illuminated by torches in sconces, they continued in silence until they reached a large stairway leading down into the lower portion of the palace. Several of the men moved away, leaving the girl in the custody of de Loungville, Erik, Roo, Duncan, and Jadow.

Half pushing, half throwing her, Erik released the girl's arm as they entered an interrogation cell. Shackles hung from the wall, and if the girl had taken the time to inspect them she would have seen them rusty from disuse. But she turned like a trapped animal and crouched, as if awaiting an attack.

"Tough one, isn't she?" asked de Loungville.

"What about my gold?" demanded Roo.

"What gold?" said the girl.

De Loungville stepped forward. "Enough!" Looking at the girl thief, he asked, "What do we call you?"

"Anything you want," she snapped. "What's the difference?"

De Loungville said, "You've caused us a great deal of difficulty, girl." He motioned and Jadow brought over a small wooden stool, upon which de Loungville sat. "I'm tired. This has been a very long night and there are things about it I don't like much. The thing I like the least is finding you have killed the man I was going to hang tomorrow. I don't know what your cause with Tannerson was, child, but I needed him for a public hanging." Glancing at the other men, who now leaned against the walls of the cell, he said, "We need someone to hang."

Jadow said, "If we dress her up a bit in a man's clothing, and cut her hair, maybe."

If the threat reached the girl, it didn't show in her reaction. She merely glared at the men, one at a time, as if silently marking their features for some future revenge. Finally she said, "He killed my sister."

"Who was your sister?" asked de Loungville.

"She was a bar girl . . . a whore over at the Seven Flowers. Her name was Betsy."

Roo blushed. Suddenly he could see the resemblance, though this girl was far prettier than her sister had been. But Roo had been intimate with Betsy and his reaction to this revelation was surprising. He felt embarrassed and didn't want to let this girl know he had been the man her sister had been with when she had been killed.

"What's your name?" de Loungville asked again.

"Katherine," said a voice behind them, and Roo turned to see Lord James standing in the door to the cell. "Pickpocket." He walked around de Loungville and studied the girl's face. "They call you Kitty, don't they?"

The girl nodded. She had been frightened by the others, for they were hard men, but they were commonly dressed. This man, however, was dressed like a noble and spoke as if he expected to be obeyed. He studied her face, then said, "I knew your grandmother."

Kitty looked confused for a minute, then her eyes widened and she turned pale. "Gods and demons, you're the bleeding Duke, ain't you?"

James nodded and said to de Loungville, "How did you catch this little fish?"

De Loungville explained that one of his rear guard had spotted her coming down a drainpipe and had signaled they were being followed, and how the trap for her had been laid. "I just dropped Erik off in the shadows so he could grab her when she walked past him," he finished. He stood and indicated the duke should take the stool.

James sat and calmly said, "You'd best tell me exactly what happened, girl."

She told of discovering that Tannerson and his bashers had killed her sister, and of how she had arranged to lure him to a room. She had turned down the lamp and rested on the bed, and when Tannerson had entered he saw a pretty young girl and it wasn't until he leaned over her and found her dagger entering his throat he suspected anything.

She had ducked out from under him as he had fallen on the bed, and she had tried to get as much blood off her body and hands as possible before she fled out the window.

Roo interrupted and said, "Did you take any gold from him?"

"He didn't have a purse," she said. "At least, I don't think so; I didn't stop to look."

Roo swore. "Someone heard you leave, looked in, saw the blood, and took the gold."

"What about the locked door?" asked de Loungville.

It was Duke James who said, "It's a common thing to find that those latches aren't as secure as you think if you know where to find the hidden trip. Probably one of the employees at the inn has your gold, Roo. They knew how to set the latch so it fell into place when they closed the door. If you'd been there five minutes earlier, you might have caught the thief in the act. Now we could tie the thief to a spit and roast him slowly, and we won't find the gold."

Roo swore again.

James sat back. "You're something of a problem, Kitty. I had reached an accommodation with the Sagacious Man over the disposition of Tannerson and his companions, and you've managed to completely foul that up." He rubbed his chin. "Well, your career with the Mockers is at an end."

"What are you going to do?" she asked, her voice made faint by fear.

"Give you a job," he said, rising. To de Loungville he said. "We need female agents, Bobby. But keep her on a short leash for a while. If she proves untrustworthy, we can always kill her."

He left the room and de Loungville motioned for the others to follow him. Coming up to Kitty, he reached out and took her chin in his hand. "You're pretty enough under all that grime," he said.

"Looking for some sport, then, are you?" she asked, a glint of defiance in her eyes.

"What if I am?" he responded, his voice harsh and low. He pulled her face forward and gave her a quick kiss, but his eyes remained open and he watched her face carefully.

She pushed herself away. "Well, you wouldn't be the first rough man to put hands on me," she said without emotion. "I was taken young and it's all the same to me. Getting poked by one man is much like getting poked by another." She stepped back and removed her vest. Then she unbuttoned her tunic and removed it along with her boots and trousers.

De Loungville turned to the door where Erik and Roo waited and motioned for them to move away. He studied the girl a moment. She had a lithe body, small breasts, and slender hips, but there was a nice balance to her. She had a long neck and large eyes, and he said, "Yes, you're pretty enough." Turning away, he told her, "Now, get dressed and I'll have some food sent to you. Rest awhile and we'll talk some more later in the day. And think on this: you now work for me, and if I need to, I'll as happily cut your throat as take you to my bed."

He didn't look back as he left the cell, closed the door behind him, and locked it. He then moved to where the others were waiting for him. To Erik and Jadow he said, "Go back to your quarters and get some sleep. I'll need you alert in a couple of hours. With the Sagacious Man fleeing and this Tannerson murdered, we may find things getting lively in the city soon."

As they left, he turned to Duncan and Roo. "What about you two?"

Roo looked at Duncan, who shrugged. "I guess we also need to find jobs," said Roo.

De Loungville said, "You can still work for me."

"Thanks, but if I let this one setback stop me, what sort of merchant would I be?"

"True," said Robert. "Well, you can find your own way out. If you want to, grab a bite at the commons before you do; have a hot meal on the Prince with my compliments."

He walked away and as he left, he said, "But if you change your mind, you know where to find me."

Duncan waited until de Loungville was out of earshot and said, "Just what are we going to do?"

Roo sighed, long and loud. "I have no idea." He walked toward the soldiers' commons. "But if we're going to be out looking for work, we at least can do it on a full stomach."

Six

Barret's

ROO JUMPED.

The waiter coming out the door swerved expertly to avoid Roo as he came into the kitchen at Barret's Coffee House, and Roo put down his tray as he called out his order. The chaos in the kitchen stood in direct contrast to the calm evidenced in the common room and the private areas on the second floor of Barret's. The large oak double doors kept the sound away from those merchants and traders negotiating in hushed voices throughout the coffee house.

Roo had sought employment for almost a week before he thought of Barret's. Several merchant concerns had looked upon the poorly dressed former soldier with little civility, and no one seemed interested in taking on even the most junior of partners without receiving a large sum of capital as an incentive. Promises of hard work, diligence, perspicacity, and loyalty were far less important than gold to these men.

Most merchants either had sons or apprentices, and few had any work available save as guards or menials. Roo felt close to defeat before he remembered the young waiter at Barret's named Jason who had directed Erik and Roo to the horse trader by the city gate.

Roo had returned to Barret's, found the man in charge of the waiters, mentioned Jason by name, and after a short consultation with Sebastian Lender, the manager of Barret's—a man named Hoen—offered Roo a tryout as a waiter.

Roo quickly learned his way around the floor, with Jason acting as his tutor. Roo had come to like Jason, the youngest son of a merchant in another part of town. McKeller, the headwaiter, had told Jason to "show the new boy the ropes." Roo disliked being referred to as a "boy," but given McKeller's age, he supposed it was reasonable. Duke James would appear a boy next to McKeller.

Jason had proven an easygoing teacher, one who didn't presume Roo was stupid because he didn't know his way around the coffee house. Roo's years of growing up around Erik's family at the Inn of the Pintail helped, as he wasn't completely ignorant of what went on in a kitchen or in a common room.

Still, there was much about Barret's that was unusual to Roo. First of all, he had been required to swear an oath, on a relic from the temple of Sung, the Goddess of Purity, promising he would never reveal to anyone what he might overhear while waiting tables. He was next fitted for the standard uniform of tunic, trousers, apron, and boots—his own were considered too worn—and was informed the price of his clothing would be deducted from his pay. Then he was taken into the kitchen and introduced to the vast variety of coffees and teas, baked goods, and breakfast, lunch, and dinner items offered to the clientele of Barret's.

A quick study, Roo memorized as much as he could, confident he would learn the rest as he needed. The organized chaos of the coffee house at its busiest reminded Roo of a battle in many respects. The orders came in from each waiter, who was expected to remember everything a customer requested and who would also remember which table to return to and which gentleman or nobleman received which item. Mostly it was coffee, or an occasional sweet roll, but often it was a complete breaking of fast or a noontime meal. Rarely did anyone eat an evening meal at Barret's, as most businessmen preferred to eat at home with their families, but sometimes the late afternoon business ran long, and waiters and cooks could be working until two or three hours after sunset before the last customer left and the doors were locked. That was the custom at Barret's, that the doors remained open so long as one customer remained, and a few times over the years, at the height of financial crisis in the Kingdom, the coffee house had remained open around the clock, with the wait staff expected to remain alert, neatly dressed, and ready to answer the call of the frantic businessmen and nobles crowding the floor of the common room.

The cook said, "Your order's ready."

Roo grabbed his tray from off the counter, double-checked the order, and moved toward the door. He paused a beat to ensure the slight swing of the door was the result of the last waiter moving through it and not because some fool had forgotten which door to pass through—always keep to the right, he had been told. Jason had told him the biggest problem was caused by customers, who occasionally would mistake the kitchen door as an entrance to the jakes or a back way out, and the resulting collision was usually both loud and messy.

Just before reaching the door, Roo turned and backed through, as if he had been doing this for years, and moved with a fluid grace into the commons. Only his battle-trained reflexes prevented a collision with a customer who turned and moved across the aisle down which Roo moved. "Excuse me, sir," Roo intoned, when what he wanted to say was "Watch where you're going, fish brain!" He forced a smile.

Jason had impressed upon him that while his salary from Barret's was modest by any measure, the true source of income for the waiters was the gratuity. Quick, efficient, polite, and cheerful service could earn a waiter a week's wages in a day if business was particularly good. Occasionally a single table would provide enough income for a waiter to invest in one of the common undertakings.

For which reason, Roo, as the newest member of the staff, had the poorest section of the common room. He glanced longingly up to the galleries where the business associations, brokers, and partnerships gathered. Among their number were several bright young men who had begun their business lives as waiters at Barret's. It might not be as quick a rise as seeking treasure in far lands, but it could be as dramatic as that in results.

Roo placed his order expertly in front of each businessman, as he had been instructed, and they all but ignored him as they continued their discussion. He heard enough to realize they were discussing the extramarital adventures of an associate's wife rather than matters of business, and he ignored them. A single copper piece more than the price of the coffee and rolls was placed upon his tray and Roo nodded once and backed away.

He moved through his area, inquiring politely if anyone needed anything, and when he had made his way around his area and had received no new orders, he stationed himself quietly in plain sight, ready to answer the call of any customer who needed him.

For a few minutes he had time to himself and he again looked around the room, memorizing faces and names, certain that someday such information might be useful. From across the room a figure waved at him. Roo recognized him as another waiter, Kurt, a tall, nasty-tempered bully who had most of the younger waiters cowed. He was also a suck-up and had both Hoen and McKeller convinced he was a competent and pleasant waiter, while he was neither. He managed to get the younger waiters to do as much dirty work as possible while avoiding work at every turn. Roo wondered how such a lout had come to such a senior position at Barret's.

Roo ignored the wave, and at last Kurt came across the room toward him. As he approached, Kurt forced a smile for the benefit of the patrons. He would have been a handsome young man, Roo judged, had he not had such a mean turn to his smile and such narrow eyes.

"I was signaling you," he hissed between clenched teeth.

"I noticed," Roo answered without looking at him. He kept his eyes on the customers in his section.

"Why didn't you come?" asked Kurt in what he must have assumed was a threatening tone of voice.

"Last time I looked, you weren't paying my salary," answered Roo, moving to the elbow of the customer who had just tipped him a single copper coin. He nimbly filled the man's half-empty cup without being asked and the two businessmen at the table barely noticed him doing his job.

Kurt put his hand on Roo's arm as he turned. Roo glanced at the hand and said, "I would advise you not to touch me again."

Kurt almost snarled as he quietly said, "And what if I do?"

"You don't want to find out," Roo answered calmly.

Kurt said, "I've eaten bigger men than you for breakfast."

Roo said, "I have no doubt. But I'm not interested in your love life." He dropped his voice. "Now get your hand off my arm."

Kurt withdrew it and said, "You're not worth a scene at work. But don't think I've forgotten you."

"I'll be here every day to remind you in case you do," said Roo. "Now, what did you want me to come over for in the first place?"

"Shift change. You're on the door."

Roo glanced at the large fancy timepiece that was hanging from the ceiling. A water clock fashioned in Kesh, it displayed the hour and the minute by a rising column of blue water that dripped into a transparent tube marked with the hours at a controlled rate. One of his jobs, as juniormost waiter, was to be in the common room at dawn to quickly flip the valve that caused the strange device to pump water back to the tank above, while the second tank began dripping, so that the time was always accurate. Roo had been uncertain why it was so critical for these businessmen always to know what time it was, but he was fascinated by the device and the fact that he could see what time of day it was with a glance to the center of the room.

"Why the change?" he asked as he headed for the kitchen, Kurt a step behind him. "We're not due for a shift change for another hour."

"It's raining," answered Kurt with a smug grin as he brushed his black hair away from his forehead and took up his own tray. "New boy always gets to wipe up the mud."

Roo said, "Fair enough, I guess." He didn't think it was fair at all, but he was damned if he was going to give Kurt the satisfaction of seeing him distressed by the news. He left his own tray and cleaning cloth on a shelf designated as his, and moved quickly through the large kitchen door and crossed the commons to the front door.

Jason was waiting for him, and Roo looked out to see that a tropical storm up from Kesh had swept across the Bitter Sea and was now dumping massive amounts of warm rain on the Prince's City.

Already a pile of damp rags were tossed into the corner and Jason said, "We try to keep the floor as clean as possible before the rail so we don't have to mop down the floor completely throughout the coffee house."

Roo nodded. Jason tossed him a rag and knelt and began to clean up the mud that was splashing in from the force of the rain, along the edge of the doorway on his side. Roo duplicated his actions at his own door and knew it was going to be a long, frustrating morning.

After the fourth cleaning of the portal, a large carriage turned the corner at high speed, just a few feet from the doorway to Barret's. The splash of mud through the door barely missed Roo's boots. He quickly knelt and used a rag to get as much of it off the wood as possible. The rain continued its steady tattoo, and little splatters of dirty water continued to edge the wooden floor with grime, but the majority of the entrance hall to the coffee shop was still clean.

Jason tossed Roo a fresh rag. "Here you go."

"Thanks," answered Roo, catching it. "This seems a bit pointless," he added, nodding through the open door to where the rain was picking up in intensity. It was a typical fall storm off the Bitter Sea and it could mean days of unrelenting rain. The streets were becoming rivers of mud, and each new arrival at Barret's tracked increasing quantities of the dark brown ooze onto the wooden floor of the entranceway.

"Think how it would look by now if we didn't keep at it," suggested Jason.

"What else do we do besides fight mud?" asked Roo.

Jason said, "Well, we help customers out of coaches. If one pulls up on your side, first see if it's driven by a coachman alone, or if there's a footman riding on the back. If there's no footman, open the carriage door. If the coach has one of the new fold-down steps, lower it for whoever's inside. If there's no step, get that box over there and carry it to the coach." He pointed to a small wooden box kept in the corner of the entrance for such use. It sat next to some dirty towels in a larger metal pan.

A coach pulled up, and Roo glanced at Jason, who nodded; there was no footman, as this was a hired coach, and Roo could see there was nothing like the fancy swing-down step in evidence. He grabbed up the box and, ignoring the rain, placed the box below the door, then pulled down on the handle as instructed. Swinging the door open, he waited. An elderly gentleman climbed quickly down from the coach and took the two steps into the relative shelter of the entranceway.

Roo grabbed the box and was barely a stride away as the coach moved on. He reached the entrance in time to hear McKeller greet the newly arrived patron: "Good morning to you, Mr. Esterbrook."

Jason was already cleaning the mud from Mr. Esterbrook's boots as Roo replaced the box in the metal pan designed to confine water and mud. He then took up a rag, and by the time he had it in hand, the client had moved into the inner sanctum of Barret's.

"That's Jacob Esterbrook?" asked Roo.

Jason nodded. "You know him?"

"I know his coaches. They'd come through Ravensburg all the time."

"He's one of Krondor's richest men," confided Jason as they finished cleaning up the floor. "He's got an amazing daughter, too."

"Amazing how?" said Roo, putting away the muddy rag.

Jason was a young man of middle height, a lightly freckled, fair complexion, and brown hair, one who Roo judged unremarkable in appearance, but his expression became close to transfixed as he answered, "What can I say? She's the most beautiful girl I've ever seen."

Roo grinned. "And you're in love?"

Jason blushed, which amused Roo, though he kept any jibe to himself. "No. I mean, if I could find a woman who looked like that who would give me a second glance, I'd tithe to Ruthia"— the Goddess of Luck—"for the rest of my life. She's going to marry some very rich man or a noble, I'm certain. It just that . . ."

"She's someone to daydream about," supplied Roo.

Jason shrugged as he put away his cleaning rag. He then glanced at Roo's feet and said, "Boots."

Roo looked down, saw that he was tracking mud on the floor they were trying to clean, and winced. Taking the rag out of the metal pan, he cleaned his own boots and then the tracks he had made. "You don't do much of this when you spend your life barefoot."

Jason nodded. "I guess."

"Now, about this wonder . . ."

"Sylvia. Sylvia Esterbrook."

"Yes, Sylvia. When have you seen her?"

"She sometimes travels here with her father, on her way to shop in the city. They live out on the edge of the city, near the Prince's Road, on a large estate."

Roo shrugged. He knew that in Krondor the King's Highway was called the Prince's Road, and he had traveled it with Erik the first time he had come to Krondor, though they had left the highway and cut through the woods and some farmland. Later travels had been by the southern road to the training ground where he had learned the soldier's trade, so he had never seen the estate of which Jason spoke.

"What's she look like?"

"She has the most amazing blue eyes and blond hair that's almost pale gold in color."

Roo said, "Blue, not green? Blond hair?"

"Blue eyes, blond hair," answered Jason. "Why?"

"Just checking. I met a really beautiful woman who almost got me killed. But she had green eyes and dark hair. Anyway, go on."

"There's nothing more to say. She rides up with her father and then goes off after he gets out. But she smiles at me, and she even took a moment to speak to me once."

Roo laughed. "That's something, I guess."

A shout and the sound of a large wagon moving near caused Roo to turn. Heaving around the corner, looking for a moment as if it were about to attempt to enter the building, came a horse, as tired, old, and ragged a creature as Roo had ever beheld. A loud grinding of wood upon wood was punctuated by oaths and the sound of a lash as a wagon wheel ground across the open portal and the driver came into view.

An instant was all Roo needed to realize this man didn't possess even the most rudimentary knowledge of driving a wagon and had tried to turn the corner too sharply, jamming the wagon against the side of the building.

Ignoring the driving rain, Roo turned and moved in front of the horse, grabbing the animal by the bridle, while shouting, "Whoa!"

The animal obeyed, as it was hardly moving at all because of the jamming of the wagon against the corner, the deep mud, and near-total exhaustion. "What's this?" demanded the driver.

Roo look up at a young man, only a few years older than Roo, thin and soaked through to his skin from his appearance. It was also obvious he was a sailor, as he wore no boots or shoes and was sunburned and drunk.

"Heave to, mate," cried Roo, "before you run ashore."

Trying to look threatening, the young sailor shouted belligerently, "Clear away! You're fouling my rig!"

Roo moved around the animal, its sides heaving from the exertion, and said, "You cut that too sharp, friend, and now you're hung up. Do you know how to back this animal?"

It was obvious he didn't. The sailor swore and jumped down, losing his balance and falling facedown into the thick ooze. Cursing and slipping as he tried to stand, he at last regained his feet and said, "Damn the day I tried to do a favor for a friend."

Roo looked at the overloaded wagon, now up to the wheel hubs in mud. It was piled high with crates, all covered and lashed down with a canvas cover. "Your friend did you no favor. That load needs two horses or, better, four."

Just then Jason yelled, "What is all this?"

Before Roo could answer, he heard Kurt's voice shouting, "Yes, Avery, what is this?"

"A blind man could see we have a wagon stuck in the doorway, Kurt," he answered.

An inarticulate growl was the best reply he got. Then McKeller's voice cut through the sound of the driving rain. "What have we here?"

Roo hurried away from the mud-covered sailor and ducked under the neck of the still-panting animal. Without bringing more mud into the entrance, he peered into the coffee house. McKeller and some of the waiters stood there just beyond the splash of mud and rain and watched the spectacle of a horse almost inside the establishment. "The driver is drunk, sir," explained Roo.

"Drunk or sober, have him get that animal out of here," demanded the ancient headwaiter.

Roo could see Kurt smirking at the order.

Roo turned and saw the sailor starting to walk away. He took three quick steps—as quick as possible in the ankle-deep mud— and overtook the man. Swinging him around by the arm, he said, "Wait a minute, mate!"

The sailor said, "Yer no mate of mine, bucko, but for all of that, I'll not hold it against you. Care for a drink?"

"You need a drink like that horse needs another lashing," said Roo, "but, drunk or not, you need to get that wagon from out of my employer's doorway."

The sailor looked halfway between anger and amusement. He took that pose of control assumed by drunks who don't wish to appear drunk, and slowly said, "Let me explain to you, me lad. A friend of mine named Tim Jacoby—a boyhood chum I just met today—convinced me that it would be better to be a wagon driver in his father's employ than to risk another voyage."

Roo glanced back and with alarm saw the horse was attempting to kneel in the mud, an impossible act because of the confining traces. "Oh, gods!" he said, grabbing the sailor's arm and trying to pull him back toward the wagon. "He's colicking!"

"Wait a minute!" shouted the sailor, pulling away. "I haven't finished."

"No, but the horse has," said Roo, grabbing the man again.

"I was saying," continued the sailor, "I was to deliver this wagon to Jacoby and Sons, Freight Haulers, then get my pay."

The horse started making a sick, squealing noise as McKeller's voice sounded from the doorway, "Avery, move along, will you now? The customers are starting to be annoyed."

Propelling the sailor back to the wagon, Roo found the old animal down on its knees, with its back legs trembling furiously. Pulling a knife from his tunic, Roo quickly cut the traces, and as if sensing freedom, the horse struggled to its feet, staggered forward, then collapsed into the mud. With a sigh that sounded like nothing so much as relief, the horse died.

"Damn me," said the sailor. "What do you think of that?"

"Not bloody much," said Roo. The horse had managed to stumble around the corner, so that now the other entrance was half-blocked. The exiting and entering patrons could now choose how they would get soaked and muddy: climbing around a filthy wagon or over a dead horse.

McKeller said, "Jason, you and the other boys pull that animal and that wagon away from here."

Roo shouted, "No!"

McKeller said, "What did you say?"

Roo said, "I meant to say, I wouldn't advise that, sir."

Roo could see McKeller peering past the wagon from the doorway as he said, "Why is that?"

Hiking his thumb toward the horse, Roo replied, "That animal was old and sick, but it's a draft horse. It weighs fourteen hundred pounds if it weighs an ounce. The entire staff's not going to be able to pull it from that sucking mud. And that wagon was too heavy for it to pull, so we won't be able to move it."

"Do you have a suggestion?" called McKeller to the now completely soaked Roo.

Roo's eyes narrowed and a slight smile crossed his face for a moment as he said, "I think I do." He turned to the sailor. "Walk to your friend's company and tell him that if he wants his cargo he can come here to claim it."

"I think I'm going back to sea," said the sailor. He reached inside his tunic and pulled out a leather wallet, bulging with documents. "You can have this, sir," he added with a drunken half-bow.

"You do and I'll hunt you down myself and kill you," said Roo. He took the wallet and said, "Go tell your friend's father his freight is here at Barret's and to ask for Roo Avery, then you can go drown yourself in ale for all I care."

The sailor said nothing as Roo shoved him away, but he turned in the direction he had indicated Jacoby's lay and not back toward the harbor.

"Jason!"

"Yes, Roo?"

"Run and find some knackers—wait!" he corrected himself. Knackers would charge money to cut up and haul away the animal. "Run to the Poor Quarter and find a sausage maker. Tell him what we've got here and that he only has to come and haul it away. The knackers are going to sell the meat for sausage anyway; why pay a middleman?"

Jason's voice could be heard asking McKeller if that was all right, and when the answer came in the affirmative, he ran out into the rain and disappeared quickly toward the Poor Quarter.

Roo quickly inspected the wagon and knew that it would never be moved until it was unloaded. "I'm going for some porters," he shouted to McKeller. "We need to unload the cargo before we can move this rig."

McKeller said, "Very well. As quickly as possible, Avery."

Roo hurried down to the next street, then one street over, until he came to a Porters' Guild hiring office. Stepping inside, he saw a dozen burly men sitting around a fire, waiting for work. Moving to the small desk where the Guild officer sat, he said, "I need eight men."

"And who are you?" asked an officious little man sitting on the stool behind the desk.

"I'm from Barret's and we have a wagon stuck in the mud in front of the coffee house. It needs to be unloaded before it can be moved."

At the mention of Barret's, the man lost some of his officious manner. "How many men did you say?"

Years of being around teamsters and porters served Roo well, as without hesitation he said, "Your stoutest eight men."

The officer quickly singled out eight of the twelve men and said, "There's an extra charge for the weather."

Roo narrowed his gaze. In his best no-nonsense tone he said, "What? They're now tender boys who can't stand to get wet? Don't try to hold me up so you can cadge some extra drinking money, or I'll be talking to the Guild Masters about how many other clever little schemes you may have conceived over the years. I was loading and unloading wagons since I could reach a tailgate, so don't be telling me about guild rules."

Roo actually had no idea what he was talking about, but he could smell a con in his sleep. The man's face turned red as he made an inarticulate sound in his throat and said, "Actually, that is for snow and ice, not rain, now that I think on it. Sorry for the misunderstanding."

Roo led the eight men back into the storm to the wagon. He unhitched the tailgate and pulled up the canvas. "Oh, damn," he said. The cargo was mixed, but right before him was a large pile of fine silk, worth more gold than he'd make this year and the next, if he was any judge of fine fabric. But once wet and muddied, it might as well be homespun for the price it would command.

He said to the lead porter, "Wait here." Rounding the wagon, he found McKeller still at the door with a mixed company of waiters and customers, the latter watching the performance with some amusement.

"I need one of the large, heavy tablecloths, sir."

"Why?"

"Some of the cargo will have to be kept dry and . . ." He glanced around. Seeing the unused building catercorner to Barret's, he continued, "and we can put it there for the afternoon. But we'd probably have less difficulty if we kept the cargo undamaged. They might claim we damaged their goods and should have let it sit where it was until they came to collect it."

That argument might not have convinced any inn or tavern keeper in Krondor that it was a good idea to possibly ruin a precious tablecloth, but Barret's was an establishment founded on protecting cargo, among other investments, and McKeller nodded. With dozens of litigators among his clientele, he wanted nothing to do with a possible hearing before the local magistrate. "Fetch a large tablecloth," he instructed Kurt.

Looking pained to have to do anything to help Roo, Kurt turned and moved between the patrons, returning a few minutes later with a large cloth.

Roo held it close to his chest and hunched over in an attempt to keep it as dry as possible as he ran to the back of the wagon. He pushed it under the tarp and then loosened the two end tie-downs. Holding the canvas up with one hand, he climbed awkwardly into the back of the wagon, making sure he didn't touch the precious silk. He motioned to the nearest porter and said, "Climb up here, but be cautious you touch nothing. Get any mud on this cloth and you'll be discharged without pay."

The porter knew from the exchange in the hall that this boy knew a thing or two and that one of the Porters' Guild's reasons for existing was for goods to be carried without damage, so he was cautious enough to be almost slow in getting up next to Roo.

"Hold the canvas so it keeps this dry," Roo said, pointing at the silk. Roo tried to examine the balance of the cargo, which was difficult in the dim afternoon light of this heavy storm. After a moment, he was convinced it could withstand a little water. He unfolded the table cloth and made sure that only the clean side, not the mud from his tunic that had gotten on it, touched the silk. It took him nearly ten minutes to get the entire bundle covered and turned over and covered again by the large linen cloth, but when it was as protected as it was going to be, he said, "Now untie the rest of the tie-downs."

The other porters hurried to obey, and when the job was done, he said, "Wrap this canvas around the bundle."

Two porters jumped into the wagon and did as instructed, while Roo jumped down and started across the street. "Bring it here!" he shouted to the porters, urging them to move as quickly as possible.

He reached the door of the abandoned building and saw that there was a small, decorative lock on the door. He inspected and then rattled it. With no idea how to pick such a lock, he sighed, raised his boot, and kicked as hard as he could. The lock remained intact, but the small hasp's four screws pulled from the wood as the door swung inward.

Roo stepped inside the abandoned house. The faded grandeur of the entrance was nothing short of spectacular to Roo. A large staircase wound up from the hallway to a railed landing on the second floor, and from the vaulted ceiling of the entranceway a large crystal chandelier hung, dust dimming whatever sparkle the faint afternoon light might have imparted.

The sound of the porters coming up behind him caused Roo to forgo exploring the upper hall for a moment as he crossed the entranceway and opened a large sliding door. A formal sitting room, devoid of furnishings, lay below the balcony. But it was dry, as both large windows on the opposite wall were intact.

Roo told the porters, "Bring that in here, and put it against this wall." He indicated the farthest wall from the windows, just in case someone managed to break one of them. Salvaging this silk would be worth something to him only if he kept it undamaged. The porters put the bundle of cloth down and Roo said, "Get the rest of the cargo and haul it over here."

It took the eight men less than a half hour to unload the wagon. Roo had opened the wallet and found the inventory list, as he had expected, but with one significant difference: there was no bill of lading for the bolts of silk. Each of the boxes bore a customs stamp and had a corresponding paper also bearing a stamp and signature. But as far as the Royal Customs were concerned, that silk did not exist.

Roo considered this, and after the last load was brought into the building, he had the workers pick up the silk again and move it to another room, a small storage closet under the stairs, next to an old metal pail and dried-out mop.

He led the men back outside and secured the door by pushing the hasp screws back into the stripped-out holes in the wood. There was no security in it, but any casual passerby might think the lock still intact.

By then Jason had returned with a sausage maker and a half-dozen apprentices and workers, as unsavory a band as Roo had seen this side of the war in Novindus. Leading the porters over to where Jason stood, now as drenched as Roo was, he said, "Remember to tell me where you got this crew so I never buy sausage there."

Jason made a face. "One step inside his shop would do it." He watched in revulsion as they set to the horse with large knives. "I may never eat a sausage again, even if it's from the King's own table."

Horses, dogs, and other animals died in the streets of Krondor often enough that the bloody spectacle of the sausage makers cutting up the horse did little but cause a few passersby to look twice, but it would have been a major embarrassment for Barret's to have its customers have to move around a dead animal to enter or exit. Over his shoulder, the sausage maker shouted, "Do you want the hooves, skin, and bones?"

"Take it all," said Roo as the lead porter came up to tap him on the shoulder.

"You owe us eight sovereigns," said the porter.

Roo knew better than to argue price. The guild official working behind the desk might try to net a little extra gold out of him, but this worker would be quoting guild rates and no merchant in the Kingdom would get the guild to come down a copper piece from those rates.

Roo said, "Not quite yet."

He motioned for the porters to follow him back to the wagon. "Pull this out and get it to that courtyard behind the building where we put the cargo."

"We're porters, not bloody horses!" said the lead porter.

Roo turned and gave the man a dark look. "I'm cold, wet, and in no humor to argue. You can pick it up and carry it like porters for all I care, but move it over there!" he shouted.

Something in this little man's manner impressed the porter, for he didn't argue and signaled his men to form up. Four took the ruined traces, while the other four moved to the rear of the wagon. They raised the tailgate and two got ready to push while the other two moved to turn the rear wheels by hand.

It took some struggling and a great deal of swearing, but after a bit of work, the wagon was broken loose from the mud and was half rolled, half dragged through the mud across the street and down the little alley that led to the rear courtyard of the abandoned building.

"How did you know there was a courtyard behind that house?" asked Jason.

Roo grinned. "I told a friend I might buy that place someday, so I got curious and looked around. There's a little alley that leads around it, and two windows that look out of the sitting room over it. Might be a nice place for a lady's flower garden."

"Going to marry a fine lady?" said Jason in only slightly mocking tones.

"I don't know," said Roo. "I might marry that Sylvia Esterbrook you speak so highly of."

Soon the sausage maker and his half-dozen apprentices and workers were finished with their bloody work, and they carried off the horse, leaving some scraps of skin and entrails behind. Roo said, "The rain will clean things up quick enough."

He led Jason back toward the entrance as the porters returned. "Here, now!" shouted the seniormost porter. "About our pay . . . ?"

Roo motioned for them to follow and led them across to the portal to find McKeller still there. "Sir, these men need to be paid."

"Paid?" said the headwaiter. It was obvious to Roo that the old man hadn't given a thought to cost when Roo had gone to get the porters.

"These are *guild* porters, sir."

At mention of that word, McKeller almost winced. Like every other person in business in Krondor, he was used to the many guilds in the city, and no business could long endure if it found itself at odds with the guilds of the city. "Very well. How much?"

Before the head porter could answer, Roo said, "Ten gold sovereigns, sir."

"Ten!" said McKeller. That was more than a skilled craftsman might expect to earn in a week.

"There are eight of them, sir, and it is raining."

McKeller said nothing as he removed a large purse from his belt and counted out the coins, handing them to Roo.

Roo went to where the porters stood and gave the head porter nine. The man frowned. "You told the old coot—"

In low tones, Roo said, "I know what I told him. You take the nine and give eight to your guild scribe, and he gives you back your share. He doesn't complain about the ninth coin he doesn't know about and you don't complain about the tenth."

The man didn't look pleased, but he didn't look that unhappy either. The extra few silver royals each man would get were a proper bonus. He slipped the money into his tunic and said, "I get you. We'll hoist a drink to you this evening."

Roo turned away and moved back to the entrance, where Jason was toweling himself dry. Roo stepped into the area and saw it was now filthy with mud and rain. The wind was picking up, and McKeller said, "We'd better close the shutters and then we'll clean up this mess." He signaled for Kurt and another waiter. "Clean up this area." To Roo and Jason he said, "Go around back and come into the kitchen from the alleyway. I don't want you tracking mud across the floor. Change into clean clothing and get back to work."

Roo tossed his dirty, wet towel back into the metal pan and saw Kurt glowering at him, as if this extra work was Roo's fault and not the result of the weather. Roo grinned at him, which deepened Kurt's irritation.

As he started to leave, McKeller said, "Avery?"

Roo turned. "Sir."

"You thought and acted quickly. You did well."

"Thank you, sir," said Roo as he and Jason stepped back into the storm.

As they headed for the alley behind the coffee house, Jason said, "That's rare."

"What?"

"You don't often hear McKeller compliment one of us. Sometimes he calmly tells us how we're lashing things up, but most of the time he says nothing. He expects us to do the right thing. You've impressed him."

Roo rubbed his nose. "I'll remember that when I'm dying of a cold tonight."

They turned the corner and moved down the alley, reaching the large delivery yard behind the coffee house. They climbed up on the loading dock and then moved into the kitchen. After the time spent in the cold storm, the kitchen felt hot to them. They went to where they kept dry clothes and started to change.

As Roo finished dressing, Kurt came into the kitchen to where Roo and Jason were tying on their aprons. "Well, I had to clean up your mess, Avery. You owe me for that."

"What?" said Roo, his expression a mix of amusement and irritation.

"You heard me. I don't get door duty, but because of you I'm mopping up more mud than I've seen since I started working here."

"I don't have time for this," said Roo, pushing past him.

Kurt's hand fell on his arm. Roo turned and, using a hold taught him by Sho Pi when they were traveling across the sea in Calis's mercenary band, he bent Kurt's fingers back to a very uncomfortable angle, just short of causing him injury. But the pain gained him instant results. Kurt's face drained of color and his eyes began to water as he dropped to his knees. Roo calmly said, "I told you you didn't want to find out what would happen if you touched me again." He caused Kurt another moment of pain, then released his fingers. "Next time I'll break your hand, and then we'll see how fit you are for waiting tables."

Kurt whispered, "You're mad!"

Roo saw fear in Kurt's eyes. Like all bullies, he didn't expect any resistance, and when it came from a small man like Roo, he was doubly shocked. "Very mad," said Roo. "And capable of killing you with my bare hands. Remember that and keep your mouth shut when I'm around and we'll get along just fine."

Roo didn't wait for a response or to say anything to the kitchen staff, who had turned to stare at the sight of Kurt being forced to his knees. Roo knew he now had an enemy, but he didn't fear Kurt. He had lost all fear years before, and it would take something a great deal more frightening than a pumped-up town bully to make Roo Avery know it again.

Seven

Opportunity

ROO SMILED.

The man had come looking for him about midmorning, and McKeller had summoned him from the kitchen, where he was learning to brew coffee to Mr. Hoen's satisfaction. Without introducing himself, the man said, "Are you the boy who stole my wagon?"

Roo halted and studied the man. He was of middle height, only a head taller than Roo, was stocky, and had a round face. His hair was cut short, but slicked with some pomander oil in a Quegan style, with ringlets across his forehead. He wore a shirt with a collar that was too high for him, given his thick neck, and with far too much lace down the front. With his cutaway jacket and tight trousers, he looked comic to Roo. Two less than comic bodyguards stood behind him. Each wore only a long belt knife, and otherwise were unarmed, but Roo could see instantly these were killers—exactly the sort of men Roo had served with in Calis's company.

The man who had spoken might have dressed the part of a young city dandy, but his anger and his narrow eyes caused Roo to sense he was as potentially dangerous as the two men who served him. Roo said, "And you are . . . ?"

"I am Timothy Jacoby."

"Ah," said Roo, making a display of wiping his hands on his apron before offering his right to shake. "Your drunken friend mentioned you by name. Did he ever get to your shop last night?"

Instantly anger was replaced by confusion. It was obvious to Roo that the man had expected some denial. He reluctantly took Roo's hand and shook in a cursory fashion, then let go. "Friend? He was no friend, just a sailor who I bought some drinks, who . . . who did me a favor."

"Well, he obviously felt that returning to sea was a better choice than telling you he almost drove your wagon into Barret's Coffee House."

"So I heard," Jacoby answered. "Well, if he ran off, that explains why I had to buy information from a rumormonger. She said someone had unloaded my wagon in front of Barret's and moved all the cargo. I thought the sailor had been overcome by robbers."

Roo said, "No. Your goods are safe." Reaching into his tunic, he removed the large leather wallet and handed it to Jacoby. "Here are the customs documents. The entire cargo is in that house across the way, safely dry."

"Where's the horse and wagon?" asked Jacoby.

"The horse died. We had to cut it out of the traces, and knackers slaughtered it and hauled it away."

"I won't pay a dime for the knackers!" said Jacoby. "I never authorized that. I could have sent another team and hauled it away myself!"

"No bother," said Roo. "The wagon was ruined"— which he knew to be a lie— "so I had it hauled away. Let me have it for scrap to cover the cost of the porters and knackers, and we'll call it even."

Jacoby's eyes narrowed. "Ruined, you say? How do you know?"

"My father was a teamster," said Roo, "and I've driven enough to know yours wasn't serviced regularly"—which he knew to be the truth—"and with the traces all cut up, there's not a lot but four wheels and a flatbed"—which was also true.

Jacoby was silent a minute, his dark eyes studying Roo while he thought. "How many porters?"

"Eight," said Roo, knowing Jacoby could check with the Porters' Guild easily enough.

Jacoby said, "Show me my goods."

Roo looked back to where McKeller stood. The old man nodded and Roo moved across the street. The storm had halted late the night before, but the streets were still deep in mud. Jacoby had arrived by carriage, and Roo took silent delight as the fancy boots and the lower half of his trouser legs were fouled by the thick muck.

Reaching the door, Jacoby looked at the heavy lock. "How'd you get the key?"

"I didn't," said Roo, easily pulling the hasp away. The screws came out and one fell to the porch. Roo picked it up and stuck it back in the hole. "The owner obviously thought no one was likely to steal his house."

He pushed open the door and led Jacoby to where his cargo was hidden. Jacoby did a quick inventory, then said, "Where's the rest?"

"Rest?" said Roo innocently.

"There was more than this," said Jacoby, anger barely held in check.

Roo then knew for certain what the plan had been. The silk had been smuggled in from Kesh to the Krondorian docks. From there it had to get to the trader's office, with the sailor duped into driving the wagon for some quick gold. If Royal Customs arrested the sailor, Jacoby could claim that he knew nothing of the silk and that the sailor was smuggling it in Jacoby's wagon without his knowledge. Any guild teamster, or even an independent such as his father had been, would have checked the cargo against the manifest, to ensure that he was not accused of stealing something never loaded. But a drunken sailor who was lying about his ability to drive a single horse-drawn wagon was likely not even to think about what was in the back.

Roo looked at the man and calmly said, "Well, if you'd like to go to the constable's office and swear out a complaint, I'll be more than happy to accompany you. I'm sure he will be almost as interested as the Royal Customs office to know why you're concerned with something not accounted for on this bill of lading."

Jacoby fixed Roo with a dark stare, but after a moment it was clear he could do nothing. Both men knew what was going on, but at this point Jacoby had only two options left open to him, and he took the obvious choice.

Jacoby nodded once to the man on his right. From within his jacket he produced a dagger as Jacoby said, "Tell me what you did with the silk or I'll have him cut your heart out."

Roo moved to the center of the room, giving himself space to defend himself. He had a dagger secreted in his own boot, but waited to pull it. Jacoby's two thugs might be dangerous to an untrained man in a tavern brawl or if they had the drop, but Roo knew his own abilities, and unless these men were as skilled as the men Roo had trained with, Roo knew he could defend himself.

"Put that away before you hurt yourself," Roo said.

Whatever reaction Jacoby had expected, that wasn't it. "Cut him!" he said.

The first thug lunged forward while the second pulled his belt knife. The first attacker found Roo's hand on his wrist, and suddenly pain shot up his arm as Roo dug his other thumb into a particularly delicate set of nerves in his elbow. He quickly wrestled the knife from the man's hand and let it fall to the floor, deftly kicking it aside. He then disposed of the first guard with a kick to the man's groin, causing him to groan as he collapsed.

The second thug was disposed of as quickly, and Jacoby pulled his own knife. Roo shook his head as he said, "You really shouldn't do this."

Jacoby's temper got the best of him and he made a growling sound as he lunged at Roo. Roo easily got out of the man's way, gripped his arm as he had the first man's, and found the same bundle of nerves. But rather than jabbing to force the fingers limp, Roo ground his thumb into his elbow, ensuring as much pain as possible. Jacoby cried out softly as his knees buckled and his eyes filled with tears. Then Roo released his grip and the dagger fell from limp fingers. Roo calmly picked it up.

Jacoby knelt, holding his right elbow with his left hand. Roo calmly took the dagger and reversed it, handing it to Jacoby. "You dropped this." The first thug was slowly trying to regain his feet and Roo could tell he would need to soak in a cold bath to reduce the swelling in his groin. The second guard looked at Jacoby with uncertainty written on his face.

Jacoby said, "Who are you?"

"Name's Avery. Rupert Avery. My friends call me Roo. You can call me Mr. Avery." He waved the dagger.

Jacoby took the dagger and looked at it a moment.

Roo said, "Don't worry, I can take it back any time I want."

Jacoby got to his feet. "What kind of waiter are you?"

"The former-soldier kind. I tell you so you don't think about sending these two buffoons with some friends tonight to 'teach me a lesson.' Then I'd be forced to kill them. And then I'd have to explain to the city watch *why* you were trying to teach me a lesson.

"Now, I suggest you get back to your office and get another wagon and team and get this cargo out of here. The owner of this building might want to charge you rent if he finds you warehousing your goods here."

Jacoby signaled to his guards to go on outside and, after they had left, followed them to the door. He paused and regarded Roo over his shoulder before leaving. From outside the door he said "The wagon?"

Roo said, "Do you see a wagon anywhere around here?"

Jacoby said nothing for a long moment, then spoke. "You've made an enemy, *Mr. Avery.*"

Roo said, "You won't be my first, Jacoby. Now get out of here before I get irritated with you, and thank Ruthia"—he invoked the Goddess of Luck—"that someone hasn't taken *all* your cargo and vanished with it."

After Jacoby left, Roo shook his head. "Some people. He didn't even say thank you."

Returning to the door, he closed it and crossed the street. McKeller was waiting for him and said, "You were gone a long time." It wasn't a question.

Roo said, "Mr. Jacoby seemed to think some of his cargo was missing and was ready to claim Barret's was responsible for the loss. I carefully accounted for every item on the manifest and he was satisfied when he left."

If McKeller wasn't completely convinced, he seemed ready to accept the lie at face value. With a nod of his head, he indicated Roo should return to his duties. Roo moved back toward the kitchen and found Jason standing next to the door. "You taking a break this hour?"

Jason nodded.

"Do me a favor if you've a mind to: go to the hiring hall and see if my cousin Duncan is still in town." After the destruction of the wagons of wine, Duncan had decided Roo's get-rich-quick plan was over and was seeking guard duty on a caravan heading eastward.

"If he is?" asked Jason.

"Tell him we're back in business."

If Jacoby had revenge on his mind for Roo, he didn't attempt to extract it quickly. The night passed with Roo sleeping lightly in the loft he rented above the kitchen at Barret's. Duncan had returned with Jason, complaining that he had been about to leave on a large caravan heading to Kesh, and was sleeping next to his cousin.

Roo suspected it was a lie, as Duncan was inclined to aggrandize his own discomfort and diminish others', but he didn't mind. He knew that the silk he had hidden in the building was worth a great deal more than he had first thought. Otherwise why would Jacoby have been so desperate to regain it? So having Duncan around was important; Roo knew he needed someone reliable to guard his back as he entered into the world of commerce.

The night passed slowly as Roo lay awake making and discarding plan after plan. He knew that the silk would be his recovery from the disaster of his wine venture, and that while sound in theory, the manner in which he had undertaken to build up his wine trade revealed to anyone who cared to look just how unpracticed Roo was in matters of business.

As dawn approached, Roo rose and dressed. He went out into the predawn morning, listening to the sounds of the city. A village boy from a small community in the mountains, he found the strange sounds of Krondor exhilarating: the squawk of the gulls flying in from the harbor, the creaking of wagon wheels moving over the cobbles of the street as bakers, dairymen, and fruit sellers brought their wares into the city. The occasional craftsman, moving cautiously through the gloom of the streets on his way to work, passed by, but otherwise the street was abandoned as Roo moved across to the old building. He had felt a strange attraction to the once-rich domicile from the first moment he had seen it. He had visions of himself standing at the large windows on the second floor, looking down upon the busy intersection that stood between the home and Barret's. Somehow that house had become a symbol for Roo, a concrete goal that would show the world he had become a man of importance and means.

He entered the dark house and looked around. The grey light that came in the doorway barely outlined the stairway under which he had stored the silk. He suddenly wondered at the upper room and moved up the stairway.

He paused as he reached the top of the stairs, as they bent to the right to form a balcony overlooking the entryway. He could see the shadowy form of the chandelier and wondered what it would look like with the candles ablaze.

He turned and saw that the hallway led into pitch darkness. He could barely see the handle to the first door on the right, the one that would provide a window view of the city street. He opened the door and saw the room in the dim light of the grey morning.

The room was empty save for some rags and a few shards of broken crockery. Roo walked to the window and looked out. In the morning gloom he saw the doorway of Barret's. A thrill ran through Roo and he put his hand out and touched the wall.

He held motionless as the sun rose in the east, until at last the street below him filled with citizens of the city about for the day. The noise of the quickly building throng below robbed him of the secret quiet he had taken for himself, and he resented it for that.

He moved quickly through the other rooms, curiosity making him want to know every inch of the town house. He discovered a master suite in the rear, several other rooms, a garderobe, and a rear servants' stairway. A third floor seemed equally divided between a storage area and what might pass as a workspace for the servants; at least, there were shreds of fine clothing and a thimble to convince Roo he had found where the lady of the house had once met with her seamstress.

Roo worked his way through the house, and when he was done, he left with a twinge of regret. He closed the door behind him and promised himself that he would return someday as the owner.

As he reached the center of the street, he realized he was holding a small shred of cloth. He examined it. It was a faded piece of once-fine silk, now yellowed by age and dirt. Without understanding quite why, he slipped it inside his tunic and moved past the doorway to Barret's.

The doors swung open as he passed through the side street and he knew he was late. He should have been among those opening the coffee house.

Roo returned to his quarters, put on his apron, and hurried to the kitchen, where he slipped in with the other waiters without attracting attention. Duncan had not stirred for a moment and the silk was still safe below the stairway.

Roo knew it would be a long day until he was free in the evening and could embark on making his fortune.

Duncan found him during his lunch break. Roo moved into the rear courtyard of the coffee house and said, "What is it?"

"It's less than diverting sitting in that cramped loft, cousin. Maybe I could be about seeing if there's a buyer for—"

A warning glance from Roo silenced him. "I have plans already. If you really want to get something done, return to the house across the way and inspect the wagon. Let me know what you think we need to repair the traces. You're no teamster, but you've been around enough wagons to have some sense of it. If we need to buy new leathers, let me know. And if we can repair what's there, so much the better."

"Then what?" asked Duncan.

Roo reached into his tunic and pulled out the gold piece he had acquired from McKeller the day before. "Get something to eat, then buy what we need to refit the wagon. I need enough for two animals."

"Why?" said Duncan. "That won't buy what we need and get us horses. Besides, what are we going to haul?"

Roo said, "I have a plan."

Duncan shook his head. "Your plans seem to lead nowhere, cousin." Roo's features clouded and he was about to say something in anger, but Duncan said, "Still, it's your gold and I've nothing better to do." His smile caused Roo's anger to flee before it was fully formed. Duncan's roguish ways always brought a smile to his lips.

"Get on with you," said Roo. "One of us has to work for a living."

Roo returned to the kitchen as he was due to return to the floor, and he regretted he had spent his few free moments talking with Duncan rather than grabbing a bite to eat, as was the purpose of the break. Suddenly he was hungry and that only made the day pass even more slowly.

*   *   *

"Are you sure you know what you're doing?" asked Duncan.

Roo said, "No, but I can't think of anything else to try." He adjusted the end of the silk bolt he carried under his arm.

They stood before a modest home, located as far from Barret's as one could live without leaving the Merchants' Quarter. Duncan carried the other end of the long bolt of silk, still wrapped in canvas and linen, and glanced around. They were not in a particularly rough part of town, but it wasn't a completely safe area, either. Only one street over, a traveler would find the homes less cared for, occupied by working families, often several to a dwelling, four or five people living in a room. Roo shook his head as he realized this house was totally in keeping with what he would expect from Helmut Grindle.

Roo knocked on the door.

After a minute, a woman's voice said, "Who is it?"

Roo said, "My name is Rupert Avery and I seek Helmut Grindle, a merchant with whom I am acquainted."

A cleverly hidden peephole opened in the door—Roo noticed it only because of a tiny glint of light—then, after a moment, the door opened.

A plain-looking young woman, plump, with light brown hair pulled back under a modest fillet of dark cloth. Her blue eyes were narrow with suspicion, but she said, "Wait inside, sir."

Roo and Duncan stepped inside. The girl turned and Roo noticed she wore simple but well-made and well-cared-for clothing. A possibility crossed his mind and he let his face cloud over.

"What?" whispered Duncan when they were alone.

"I hope that's the maid" was all Roo said.

A few minutes later a narrow-shouldered, stooped-over man entered, glanced at Roo, and said, "Avery! I had heard you'd been hung."

"Pardoned by the King himself," said Roo, "and any who don't believe me are free to inquire at the palace. Tell them to ask for my good friend Duke James."

A lively light came into Grindle's eyes. "I may have someone do that." He motioned through a curtained doorway. "Come inside."

They left the plainly decorated hallway and entered a very finely finished sitting room. The decor was what Rupert expected, and was consistent with what he had learned of Grindle when he and Erik had ridden along with him on the road to Krondor.

Grindle was a merchant who specialized in luxury goods, small and easily transported, which he moved across the Kingdom in ordinary wagons that looked to be carrying unremarkable wares. In fact they contained more gold in value per square foot than Roo had seen in any cargo during a young lifetime spent loading and unloading wagons.

The young woman returned and Grindle said, "Karli, bring us a bit of wine." He motioned for the two men to sit, and Duncan did. Roo introduced his cousin to the merchant, then said, "I hope we're not intruding."

"Of course you're intruding," said Grindle with no hint of tact. "But I suspect you've got some scheme or another that you think would interest me, and I find that sort of nonsense occasionally diverting." He glanced at the bundle that Duncan and Roo had put down, now propped against the side of Duncan's chair, and said, "I suppose it has something to do with whatever you have in that large canvas bundle."

The girl whom Roo—with an an inward sigh of relief—took to be the maid, returned with a tray, three silver cups, and a carafe of wine. Roo sipped and smiled. "Not your best, but not your worst, either, Master Merchant?"

Grindle smiled. "You're from Darkmoor, now that I think on it. Wine country. Well then, maybe if you can show me something worthwhile, I'll pull the cork on something rare. What is your plan and how much gold do you need?"

His tone remained light, but Roo could see the suspicion in his eyes. This was as shrewd a man as Roo had ever encountered and one who would smell a confidence job before Roo could dream it up. There was nothing to be gained by trying to dupe the man.

Roo nodded and Duncan put down the bundle and slowly un-wrapped it. When he had the canvas open, he began unwrapping the linen, and when at last the silk was revealed, Duncan stepped away.

Grindle quickly knelt and inspected the cloth, gently picking up a corner and thumbing the weave. He moved part of the bolt and calculated the weight and from that the length. From the size of the bolt, he knew the width. "You know what you have here?" he asked.

Roo shrugged. "Keshian, I'm guessing."

"Yes," said Grindle. "Imperial. This silk is supposed to go to the Plateau of the Emperor. It is used to weave the little skirts and other light clothing worn by the Keshian Truebloods." A calculating look entered his eyes. "How did you come to possess this?"

Roo said, "Something like salvage. No one appeared who could prove ownership—"

Grindle laughed as he sat back down in his chair. "Of course not. It's a capital offense to smuggle this silk from the Empire." He shook his head. "It's not that it's the best in the world, you understand, but the Truebloods have a strange sense of ownership with anything associated with their history and traditions. They just don't like the idea of anyone but one of their own possessing such items. Which makes them all the more valuable for those vain nobles who want something they're not supposed to have."

Roo said nothing. He simply looked at Grindle. At last the old man said, "So, what does this rare bit of contraband have to do with whatever plan you have rattling around in that devious skull of yours, Rupert?"

Roo said, "I don't really have a plan." He outlined his attempts to import wine from Darkmoor in bulk, and, surprisingly enough, Grindle didn't comment unfavorably on the idea. When he explained his encounter with the Mockers and the fatal outcome for Sam Tannerson, Grindle waved him to a halt.

"You're at the heart of the matter, now, boy." He sipped his own wine. "When you deal with this sort of item"—he waved at the silk—"you're dealing with the Mockers or those businessmen who must needs deal with them regularly." He tapped his chin with his bony finger. "Still, there are dressmakers who would pay dearly for silk of this quality."

Duncan said, "What makes it so dear, besides the Imperial exclusive, I mean?"

Grindle shrugged. "It is rumored to come from giant worms or spiders or some other fantastic creatures, rather than from the usual silkworms. I have no idea if any of that is true, but there is this one thing: it'll wear for years without losing its luster or shape. No other silk I know of can claim that."

Again silence fell on the room, then Grindle said, "You still haven't said what you wish of me."

"You've already been a great help," said Roo. "Truth to tell, I have a wagon but no horses and I was thinking of selling this. I thought perhaps you might suggest a likely buyer and a fair price."

A calculating looked crossed the merchant's face. "I might." He then nodded once and added, "Yes, I just might."

Duncan covered the silk again, and Grindle called out, "Karli!" The girl appeared a moment later and Helmut Grindle said, "Daughter, bring me a bottle of that vintage from Oversbruk, what year was it?"

"I know the one, Father."

Looking from father to daughter, Roo forced a smile. He had two reasons not to smile. The first was the girl wasn't the maid but the daughter. He sighed inwardly, and turned to smile in her direction. The other reason was the choice of wine. He knew exactly what Grindle was proposing to do: drink one of the very sweet Advarian-style wines that flourished in the cold climates of Grindle's ancestors. Roo personally had had limited experience with sweet wines, and had only drank such on one occasion, a bottle he had stolen from his father's wagon the last time the rare hand-picked berry wine had been transported into Ravensburg. He had suffered the worst hangover of his young life from drinking too much, but he knew that right now he wanted nothing more in life than Helmut Grindle's approval, and he would drink the entire bottle if asked. Then, glancing at the plump and plain girl, he knew he also wanted the girl's approval as well.

His steady gaze caused the girl to blush as she left the room, and Grindle said, "None of that, you young rogue."

Roo forced a grin. "Well, it's hard to ignore a pretty girl."

Grindle erupted in laughter. "I told you once before, Avery, that your biggest fault was in thinking other people were not half as clever as you."

Roo had the good grace to blush, and when the girl returned with the sweet white wine, he said nothing. When they had hoisted a toast, Duncan offering up some meaningless pledge of good faith and hope for good fortune, Roo said, "Then I guess we're going to do some business?"

Helmut Grindle's expression turned from an affable smile to stony coldness as he said, "Perhaps." He leaned forward. "I can read you like a parchment nailed to the side of a tavern, Roo

Avery, so let me set you straight on some things.

"I spent enough time with you and your friend Erik on the road to have a good sense of you. You're smart, and you're clever, and those aren't the same thing; you have a cunning nature but I think you're willing to learn." He lowered his voice. "I'm an old man with a homely daughter and no one pays court to her who doesn't have his eye on my purse." He halted, and when Roo said nothing in protest, he nodded once and continued. "But I won't be around forever and when I'm dead I want grandchildren at my bedside shedding tears. If the price of such vanity is finding my son-in-law among those who have an eye on my purse before my daughter, so be it. But I'll pick the best of them. I want a man who will take care of my grandchildren and their mother." He spoke even softer. "I need someone to take over my trade and to care for my girl. I don't know if you're the lad, but you might be."

Roo looked back into the old man's eyes and saw in them a will as hard and unyielding as any he had encountered, including Bobby de Loungville's. He only said, "If I can be."

"Well then," answered Grindle, "the cards are on the table, as the gamblers say."

Duncan looked as if he wasn't quite sure what he was hearing, but he continued to smile as if this had been but another friendly chat over wine.

"What should I do with the silk?" Grindle asked.

Roo considered, then answered: "I need a start. Take the silk, and give me horses, refit my wagon, and give me a cargo and a place to take it. Let me prove myself to you."

Grindle rubbed his chin. "That silk is decent collateral, no doubt." He waved his hand in the air, as if calculating figures in his mind. Then he said, "One more thing before I say yes or no. Who will be looking to find you for loss of that silk?"

Roo glanced at Duncan, who shrugged. Roo had told him of the run-in with Jacoby, and Duncan didn't seem to think it worth holding back.

Roo said, "I think Tim Jacoby had the silk smuggled in from Kesh. Or he was to receive it from whoever did. In any event, let's say he's less than pleased with not having it tonight."

"Jacoby?" said Grindle. Then he grinned. "His father and I are old enemies. We were boys together, friends once. I hear his son

Randolph is a decent enough boy, but Timothy is a different sort; he's a bad fellow. So I gain no new enemies by supporting you in this."

"Then we're in business?" asked Roo.

"Seems we are," answered Grindle. He poured more wine. "Now, another drink."

They drank, and after the second glass, Duncan said, "You wouldn't have another daughter, then, would you? A pretty one, perhaps?"

Roo covered his eyes but was taken aback when Grindle laughed. He uncovered his eyes and was surprised to see Helmut Grindle genuinely amused at the question.

They drank the bottle dry and spoke of many things, but mostly Helmut Grindle and Rupert Avery made plans, discussing various trading strategies and cargoes, which routes to take, and after a while neither man noticed that Duncan had fallen asleep in his chair or that Karli Grindle had come down, removed the bottle of wine, replaced the low, guttering candle, and retired, leaving the two men to talk late into the night.

Roo said, "Look alert."

Duncan nodded. "See them."

They were driving a wagon along the coast road, just south of the town of Sarth, the next safe harbor north of the city of Krondor. The wagon had been restored to Roo's satisfaction and the horses were fine animals, and Grindle assured him that his share of the profits from the silk would prove ample for his participation in this undertaking.

A band of armed men gathered near the roadside, holding some sort of discussion. As the wagon approached, one of the armed men called it to the attention of the rest, so that by the time Roo and Duncan were upon the group, the men were arrayed across the road, with one in front holding up his hand.

"Who disputes my right to pass on the King's Highway?" demanded Roo.

"No man," said the leader, "but these are difficult days and we need to ask if you've seen armed men riding past to the south."

"None," said Duncan.

"Who are they?" asked Roo.

"Bandits, and they hit us late last night. A full score of them, or more," said a man nearby.

The leader threw the man a black look over his shoulder, then said to Roo, "Bandits. Late last night they robbed a couple of merchants, ransacking their stores, then robbed the two inns in the town."

Roo glanced at Duncan, who looked amused. It was nearly mid-afternoon, and there was a small ale cask nearby, so Roo was pretty convinced these "soldiers" had been debating the best course of action since dawn.

"You're the town militia?" asked Roo.

The leader puffed up a bit. "Yes, we are! In service to the Duke of Krondor, but freemen protecting our own."

"Well then," said Roo, as he urged his horses forward, "you had better get right after them."

The man who was doing the talking said, "Well, that's the problem, then, isn't it? We don't know where they went. So we're not too sure which is the best way to take out after them."

"North," said Roo.

"That's what I said!" The man who had presumed to talk before was speaking again.

"Why north?" demanded the leader of Roo.

"Because we've been on the road since leaving Krondor. If raiders had hit you, then fled south, they would have passed us on their way. None came by us this morning, so it's safe to assume they're heading north up toward Hawk's Hollow or Questor's View." Roo was no student of geography, but he knew enough about trade routes to know that once past the northeast branch road that led up the eastern edge of the Calastius Mountains, there was no easy route across them south of Sarth.

One of the more drunken soldiers said, "Why not west or east?"

Roo shook his head. To the leader he said, "Sergeant?" The man nodded. "Sergeant, if they were heading west, they would have been in boats, not on horseback, and to the east lies what?"

"Only the road to the Abbey of Sarth and more mountains."

Roo said, "They've gone north. And odds are they're bound for Ylith, for where else would they fence what they've stolen here?"

That was enough for the leader, who said, "Men, we ride!"

The deputation of town militia moved in something like haste, though some of the defenders of Sarth were having difficulty moving in a straight line.

Roo continued up the road, and watched as the little squad headed for various locations around the town, to get their mounts.

"Think they'll find the bandits?" asked Duncan.

"Only if they are very unfortunate," said Roo.

"Where's the Prince's army?" asked Duncan.

Roo said, "Off on the Prince's business, I should think." Sarth lay within the boundaries of the Principality of Krondor, which meant it had no local earl, baron, or duke to answer to, and to provide protection. Krondorian soldiers would ride a regular patrol from the boundary between the Principality and the Duchy of Yabon to the north to the City of Krondor itself. But for local problems, a militia, watch, or town constable would have primary responsibility to keep the peace until such a patrol arrived, or answered a request for help.

Roo and Duncan had been pleased with the beginning of the journey. Roo had tendered his resignation from Barret's, and had been surprised to hear something akin to regret from McKeller. He promised Jason that should fate take a kind turn, he might find him a position that matched his wit someday.

Helmut Grindle had been straightforward enough about bringing Roo into the business. He had spoken several times of matching the boy, as Grindle called Roo, with his daughter, Karli. A couple of passing references had caused the girl to blush when she was in earshot, but Grindle had at no time bothered to ask his daughter what she thought of the matter.

Roo had joked with Erik about marrying Helmut Grindle's ugly daughter, and now that the reality was before him, he wondered at his quips. The girl wasn't ugly, just not very attractive, but then neither was Roo, so he didn't think much about that. He knew that if he were to become rich enough he could afford pretty mistresses, and that his primary obligation to Grindle would be to keep his daughter fat with child and ensure that the old man's grandchildren were well fed and provided for. Roo also knew that if he could build upon what Grindle already had in his possession, he stood to inherit—or, rather, Karli stood to inherit, which would be the same thing—quite a tidy sum, and that with that to work with, why, there was no limit to his future.

Roo had talked with Duncan about several plans he had, but Duncan's interest in business was cursory, beginning and ending with when he would be paid and how much, and where the nearest whore or willing barmaid might be found. Traveling with Duncan had been an education for Roo, and he found himself more likely to spend the night with a tavern wench than alone because of Duncan's influence, but he was constantly amazed at how focused Duncan could become on wooing an innkeeper's pretty daughter. The man had a passion for women that far exceeded Roo's normal young male appetite.

Duncan, on the other hand, had absolutely none of Roo's passion for riches. He had traveled, fought, loved, drunk, and ate, and his dreams were not shared. But while easy money appealed to him, hard-earned money was something that would never come his way.

Roo drove through the south end of Sarth, and when he saw a store with a broken-in door, he pulled over. "Keep an eye on things," he said to Duncan as he jumped down from the buckboard.

He entered the establishment and saw at once it had been totally ransacked. "Good day," he said to the merchant, who looked at him with an expression halfway between irritation and hopelessness.

"Good day, sir," said the merchant. "As you can see, I am unable to conduct business in my usual manner."

Roo studied the merchant, a middle-aged man with an expanding middle. "So I've heard. I'm a trader, by name Rupert Avery," he said, sticking out his hand. "I'm on my way to Ylith, but perhaps I may be of some service."

The merchant shook in a distracted manner and said, "I'm John Vinci. What do you mean?"

"I am a trader, as I said, and I am able perhaps to provide some goods that you may need to replace your pillaged stores."

The man's manner changed instantly, and he regarded Roo with a studied expression, as if suddenly he had wagered every coin he owned on the outcome of a bet. "What sort of goods?"

"Only the finest, and I am embarked upon a journey to Ylith, and was planning on purchasing goods to return to Krondor, but I may be able to add a leg, as it were, providing you can, in turn, trade with me those goods I was seeking to purchase in Ylith."

The man said, "What manner of goods?"

"Goods easily transported in small quantity, but of high enough quality to ensure me a profit."

The merchant studied Roo a moment, then nodded. "I understand. You trade in high-priced baubles for the nobility."

"Something like that."

"Well, I need little in the way of finery, but I could certainly use a dozen bolts of sturdy linen, some needles of steel, and other goods required by the townspeople."

Roo nodded. "I can take a list with me to Ylith and return within two weeks. What have you to offer?"

The merchant shrugged. "I had a small cache of gold, but those bastards found it quickly."

Roo smiled. The merchant had most certainly left a small strongbox of gold poorly hidden to let the raiders think they had captured his only treasure, but almost as certainly had another, richer, deposit of coins nearby. "Some items of worth?"

The merchant shrugged. "A few articles, perhaps, but nothing that might be called unique."

"Unique is for the very rare client," said Roo. He rubbed his chin and said, "Just something that might wait a long time to find a buyer here, but that might find a quick home in Krondor."

The merchant stood motionless for a moment, then said, "Come with me."

He led Roo through the back of the store and out across a small courtyard and into his home. A pale woman worked in the kitchen while two small children fought over possession of a toy. The man said, "Wait here," without bothering to introduce his wife to Roo, and went up a narrow flight of stairs. He returned a few moments later and held out a leather-covered box.

Roo took the box and opened it. Inside was a single piece of jewelry, an emerald necklace, closer to a full choker, of matched stones. It was set with cut diamonds, tiny but brilliant, and the goldwork was fine. Roo had no idea of its real worth, but calculated it was probably of fine enough quality to warrant a second look from even the most jaded dealer in gems.

"What do you want for it?"

"I was keeping this as a hedge against a disaster," said the merchant, "and this qualifies as one, I guess." He shrugged. "I need to restock, and quickly. My business will be nonexistent if I can't provide goods to the townspeople."

Roo was silent for a minute, then said, "Here's what I'll do. Give me a list of what you need, and we'll go over it together. If we can agree upon a price, then I'll bring back the goods from Ylith, within two weeks, perhaps as quickly as ten days, and then you'll be back in business."

The man frowned. "There's a Quegan trader due in less than a week."

"And what assurance have you he'll have any of the goods you need?" said Roo instantly. "What good would it do you if he's a slaver?"

The man shook his head. "None, but then again, we don't see a lot of slavers in these parts." Slavery was banned in the Kingdom, save in the case of condemned criminals, and the importation of slaves from Kesh or Queg was illegal.

"You know what I mean," said Roo. "For a small premium, I can bring you exactly what you need."

The man hesitated, and Roo said, "The children will continue to eat."

The merchant said, "Very well. Go to the inn at the end of the street and find a room. I'll meet you for supper and we'll go over the list together."

Roo shook hands with the man and hurried to where Duncan waited. Duncan was half-dozing when Roo climbed aboard the wagon. "What?" he said in sleepy tones.

"The inn," said Roo. "We find ourselves a room and make a deal."

Duncan shrugged, "If you say so."

Roo grinned. "I say so."

Helmut Grindle looked up when Roo entered his study. "And how did we do, young Rupert?"

Roo sat and nodded in appreciation when Karli entered with a glass of wine for him. He sipped at it and said, "Very well, I think."

"You think?" asked Grindle, sitting back in his chair. He glanced through the window where Duncan stood watch over the wagon. "I don't see a wagon large with cargo, so I must assume you found something tiny but valuable."

Roo said, "Something like that. I took our goods to Ylith and, after three days of shopping them around, made trades I thought were most profitable, and restocked with goods."

Grindle's eyes narrowed. "What manner of goods?"

Roo grinned. "Twenty bolts of fine linen, two hogsheads of steel nails, ten dozen steel needles, a dozen hammers, five saws, one gross spools of fine thread—"

Grindle interrupted. "What?" He held up his hand. "You speak of common inventory! What of the long discussions we had on rare items of value for wealthy clients?"

Roo said, "I got a little gold as well."

Grindle sat back in his chair and fingered his shirtfront. "You're holding back something. What is it?"

"I took those items mentioned and traded them in Sarth for this." He held out the leather box.

Grindle took it and opened it. He sat silently for a very long time, examining the necklace. After a moment he said, "This is very fine." He calculated in his head. "But not worth enough more than what I sent north to make this a very profitable journey."

Roo laughed and reached inside his tunic. He pulled out a large purse, which he tossed on the table. It landed with a heavy clank. "As I said, I got a little gold as well."

Grindle opened the purse and quickly counted. He sat back with a smile. "This is a profit to be reckoned with, my boy."

"I got lucky," Roo said.

"Luck is when those who are prepared take advantage of the moment," answered Grindle.

Roo shrugged, trying hard to look modest and failing.

Grindle turned toward the rear of the house and called, "Karli!"

After a moment the girl appeared. "Yes, Father?"

"Karli, I've given young Avery here leave to pay court to you. He will come to escort you out next Sixthday eve."

Karli looked at her father, then Roo, uncertainty etched on her features. She hesitated, then said, "Yes, Father."

Looking at Roo, she said, "Sixthday, then, sir."

Roo sat awkwardly, not knowing what to say. Then he nodded, saying, "After the noon meal."

The girl fled through the curtains at the rear of the room, and Roo wondered if he should have said something pleasant, such as he looked forward to it, or she looked attractive in her gown. He shook off the irritation that this uncertainty brought, and counseled himself to quiz his cousin Duncan on what to say to the girl, then returned to matters at hand.

Grindle poured them both a stiff drink of sweet wine and said, "Now tell me how you did this, my boy. Every step of the way."

Roo smiled, basking in the approval written in Grindle's eyes as he beamed at Roo, occasionally looking down at the necklace.

Eight

Players

Roo POINTED.

"I see Greylock!" he said.

Erik, Jadow, Duke James, Robert de Loungville, and Knight-Marshal William waited upon the royal dock as *Trenchard's Revenge* was approaching the waiting party. Anxious eyes scanned the distant ship, looking for those other members of Calis's company who might have somehow survived the Emerald Queen's attack on the distant city of Maharta.

"Easy to see that grey streak," said Roo, shading his eyes against the bright afternoon sun. In the last month, since he had become veritable partners with Helmut Grindle, Roo had been too busy to think overly long on his former companions, but when Erik had sent word that the other ship from Novindus was sighted coming across the harbor's outer boundary, he left Duncan to oversee the loading of wagons for a short trip up the coast to Sarth, and hurried to see the ship put in. Like Erik, he felt the loss of those other men who had endured the hardship of that long voyage across the sea two years before. Then he saw a familiar figure near Greylock, and he shouted, "Luis! It's Luis!"

Jadow said, "You're right, man. It's that foul-tempered Rodezian mother-lover or I'm a priest of Sung."

Roo waved and Greylock and Luis waved in return. Then the mood darkened as Roo realized there were no other members of his company on deck. As if sensing his boyhood friend's thoughts, Erik said, "Maybe some of them are ill belowdecks."

"Maybe," agreed Roo, but his tone revealed he had little hope that was true.

Time passed slowly as the ship came closer to the royal docks. Unlike Admiral Nicholas, the captain of the *Revenge* seemed disinclined to ignore the prerogatives of the Harbormaster and his pilots, so the ship slowed until it was close enough to the docks to be towed by longboat, then hauled into place.

As soon as the gangplank was run out, Greylock and Luis came down. Greylock saluted Duke James and Knight-Marshal William, while Luis, Jadow, Erik, and Roo all slapped each other on the back, weeping unashamedly at the sight of one another.

Then something odd about Luis struck Roo and he said, "Your hand?"

Luis wore a long-sleeved jacket and black gloves. The former Rodezian courtier turned murderer lifted his right sleeve, letting it fall away. His right hand was fixed in a half-claw, the fingers unmoving. A moment of regret shown in his eyes, but all he said was "Buy me a drink and I'll tell you about it."

"Done!" said Erik, then turned to de Loungville. "If you don't need us right now, Sergeant?"

De Loungville nodded. "Don't get too drunk. I need you and Jadow clearheaded tomorrow. And bring Luis back with you. I'll have a few questions for him, and there's the matter of his official pardon."

"Pardon?" said Luis. "I remember the Captain saying something but doubted he'd get it done."

"Come along," said Roo. "We'll tell you about it and try to keep you from getting hung by the city watch before tomorrow."

Erik said, "Master Greylock, it's good to see you."

"I'll be around," answered the former Swordmaster of the Baron of Darkmoor. "We can catch up tomorrow." A momentary sadness passed over his face. "We have a lot to talk about."

Erik nodded. Obviously, he had news about those who hadn't survived the sack of Maharta or the exodus to the City of the Serpent River.

The reunited members of Calis's company were quickly free of the royal docks, and Erik led them to an inn close by often used by soldiers from the palace. Erik suspected that every employee of the inn was in the Prince's service; de Loungville had made it clear he preferred his men to frequent the inn of the Broken

Shield rather than others farther into the city proper. As the drink was decent for the money, the women were friendly and agreeable, and it was close enough to visit without neglecting his duties at the palace, Erik was satisfied to give the inn his business.

Since it was early in the afternoon, business was light. Erik signaled to the barman for a round of ales, and as they sat, Roo asked, "Luis, what happened to you? We thought you lost crossing the river."

Calis's company had been forced to swim across the mouth of the Vedra River to reach the city of Maharta, each man fully armed, and many had not reached the far shore. Luis rubbed his chin with his good hand.

"I nearly was," he said, his Rodezian accent lending an oddly musical quality to his words. "Cramped up just a few yards short of that little island you all crawled onto before you continued on, and by the time I got my head back above water, I'd been swept south of it. So I tried to reach the far shore and started cramping again after a while."

He shook his head, and suddenly Roo realized how much older he looked. A man of not yet middle years, he now had noticeable grey in his hair and mustache. He let out a long sigh as the bar man set pewter jacks of ale before them. He drank deeply and continued. "I didn't wait when the second cramp hit. I dropped my shield and sword, pulled my belt knife, and started cutting off armor. When I could get above water again, I was half-drowned, and I didn't know where I was.

"The sky was dark and all I knew was I didn't have much left. I saw a boat and swam for it." He held up his ruined right hand. "That's how I got this. I reached out for the gunwale and got a hold of it, when a fisherman smashed it with an oar."

Erik visibly winced and Roo said, "Gods!"

"I must have shouted," said Luis. "I blacked out and should have drowned, but someone hauled me in, as I came to on a boat full of refugees, sailing out into the open sea."

"How did you get to the City of the Serpent River?" asked Roo.

Luis told his story, about the desperate fishing folk who sailed past the warships heading after those fleeing the harbor proper, ignoring the little boats that were fleeing the estuary near the city. "We started taking on water," he said, looking off into space as he remembered. "We landed a day northeast of the city, and those of us not inclined to trust their future to the sea went ashore. They repaired the boat, I suppose, or they were taken captive by the invaders. I didn't stay around long enough to find out."

He sighed. "I owed someone there my life and never did find out who it was who pulled me out and why. We were all brothers and sisters in misery." He held out his hand. "Besides, this was starting to throb and puff up, black and angry."

"How did you fix it?" asked Roo.

"I didn't. I considered cutting it off, truth to tell, it hurt so much by the third day, and I was sweating from the fever. I tried the reiki Nakor taught us, and it helped the pain, but it didn't keep me from burning up. But the next day I found this camp with a priest of some order I've never heard of. He couldn't magic it, but he did bathe it, then wrapped it in a poultice of leaves and herbs. Gave me something to drink that broke the fever." He was silent a moment, then said, "He told me it would take some powerful healing magic to restore my hand, the kind the temples charge a lifetime's gold to undertake, and he also said it would be a chance thing; it might not take." Luis shrugged. "As I am unlikely ever to have the wealth needed, I will never know."

He pushed his now empty ale jack away and said, "So now I am here, and as I understand it, a soon to be pardoned and freed man, and I must consider my future."

Erik signaled for another round of ale. "We all faced that."

"If you don't have any plans," Roo said, "I could use a man with a good head and some familiarity in dealing with people of importance."

Luis said, "Really?"

Erik laughed. "Our friend has realized his ambition and is currently working hard at marrying the ugly daughter of the rich merchant."

Jadow fixed Roo with a narrow gaze. "You're not taking liberties with that tender child, are you?"

Roo held up his hands in mock defense. "Never." He shook his head. "Fact is, she appeals to me little more than you do, Jadow. She's a nice enough girl. Very quiet. Not as ugly as I imagined, really, and there's a hint of something when she manages a smile, but right now I'm fighting a two-front battle."

"Oh, this sounds desperate," offered Erik.

"Well, I'm trying to be as capable as I can, to impress her father, but the girl knows I'm about to be hand-picked to marry her, and I don't think she's happy about it."

"Make her happy," offered Luis.

"How?"

"Court her as much as you're obviously courting her father," said the Rodezian. "Bring her small gifts and talk to her of something besides business."

Roo blinked, and it was obvious to those at the table that this thought had never occurred to him. "Really?"

The other three men laughed and after they were finished, Luis said, "Who else made it?"

Erik lost his smile, and Jadow's grin faded to a scowl.

"Not many," said Roo.

Erik said, "The Captain and the sergeant. Nakor and Sho Pi. Those of us here, and a few others from some of the other squads, but of our original six, only we three." He indicated Roo, Luis, and himself.

Jadow said, "That's better than the rest of us." They all nodded. Jadow's original company had perished in a holding action with the Saaur while he carried word to the Captain, and he lost his other companions during the final battle at Maharta.

"Tell him about Biggo," suggested Roo, and Erik told Luis about the last of their squad to die. By the time he finished, they were smiling again.

"I swear he looked surprised. After all that talk about the Goddess of Death and how pious he was," Erik said, "and this and that, he looked as if . . ."

"What?" asked Roo, who hadn't been there but had heard the story before.

"As if he was saying"—Erik lowered his voice to sound like Biggo's—"'Oh, *this* is what it's like!'" He widened his eyes in mock astonishment.

The others chuckled. After the next round was served, Luis picked up his jack of ale and said, "To absent companions."

They drank and for a moment were silent.

"What are you two doing?" asked Luis.

"We're helping the Captain build his army," said Jadow. "Erik and me are corporals."

Erik removed a small book from within his tunic. "Though they have us doing some odd things."

Luis picked up the book and looked at the spine. "Keshian?" he asked.

Erik nodded. "Not that hard to learn to read after you learn to speak it. But it's slow going. I never was the reader Roo was when we were boys."

"What is it?" asked Roo.

"An ancient book on warfare, from the Lord William's library," Jadow said. "I read it last week. This week he's got me reading something called *The Development of Effective Lines of Supply in Hostile Territory* by some Quegan lord or another."

Luis seemed impressed. "Sounds like they're making a couple of generals out of you."

"I don't know about that, but it matches what Natombi told us when we were on the march in Novindus," said Erik.

Luis nodded. Natombi had been another of their company, but he had come from the heart of Kesh and had served with the Inner Legion, the most effective army in the history of Great Kesh, one that had conquered more than two thirds of the continent of Triagia. He had spent many hours talking to Erik about the manner in which the ancient legions deployed their forces and fought their many campaigns. Given the close quarters of their tiny six-man tent, Luis and Roo had heard every one of those conversations, save when they were serving guard duty.

Jadow said, "We're building an army like none seen before." He lowered his voice. "And you know why?"

Luis half laughed and shook his head. "Better than you do, I think." He glanced from face to face. "I only got away from their advanced units by minutes a half-dozen times. And I watched as they butchered those trying to get away." He closed his eyes a second. "I'm a hard man, or so I thought, but I saw things down there I couldn't imagine. I've heard sounds I can't get out of my ears, and I've smelled odors that linger in the nose no matter how much spice you burn or wine you drink."

The mood was now somber, and after a quiet minute, Roo said, "Well, yes, we know what's going on. Still, we have to get on with our lives. Do you want to work with me?"

Luis shrugged. "Doing what?"

"I need someone with court manners who can present certain goods to men and ladies of breeding, nobility even. And who can negotiate prices."

Luis shrugged. "I've never been much of one to haggle, but if you show me what you want, I think I can do this."

Conversation ceased as the front door opened and Robert de Loungville entered, a slender girl at his side. The four men at the table regarded the unlikely pair: the short, stocky, and pugnacious sergeant, and the almost frail but attractive young woman. She wore common clothing, a homespun dress and simple shoes. Other than unusually short hair, her appearance was unremarkable.

But Erik's face showed he recognized her. "Kitty?" he said.

De Loungville held up his hand. "This is my fiancée Katherine, and if any of you murdering scum so much as look at her in a way to cause her to blush, I'll have your liver on a stick."

He said this with a casual tone, but his eyes clearly instructed the men: there is something going on you do not need to know anything about; and wise men heeded even the vaguest warnings. The girl looked irritated at being referred to as de Loungville's fiancée but said nothing.

He took the girl to the barman and spoke to him. He nodded and directed the girl toward the kitchen. She threw one last black look at de Loungville, then went into the kitchen.

De Loungville returned to the table and pulled up a chair. "She's going to work here. So if one of you lot causes her *any* trouble . . ." He let the threat go unfinished.

Roo shrugged. "Not me. I have a fiancée of my own."

"Oh, is that a fact," said de Loungville, evil delight showing in his eyes. "And does she know her intended is a former gallows rat?"

Roo had the good manners to blush. "I haven't told her everything."

"And he hasn't proposed," said Erik. "He's assuming a bit here."

"Well, that's our Rupert," said de Loungville, signaling for an ale.

Luis said, "They were telling me that not many of our friends came back."

De Loungville nodded. "Not many. But we've gone through this before." His features darkened as the barman placed an ale before him. "I've been down under to that bloody continent twice now, and I've left nearly two thousand dead men behind, and I'm sick of it."

"Is that why you and the Knight-Marshal have us reading these?" asked Jadow, indicating the books he and Erik held.

De Loungville's manner changed and he grinned as he reached out and pinched Jadow's cheek. "No, ducky, it's so I can watch your lips move. It amuses me."

Erik laughed. "Well, whatever the reason, there's a lot of interesting things in these books. I'm not sure I understand it all."

"Then talk to the Knight-Marshal," said de Loungville. "I've orders that if any of the corporals need to discuss what they've read, they're to go to Lord William's office." De Loungville took a long drink and smacked his lips with exaggerated satisfaction.

"The Knight-Marshal?" asked Erik. He was the most important military leader in the West after the Prince of Krondor. One of the two of them carried the title Marshal of the Armies of the West in time of war, and historically it was the Knight-Marshal as often as it was the Prince. For any soldier he was something of a figure of awe. Despite having spoken to the man a half-dozen times, Erik had never spoken with him in private or for longer than a few minutes. The prospect of trying to hold a conversation about something he didn't understand obviously caused Erik some distress.

"Don't worry," said De Loungville. "He understands how stone-headed you lot are and he won't use any big words."

Roo and Luis laughed, while Erik said nothing. "Just seems strange that you and the Captain think we need to learn this, Sergeant," said Jadow.

De Loungville glanced around the room. "If you haven't puzzled it out yet, this inn is owned by the Duke. Every man and woman working here is one of James's agents." He hiked his thumb toward the bar. "Katherine is here to alert us to any Mockers who might come snooping around. After our set-to with them last month, we need to make sure they don't cause us more problems.

"What I'm trying to say is this is the safest place outside the palace to talk about what we all know from our last voyage"—his voice lowered—"but there's nowhere that's safe in all ways." He paused. "You need to learn as much as you can, because we're building an army like no other in history. You need to be able to take command of as many men as are there, and if that means that everyone in the chain of command above you is dead, you're going to be a general. So if you find yourself in command of the Armies of the West, and the fate of the Kingdom, and the entire world for that matter, is suddenly in your hands, you'll not muck things up too badly."

Erik and Jadow exchanged glances but said nothing.

Roo pushed back from the table. "Makes me glad I chose a life of commerce," he said. "Well, it's been wonderful, but I have wagons to see to." He asked de Loungville, "Can I take Luis with me now?"

De Loungville nodded. "Come by in the morning and we'll have your pardon signed," he said to Luis.

He motioned for Luis to accompany him. He bade the others good-bye and left the inn.

As they walked, Luis said, "Wagons?"

"I'm a trader now, Luis, and I deal in items of value. I need someone to teach me to talk to the nobility as well as act as my agent."

Luis shrugged. He held up his right hand. "I guess I don't need this to talk."

"How bad is it?" asked Roo as they maneuvered through the busy street.

"I can still feel things, but it feels like I'm wearing heavy gloves. I can't move any finger much."

With a sudden movement, he had a dagger in his left hand. "This one still works, however."

Roo smiled. He knew Luis to be the best man with a short blade he had ever seen and realized that while Luis could not soldier as he used to, he was far from helpless.

As they headed toward Helmut Grindle's establishment, Luis asked, "Where are Sho Pi and Nakor?"

"With the Captain."

"And where is the Captain?"

Roo shrugged. "Off on some errand for the King. I hear he headed down toward Kesh. Stardock maybe."

They continued on.

"You can't go in there," said the student.

Calis pushed past the door guard, Nakor and Sho Pi following after, and kicked open the large door to the inner chamber of the Council of Magicians, the ruling body of the Academy of Magicians at Stardock.

Five magicians looked up and one half rose. "What is this?" he said.

"Kalied," said Calis in a cold, even tone of voice, "I have been patient. I have been waiting for weeks for some indication from this body that it understands the problems confronting us and is willing to aid us."

Another magician, an older man with nearly white beard and hair, spoke. "Lord Calis—"

"Captain," corrected the half-elf.

"Captain Calis, then," said the elderly magician, named Chalmes, "we appreciate the gravity of your warning and have considered your King's request—"

"*My King?*" said Calis in a tone of astonishment. "He's your King as well, need I remind you?"

Kalied held up his hand. "The Academy has long considered our relationship with the Kingdom to have terminated with Pug's departure—"

"No one bothered to inform the Kingdom," observed Nakor.

The five at the table looked at him with a mixture of irritation and discomfort. Nakor had once sat at that same table, when most of those now in control of the Academy had been either students or teachers. Of the five now ruling Stardock, only Chalmes had been a contemporary of Nakor's.

Calis held up his hand to silence further comment. "More to the point, no one bothered to inform His Majesty." He glanced from face to face. The council chamber was a high-ceilinged circular room, and the deep-ensconced torches cast flickering light across the room. Only the presence of a circular overhead wooden candle holder provided enough light to see clearly each man's features.

But Calis's eyes were more than human and he could see the telltale flicker around the eyes, the quick sidelong glance. Kalied might be the one to speak first, but Chalmes was the leader of this committee. Nakor had filled him in on each of these men, over the weeks they had been waiting for some declaration that the Academy at Stardock understood the gravity of the warning carried there by Calis and his companions. Chalmes had been a student of Korsh, one of the two Keshian magicians who along with Nakor had ruled the island community for five years after Pug's departure. His first acolyte, Chalmes, had risen to the council upon Korsh's death, and had showed every sign he was just as conservative and intractable as his predecessor had been. The others Nakor had known as students while he had taught at the Academy, before finally leaving in disgust at the insular tendencies of the administration.

Calis said, "Let me make this simple, so there can be no misunderstanding. You may not sever your ties with the Kingdom. Despite your having come from many nations, this island"—he pointed downward for emphasis—"belongs to the Kingdom. It is a Royal Duchy, and while Pug lives, it will remain so. Despite his absence, he is still a Royal Prince of the Kingdom by adoption and a Duke of the Royal Court. And if Pug dies, it will pass on to his son, the King-Marshal of Krondor, or whoever else the King deems fit to assume the title."

He leaned forward, knuckles upon the table, and said, "You've been granted free reign to conduct your affairs as you like, but by no means does this allow you unilaterally to declare yourself free of Kingdom rule.

"Is this clear, or do I have to send to Shamata for a garrison of soldiers to occupy this island while the King decides which of you traitors to hang first?"

Naglek, the youngest and most quick-tempered of the magicians, sprang out of his chair. "You can't be serious! You come into our council chamber and threaten us?"

Nakor grinned. "He's telling you how things are," he said. He waved Naglek back into his chair. "And don't bother to bluster about your magic powers. There are other magicians who would happily support the Kingdom's efforts to regain control of this island."

He circled around the table and stood next to Naglek. "You were one of my better students. You were even leader of the Blue Riders for a while. What happened to you?"

The man blushed, his fair skin coloring up to his reddish brown eyebrows. "Things change. I'm older now, Nakor. The Blue Riders have been—"

"Their activities have been curtailed," said Chalmes. "Your more . . . unconventional views caused friction among the students."

Nakor made a waving motion with his hand and Naglek stepped away. Nakor sat down and motioned for Sho Pi to come stand next to him. "Now, what are we going to do about this?" he asked.

Chalmes said, "Captain Calis, we are certainly alarmed at some of the things you've reported regarding your voyages across the ocean. We agree that should this Emerald Queen you spoke of attempt to cross the seas and invade the Kingdom, the situation would become most difficult. I think that should these events come to pass, you can tell His Majesty we will give the most serious consideration to his requests."

Calis was silent a minute. Then he looked at Nakor.

"I told you this would happen," Nakor said.

Calis nodded. "I thought we should give them the benefit of the doubt."

Nakor shrugged. "We've wasted nearly a month here."

Calis nodded. "You're right." To the other magicians in the room he said, "I am leaving Nakor here as the Crown's duly appointed representative. He will act as a ducal regent in my absence."

"You can't be serious," said Kalied.

"Most serious," said Nakor.

"You don't have such authority," said a magician named Salind.

Nakor grinned. "He's the Eagle of Krondor. He's the King's personal agent. He holds the rank of Duke of the King's Court in addition to being a Knight-Captain in the Armies of the West. He can have you all hung for treason."

"I'm returning to Krondor," said Calis, "to report to the Prince and to get further instruction as to what we are to do with you until such time as Pug returns."

"Returns?" said Chalmes. "It's been nearly twenty years since we last saw Pug. What makes you think he will return?"

Nakor shook his head. "Because he will need to. Are you still so narrow of vision—" He stopped himself. "Stupid question. Pug will be back. Until then, I think I shall have to see what needs to be changed around here."

Nakor had been snooping, as was his habit, since the day they arrived, so everyone in the room knew instantly he already had a long list of things he would change. The magicians glanced at one another; then Chalmes and the others rose. "Very well," said Chalmes to Calis. "If you expect such behavior will bring the results you wish, you are wrong, I fear, but we shall not actively oppose you. But if you're leaving this . . . gambler in charge, then let him be in charge." With that, he led the other four magicians from the chamber.

Calis watched them depart, then turned to Nakor and Sho Pi. "Will you two be all right?"

"I will protect my master," said Sho Pi.

Nakor made a dismissive gesture. "Bah. I need no protecting from that group of old ladies." He stood up. "When do you leave?" he asked Calis.

"As soon as I can get my horse saddled in town and get started back to Shamata. There's still a half day ahead."

Nakor said, "I knew I was hungry. Let's get something to eat."

The three of them walked down a long hall, past the now totally confused door guard, and at the end of the hallway they stopped. Calis would head outside to gather the soldiers he had brought with him to the island and take the ferry to town. Nakor and Sho Pi would head in the other direction, toward the common kitchen.

"You take care," said Calis. "They gave up too easily."

Nakor smiled. "Oh, they're all up in Chalmes's room this moment, plotting away, no doubt." He shrugged. "I've lived far longer than any of them and not because I was careless. I'll keep an eye out for surprises." Then his mood turned serious. "I've had enough time to look around to know this much: tell the Prince that there are only a few here who have the talent and the temperament to be of any help to us. The rest might be useful in some minor ways, moving messages and the like, but there are only a few real talents here." He sighed. "I thought after twenty years they might have developed dozens of students around here, but I suspect those with genuine ability leave as soon as they can."

"Well, we need someone."

"We need Pug," said Nakor.

"Can we find him?" asked Calis.

"He'll find us." He glanced up and down the hall. "And he'll find us here, I think."

"How will he know we need his help?" said Calis. "The Prince tried using the charm Pug gave Nicholas, and Pug didn't answer."

"Pug will know," said Nakor. Glancing around again, he added. "He may already know."

Calis stood silent a moment, nodded, turned, and without another word walked down the hallway.

Nakor took Sho Pi's arm in his hand. "Let's get something to eat."

"Yes, Master."

"And don't call me master," insisted Nakor.

"As you wish, Master."

Nakor sighed, and they walked down the hallway.

"What do you see?" asked Miranda.

Pug laughed. "Nakor's up to his old tricks. I can't hear what they're saying, but I saw Chalmes and the rest of them stalk out of the council chamber. I suspect Calis left Nakor in charge."

Miranda shook her head and a rain of droplets fell around Pug's head and shoulders, striking the calm pool of water he had used for his scrying. The faint image of the distant chamber room vanished in the ripples.

"Hey!" Pug feigned irritation.

Miranda laughed and shook her head harder, making more water fly. She had just emerged from swimming in the warm ocean and had found Pug spying on the doings at Stardock in a still pool.

Pug turned and grabbed for her, but she danced quickly backwards, avoiding him. Pug's laughter joined hers as she turned and started running down the beach, back toward the waves.

Pug felt his breath tighten for an instant at sight of her slim but muscular body, glistening with water, as she raced ahead of him. Almost a year of living on this island had browned both of them deeply.

She was a far better swimmer than Pug, but he was faster of foot. He tackled her just as she reached the water's edge and they both went down in a heap. Her shrieks of mock outrage joined with his laughter. "You monster!" she shouted as he rolled her over and playfully bit her on the neck near her shoulder.

"You're the one who started it," he pointed out.

Lying back as the soft waves came in to cover both of them,

Miranda studied Pug's features. In the year they had been together they had become lovers and confidants, but there were still secrets between them. Pug knew almost nothing of her past, for she was adept at avoiding direct answers to many of the questions he had asked. When it had become clear she didn't wish to speak of her life before meeting him, he ceased asking. Pug held part of himself back as well, so the relationship was equitable.

"What is it?" he asked. "You've got that look."

"What look?"

"The trying-to-read-my-thoughts look."

"Never learned that trick," she said.

"Few do," said Pug. "Though Gamina always could."

"Read minds?"

"Mine, anyway," he said, turning so he could lie back on his elbows next to her. "It was something of a problem when she turned . . . thirteen or so, and didn't go away until she was nearly twenty." He shook his head as he remembered his adopted daughter's childhood. "She's a grandmother now," he said softly. "I've got a grandson, Arutha, and great-grandsons, James and Dashel." He fell into a reflective silence. The sun beat down on their bodies while the waves rose higher with each turn of the tide, and they were content to be silent for a few moments. When the rising tide threatened finally to wash over them, Pug stood and Miranda followed.

They strolled down the beach in silence for a while. Finally Miranda said, "You've been peeking in at Stardock more often lately."

Pug let out a slow breath, "Things are starting to . . . get more serious."

Miranda slipped her arm into his, and as he felt her skin touch his, Pug's chest tightened again. He had loved his wife as he had thought he could love no other, but this woman, despite her mysterious past, reached parts of him he had not thought anyone could reach. After a year together she still excited and confused him as if he were a boy, not a man in his eighties.

"Where did we leave our clothing?" she asked.

Pug stood up and glanced around. "Over there, I think."

They had occupied the island, in a rude hut Pug had fashioned out of palms and bamboo, and had traveled at will between it and his home at Sorcerer's Isle to restock their supplies of food. Most of their time together had been given over to play, lovemaking, and talking of many things. But Pug had always known that this was only a respite, a time to let troubles be forgotten, while they rested and prepared to face dark horrors once more.

Pug followed Miranda to where their clothing lay in a heap, and watched with a moment of regret as she slipped her dress over her head. He donned his black robe and said, "You're thinking."

"Always," she said with a wry smile.

"No, I mean something specific. And your expression is one I've not seen before. I don't know if I like it."

Worry lines marred her usually smooth forehead. She came to him and put her arms around him. "I'm leaving for a time."

"Where are you going?"

"I think I must go find Calis. It's been too long since I have seen him. I must see what more needs to be done with him."

At the mention of the son of Pug's boyhood friend Tomas, the magician said, "You say this with more than one meaning."

Miranda's green eyes locked with Pug's dark brown ones, and after a moment she nodded, once, quickly. "Yes." She said nothing more.

"When will I see you again?" asked Pug.

She kissed his cheek. "Not as soon as either of us would like, I fear. But I will be back."

Pug sighed. "Well, it was bound to come to an end."

She hugged him. "Not ended, just interrupted. Where will you go?"

"My island, first, to confer with Gathis; then I will return to Stardock for a while. After that I must begin my quest."

Miranda knew he meant to search for Macros the Black. "Do you think you can find the sorcerer? It's been, what? Nearly fifty years?"

Pug nodded. "Since the end of the Great Uprising." Glancing toward the blue sky, he said, "But he's out there somewhere. There are a few places I have yet to search, and there's always the Hall."

At mention of the Hall, Miranda started to laugh. "What is it?" asked Pug.

"Boldar Blood. I left the mercenary at Trabert's in Yabon. I told him to wait there until I sent for him."

"For a year?"

"You're very distracting," she purred, nipping at his earlobe.

"Stop that, unless you want to postpone your departure."

She said, "Well, an hour or two won't make much difference."

As their garments fell to the sand again, Pug said, "How are you going to pay Boldar? Hall mercenaries don't come cheaply."

Grinning at Pug, she said, "I have a lover who's a duke."

Pug smiled ruefully and said, "I'll see what I can do," as he gathered her into his arms.

Nine

Growth

ROO SMILED.

Robert de Loungville walked into the shop, which was filled by the sound of workmen hammering. The building had once been a prosperous establishment, a brokerage for traders that had fallen upon hard times. Roo liked it because there was a small kitchen in the rear, so that he, Duncan, and Luis could fix meals, since they used a corner of the large warehouse as sleeping quarters, saving him the expense of hiring guards and paying rent for quarters.

"Sergeant," said Roo, loud enough to carry over the sounds of the workmen.

De Loungville glanced around. "This your latest enterprise?"

Roo smiled. "Yes. We're expanding, and there's no longer any room behind my partner's house for more than two wagons."

"How many do you have?" asked Bobby.

"Six," answered Roo. "I'm now supplementing our more exotic trade with other traffic."

"That's why I'm here," said de Loungville.

Roo's interest picked up at once and he signaled for his guest to follow him to the rear of the office. Inside the large warehouse behind the office the noise wasn't any less deafening, but they could find a relatively peaceful corner in which to converse. "How may I be of service?" asked Roo.

De Loungville said, "We've had some trouble with our freight shipments into the palace."

Roo's gaze narrowed. "Trouble?"

"Trouble," was all de Loungville replied.

Roo nodded. Agents of the Pantathians had long been a constant source of concern to the Prince and Duke, and while every step was taken to ensure that no one outside those most trusted had any sense of what was being planned by the Prince, there were just too many people needed around the palace on any given day to guarantee privacy. De Loungville and Calis had decided after the return from Novindus that it would be less risky to keep the garrison of Calis's new army at the palace and watch closely who had contact with those men.

"We need a new freight hauler to deliver key shipments to the palace."

Roo hid his delight. He knew that he had no competition. There wouldn't be another freight hauler who could be trusted not to say anything about what he saw at the palace.

"Drivers," Roo said.

De Loungville nodded. "It's a problem."

Roo said, "Maybe there are some men you're training who really aren't suited for whatever it is you're planning"—he kept his voice low enough that no one would be able to overhear—"but who are trustworthy enough to run such shipments."

"You want us to give you a contract and then provide you with drivers?" said de Loungville.

Roo grinned. "Not quite, but if you've already had trouble with your present freight hauler, you know that I'm going to run the same risks with any new drivers I hire. Right now it's only myself, Luis, and Duncan with the valuable goods, and three fairly reliable lads I've employed for the other three wagons. But I'm not willing to vouch for them."

"Understood," said de Loungville. "Well, we've convinced James to open an inn, so why not provide you with some drivers?"

"Why not just set up your own operation and staff it with soldiers?" asked Roo.

"Because it's too obvious," said de Loungville. "The reason you're here is because we need an already established freight company to cover what you're doing. Grindle and Avery has been expanding for several months now and you've made a name for yourself. We'll call for a new contract, keeping the news low-key, but not trying to hide anything."

Roo nodded. "So I'll bid, and win."

"You're not as stupid as you look, Avery." De Loungville lowered his voice even more and put his hand on Roo's shoulder. "Look, you know why we have to be careful, and you also know what's at risk." Roo nodded, though he tried to think little about what he had gone through across the sea when he was a soldier in Calis's company. "Here's the deal: you make sure that whatever we need gets delivered in timely fashion and I'll make sure you get paid in timely fashion. And don't go thinking you can charge us outrageous prices, else we'll try our hand at freight hauling." De Loungville grinned, and it was an expression Roo knew all too well: what he was about to hear wasn't going to be funny. "After the Duke and I contrive a way to either put you out of business or get you hung for some crime or another."

Roo had no doubt at all that should conditions warrant it in de Loungville's judgment, he would happily hang Roo on a trumped-up charge. The man was single-minded in his desire to protect the Kingdom to a point bordering on the fanatical.

Roo said, "Just getting paid in a timely fashion would be novel. You can't believe what I have to go through collecting some of these bills."

De Loungville's grin broadened, and this time there was humor in it. "Certainly I can. Just because a man has a title doesn't mean he has two coins to rub together." He inspected the yard and asked, "How many wagons can you devote to your new service to the palace?"

"How many deliveries a week do you need?" asked Roo.

De Loungville reached into his tunic and pulled out a parchment, handing it to Roo. "This ship's due in tomorrow from Ylith. This is the cargo heading to the palace. We should be looking at similar deliveries two, three times a week from now on."

Roo's eyes widened at the size of the cargo. "Some army you're building, Sergeant. You've enough swords here to invade Kesh."

"If we need to. Can you do it?"

Roo nodded. "I'm going to have to buy three, maybe four more wagons, and if you step up your demand for unloading..." He studied De Loungville's face. "What about incoming caravans?"

De Loungville said, "We're unloading them at the city gate, and we'll need you to transport the freight through the city."

Roo shook his head in wonder. "I'd better get five wagons." He calculated in his head and realized he was short of gold. Without changing expression, he said, "I'll need some gold to close the deal."

De Loungville said, "How much?"

"A hundred sovereigns. That'll get me the wagons and mules, and hire some drivers, but make sure you do get me paid quickly, because I don't have any reserves."

"Well, we'll make it a bit more," said de Loungville. "I can't have you going insolvent because you weren't ready for trouble." He drew a purse out of his tunic and handed it to Rupert. Then he put his hands on Roo's shoulders, leaning close. "You're far more important to us than you think, Avery. Don't create any problems for yourself or for us and down the road you're going to be a very rich man. An army needs quartermasters and paymasters as much as it needs sergeants and generals. Don't make a mess of this, understand?"

Roo nodded, not quite sure he did.

"Let me put it another way: if you cause me or the Captain the slightest problem, anywhere along the way, the trivial fact you are no longer a soldier in our command will spare you no pain whatsoever. I'll have your guts on a stick as if you were just down from the gibbet that first day I took your life and made it mine. Now do you understand?"

Roo's expression darkened. "Yes, but I still don't care for threats, Sergeant."

"Oh, those aren't threats, my pretty. Those are merely the facts of life." Then he grinned. "You can call me 'Bobby' if you wish."

Roo mumbled something, and then said, "Very well, *Bobby*."

"How's your love life? Any wedding plans soon?"

Roo shrugged. "I asked her father and he said he'd consider it; if he says yes, then I'll ask her."

De Loungville rubbed the stubble on his chin as he said, "From what you said a few weeks ago, I thought it already agreed."

Roo shrugged. "Helmut has made me a partner and I dine with him and Karli twice a week, and I escort her down to the town market or square on Sixthday, but . . ." He shrugged.

"Go on with it," instructed De Loungville.

"The girl doesn't like me."

"Doesn't like you or doesn't like the idea you're marrying her for her father's business?"

Roo shrugged. "Luis says I need to win her, but . . ."

"But what?"

"I just don't find her very interesting," said Roo.

De Loungville was quiet a moment, then said, "When you're taking her about and trying to woo her, Avery, what do you talk about?"

Roo shrugged again. "I try to make myself interesting to her, so I talk about what we're doing, her father and I, or what I did during the war." As De Loungville's expression darkened, he added, "Nothing that would displease the Captain, certainly. I'm more discrete than that."

De Loungville said, "Here's a suggestion. Ask her a question."

"What question?"

"Any question. Ask her something about herself. Ask her opinion on some subject." De Loungville grinned. "You might discover that you're not as captivating a topic of conversation as you seem to think you are."

Roo sighed. "I'll try anything." As they walked toward the door to the office, he added, "I'll have wagons at the docks at first light. You'd better have your five drivers here an hour before dawn."

"They'll be here," said de Loungville without looking back as he passed through the door into the front office. The door closed. Roo glanced at the bill of lading and began to calculate.

An hour later, Helmut Grindle entered the workshop area and signaled to Avery, who was overseeing the installation of iron gates on the front of stalls where valuables would be warehoused before shipping.

Roo crossed to stand before his partner and, he hoped, soon-to-be father-in-law, and said, "Yes?"

Helmut Grindle said, "I'm taking the shipment of valuables to Ravensburg myself. Some of the more expensive items are to be shown to the Baron's mother, and given your past relationship, I thought it best if you didn't make this journey."

Roo nodded. "A good idea." Glancing around, he said, "And there's still too much work to oversee here for me to leave."

"Are you stopping by for dinner?" asked Grindle.

Roo considered. "I think I'll stay here and make sure we're well along on the work. Would you be so kind as to tell Karli I'll call on her tomorrow?"

Grindle's eyes narrowed and his expression became unreadable. After a moment he said, "Very well."

Without further remark he departed and Roo turned his attention back to the matters at hand. He had come to know his older partner well over the months they had been working together, but when it came to matters concerning Karli, Roo wasn't entirely sure what the old man thought. Several times in the course of the evening he wondered what had been passing through his wily partner's mind at that minute.

Roo sat quietly in the parlor. With her father taking a wagon of luxury goods to Darkmoor, Karli and Roo were alone in the house for the first time. Previously either they had dined with her father or Roo had escorted her out, to one of the fairs in the city or to the market.

Roo spent much of the early part of the evening alone, since Karli insisted on taking charge of the kitchen herself. As Roo had discovered, there was a cook as well as a maid living in the outwardly modest Grindle home, but Karli had never allowed anyone to care for her father but herself.

Now that supper was over, they sat quietly in a room Helmut used to entertain business guests, one he called the "sitting room." Still, Roo now admitted that the comfort and privacy of the room made it easy to relax. He sat on a small divan and Karli sat on a chair next to it.

Karli spoke softly, as she always did. "Is there something wrong?"

Roo came out of his reverie. "No, nothing, really. I was just thinking about how odd it seems, having an entire room of a house devoted to doing nothing but sitting and talking. Back in Ravensburg the only time we got to talk was over meals at the inn where Erik's mother worked, or when we were out doing something."

The girl nodded, and kept her eyes down. Silence fell.

After a moment Roo said, "When is your father expected back?"

"Two weeks, if all goes as planned," she answered. Roo studied the plump girl. She kept her hands quietly in her lap, and her posture was upright but not stiff or rigid. Her downcast eyes gave him a moment to study her face again. He had been looking for something in that face to arouse him since the day he had met her. He had a coldly calculated plan here, to woo and win this girl and use her father's good offices to rise as a merchant, but each time he found himself with any opportunity to press his suit to her, he could think of nothing to say. He had at last come to the realization that he found nothing remotely attractive in her.

He had coupled with whores far uglier than Karli, with the taste of sour wine and bad teeth on their breath, but that had been on the trail, during war, and the prospect of looming death made each encounter urgent. This was different.

This was a commitment of a lifetime and carried with it great responsibilities. He was contemplating marriage and having children with this girl, yet he knew almost nothing about her.

Luis had said woo her, and de Loungville had said to stop talking about himself. Finally Roo said, "Karli?"

"Yes?" she glanced up at him.

"Ah . . ." he began, then, in a rush, "What do you think of this new contract with the palace?"

Roo cursed himself for an idiot before the words had finished echoing in the air. Here he was trying to convince this girl he would be a fit lover and husband, and the first question he asked was about business!

But instead of looking put out, she smiled slightly. "You want to know what I think?" she asked shyly.

"Well, you know your father," he quickly said. "You've been around his work . . . all your life, I guess." He found himself feeling more like an idiot each passing second. "I mean, you must have come to a conclusion or two on your own. What do you think?"

The girl's smile broadened a little more. "I think having a steady flow of income, even a modest one, is far less risky than continuing to depend on luxuries."

Roo nodded. "That's what I thought." He decided she didn't need to understand that he was the only freight hauler in the city the Prince would trust to bring in those critical supplies.

"Father always talks of maximizing profits, but when he does he also takes great risks. He's had setbacks that have made it very difficult at times." Her voice lowered as she realized she seemed to be criticizing her father. "He tends to remember the good times and forget the bad."

Roo shook his head. "I'm the opposite, I think. If anything, I remember the bad all too easily." Then he realized something about himself. "Truth to tell, there haven't been all that many good times." She was silent, and he shifted the topic of conversation. "So you think this contract with the palace a good one?"

"Yes," she said, and then fell silent again.

Trying to think of the best way to draw her out, Roo at last said, "What about the contract is good?"

She smiled; for the first time since he had met her, Roo saw genuine amusement in her expression. And he was surprised to discover that she had dimples. For a brief instant he discovered that when she smiled she wasn't anything close to being as plain as he had thought.

Suddenly finding himself flushing, he said, "Did I say something funny?"

"Yes." She lowered her eyes again. "You didn't tell me anything about the contract, so how would I know what about it could be good?"

Roo laughed. Obviously she just knew the basics of the contract, and given how little he had been able to share with Helmut, he realized she knew even less. "Well, it's like this," he began.

They talked, and Roo was astonished to find that Karli knew a great deal more about her father's business than he ever would have suspected. More, she had a good mind for business; she asked questions at key moments and discovered weaknesses that Roo hadn't anticipated.

Somewhere during the course of the night, Roo had opened a bottle of wine and they sipped at it. He had never noticed Karli drinking before, and he recalled with some self-condemnation that he had never really paid attention to the girl. Over the weeks he had been coming to pay court to her, he had really been trying to impress her, not to get to know her.

At one point he noticed she had risen to trim the wick in a lamp, then before he realized it, he heard a cock crow. Glancing at the window, he saw the sky beginning to lighten, and said, "Gods! I've been talking to you all night."

Karl laughed and blushed. "I've enjoyed it."

"By Sung"—Roo invoked the Goddess of Truth—"so have I. It's been a long time since I've had anyone to talk to. . . ." He halted. She was now staring at him—and smiling.

On an impulse he leaned over and kissed her. He had never tried before and almost drew back, fearful that he had overstepped his bounds.

She didn't resist, and it was a tender, soft kiss. Roo slowly pulled away, now completely confused. "Ah . . ." he said, "I'll call for you tomorrow—tonight, if you don't mind. We can visit the evening market. If you like!" The last came out in a rush.

She lowered her eyes, again now embarrassed. "I would like that."

He moved toward the door but kept facing her, as if he were fearful of turning his back. "And we can talk," he said.

"Yes," she answered as she rose to follow him to the door. "I would like that, very much."

Roo almost fled, he was so confused. Outside, the door safely closed between them, he paused and wiped his forehead. He was perspiring and felt hot to his own touch. What is this? he wondered. He decided he needed to consider more fully the consequences of this campaign he had started of winning Helmut Grindle's daughter.

As the city awoke around him, Roo returned to the office and the seemingly endless work ahead.

Six wagons rolled to the gate and a guard waved Roo to halt. The guard wore the usual tabard of the Prince of Krondor, the yellow outline of an eagle soaring above a peak, contained in a circle of dark blue. The only change Roo noticed was that the grey tabard was now trimmed in royal purple with yellow. For the first time in memory, a Crown Prince, heir to the throne of the Kingdom of the Isles, now ruled the Western Realm.

Roo struggled to remember what that meant; he was vaguely aware that tradition held that the Prince should rule in Krondor until assuming the throne, but that recent history had placed Arutha, father to the King, on the throne of Krondor, but he wasn't heir to the crown. Roo thought he might ask someone about that, if he remembered.

The guard said, "Your business?"

"Delivery for Sergeant de Loungville" was all Roo had been instructed to say.

At mention of that name, Jadow Shati seemed to materialize out of nowhere, though he merely had been in the shadow of the guardhouse next to the gate. He wore the black tunic of Calis's special forces, with only the crimson eagle above his heart for marking. "Let them in," he said in his deep voice.

He grinned at Roo. "They'll get used to your face, Avery."

Roo smiled back. "If he got used to yours, mine will be easy."

Jadow laughed. "And you're such a handsome fellow, after all."

Then Roo noticed the sleeve on his old companion's tunic and said, "You've got a third stripe! You're a sergeant?"

Jadow's broad smile seemed to widen. "That's the truth, man. Erik, too."

"What about de Loungville?" asked Roo as the gates swung wide. He urged his team of mules forward.

"He's still our lord and master," said Jadow. "But he's now called the Major Sergeant, or Sergeant Major; I can never remember which." As the first wagon with Roo aboard passed, he said, "Erik will tell you. He's going to oversee the unloading."

Roo waved and steered his team into the yard. This was not his first delivery to the palace, but it was his biggest. A caravan of trade goods from Kesh and the Vale of Dreams had arrived from the south, and attached to it had been goods marked for the palace, specifically for Knight-Marshal William. It was now a standing order that anything earmarked for Calis's special force was to be shipped to the Knight-Marshal. The palace brokers who controlled the flow of goods in and out of the harbor and the caravanserais outside the city were notified that all such cargo was to be shipped directly to the palace via wagons owned by Grindle and Avery.

A newly erected warehouse stood alongside the outer wall of the palace, cutting the marshalling yard in half for its entire length. Roo had puzzled over its construction the last few times he had visited the palace, but had said nothing. He pulled his team up before the entrance, where three figures waited.

Erik waved, as did Greylock, once Swordmaster to the Baron of Darkmoor. Next to them stood the Knight-Marshal himself, and behind him squatted his pet, the green-scaled flying lizard, as Roo thought of it.

"Gentlemen," said Roo as he dismounted the wagon, "where do you want this unloaded?"

Greylock said, "Our men will unload. It's going in here." He waved toward the newly finished warehouse.

Erik signaled and a full squad of soldiers in black tunics hurried and untied the lash-down covering the wagon. They lowered the tailgate and began to unload cargo.

Roo said, "Jadow said congratulations are in order."

Erik shrugged. "We've been promoted."

Greylock put his hand on Roo's shoulder. "They both need the rank. Our chain of command is beginning to emerge."

The Knight-Marshal's pet hissed, and Lord William said, "Hush, Fantus. Rupert has served with us before. Captain Greylock isn't spilling state secrets to the enemy."

As if he understood, the creature, a firedrake, Roo now recalled, settled down at the King-Marshal's boots. He stretched forth his neck and Lord William scratched him behind the eye ridges.

"Captain Greylock?" said Roo. "What is this?"

Greylock shrugged. "It makes things easier in dealing with the normal army command. Our unit is . . . unusual," he said, glancing at Lord William to see if he was overstepping his authority by talking to Roo. When the Knight-Marshal ignored him, Greylock continued. "I have a lot of things to do, and this way I never have to ask anyone's permission."

Lord William smiled and said, "Except mine, of course."

"And the Captain's," said Erik.

"Which Captain?" asked Roo.

Greylock smiled. "I'm 'a' captain, Roo. There is only one man who's 'the' Captain. Calis."

"Of course," said Roo as the second wagon was unloaded. He waved to the driver and shouted, "Take it back to the warehouse. I'll be along shortly."

The driver, one of the former soldiers of this very command, waved in reply and moved the mules ahead, turned them in a half circle, and headed back toward the gate.

"Where is *the* Captain?" asked Roo.

"In the palace, talking with the Prince," said Greylock. At that, Knight-Marshal William glanced at Greylock and gave a slight shake of his head.

Roo looked at Erik, who seemed to be intently watching the exchange. After a moment Roo audibly sighed. "Very well. I won't say anything. But when are you leaving?"

Knight-Marshal William took one step and put himself right before Roo. "What do you mean leaving?"

Roo smiled. "I may not be a student of the military, like my good friend Erik here, my lord, but I was a soldier." He glanced at the mounting pile of goods in the warehouse. "This isn't usual provisions for an extra garrison here in the palace. You're mounting an expedition. You're going down"—he glanced from face to face—"there again."

Knight-Marshal William said, "You'd be advised to keep your speculation to yourself, Rupert Avery. You're trusted, but only to a point."

Roo shrugged. "I'm saying nothing outside these walls, so don't worry." Then he considered something and added, "But I'm not the only one who can figure this out, just watching what comes in and what doesn't go out."

Knight-Marshal William looked irritated at that observation. Turning to Greylock and Erik, he said, "Take care of that. I think I need to speak with Duke James." He snapped his fingers and pointed skyward, and the firedrake sprang into the air, his wings beating down with furious power. William said to the startled Roo, "I told him to go hunt. He's old and claims he can't see as well as he used to, but the truth is he's lazy. If I let the kitchen staff feed him scraps, he'd be as big as one of your mules and unable to get off the ground."

The last was said with a rueful smile. The Knight-Marshal walked away, and Roo said, "He claims he can't see as well as he used to?"

Erik laughed. "Don't underestimate the Knight-Marshal. I've heard stories from the palace staff."

Greylock laughed as well. "They say he can speak to animals and they can speak to him."

Roo looked to see if he was being made fun of; Erik recognized his boyhood friend's expression and said, "No, he's serious. I've seen him do it, with the horses." Shaking his head emphatically, he said, "Truth of the gods!" Looking after the retreating back of the Knight-Marshal, he said, "Think of what a horse healer he would have been."

Greylock put his hand on Erik's shoulder. Erik's gifts in healing horses were what had brought him to Greylock's attention years before, and had caused them to become friends. "It takes more than knowing the animal's in pain, Erik. What's a horse going to tell you about a bruised bone beneath the hoof or an abscess? 'It hurts' is about as much as Lord William gets, from what I've heard. You still have to know what to do to find the problem and heal it."

"Maybe," said Erik. He turned to Roo. "Do you have any suggestions about ways to mask what we're doing here?"

"Off the top of my head, no. Maybe if you let me pick up a few other shipments—and if you route a few false ones with the notation about the Knight-Marshal on them." He pointed past his last wagon, toward the gate into the palace. "Route them through that gate, send them somewhere else in the palace, but let them see this." He pointed to the front of the warehouse.

"Let them see it?" said Greylock.

"Yes," said Roo. He smiled a smile familiar to Erik.

Erik's own smile broadened until the two old friends stood grinning at each other. "Let them see it." He turned to Greylock. "Captain, let them see it! Yes. We'll let them see what's here, but it will be what we want them to see."

Greylock rubbed his chin with one hand. "Perhaps. What would we have them see?"

Roo said, "Look, those lizard people know we're getting ready for them." He waved his hand around the façade of the building. "Make this look like a new barracks. A place to house a large army inside the palace won't get their attention much."

Greylock nodded. "That might work."

Erik shrugged. "We know they've got agents in the city. We've always assumed they have, anyway."

Just then a guard ran from the gate toward them. "My lord," he called.

Greylock smiled self-consciously. "I'll never get used to that."

"My lord?" echoed Roo.

Erik grinned. "We've all got some sort of court rank or another, to keep the minor officials out of our hair. Nobody is quite sure who is who, so we all tend to be addressed that way by those outside our command."

"What?" shouted Greylock.

"A man without the gate, my lord, demanding to see the master of this freight company."

Roo said, "Who is it?"

"He says he's your cousin. . . ." After a moment's hesitation, the soldier added, "sir."

Roo didn't wait and started running toward the gate. He passed his own wagons heading out and ran to the outer gate. Just outside he found Duncan sitting on his horse, looking fretful.

"What is it?" demanded Roo.

Duncan said, "It's Helmut. He's been injured."

Roo said, "Where?"

"He's back at the house. Karli sent me to fetch you."

Roo said, "Get down!"

Duncan complied and said, "I'll ride back with the wagons."

Roo nodded, set heels to the horse's flank, and was off at a gallop before the words were out of Duncan's mouth.

Roo nearly ran down a half-dozen people on his mad dash though the city to his partner's house. He found two of his workers outside the door and tossed the horse's reins to one of them, passing the other man as he made his way through the entrance.

Luis was waiting for him and told him, "He was ambushed."

"How is he?" asked Roo.

Luis shook his head. "Bad. Karli is upstairs with him."

Roo hurried up the stairs and realized he had never been up to the second floor of the house before. He glanced into one door and saw a small room furnished in a plain fashion, which he guessed was the maid's room. The next was decorated with silk draperies, colorful wall hangings, and warm woolen rugs; he guessed it was Karli's room.

He heard her voice as he reached the end of the hall. The door was open, and as he entered the room he saw his business partner lying on a bed, his daughter at his side. Karli was drawn and pale, but she wasn't crying. On the other side of the bed stood a priest of Kilian, Goddess of Farmers, Foresters, and Sailors. As a deity of nature, her priests were reputed to be healers, though often as not the patient died.

"How is he?" asked Roo.

Karli only shook her head, while the priest said, "He has lost a great deal of blood."

Roo went to the side of the bed and glanced down at the older man. He looked positively frail! Roo thought with alarm. Where before he had seemed only an older man, now he appeared ancient. His head was bandaged, as was his chest.

"What happened?" asked Roo.

"He was attacked last night, outside the city," said Karli, her voice sounding like a child's. "Some farmers found him in a ditch and brought him in after you had already left for the palace this morning. I sent for the priest and, when he got here, sent Duncan to find you."

Roo hesitated, then, remembering the lessons taught him by Nakor while they served together, made a couple of signs in the air and placed his hand upon Helmut's chest. Instantly he felt the connection as energy flowed from his hands.

The priest looked at him and his expression became one of suspicion. "What are you doing?" he asked.

"This is a healing I was taught," answered Roo.

"Who taught you?" asked the priest.

Rather than try to explain Nakor to anyone, Roo simply said, "A monk of Dala taught me this."

The priest nodded. "I thought I recognized the reiki." Shrugging it off, he said, "It can't harm him. It will either help his healing or aid him in leaving this life."

Turning to Karli, the priest directed, "If he regains consciousness, have him drink the herbs in a warm cup of water. As soon as he can, get him to eat something: a little broth and bread."

Karli's eyes were suddenly suffused with hope. "Will he live?"

The priest's manner bordered on the brusque, but he kept his voice low as he replied, "I said, 'If he regains consciousness.' It's the goddess's will."

Without another word, the priest departed, leaving Karli and Roo alone. Time passed. After nearly an hour of doing what he could for Helmut, Roo removed his hands, which still tingled from the energy he had given the stricken man.

Leaning over, he whispered in Karli's ear, "I'll be back. There are some things I need to see to."

She nodded as he left the room and went downstairs, to find

Duncan and Luis waiting. "How is he?" asked Duncan.

"Not good," Roo answered. He shook his head, indicating the old man might not regain consciousness.

"What now?" asked Luis.

Roo said, "Get back to the office and make sure everyone is doing what they're supposed to be." Luis nodded and departed. To Duncan, Roo said, "Head down to the inns near the gate. See if you can find anyone who knows anything about what happened. Especially see if you can find out who those farmers were that found Helmut. I want to talk to them."

Duncan said, "You don't think bandits . . . ?"

"This close to the city?" replied Roo. "No. I think . . . I don't want to think." He took his cousin by the arm and moved him toward the door. "I'm so tired I can't see, and this day is only half over." He sighed. "Find out what you can. I'll be here."

Duncan patted his cousin on the shoulder and departed. Roo found the maid standing near the kitchen, her distress clearly showing.

"Mary," said Roo, "bring Karli some tea." As the girl hesitated, Roo said, "Thank you." The girl nodded and returned to the kitchen.

Roo mounted the stairs and came to stand behind Karli. He hesitated, then put his hand on her shoulder. "I asked Mary to bring you some tea," he said.

"Thank you," she answered, but never took her eyes from her father.

The day passed slowly and as the afternoon shadows lengthened into night, Duncan returned. He had found nothing useful from any of those claiming to know something about the injured man fetched into the city that morning. Roo told him to return to the inns near the gate and start looking for someone spending money freely or boasting about sudden wealth. Roo had no idea what Helmut might have been carrying back from Darkmoor, but he knew exactly what the items he had taken were worth; whoever had robbed Roo's partner had pillaged Grindle and Avery of more than two thirds of their current net worth. More than a year's profits were gone.

Night came. Mary brought supper, but neither of them ate. They watched the still form of Helmut as he fought for life. His breathing seemed easier—at least, Roo thought so—but through the early hours of night the man barely moved.

Karli dozed, her head on the side of her father's bed, while Roo slept in a chair he had fetched in from the sitting room. He stirred as he heard his name.

Suddenly awake, he came to stand over Karli as Helmut's eyes flickered open. Then he realized it had been the old man speaking his name.

Karli said, "Father!" and leaned over him.

Roo said nothing as the girl embraced her father. The old man whispered and his daughter moved away, "He said your name."

Roo leaned over. "I'm here, Helmut."

The old man reached out and whispered, "Karli. Care for her."

Roo glanced back and saw the girl hadn't heard what her father had said. Roo whispered, "I will, Helmut. You have my word on it."

Then the old man whispered a word. Roo stood up and he knew his face had become a mask of outrage, for the girl looked at him and said, "What is it?"

Roo forced himself to calmness and replied, "I'll tell you later." Glancing down at the old man, whose eyes were fluttering, he said, "He needs you."

Karli moved to stand next to her father and took his hand. "I'm here, Father," she whispered, but the old man had lapsed back into unconsciousness.

Just before dawn, Helmut Grindle died.

The ceremony was simple, as Roo knew the old man would have wanted. Karli wore the black veil of mourning and watched in silence as the priest of Lims-Kragma, Goddess of Death, pronounced the benediction and then lit the funeral pyre. The inner courtyard of the temple was busy that morning, for a half-dozen funerals were under way. Each was contained in a marked-off area of the temple park, but above the shielding hedges the smoke rising from other flaming biers could be seen.

They waited in silence, Karli, Roo, Duncan, Luis, Mary, and two of the workmen who represented the employees of Grindle and Avery. Roo glanced around and thought to himself that this was a modest enough turnout for a man who had spent his life selling riches to the powerful and influential of the Kingdom. A few notes of condolence from other businessmen had arrived over the last two days, but not one of those nobles who had been among Helmut's best customers had deemed it appropriate to send even a single line of comfort to the merchant's daughter. Roo vowed that when he finally died, the Kingdom's rich and powerful would be in attendance.

When at last the corpse was consumed by flame, Karli turned and said, "Let's go."

Roo gave her his arm and escorted the girl to a rented carriage. Once she and Mary were inside, he said, "Tradition says I have to stand the employees to a farewell drink. We're doing it at the warehouse. Will you be all right?"

"I'm fine," Karli said. Despite her pale appearance, her voice was calm and her eyes free of tears. She had finished crying the day before and showed a strength that Roo found surprising.

"I'll be along later," he said. Then he added, "If you don't mind, that is."

"I'd like that," she said with a smile.

Roo closed the carriage door and said, "Driver, take her home."

Duncan, Luis, and the workmen accompanied Roo in silence as they walked from Krondor's temple square. When they were free of the center part of the city and halfway back to the warehouse, Luis said, "Gods, I hate funerals."

Duncan said, "I doubt even the priests of the Death Goddess are overly fond of them."

Roo said, "I'll stink of woodsmoke for a week."

One of the workers said, "And death."

Roo threw the man a glance, but nodded. One of the features of the temple of the Death Goddess was the ever-present woodsmoke that hung around the place. Herbs and other scented woods were placed in the fire, but there was always a hint of something else in the fumes, something that Roo would rather not think of. He had smelled enough of it during the sack of Maharta to recognize the stench of burning flesh.

Reaching the warehouse, they entered and found the drivers and other workers standing around. Several bottles of strong ale were arrayed upon a bench and were quickly opened and passed around. When each man held one, Roo said, "Helmut Grindle. Hard but fair, a good partner, a loving father, and deserving of kindness."

"May Lims-Kragma be merciful," said Luis.

They drank to Helmut's memory and talked of him. No one had worked for the man longer than Roo. As successful as Helmut had been, until he had joined forces with Roo he had always operated alone. In less than a year, Roo had more than tripled Grindle's income, and now seven men besides Duncan and Luis worked full time for Grindle and Avery.

Given there was not much history among the men who now worked for Roo, the discussion quickly turned to wondering how the old man had died. Roo listened awhile, then sent the workers home early.

When the workers had gone, Roo held a quick conference with Luis and Duncan, sharing with them what Helmut had said. They discussed what they needed to do, and when at last plans had been made, Roo departed.

He was so filled with anger and dark purpose that he nearly walked past Karli's house. He knocked upon the door, and when Mary opened the door, she instantly stepped aside so that Roo might enter.

Karli had changed from the traditional black clothes of mourning to something that bordered on the festive, a bright blue gown with lace trim. Roo was amazed to find a full dinner waiting and suddenly discovered he was famished.

They ate in near silence. Finally Karli said, "You seem so distant."

Roo blushed and said, "I'm so caught up in my own anger about your father I haven't given any thought to what you must be going through." He reached across the corner of the table that separated them and took her hand. He gave it a gentle squeeze and said, "I am sorry."

She returned the squeeze. "No need. I understand."

They finished eating and Mary cleared the table, while they moved to the sitting room. Roo said nothing as she fetched him a brandy, far finer than anything her father had ever served. In a moment of surprisingly strong feeling, Roo said, "Helmut," held up the goblet a moment in salute, then drank the brandy quickly.

Karli sat and said, "I'm still unable to think that he will not walk through that door in a moment."

Roo glanced toward the door and nodded. "I understand." He felt the same way.

Suddenly Karli said, "What am I going to do?"

"What do you mean?" asked Roo.

"With Father gone . . ." Suddenly she was in tears again, and Roo found himself with his arms around her shoulders while she sobbed against his chest.

After a moment he said, "I promised your father I would take care of you."

Karli said, "I know you meant well, but you don't need to say something you'll be sorry for later."

Roo said, "I don't understand."

Karli forced her voice to calmness. "I know Father intended us to marry, Rupert. You're the first of those who came to see him that he took a liking to. But I also know that he was getting on in years and worried about just this circumstance. He never talked to me, but it was clear that after a while he expected we would simply . . . decide to wed.

"But the business is now yours. You needn't feel any obligation."

Roo felt as if the room were turning on its side. He didn't know how much of that was the brandy, the long hours, the anger he felt, or his dealing with this strange, often unreadable girl.

"Karli," he said slowly, "I know your father had plans for us." He lowered his eyes, "And truth to tell, when I first came here I was ready to court you to win his approval, without thought for you or your feelings."

He fell silent a moment, then said, "I don't know if this is something I can explain, but I have come to . . . value you. I find I . . . enjoy the time we spend together. I do feel some obligation to your father, but my feelings toward you are more than that."

She regarded him a moment, then said, "Do not lie to me, Rupert."

He kept his arms around her waist. "I would not do that. I do care, Karli. Let me prove it to you."

She was silent, studying his face. As seconds passed, she looked deep into his eyes, then at last took his hand in hers and said, "Come with me."

She led him up the stairs to her room and inside. Then she closed the door behind her. She put her hand upon his chest and pushed him to the foot of her bed, until he sat down upon it. Quickly she undid the fastenings of her gown and let it fall to the floor. Then she undid the shoulder ties of her short chemise and, with a single shake, caused it to fall atop the dress. Nude, she stood before him in the light of the single candle on the nightstand.

Karli's breasts were young and firm, but her waist was thick, as were her hips and thighs. Her face still lacked any quality that any man would call pretty, save her eyes, which were shining in the light.

"This is what I am," she said, her voice full of emotion. "I'm plain. And fat. And I don't have a rich father anymore. Can you love this?"

Roo found his own eyes filling as he rose and took her into his arms. Swallowing hard, he willed his voice to calmness as he said, "No one has accused me of being any lady's fancy." A single tear fell down his cheek as he said, "I used to be called 'rat face' and worse. Looks aren't everything."

She put her head on his chest and said, "Stay."

Later, Roo lay staring upward in the dark while Karli slept in his arms. They had made love, awkwardly and with a frantic edge that was more a demand for acceptance than anything freely given. Karli had shown no skills, and Roo had forced himself to be more attentive than he had wished.

At some point he had promised to marry her, and he was vaguely aware that he was now engaged to be married after the mourning period was over. But in the darkness his mind turned once more to his anger and the plans he, Duncan, and Luis had made. For the one thing he had not told Karli was what her father had whispered to him before he died.

It had been a name. "Jacoby."

Ten

Plans

ROO HELD UP HIS HAND.

"There are three things I need to discuss with you," he said.

Karli had given him permission to use her dining room to hold a meeting with Luis and Duncan. She even managed not to look disappointed when he asked her to leave them alone.

Luis glanced at Duncan, who shrugged, indicating he had no idea what was coming.

"We're here instead of at the warehouse because I wanted to be certain there was no chance of anyone overhearing us."

"You suspect one of our workmen of something?" asked Luis.

Roo shook his head. "No, but the fewer of us who know what we plan, the less risk we have of our enemies finding out."

"Enemies?" said Duncan. "Who are we at war with now?"

Roo lowered his voice to just more than a whisper. "There's a piece of walking scum named Tim Jacoby who had Helmut killed."

Luis said, "Jacoby?"

Duncan nodded. "Son of a trader named Frederick Jacoby. Jacoby and Sons."

Luis shook his head. "I've not heard of them."

Roo said, "Spend a few more months working in Krondor in the freight-hauling trade and you will. They are not our biggest rivals, but they are important." Roo leaned back and obvious frustration showed on his face. "Helmut told me it was the Jacobys who robbed his wagon."

"Can we go to the City Watch?" said Luis.

"With what?" said Duncan. "We have no proof."

"We have a dying man's declaration," said Luis.

Duncan shook his head. "That might do if Roo here was a noble or some such, but without someone important having heard it, a priest or city watchman at the least, it's Roo's word against this Jacoby."

"And his father is very well connected," said Roo. "They're working with some of the bigger trading concerns in the Western Realm, and if I said anything to anyone they'd claim it false and say I was just trying to hurt their business."

Luis shrugged. "It is always this way with the powerful; they can do what the rest of us cannot."

Roo said, "I've half a mind to go pay Tim Jacoby a visit this night."

Luis shrugged. "You can always do that, young Roo." He leaned forward, his deformed hand lying on the table before him, as he pointed with his left forefinger at Roo. "But ask yourself: what good would it do save to get you back to the gallows?"

"I've got to do something."

Luis nodded. "Time will bring an opportunity for revenge." He considered. "You said Jacoby and Sons, Duncan. Is there a brother?"

Duncan said, "Yes. Tim's the elder. Randolph, the other, is a decent enough man, from what people say, but he's fiercely loyal to his family."

Luis said, "In Rodez, when a man wrongs another man, we fight a duel. But when a family wrongs another family, we wage war. It may be a quiet war, one that lasts for generations, but ultimately one family is destroyed."

Roo said, "I'm going to have to struggle to keep this business alive, Luis. Waging war is costly."

Luis shrugged. "The war has begun. It may not be stopped until you either win or are defeated, but no one says the next battle must be tonight. Bide your time. Build your strength. Reduce your enemy's position. When you finally have the opportunity, then seize the moment." He made a crushing gesture with his good hand. "Often you'll hear it said that revenge is a dish best served cold. This is a mistake; you must never lose the heat of rage that drives you to revenge." He studied Roo's face. "Forgiveness is a virtue in some temples. But if you are not virtuous, then study your enemy." He tapped his head. "Think.

Think about what drives him and what his strengths and weaknesses are. Keep the fires within banked, and plot coolly, but when everything is in place, unleash the fire and enjoy the hot flush of revenge."

Roo blew air out of his mouth slowly, as if letting his anger escape. "Very well. We wait. But make it known to our men that any rumors concerning Jacoby and Sons should be shared with us."

"What's the next thing?" asked Duncan. "I've got a lady to visit. . . ." He grinned.

Roo smiled. "Helmut kept our books and records. I have some sense of it, but I'm no expert. Can either of you keep books?"

Luis shook his head and Duncan laughed. "I've never been one for sums. You know that."

"Then we need to hire someone."

"Who?" asked Duncan.

Roo said, "I don't know. Maybe Jason, over at Barret's. He was good with figures when we worked together; McKeller had him doing inventories more often than anyone else. He could remember things . . . costs and numbers of sacks of coffee and details that I had no clear picture of. I'll ask him. He's ambitious. Maybe he'll work for us."

"Can we pay him?" Duncan asked with a laugh.

Roo said, "We have the contract with the palace. I'll ask de Loungville to make sure we get paid on time, and we'll get by."

"What's the third thing?" asked Luis.

Roo's face underwent a change of expression, from anger and worry to self-consciousness. "I'm getting married."

Luis said, "Congratulations." He held out his hand and Roo gripped it.

Duncan said, "Karli?"

"Who else?" said Roo.

Duncan shrugged. "When?"

"Next Sixthday. Can you join us?"

"Certainly," said Duncan, standing up. "If we're done?"

"You can leave," said Roo, feeling disappointed at his cousin's lack of enthusiasm.

After Duncan left, Luis said, "This is a difficult responsibility to assume, Roo."

"What do you mean?"

Luis said, "It is not my business. I'm sorry I spoke."

Roo asked, "What's on your mind?"

Luis said nothing for a moment, then said, "You seem to like the girl. But . . . are you marrying her because you feel someone must take care of her and you're the only one?"

Roo started to deny it, then found he couldn't. "I don't know. I like her, and a wife . . . well, a wife is a wife, right? I need a wife, and some children."

"Why?"

Roo looked completely confused. "I . . . well, I just do. I mean, I plan on being a man of some importance in the city, and I need a wife and children."

Luis studied the young man awhile. "As you say. I will return to the office and mention to the men there will be a wedding on Sixth-day."

Roo said, "I'll tell Erik and Jadow tomorrow. Maybe the Captain will come if he's still in the city."

Luis nodded. As he passed behind Roo's chair, he stopped and put his hand on the younger man's shoulder. "I wish you happiness, my friend. I really do."

"Thank you," said Roo as Luis left.

A moment later, Karli entered the room. "I heard them leave."

Roo nodded. "I told them we were getting married on Sixthday."

Karli sat down in the chair Duncan had occupied. "Are you certain?"

Roo forced a smile. "Of course I am," he said, patting her hand, but inside he felt like nothing more than leaving this house and running for all he was worth. "Of course I am," he repeated.

He glanced out a curtained window as if he could see through the fabric, and in his mind's eye he saw the pale face of Helmut as he lay on his deathbed. His skin was bone-white, the same color as the large bolt of silk Roo had stolen, and in his heart Roo knew that there was a thread leading from that bolt to Helmut and that Karli's father's death lay at his feet. Patting the girl's hand, Roo knew that even if he hated the girl, he would marry her to make up for the wrong he had caused.

Calis pushed himself back from the table, stood up, and moved to a window. Staring out at the marshalling yard below, he said, "I've got a bad feeling about all of this."

Prince Nicholas sat back in his chair, glanced at his nephew, then to Knight-Marshal William, who nodded agreement. "It's a desperate gamble," said William.

Patrick, who sat at the head of the council table, said, "Uncle, you've seen this personally. You've traveled to that distant land more than once." He glanced around the room. "I'm prepared to admit that some of my reluctance comes from not having . . . first-hand experience, I should say, with these Pantathians."

Nicholas said, "I've seen what they can do, Patrick, and I scarcely believe what we're told." He waved at a pile of papers on the table before them. Dispatches had arrived by fast courier, as a relay of ships wended their way between Krondor, the Far Coast, the Sunset Islands, and the distant continent of Novindus. The reports that had arrived the morning before had been sent from Novindus less than a month after Greylock and Luis had departed. And the news was not good.

Duke James, who sat beside Knight-Marshal William, said, "We know that our guesses were overly optimistic. Destroying the shipyards at Maharta and the City of the Serpent River didn't buy us as many years as we thought."

"Ten years," said Calis. "I remember thinking it would take them ten years to rebuild and refit and launch a fleet big enough to carry that host across the ocean."

Patrick said, "What do you judge now, Captain?"

Calis sighed, the first outward display of emotion any in the room had seen from him since his return from Stardock. "Four more, maybe five."

Nicholas said, "We didn't count on an enemy who was willing to turn every resource at hand to rebuilding those yards and starting that fleet."

"We didn't count on an enemy who doesn't care if her population dies to the last man," said William. He pushed himself away from the table and stood, as if he, too, could no longer sit still. "We're preparing to defend, and we're making it obvious enough the Pantathians may think we're done taking the fight across the ocean to them."

He came to stand next to Calis. "But we have one advantage they are unaware of; they don't know we know where their home is."

Calis smiled a half-smile, lacking any humor. "I don't think they care." He moved past William and stood opposite Nicholas, but addressed his remarks to Prince Patrick. "Highness, I am not certain this mission will win us anything."

Patrick asked, "You think this wins us nothing?"

William said, "Our presumption is they will not expect this, slipping in behind them and destroying their nest."

Calis held up a finger, like a schoolmaster, "That's the word: *presumption*." He turned to look at William. "Everything we have ever seen from these creatures tells us they think like no others. They die as willingly as they kill. If we slaughter them to the last child when they're seizing the Lifestone, they will not care. They believe they will return as demigods in the service of their 'Lady,' and death holds no fear for them."

Turning back toward Patrick, he said, "I will go, Patrick. I will go and kill for you and, if I must, die. But even if I get in and get back out, those left alive will come after us. I think we will never understand these creatures."

"Do you have a better idea?" asked Nicholas.

William put his hand on Calis's shoulder. "Old friend, our only other choice is to wait. If they come anyway, what have we lost by undertaking this raid?"

Calis's voice was neutral. "Just the lives of more good men."

William said, "It's what soldiers do, Captain."

"It doesn't mean I have to like it," he answered.

Despite the differences in rank, the two men were old friends and William showed no irritation at his friend's tone or lack of deference. In this private council rank was put aside, and everyone had proven his worth to the Crown and his reliability many times before. Despite his youth, barely twenty-five years of age, Patrick had served three years on the northern border, fighting goblins and dark elves. Calis was roughly the same age as William, though William looked to be in his late fifties while Calis looked barely older than Prince Patrick.

"What if it doesn't work?" asked Calis.

It was James who answered. "Then it doesn't work."

Calis studied the old man and laughed ruefully. Glancing at his old friend, he said, "I remember when you used to ask questions like that, Nicky."

Nicholas said, "None of us is as young as he once was, Calis."

Patrick said, "When will you go?"

Calis said, "We're still months away from being ready. I've got only four men I can count on besides those of us here in this room: De Loungville, Greylock, Erik, and Jadow. All have seen what's down there and know the risks. There are a couple of other veterans from the last two campaigns, but those four are leaders, though Erik and Jadow don't know it yet. But the rest are men who just follow orders. Fine for soldiers, not enough for leaders."

Patrick said, "How are you going to proceed?"

Calis smiled. "Come at them from behind." He crossed to a large map on the wall, one redrawn many times over the last twenty years as new information came from the continent on the other side of the world. "We'll sail from the Sunset Islands, as usual, but here"—he pointed to a seemingly empty place on the map four hundred miles south of the long island chain—"is an uncharted bit of land with a lovely harbor. We'll meet there and transfer to another ship."

"Another ship?" asked Patrick.

Nicholas answered. "By now our enemy has an inventory of every ship in the Western Navy. They can probably identify the outline on the horizon of each one from their rigging. And I have no doubt they know which of our 'trading ships' are really royal warships in disguise."

"What have you got down there?" asked Patrick. "A new ship?"

"No, a very old one," said Calis. "We're going to go as Brijaners."

"Brijaners? Keshian raiders?" said William with a half-smile.

Nicholas said, "We have one of their dragon ships. The navy of Roldem captured one during a raid two years ago." Roldem was a small island kingdom to the east of the Kingdom of the Isles that was a longtime ally. "The King of Roldem has agreed to 'lend' it to us. It was quietly sailed around lower Kesh." Nicholas smiled. "A couple of times, according to reports, other Brijaner dragon boats sailed within hailing distance. The Roldem captain waved and smiled and kept right on going, no questions asked or answered."

William laughed. "The arrogant swine couldn't imagine someone sailing in their waters who wasn't one of them."

Calis said, "I'm hoping we get the same reaction."

"What?" asked Patrick.

"I'm not sailing west to get to Novindus. I'm sailing east, under the Horn of Kesh, then across what is now known as the Green Sea, to a small village near the city of Ispar." He pointed at the map as he spoke. "We'll be sailing in from their west. I hope if they're looking for our ships, they're looking in the other direction. We have always sailed out of the City of the Serpent River. If we're intercepted, we're Brijaner traders who were blown off course and are working our way around their landmass."

Patrick said, "Do you think they will accept that?" Calis shrugged. "It's happened before, I've been told. There's a fast-running current that moves eastward down near the ice floes, and if you catch it south of Kesh you can ride it across the Green Sea to a great mass of ice that points like a finger right at Port Grief. We won't be the first party of Keshian sea raiders to show up there, but they won't have been so common that locals will notice any differences."

Patrick said, "Then what?"

Calis said, "We buy some horses, change clothing, and sneak out of the city one night, and head north." He pointed to the south end of the mountain range that ran down to the sea west of Ispar. "I can find the entrance we used to get out of those caverns on our last journey, without too much trouble."

No one doubted him. His tracking skills were considered legendary. Calis's heritage was unique and in no small measure supernatural.

Patrick said, "Very well. What then?"

Calis shrugged. "The destruction of the Pantathians."

Patrick's eyes widened. "How many men were you planning on taking?"

"Ten squads. Sixty men."

"You plan on destroying a nation of these creatures, magic users from every report I've studied, with sixty men?"

Calis said, "I never said it would be easy."

Patrick looked at Nicholas. "Uncle?"

Nicholas said, "I learned twenty years ago that if Calis says a thing can be done, it can be done." Looking at Calis, he asked, "What is your thinking?"

"My thinking," said Calis, "is that the bulk of their forces will be with the armies of the Emerald Queen." He made a sweeping motion with his hand on the map between the city of Maharta and the

City of the Serpent River. "We've never seen them in numbers. The squad I saw in the caverns was no more than twenty in one place, and that was the single largest concentration we've encountered. We've judged them by their ability to visit evil on us, but never have we questioned their strength of numbers." He let a distasteful expression cross his face. "When I caught sight of one of their crèches it was poorly guarded. A half-dozen adults, a dozen or more infants, and a score of eggs. I saw nothing of their females."

Patrick said, "What does all this mean?"

Calis said, "Pug and Nakor both hold that these creatures aren't natural." He returned to the table and sat. "They claim that these were created by an ancient Dragon Lord, Alma-Lodaka." Calis let his eyes drop a moment, and William and Nicholas both understood that this strange man, half-elf by birth, was revealing lore to non-elves that no full elf would volunteer. His half-human nature felt no such prohibition, and he knew that he served a greater good by being frank in all matters concerning the Serpent Men, but that still didn't make it any easier for his elven half to accept. Those things were not taught; they were inbred. "If this is so, that may explain a low birth rate. Or perhaps they have never had a large population. They may even have some queens, as insects do, or there may be a special holding area for females. We don't know. But if there is a crèche, the females can't be far away."

Patrick said, "I'm still unclear on one thing. If the majority of fighting men and magicians are with the army of the Emerald Queen, what do we gain by raiding those birthing caverns . . . ?" His words trailed off as his eyes widened. "You're going to slaughter the young?" he asked, almost gasping in shock.

Calis's expression remained calm. "Yes."

"You're talking about waging war against innocents!" said Patrick, his voice taking on an angry tone. "Keshian Dog Soldiers may slaughter women and children in their rampages, but the last man caught at that during a Kingdom war was hanged before the assembled rank and file of the army."

Nicholas glanced at Calis, who returned the look, then nodded.

Duke James said, "Patrick, you're new here, and you don't have all the information—"

"My lord," interrupted the Prince, "I realize you've held high office since Grandfather's youth and were my father's chief adviser in

Rillanon, but *I* am now the ruler of the Western Realm. If there is something you think I should know, why have I not been informed?"

Duke James looked at Prince Nicholas.

Nicholas sat back, recognizing his nephew's mood. The new Prince of Krondor was revealing himself to be a young man of some temper, touchy disposition, moods, and not terribly secure in his position, so he tended to magnify every slight, real or imagined.

Knight-Marshal William took charge. "Your Highness," he began, formally emphasizing the young man's title, "what I think Calis means is that we were all here during these events, which are only dry reports on paper before you." He paused, then went on, "We've seen the damage these creatures can do firsthand."

It was Calis who said, "Would you not kill a poisonous snake because it was its nature to be a viper?"

Patrick looked at Calis. "Say on."

Calis said, "You've cities within your borders that were once Keshian. But those who live there are Kingdom by birth, though their ancestors were loyal to the Emperor of Great Kesh. To them it makes no difference. They were raised within the Kingdom, they speak the King's Tongue, and they think, as we all do, that this is their homeland."

"What has this to do with the matter under discussion?" asked Prince Patrick.

"It has everything to do with it," said Calis. He leaned forward, elbows on the table. "You may somehow think that these creatures are born innocent. That is not the case. Everything we know about them says they are born hating from the moment they hatch from their eggs. They are created to be the way they are. If we killed every adult and child, and took the eggs, and hatched them in this palace, raising those who were born here, they would come to consciousness hating us and seeking to reclaim this 'lost goddess' they so mistakenly believe in. It is their nature to be this way, as it is the nature of a viper to bite and poison. They cannot help it any more than can the viper."

Seeing that the Prince's objections were wavering, Calis pressed on. "You may someday forge a treaty with the Brotherhood of the Dark Path, as you call the moredhel. You may see goblins obeying Kingdom law and visiting our town markets in some dimly imagined future. You may see open borders with Great Kesh and free travel between the two nations. But you will never know a moment's peace in this world so long as a Pantathian draws breath. Because it is in his nature to scheme, kill, and do whatever needs to be done to seize the Lifestone in Sethanon and reclaim the 'lost goddess' Alma-Lodaka, the Dragon Lord who created him."

Patrick was silent a long moment, then said, "But you're talking of genocide."

Calis said, "I'm not leaving for at least six months, Highness. If you conceive of a better plan, I will be here to listen." He let his voice fall, the low tone making his next sentence that much more urgent. "But forbid me this, and I will go anyway. If not in a Kingdom ship, then in one from Queg or Kesh. If not this year, then the next, or the one after. Because if I do not, then sooner or later the serpent priests will gain the Lifestone, and then we shall all perish."

Patrick sat motionless for a very long time. At last he said, "Very well. There seems no other course. But if any one of you learns anything that changes this matter, I wish to know of it at once." He stood up and said to William, "See that things stay calm, but begin preparations."

The Prince departed. James turned to William. "There's something else going on we need to discuss."

William smiled and looked up at the slightly taller Duke. "What's going on, Jimmy?"

James looked at Calis and Nicholas, then at William. "Helmut Grindle was killed last night outside the city gates."

William said, "Grindle? He's Roo Avery's partner."

Nicholas said, "Exactly, and a potential ally. We are going to need the support of merchants like him."

William looked at James. "Any suspects?"

"Our agents are almost certain Frederick Jacoby or one of his sons is behind the death of Grindle, and the Jacobys are presently allied with Jacob Esterbrook. Esterbrook is a very influential man, both here and down in Kesh." James was silent for a second, then said, "For the time being, let's hope Mr. Avery doesn't discover too much about who killed his partner."

"What if he already knows or has suspicions?" asked Calis. "I know Roo Avery. He's clever, and Grindle may have regained consciousness long enough to identify his killer."

"Perhaps, but as long as Mr. Avery doesn't cause any problems with Jacob Esterbook and his friends, it won't matter." He smiled. "We need merchants hard at work making profits for us to tax, not killing one another."

William said, "With that in mind, will they cooperate when it comes time to put that wealth at risk for our benefit?"

James looked at his old friend. "You take care of the war, Willy, and I'll see it's paid for. The merchants of the Kingdom will come to heel once we make it clear they're going to lose everything if they don't help us." He glanced around the room. "I now have the Mockers where I want them; I have the throne where I want it; and soon I'll have the wealth of the Kingdom to use as I need. And if I must bleed our people white to finance this war, I will. Remember, I am the only one in this room who was at Sethanon."

No one else needed to hear any further explanation. Nicholas's, William's, and Calis's fathers had been at Sethanon, and they had heard in detail over the years what had happened when the Pantathians had tried to seize the Lifestone for the first time, but James had been there.

William said, "I'm due in court soon, too. If you'll excuse me, I'd like to see to some other matters before that. James?"

The Duke nodded. After William had left, James said to Calis, "Who are you taking with you on this suicide mission?"

Calis knew whom he spoke of. "Bobby, Greylock, and Erik. Of the two junior sergeants, he's the smarter one."

"Then leave him here," said James. "If you're going to kill off one of them, leave the smarter one alive to serve me here if you fail. Take Jadow with you instead."

Calis nodded. "Done."

"And leave Bobby here."

Calis said, "He'll never stand for it."

"Order him."

"He'll disobey."

James said, "You serve a unique function here, my friend, but as much as I need the Eagle to return unharmed, I need your vicious Dog of Krondor." He glanced out the window. "I need a sergeant now more than I need a General"—he glanced at Calis—"or a Captain."

Calis smiled slightly. "He's going to make your life living hell."

James returned the smile. "What else is new? It's not as if I have any choice."

"Very well," said Calis. "I'll leave Bobby and Erik here and take Jadow and Greylock."

The three were starting toward the door when James said, "What about Nakor?"

Calis said, "He'd go back if I asked, I'm almost certain, but I think he'll serve us better down in Stardock. Those magicians are far too full of themselves, and he's just the man to sort them out and remind them they're living on a Kingdom island in the middle of that lake of theirs."

"Very well, but you're going to face some powerful magic, by everything you've said. What do you plan?"

Calis seemed almost embarrassed when he answered, "Miranda has agreed to come along."

James studied Calis, then laughed. "For all your years, you do at times remind me of my son."

Calis had the good grace to smile. "Speaking of whom, when is Arutha due?"

"Any time now," answered James. "I think I may send him down to Stardock to run things a while." His smile turned rueful. "And my grandsons are coming with him."

Calis nodded. "Jimmy and Dash must be men now."

"So they think," said James. Turning to Nicholas, he said, "You have no idea what you've missed by never getting married."

Nicholas said, "I'm not too old now. Amos married my grandmother when he was nearly seventy."

"Well, you'll miss the joy of children if you wait that long," answered James as he moved toward the door. Then he made a sour face. "As I think of Jimmy and Dash, you might not."

As they left the conference hall, James turned to Calis and said, "Like others before me, I'm not all that pleased that this magical lady friend of yours has so many secrets, but as she's proven a worthy ally over the years, I'll say nothing more than 'Be careful.'"

Calis nodded, lost in his own thoughts as James and Nicholas returned to speaking of families and children.

Roo looked around and Erik laughed. "You look as if you're ready to run."

In low tones, Roo said, "Truth to tell, I've felt that way since the minute I proposed."

Erik tried to look understanding, but he couldn't hide his amusement. Roo said, "You wait. One of these days you'll propose to that whore—"

"Wait a minute," began Erik, his good humor vanishing.

"Wait, wait," said Roo. "I'm sorry. I'm just not sure this is such a good idea."

Looking around the temple, where Karli and Roo were about to be married, Erik whispered, "It's a little late for that."

Karli was entering the temple from a side door, as brides were required to do by the followers of Sung the White. At her side was Katherine, the girl de Loungville had captured and turned to the Prince's service. Karli had no friends to speak of, and it wouldn't have been proper for Mary, the maid, to serve as her companion. So Erik, as Roo's companion, had asked the serving girl to substitute. To his surprise, the girl had said she would.

"Well, here we go," said Roo, and he turned to march down the center aisle, Erik at his side.

The only witnesses were Luis and some of the other workers from the office, and Jadow and those soldiers who had served with Roo in Calis's company. They watched as the priest, obviously bored by the fifth or sixth such ceremony of the day, hurried through the rites.

Roo vowed to care for Karli and be true to her, and she the same, and suddenly the priest was saying that the White Goddess was pleased and they could now leave. Erik gave the priest the votive offering required for such a ceremony, and the wedding party was ushered outside by harried-looking acolytes.

Roo and Karli were escorted to a carriage hired for the occasion, while the others made their way on foot or horseback to the Grindle house. As the carriage made its way through the streets, Roo turned to see Karli with eyes downcast, staring at her hands.

"What's wrong?" asked Roo. "Aren't you happy?"

Karli looked at him and her gaze struck him like a blow. Suddenly he knew there was anger and resentment behind the girl's bland façade. But her voice was calm and her tone almost apologetic as she asked, "Are you?"

Roo forced a smile. "Of course, my love. Why wouldn't I be?"

Karli looked out the window. "You looked positively terrified walking down the aisle."

Roo tried to make light of it. "It's the normal reaction." When she turned to look at him, he quickly added, "So I've been told. It's the ceremony and the . . . rest."

They traveled in silence as they made their way slowly through the city. Roo studied the passing cityscape, watching the changing buildings, the throng of citizens, traders, and travelers, as they moved through Krondor at a stately pace until they reached the Grindle house. Erik and the others were waiting as the carriage pulled up.

As Roo's companion, Erik opened the door, and Katherine moved to help Karli from the carriage. The girl might be a stranger, but she took her part of bride's companion seriously.

Inside, the cook had prepared a tremendous repast, and the best wine from the cellar had been uncorked. Roo awkwardly let Karli move through the entrance before him, despite the tradition that said a husband should lead his wife through the door. It was, after all, her home. When she was inside, she said, "I'll see to the kitchen."

Roo put a restraining hand upon her. "Let Mary. You will never serve again in this house."

Karli studied his face a moment, then a faint smile appeared on her lips. Roo turned and said, "Mary!"

The maid appeared and Roo said, "You may begin serving."

The guests fell to, and the food was both delicious and bountiful. After a more than satisfying meal, Erik stood. He looked around the room and saw Katherine smiling at his awkward stance. He loudly cleared his throat, and when conversation didn't diminish, he said, "Listen!"

He had raised his voice louder than he had wished and the room fell silent, then erupted in laughter. Blushing furiously, Erik held up his hand. "I'm sorry," he said, grinning at his own embarrassment. "It's my duty as the groom's companion to offer a toast to the newlywed couple." He glanced at Luis. "Or so I have been informed."

Luis nodded with a courtly smile and a wave of his hand.

Erik said, "I'm not one for words, but I do know this: Roo is my friend, more like a brother to me than any man living, and I only wish his happiness." Then he looked at Karli and said, "I hope that you love him as I do and that he loves you as you deserve." He raised his goblet of wine and said, "To the newlywed couple. May they live to an old age and never regret a moment of their lives together. May they know happiness every day of their lives."

The company drank the toast and cheered, then Roo stood and said, "Thank you." He turned to Karli. "I know this has been a difficult time," he said, referring to her father's murder, "but my earnest desire is to make the bad times fade into memory and to fill your days with happiness."

Karli smiled and blushed and Roo held her hand awkwardly.

The dinner progressed and Roo was filled with good cheer and too much wine. He noticed that Erik spent a great deal of time talking to the girl Katherine, and that Karli kept her own counsel most of the day.

Soon the guests began to excuse themselves, and after night fell, Roo and Karli were bidding good evening to Erik, who was the last to leave. When the door closed, Roo turned to his wife and found her staring at him, an expression impossible to read on her face.

"What is it?" he asked, suddenly sobering with a stab of fear. Something about her manner caused him to feel the need to draw a weapon.

She came into his arms and put her head on his shoulder. "I'm sorry."

Roo's head swam and he felt his knees wobble, but he forced himself to be alert enough to ask, "What are you talking about?"

Over the sound of sobbing, he heard Karli say, "I wanted this to be a happy day."

Roo said, "And it isn't?"

Karli didn't speak. Tears were her only answer.

Eleven

Travel

JASON POINTED.

The pile of ledgers and journals before the former waiter from Barret's was daunting. "Well, I've been through them all," he said as he pushed his chair back from the writing desk now established in the corner of the workshop.

Carpenters had built a set of shelves for Jason, as well as a low railing around his work area, so he could see anyone coming into the warehouse, despite some privacy. Roo had informed the youth that he would be responsible for the smooth operation of the freight business if he, Duncan, and Luis were all absent from the premises at the same time.

Duncan looked bored, as he usually did when it came to matters of business, unless it was getting paid, and Luis was his usual taciturn self. Roo said, "And?"

Jason said, "Well, you're in better shape than you thought, if you can get some of those who owed Helmut money to pay up." He held out a parchment upon which he had been working for days and said, "I've compiled a list and the amounts owed."

Roo glanced at it. "There are a couple of noblemen here!"

Jason smiled. "Experience at Barret's tells me they may be very slow in paying accounts." He paused a moment, then added, "If you don't mind my saying, you might just wish to let some of those debts ride until you need a favor from someone highly placed in court or with influence with another noble; that sort of thing."

Roo shook his head. "I don't mind your saying."

Holding out another list, Jason said, "I had more trouble with this."

Roo looked at the second list. "What's this?"

"People Mr. Grindle did business with in distant cities, but whose identity is unclear."

Roo's confusion was evident. "Their identity is unclear?"

Jason said, "This is not uncommon. Often those who trade in valuable goods don't wish it widely known they have rare items in their possession, or that they need to sell such. Hence the notations. It's a code, and only Mr. Grindle knew the identities of these people."

Roo puzzled over the list. "Maybe Karli knows who some of these people are. She knows a great deal more about her father's trade than I think even he was aware of."

Duncan said, "What are we doing now?"

Roo found his cousin's attitude irritating lately, as he often complained about not having as much authority as Luis. Roo wanted to give Duncan more authority, but had discovered he lacked Luis's willingness to work hard. Luis, on the other hand, rarely complained and was always meticulous in whatever task lay before him, while Duncan often was sloppy and left things undone.

Biting back a nasty reply, Roo said, "We're leaving for Salador in the morning. We have a special cargo to deliver."

"Salador?" said Duncan. "I know a barmaid there."

Roo said, "You know a barmaid everywhere, Duncan."

"True," said the former mercenary. His mood seemed to brighten visibly with the prospect of a change of scenery.

It was Luis who said, "What cargo for Salador?"

Roo handed over a rolled-up parchment. Luis snapped it open and held it up before him, and his eyes widened. "This is incredible."

The remark caught Duncan's interest at last. "What is it?" he asked.

"We're taking a load of goods from the palace to the estates of the Duke of Salador," answered Roo.

"The King's cousin?" asked Jason.

"The very same. I have no idea what it is we are carrying, but the Prince of Krondor is sending it by fast freight—us—and we need to make haste. But the price is too good for us not to go. And while there," he said, holding up the list, "we'll attempt to identify the two names in Salador." He mused over the list. "We've got a half-dozen names within a week's ride of Salador. I think we'll deliver our cargo and then nose around some in the east."

To his companions he said, "I'm going home to speak with Karli, and then Duncan and I will be departing at first light tomorrow." To Duncan he said, "Be here and be alert."

Duncan frowned, but both knew that, given a choice, he was likely to come wandering in around midday with a hangover.

To Luis, Roo said, "You're in charge while Duncan and I—"

Duncan said, "Wait a minute, cousin. Why not take Luis and leave me here to run things?"

Roo regarded his cousin a moment; that request could only mean Duncan had a new barmaid or serving wench who had caught his fancy. With ill humor Roo said, "Because I prefer to return here next month and find I am still in business."

He ignored Duncan's dark expression as he continued his interrupted instructions to Luis. "You are in charge, and if you have any unusual needs, see Karli. Jason knows what our resources are, so if something comes your way that depletes us of our money, make certain it's a sure thing."

Luis smiled. Many times he had said to Roo there were no "sure things." "Understood," he said.

Roo said, "Jason, you're doing a good job with the ledgers. Now, can you start a fresh set of accounts for me, beginning the day I took sole control of the company?"

Jason said, "I can do that."

Roo said, "Good, and label them 'Avery and Company.' " He turned to the door, then stopped. "And don't mention that last bit about the name change to Karli until I return."

Jason and Luis exchanged glances, but neither spoke. Roo left the office and began the long walk home. The city streets were crowded as sundown approached. Vendors hawked their wares, trying for that last sale before they called it a day and returned to their own homes, while messengers hurried to carry that last missive of the day.

Roo wended his way through the press, and by the time he

reached home, the sun had set behind the buildings opposite the Grindle house. He glanced around and suddenly realized how dingy this place looked, even when not overwhelmed by shadows. He once more vowed that as soon as he could afford it, he would move his wife to newer, more sumptuous quarters.

He opened the door and entered. Karli was in the kitchen, talking with the cook, Rendel, and Mary, the maid. Mary saw Roo first and said, "Oh, sir. It's the lady." Since the wedding, the maid had taken to referring to Karli as "the lady of the house," or simply, "the lady," as if she were the wife of nobility. Roo found he liked that, as well as being referred to as "the master," or "sir."

Roo took a moment and then the scene registered. Karli stood at the large chopping block that dominated the kitchen, holding tightly to the edge. Her hand was white, she was gripping so tightly. "What's wrong?" he asked.

Rendel, a huge woman of unknowable years, said, "She's off her feed, poor dear."

Roo frowned, not being quite sure he liked having his wife referred to as if she were livestock. "Karli?"

She said, "It's some sort of stomach problem. I just walked in a moment ago and the smell of food . . ." She grew even more pale, and suddenly her hand came to her mouth as she fought to keep whatever was in her stomach down. She turned and left the kitchen, hurrying out the back door toward the jakes.

Mary, a simple enough young woman of modest intellect, said, "I'm so worried about the lady."

Rendel laughed and turned back to the vegetables she was washing in a bucket in the sink. "She'll be fine."

As Roo looked at them both, obviously unsure what to do next, Mary said, "Sir, should I go see to the lady?"

Roo said, "No. I'll go," and he went after his wife out the rear door of the home.

The plain façade of the house hid, along with the interior of the home, the rich little garden that lay behind it. Karli spent a great deal of her time in the garden, which was equally divided between vegetables and flowers. At the far wall stood the modest little outhouse, from which issued the sound of Karli's retching.

As he reached the door, it opened and a pale Karli emerged. "Are you all right?" said Roo, at once regretting the question.

Karli's expression showed it to be one of the more stupid questions of Roo's life, but she said, "I'll be fine."

Roo said, "Should I send for a healer?"

Karli smiled at his obvious concern. "No, it's nothing a healer can help."

Panic revealed itself in Roo's face. "My gods! What is it?"

Karli couldn't help but laugh, despite her obvious physical discomfort. She allowed him to offer an arm and let him walk her to a tiny stone bench next to a modest fountain. "It's nothing to be alarmed over, Roo," she said. When they sat she told him, "I wanted to be sure. You're going to be a father."

Roo sat speechless for a minute. "I need to sit down."

Karli laughed. "You are sitting."

Roo stood, said, "Now I need to sit down," and sat down again. Then his narrow face split in the widest grin Karli had ever seen. "A baby?"

Karli nodded, and Roo suddenly realized he had never seen her look so lovely. He kissed her on the cheek. "When?"

"Seven more months," she said.

Roo calculated, and his eyes widened. "Then . . ."

She nodded. "The first night."

Roo said, "Imagine that." He sat motionless and speechless for a long moment. Then a thought crossed his mind, and he said, "I shall have Luis change the sign to 'Avery and Son' at once!"

Karli's eyes narrowed. "Change the name of the company?"

Roo took her hand and said, "My love, I want the world to know I have a son coming." He stood up. "I must tell Duncan and Erik, before I leave tomorrow."

He was halfway across the garden when she asked, "Leave tomorrow?"

He halted. "I'm going to run a special cargo to Salador for the Prince. I'll tell you about it when I get back, but I need to tell Erik and Duncan I'm going to be a father."

He dashed out of the garden without waiting for a reply. Karli sat quietly for a moment, then stood slowly. She asked herself, "What if it's a daughter?"

In the failing evening light, she returned to the only home she had known her entire life, feeling nothing so much as a guest in her own house.

*   *   *

Roo groaned. Duncan laughed as he snapped the reins, urging the horses out the city gates. Duncan, Luis, Erik, and Roo's other friends had feted their friend on the announcement of his coming fatherhood and now Roo was paying the price. He had been helped home by Duncan and had fallen into bed nearly comatose next to Karli. Without comment she had roused him the next day when, against expectations, Duncan had arrived on time.

They had made their way in the predawn light to the shop, hitched up the wagon, and headed out to the palace. At the gate a squad of men waited and they quickly loaded the cargo for Salador.

Then, to Roo's surprise, Erik rode up with a squad of horsemen, an escort for the cargo. All he said was "I don't know what's in there, either."

Now it was midday and the wagon rattled along at a good rate over the King's Highway, starting the long climb up into the foothills of the southern end of the Calastius Mountains. Roo said, "We need to rest the horses."

Duncan reined in the team and shouted, "Erik. Time for a break."

Erik, who had been riding a short way ahead, nodded as he turned his own horse and dismounted, signaling to the other guards to do the same. He picketed his horse by the roadside and let it crop grass.

Duncan took a large waterskin and drank, then handed it to Roo. He poured a bit over his face and wiped it off, then drank.

Erik came over and asked, "How's your head?"

"Too small to hold the pain inside," Roo replied. "Why did I do that?"

Erik shrugged. "I sort of wondered myself. You seemed to be working very hard at being happy."

Roo nodded. "Truth to tell, I'm scared witless. Me, a father." Taking Erik away from the wagon, he said to Duncan, "Check the horses, will you?"

When they were out of earshot, Roo said, "What do I know about being a father? All my old man ever did was beat on me. I mean, what am I supposed to do when the baby gets here?"

Erik said, "You're asking the wrong man. I never had *any* sort of father."

Panic surfaced on Roo's face. "What am I going to do, Erik?"

Erik grinned. "You're only going through what we all go through, I bet. It's a big change. First a wife, now a child." He rubbed his chin. "I've wondered what I would do if I fell in love and got married, had children."

"And?"

"I really don't know."

"Some help you are."

Erik put his hand upon Roo's shoulder. "Well, I did come up with one thing. I imagine if I'm ever a father and something happens that I don't anticipate, I'm going to ask myself, 'What would Milo do now?'"

Roo pondered that a moment. Then he smiled, "He's the best dad I've ever seen, the way he treated Rosalyn and you as kids."

"That's how I figure it," said Erik. "If I start to get confused, I'll just imagine what Milo would do and try to do that."

As if this somehow made the prospect of being a father less fearful, Roo brightened. "Well, I think I'll have another drink of water."

Erik laughed. "Take it easy, Roo. You have a lot of time to recover from last night."

Roo turned back toward the wagon. "So why are you in charge of this escort?" he inquired.

"I asked for it," said Erik. "Things are under control back at the palace, and the Prince seems to think this cargo needed special protection, and I haven't been home in a year."

Roo blinked. "It has been a year, hasn't it?"

Erik said, "This way we'll have two visits: a short one on the way through, and we can probably steal an extra day on the way back for a proper get-together."

Roo said, "Well, you've got your mother and Nathan, Milo, Rosalyn. Lots of friends."

"You've also got some friends, Roo."

Roo smiled. "I wonder how Gwen is doing?"

Erik's brow furrowed. "You're a married man, Roo."

Reaching under the buckboard, Roo pulled out a bag of provisions and dug out some bread. Yanking off a piece, he stuffed it in his mouth and washed it down with another gulp of water. "I'm not that married," said Roo.

Erik's expression turned dark. Roo held up one hand. "I mean I'm not so married I can't be civil to old friends just because they're women."

Erik studied his friend's face a moment, then said, "If that's what you mean."

Duncan returned from looking over the horses and reported, "Everything's fine."

Roo climbed back up on the buckboard and said, "Well, let's get moving again. The Duke of Salador is expecting this cargo and we're getting a bonus for speed."

Duncan sighed; the buckboard was about as comfortable as a moving block of stone. "I hope it's a very good bonus," he said with poorly concealed ill-humor.

The journey went smoothly. Twice the presence of Erik's guards had speeded up accounting with the local constabulary, saving Roo precious hours. The visit in Ravensburg had been a hasty one, with them rolling into Milo's Inn of the Pintail after sundown, and leaving before sunrise, without seeing Rosalyn and her family. Erik promised his mother he would linger on the way back.

In Darkmoor, if the local guards recognized Erik or Roo they said nothing. Still, Roo found he felt considerably better once that city had fallen behind them.

As a child, Roo had accompanied his father on the journey to Salador only twice, and now he saw the Eastern Realm with the eyes of an adult. The lands through which they passed had been cultivated for centuries. Farms were tidy to the point of appearing like miniatures painted by artists when seen from the distant road. Compared to this, the Western Realm was still rough-hewn, and the lands across the sea primitive and wild.

They reached the city gates at noon and Erik hardly slowed as he passed the City Watch, shouting, "Cargo from the Prince for the Duke!"

One of his soldiers had carried a pennant, which was now unfurled; it bore the crest of the Prince of Krondor. That morning the soldiers had donned the tabards they had carried in their saddlebags, and Roo saw that his escort was comprised of not just city troops but Prince Patrick's own household guard. Roo wondered again what his cargo was, but knew that he might never find out.

They rode through the city and Roo was astonished at the number of people. Krondor might be the capital of the Western Realm, but it was dwarfed in size by several of the eastern cities. Salador was the second largest city in the Kingdom after Rillanon, and it took more than an hour for Roo's wagon to roll through the press of the crowds and reach the ducal palace.

The Prince's palace in Krondor sat atop a suddenly rising prominence hard against the harbor. Salador's ruler's home also sat atop a hill, but over a mile from the harbor. A long, sloping hillside led down into the heart of the city, and far beyond that, Roo could see the harbor.

"I always forget how damn big it is," said Duncan.

"I never realized," was all Roo said.

They reached the palace and Erik announced them to the palace guard. The guard waved the wagon through while another ran to the main hall to inform the Duke. A third guard directed Roo's wagon to a large double-door entrance set off to one side of a sharply rising broad flight of stairs.

Duncan said, "Must be important people who get to walk up those steps." He leaped down from the wagon and with a nod of his head toward the door said, "For the common folks."

Roo said, "Did you expect anything else?"

Duncan sighed, rubbing his backside in exaggerated relief. "All I know is that tonight I want a hot tub to soak in and a hot woman to keep me warm the rest of the night."

Roo smiled. "I'm sure that can be arranged."

The doors to the palace opened, and down the steps came a well-dressed young man with a court retinue following behind. Then Roo noticed that the retinue was arranged in a loose circle around an elderly woman. Easily in her eighties, she still moved with a sure step and carried herself erect. She held an ornate walking stick with a golden hilt, but it was as much for effect as for support. Her grey hair was swept up in a fashion new to Roo, and set with jeweled pins of gold.

The young man moved to where Erik waited, and Erik bowed. "My lord."

"Grandmother," said the young man to the elderly woman, "it's here." The two large doors next to the steps opened, and servants in the livery of the ducal household ran forth. The young man waved his hand toward the wagon and they began to untie the tarpaulin covering the cargo. The six large boxes were carefully handed down.

The woman pointed to the first box. "Open it."

The servants complied; the woman poked into a loose assortment of clothing and moved it around with her walking stick. "This isn't much to show for a lifetime, is it?"

Roo and Duncan exchanged glances, and the young man said to Erik, "Tell cousin Patrick we are all grateful for this. Grandmother?"

The old woman smiled, and Roo saw a hint of youthful beauty that must have been something to behold. "Yes, we are thankful."

She motioned for her servants to pick up the boxes and said, "Arutha . . . he was always special to me. After my husband, I miss him most of all." She seemed lost in thought, then said, "Duncan."

Duncan stepped forward, confusion on his face, as the young man said, "Grandmother?"

"Ma'am?" asked Duncan.

The old woman glanced at the two men and smiled. "I was speaking to my grandson, sir," she said to Duncan Avery. "I take it your name is also Duncan?"

Duncan removed his hat and swept into his most courtly bow. "Duncan Avery at your service, ma'am."

To her grandson the woman said, "Tell your father I shall join his court shortly, Duncan."

The young man nodded, glanced at the other Duncan, then hurried up the stairs. Coming to stand before Duncan Avery, she peered into his face. "I know you," she said quietly.

Duncan smiled his most charming smile. "Madam, I hardly count that possible. I am certain had we met I would have no doubt about it."

The woman laughed, and Roo found it a surprisingly youthful sound from one so old. She tapped his chest with her finger. "I was right. I do know you. I married you." She turned away and, as she returned to the waiting retinue, said, "Or someone very much like you, once, a long time ago." Without looking back she added, "And if I ever see you within speaking distance of any of my granddaughters, I'll have you horsewhipped from the city."

Duncan looked at Roo with fleeting alarm crossing his face. Then the old woman looked at him as she mounted the first step, and Roo saw the mischief in her smile as she said, "Or brought to my quarters. Have a pleasant trip, gentlemen." To Erik she said, "Sergeant, tell my grandnephew I am grateful for these keepsakes of my brother."

Erik saluted. "M'lady," he said.

Roo went over to Erik. "Who was that?" he asked.

Erik said, "The Lady Carline, Dowager Duchess of Salador. The King's aunt."

Duncan laughed. "She must have been something once."

Roo elbowed his cousin in the ribs and said, "Seems she still is."

They returned to the wagons and Duncan said, "So that was the precious cargo? Some old clothes and whatever?"

Roo mounted the wagon and said, "So it seems. But she certainly seemed to set great store by it."

Duncan mounted the wagon and Roo called out, "Where to now, Erik?"

Erik said, "Inn of the Nimble Coachman. We passed it on the way here. They have the royal account."

Roo knew that meant he and Duncan would stay the night at the Prince's expense, and he smiled. Every coin he saved now would be put back into the business, to compensate for the riches lost when Helmut was murdered. At the thought of his former partner's murder, Roo's thoughts turned dark again, and he found his merriment fleeing.

The inn was modest but clean, and Roo enjoyed a hot bath after the long journey. Duncan found his willing barmaid and Roo found himself left alone with Erik and the squad of soldiers. Roo motioned for Erik to sit with him, and when he was sure he was out of earshot of the soldiers, he asked in a low voice, "Do you know what's going on?"

Erik said, "About what?"

"This 'rush' shipment of old clothing."

Erik shrugged. "I think it's just some things belonging to the old Prince that Prince Patrick thought his great-aunt would want to have."

"That part I understand," said Roo. "I understand why they want me to bring things into the palace." He left unsaid what they both knew about that contract. "But this cargo could have gone to anyone, and why the rush?"

"Maybe the old woman is ill?" said Erik.

Roo shook his head. "Hardly. She looked like she might yank Duncan's trousers down."

Erik laughed. "She was kind of outspoken, wasn't she?"

Roo said, "Is de Loungville doing me a favor?"

Erik shook his head. "Not him. He has nothing to say in this; fact is, no one in the military does, either our command or the palace. Your selection was handled by the office of the Chancellor."

"Which means Duke James."

"I guess," answered Erik, suddenly yawning. "I'm tired. Why don't you worry about this tomorrow. Besides, who cares if it's a pointless job, as long as it pays well?"

He stood and motioned for his men to retire for the night. Roo sat alone for a long minute, and a barmaid came over to see if he wanted anything. She smiled at him. He inspected her with a young man's eyes, then shook his head.

To the chair Erik had just vacated, Roo at last said, "I care."

Back in Ravensburg, the homecoming was far more festive than before. Knowing that Roo was returning, the locals planned a small party.

Erik and his guards had left Salador the morning after the delivery, while Roo and Duncan had set out to track down some of the mysterious accounts on the ledger Jason had found. A few of them had been known to Karli, and by using deduction during the conversation with those people, Roo identified all those in the Salador area in quick order. With each of those accounts he discovered a different reason for the discretion exhibited by Helmut Grindel. All but one had agreed to continue doing business with Roo's new company, and that one had paid off his account in full. Roo was satisfied with the overall outcome.

Erik had ridden ahead so he could spend a few days in Ravensburg. Roo felt no pressing need to linger in the town of his boyhood and was content to spend but one night there before moving on back to his new home in Krondor.

At least sixty people were crowded into the common room of the Inn of the Pintail, and Erik was grinning at the attention. Roo watched his friend from across the crowded room, feeling envy. Always something of a rogue in Ravensburg, Roo knew everyone but had few friends. Erik, on the other hand, had always been everyone's friend, including Roo's.

Roo smiled despite his somewhat subdued mood. Erik's mother Freida, long the resident rain cloud in Roo's life, came into the room through the kitchen door looking like a sunburst. She smiled at the sight of her son and husband talking together. Marriage certainly had agreed with Freida, Roo was forced to concede. He wondered if he would ever find such pleasure in wife and family. Thinking of Karli, he felt some concern, yet women had been having babies since the dawn of time and what could he accomplish by being near her? Making his fortune, providing for her and the child, that was the most important thing Roo could do.

"You're lost, aren't you?" asked a feminine voice.

Roo glanced up to see a familiar face. He smiled. "Gwen, hello."

The girl sat down. An old friend, she reached across the table and patted Roo's hand. "Thought I might run into you and that cousin of yours," she said. Then with a twist of her head, she indicated Duncan at the other side of the room, deep in conversation with a young girl unknown to Roo. "Seems Ellien found Duncan first."

"Ellien? Bertram's little sister?" Roo looked again at the girl and saw that she was a little younger than he had thought her to be when Duncan first began flirting with her. The last time he had seen the girl, she had been shapeless. Now, given the plunging neckline of her blouse, he could see some shape had definitely manifested itself over the last three years.

Gwen twirled a strand of her hair absently as she said, "What about you?"

Roo said, "I'm doing fine. I'm owner of a freight company now."

Gwen's smiled broadened. "Owner? How'd you manage that?"

Roo mentioned the death of his partner, and in the telling of his story, he overstated his own skills only a little. Freida came by and filled Roo's wineglass, smiling at him while she did.

Roo said, "She's changed."

"She's found a good man," said Gwen.

"What about you?" asked Roo, taking a deep drink.

Gwen sighed dramatically. Like most of the town girls his own age, Roo knew, she had spent her evenings down by the fountain in the center of town flirting with the local boys, and unlike most girls, she was still unwed. "The good ones are taken."

She feigned a pout. Drawing a fingernail across the back of Roo's hand, she said, "Things haven't been the same since you and Erik left Ravensburg."

Roo grinned. "Getting dull?"

"You could say that." Gwen glanced over at Duncan, who now was whispering something into Ellien's ear. The girl's eyes widened and she blushed, then burst out laughing, covering her mouth with her hand. Softly Gwen said, "Well, that's one little flower that's going to get plucked tonight." Her sour tone wasn't lost on Roo. It was now obvious that Gwen had heard Duncan was here and had come looking for him.

As a boy, Roo had slept with the girl a few times. Gwen was one of the more agreeable girls in that regard in the town, which had probably contributed to no boy's asking for her hand in marriage. Roo thought it was more likely that there simply were more girls than boys his age as he grew up. There were bound to be those who didn't find husbands. Still, he liked Gwen.

"Leave your father's house and find a position at an inn," advised Roo.

"And why should I do a thing like that?" asked Gwen.

Roo grinned as the wine warmed him. "Because then you might find a rich merchant passing through, whose fancy you might catch."

Gwen laughed. She took a sip of wine. "Rich like you?"

Roo blushed. "I'm not rich. I'm working hard at it, though."

"So you're going to be rich someday?" she pressed.

Feeling his spirits lifting, he said, "Let me tell you something about what I'm going to do."

Gwen motioned for Freida to bring more wine and sat back to listen to Roo spin his tales of ambition.

Roo winced at the sound of someone slamming a door down the hall. Then he shuddered as someone pounded on his bedroom door.

"What?" he croaked.

Erik's voice came from beyond the door. "Get dressed. We leave in an hour."

Roo felt the way he had the day they had left Krondor. "I've got to stop doing this," he groaned.

"What?" said a sleepy voice next to him.

Suddenly Roo was wide awake and sober. He looked to his right and saw Gwen wrapped up in the bedsheets.

"Gods!" Roo whispered.

"What?" asked Gwen.

"What are you doing here?" said Roo as he scrambled out of bed, reaching for his clothing.

Letting the sheets drop away, Gwen stretched, showing off her body to good effect, and said, "Well, come back here and I'll show you . . . again."

Roo pulled on his pants. "I can't! Gods! I didn't . . . did I?"

Gwen's expression clouded as she said, "You most certainly did, more than once. What is the problem, Roo? It's not the first time you and I have sported."

"Ah . . ." he said, not certain what he could possibly say to explain this away. He sat and pulled on his boots as quickly as he could. "Well, it's just . . ."

"What?" said Gwen, now certain she wasn't going to like what she was about to hear.

Draping his shirt over his arm and grabbing his coat off the floor, Roo said, "Well, it's just . . . I thought I might have mentioned it last night . . . but . . . I'm married."

"What!" came the shriek as he opened the door. "You bastard!" she shouted as she threw the porcelain washbowl that had rested a moment before on the nightstand next to the bed. It shattered loudly as Roo hurried down the stairs.

He found Duncan outside and said, "Is the wagon ready?"

Duncan nodded. "I told the smith's apprentice to hitch it up when you didn't come down for breakfast this morning."

Seeing the agitated condition his cousin was in, Duncan said, "Is something wrong?"

As if to answer his question, a loud shriek of outrage could be heard from inside the inn.

Freida, Nathan, and Milo, who had been saying good-bye to

Erik, glanced back at the inn, but Roo didn't look back. He climbed up into the wagon, took the reins, and said, "We're leaving."

Erik nodded, signaled his squad to form up, and motioned them to follow after Roo's wagon, while Duncan had to jump to get up on the wagon before it left him behind.

"What was that?" asked Duncan with a grin.

Roo turned and warned, "You will say nothing. Not a thing, do you understand?"

Duncan only nodded and laughed.

Twelve

Expansion

THE BABY SQUIRMED.

Erik smiled as he stood at Roo's side, while the priest of Sung the White, Goddess of Purity, blessed the child on her naming day. At the appropriate moment, Roo quickly handed the child back to Karli.

The priest said, "Abigail Avery, in this, your pure and innocent time of life, know that you are blessed in the sight of the goddess. If you remain true and good, doing harm to no one, then shall you abide in her grace. Blessed be her name."

"Blessed be," Roo, Karli, and Erik repeated, completing the ritual of greeting.

The priest nodded and smiled and said, "She's a beautiful girl."

Roo forced a smile. He had so expected a son that when, a week before, Karli had begun her labor and produced a girl, he had been completely unprepared. They had argued for hours about the boy's name, Roo wanting to call his son Rupert after himself, so that he could look upon himself as the founder of a dynasty, but Karli holding out for Helmut, after her father. Then, at the moment Karli had asked, "What shall we name her?" Roo had stood dumbfounded, without an answer.

Karli had asked, "Might we name her Abigail after my mother?" and Roo had nodded, not having words to express himself.

The priest left the bedchamber, and Karli put the child at her breast. Erik motioned for Roo to follow him and led his friend out of the room.

"She'll be a fine daughter," said Erik.

Roo shrugged as he walked down the stairs with Erik. "I guess. Truth to tell, I expected a boy. Maybe next time."

Erik said, "Don't be too disappointed. I think Karli would be very upset if you were disappointed."

"Do you?" said Roo, glancing up the stairs. "Well, I'll go back and fuss a little over the child and pretend I'm thrilled."

Erik's gaze narrowed, but he said nothing. He moved toward the door and retrieved his cloak and a broad-brimmed slouch hat. It was raining in Krondor, and he had gotten soaked coming to witness the ceremony. "I guess I might as well tell you now," he said as his hand rested on the door latch.

"What?"

"I probably won't be seeing you for some time."

"Why?" asked Roo, his face betraying something close to panic. Erik was one of the few people in the world he felt he could trust and rely upon.

"I'm leaving. Soon. It was supposed to be Jadow, but he broke his leg last week." He lowered his voice. "I can't tell you where, but I think you know."

Roo's expression revealed concern. "How long?"

"I don't know. We've got ... some bloody work ahead of us, and well, it may be a *very* long time."

Roo gripped his friend's arm as if to hold him there. After a moment he squeezed Erik's arm and said, "Stay alive."

"If I can I will."

Then Roo had his arms around his friend, hugging him closely. "You're the only damn brother I ever had, Erik von Darkmoor. I'll be very angry if I learn you're dead before you get a chance to see my son."

Erik awkwardly returned the hug, then disengaged himself from Roo. "Keep an eye on Greylock. He was supposed to go, but de Loungville threw a fit at being left behind. . . ." Erik managed a wry smile. "It's going to be an interesting trip. Sure you don't want to come with us?"

Roo laughed a humorless laugh. "I can do without that sort of 'interesting.'" He motioned toward the upstairs room. "I have people to take care of."

"So you do," said Erik with a smile. "Just see you do a good job or I'll be back to haunt you."

"Just come back and you can do what you want," said Roo.

Erik nodded, opened the door, and was gone.

Roo stood motionless, feeling an absence more profound than any he had known in his life. He remained there for a while, and when he at last broke out of his reverie, he pulled his cloak off the peg and left for the shop. He forgot to go upstairs and make a fuss over the baby.

Jason signaled to Roo, who moved across the crowded warehouse. Business had been building steadily for the last six months, and now they had twenty-six full-time drivers and a score of apprentices.

"What is it?" asked Roo.

Jason held out a parchment without any seal on it. The only marking on the outside was Roo's name. "This was just delivered. It came by royal post."

Roo took it and opened it. It said: "A Quegan trader has put in at Sarth. John."

Roo's brow furrowed as he considered the importance of the message, then he said, "Tell Duncan we leave at once for Sarth."

Jason nodded. Duncan came from the small apartment he and Luis still shared in the rear; Jason had taken Roo's space in the tiny apartment, since Roo was now living with his family. "What is it?" he asked, obviously having been wakened from a nap.

"Remember John Vinci up at Sarth?"

Duncan yawned widely as he nodded. "What of him?"

"He's sent us a message."

"What's it say?" asked Duncan.

"A Quegan trader has put in."

Duncan looked uncertain a moment; then his face lit up with a smile. "A Quegan trader in Sarth can mean only one thing." He lowered his voice. "Contraband."

Roo held up a finger indicating silence. "Something requiring discretion." To Jason he said, "After I'm gone, send word to Karli, telling her I'll be gone for a week or so."

As the newly serviced wagon was fitted, and food and waterskins loaded aboard, Roo speculated on what it was that Vinci wanted to sell him. He kept wondering as they rolled out of the yard into the city and started their way north.

*   *   *

The trip to Sarth had proven uneventful. Roo felt a strange discomfort listening to Duncan rattle on about this barmaid or that game of dice. He couldn't put his finger on it, but he felt as if there was something back in Krondor left unattended, and that vague uneasiness was growing into full-blown worry by the time they reached Sarth.

They arrived at sundown and went straight to the shop of John Vinci. They pulled up in front and Roo jumped down. "Let me talk to him a moment," he said to Duncan, "then we'll head for the inn."

"Very well," Duncan agreed.

Roo went inside, and Vinci said, "Ah, it's you. I was just about to close. Would you like to dine with my family?"

Roo said, "Certainly. Now what is this mysterious note you sent me?"

Vinci went to the door and locked it. He motioned for Roo to follow him to the back room. "Two things. As I said in the note, a Quegan trader arrived here a little over a week ago. The captain was . . . anxious to dispose of an item, and when I saw it I thought of you."

He took down a large box and opened it. Inside, Roo saw a very elegant-looking set of rubies mounted in a display case, as if for presentation. He had never seen anything like it, but Helmut had mentioned such displays to him, and he didn't need more than a moment to know what it meant. "Stolen."

"Well, the trader seemed ready to take whatever I agreed to give him before he returned to Queg."

Roo thought a moment. "What did you pay for it?"

John looked at Roo askance a moment. "What matter is that to you? What is it worth?"

"Your life, if the Quegan noble who ordered it to present to his mistress finds out you have it," answered Roo. "Look, I'm going to have to ship that to the Eastern Realm if I take it off your hands. No noble in the Western Realm is going to give those to his wife, have her wear them to a reception, and encounter some Quegan envoy who recognizes them for what they are."

John looked uncertain. "How would they know?"

Roo pointed at the stones. "It's a matched set, John. There are five brilliant matched stones, and a dozen smaller ones, but all are cut in identical fashion. The case is . . ." He took it, closed it, and turned it over. "Look, here." He pointed to a line of symbols cut into the wood.

"I don't read Quegan," said John.

"And I can fly," said Roo. "Don't lie to a liar, John. Vinci is no Kingdom name. What is it, short for Vincinti?"

John grinned. "Vincintius. My grandfather was an escaped Quegan slave who kept his master's surname." He glanced at the mark. "So this was made by commission from Lord Vasarius by Secaus Gracianus, master jeweler. Get a new box."

Roo said, "Because that gem cutter will know these rubies like he knows his own children, he has certainly let it be known they are gone. If they show up anywhere west of Darkmoor, he will know within a month who has them, and who they were purchased from. The hunt will be on. The only way you're going to keep your throat intact will be to stop pulling my finger and tell me what you paid."

John didn't look convinced. "Ten thousand sovereigns."

Roo laughed. "Try again."

John said, "Very well, five thousand."

Roo said, "I'm sorry. I can't hear you. What was it you said?"

John said, "I paid a thousand gold sovereigns."

"Where did you get a thousand sovereigns?" asked Roo.

"Some I had saved, and the rest in trade. He needed to refit."

"On his way to Kesh or the Free Cities, was he?" said Roo.

"In something of a hurry," said John. "He stole the box or had it stolen before he realized how difficult it would be to dispose of the booty." He shrugged. "His loss; our gain."

Roo nodded. "Here's what I'll do. You can have either two thousand sovereigns gold, now, or I'll give you . . . a third of what I can fetch in the East, but you'll have to wait."

John considered only a moment. "I'll take the gold now."

Roo said, "I thought you would." Reaching into his tunic, he pulled out a heavy purse. "I can give you a hundred now, and a letter of account. The gold is in Krondor."

"That's not 'gold now,' Roo."

Roo shook his head. "All right, make it twenty-one hundred: a hundred now, and two thousand on a letter."

"Done. I'm heading to Krondor next month and I'll present the letter then."

"Take it to my office and I'll see you're paid. Or you can have a line of credit."

"What, so you can have the merchants jack up the prices for a kickback and get your price discounted?"

Roo laughed. "John, why don't you work for me?"

John said, "What do you mean?"

"Let me buy this miserable shop of yours and close it up. Bring your family down to Krondor and run a shop for me. I'll pay you more than you'll ever make here. Your talents are wasted in Sarth."

John said, "Krondor? Never thought much of living in a city. Let me think on it."

"You do that," said Roo. "I'm heading for the inn. I'll come by your home later for supper. I have my cousin with me."

"Bring him along," said John. "And we can talk of that other matter I mentioned."

"Good," said Roo, letting himself out of the store. He felt good. It might take a couple of months, but those rubies would fetch him at least five thousand sovereigns' profit.

As he climbed into the wagon, Duncan said, "That took you long enough."

Taking the reins, Roo grinned. "It was worth it."

John's family was crowded into a small house a short distance behind his shop, separated from the shop by a small garden in which John's wife grew vegetables. Roo and Duncan were admitted by John, who was now puffing on a long pipe. He offered them a mug each of a fair ale while Annie, his wife, prepared dinner in the kitchen, aided by several children. Roo found the noise nerve-racking as the younger three children half played, half scuffled underfoot while John sat ignoring them.

"Don't you find this a little much?" asked Roo.

"What?" said John.

"The noise."

John laughed. "You get used to it. You obviously don't have children."

Roo blushed. "Actually, I do have . . . a baby."

John shook his head. "Then get used to it."

Duncan said, "Very nice ale."

John said, "It's nothing special, but I do enjoy a mug between closing the shop and supper."

"What's this other matter you mentioned?" asked Roo.

"While he was talking, the Quegan trader whom I did business with mentioned something I thought you might find interesting."

"What is it?"

"If you can turn this to a profit, what's my cut?"

Roo glanced at Duncan. "It depends, John. Information is sometimes very useful to one person and worthless to another."

"I know about those trading consortiums down in Krondor and you're the sort of man to be involved with them."

Roo laughed. "Not yet, but I do know my way around the trading floor at Barret's. If there's something you know that I can trade for gold at Barret's, I'll give you two percent of what I make."

John considered. "More. Take the two thousand gold sovereigns you owe me and invest it with your own gold." He leaned forward. "Make me a partner."

Roo said, "Done, for this one transaction."

"Here's what I know," began John. "The Quegan captain I talked to said that a friend of his had sailed a cargo to Margrave's Port. While he was there, rumors were spreading through the city that there was some sort of pest infesting the wheat fields outside the city." He dropped his voice as if fearing somehow to be overheard in his own house. "Grasshoppers."

Roo looked confused. "So? There are grasshoppers everywhere."

John said, "Not like these. If the farmer is mentioning grasshoppers, what they're talking about is a lot worse: locusts."

Roo sat back, stunned. "If this is true . . ." He calculated. "If that news hasn't reached Krondor yet . . ." He jumped to his feet. "Duncan, we're leaving now. John, I will invest the gold I owe you. For if this rumor turns out to be false, I'll be too poor to pay you what I owe you, anyway. But if it's true . . . we'll both be rich men."

Duncan was out of his seat, looking confused, as Annie stuck her head through the kitchen door. "Supper's ready."

"Aren't we going to eat?" said Duncan.

Roo saluted John's wife. "Regrets, Annie. We must fly."

He half pushed Duncan out of the door as Duncan complained.
"I don't follow. What's going on?"

"I'll explain it to you on our way south. We'll eat while we
drive."

Duncan made an aggravated sound as they hurried to the inn,
where they would need to tack up a tired team of horses and get
started on the hurried trip home.

Duncan said, "I see something ahead."

Roo, who had been dozing a bit while his cousin took a turn
driving the team, was instantly alert. It was an uneventful trip
despite their hurrying to the horses' limits. Usually between Sarth
and Krondor this was the case, but even though they were still
inside the well-patrolled Principality, outlaws and the occasional
goblin raid were not unheard of.

As they moved up the road, another wagon could be seen. It
was pulled over to the side of the road and the driver was waving.
Roo pulled up and the driver said, "Can you help me?"

"What's the problem?" asked Roo.

"I've got a busted hub." He pointed to the rear wheel, looking
nervous. "And my master will be furious if this cargo is late."

Roo took a second look at the wagon. "Who's your master?"

"I'm a teamster for Jacoby and Sons," answered the driver.

Roo laughed. "I know your master. Yes, he'll be upset if you're
delayed. What cargo?"

At that the driver looked very uncomfortable. "Just some trade
goods . . . from Sarth."

Roo glanced at Duncan, who nodded and jumped down. "My
friend," said Duncan, "we're in a position to be of service." He
slowly drew his sword and pointed at the wagon. "First we're going to unload your cargo and put it in our wagon, which, as you
can see, is presently empty. Then we will replace our very tired
horses with your rested and fresh animals."

The driver looked as if he was going to bolt, but Roo had come
around the other side of his horses and stood between the driver
and freedom. The timid man said, "Please don't hurt me."

Duncan smiled. "My friend, that is the last thing we wish to do.
Now, why don't you get started on unloading while my companion
inspects your bill of lading."

The man's eyes grew wide as he headed for the back of the wagon. Unfastening the last tie-down, he said, "The paperwork is . . . coming by messenger . . . later."

Roo laughed. "And the guard at the city gate who Tim Jacoby has paid off will believe that nonsense, I'm certain."

The driver nodded and sighed. "You know the routine, obviously." He lifted a large box out of the wagon and carried it over to Roo's wagon. Duncan lowered the tailgate, and the man shoved the box in, pushing it deep into the wagon. "You realize you're going to get me killed?"

"I doubt it," said Roo. "you've got a busted wheel, and when you reach Krondor, you'll have a wonderful tale to tell of the brave fight you put up against overwhelming odds."

Duncan chimed in: "Your bravery is undoubted, and you risked your life against six bandits—no, seven bandits for your master's cargo. Why, I'd buy you a drink in any inn in Krondor to hear that story again."

"What's the cargo?" asked Roo.

"Might as well tell you," said the driver as he carried the second box over to Roo's wagon. "Quegan luxuries. My master sent me up to Sarth to meet with a Quegan captain who made an unscheduled stop there. The Royal Customs house was closed, because the customs officer in Sarth is dead."

"When did that happen?" asked Roo, suddenly very interested.

"Over a year ago." The driver laughed bitterly. "For whatever reason, new Prince in the city, or some other thing, there's been no replacement up there since. Makes it easy to pick up goods there and bring them down to the city. As you said, if you know the right city gate and which guard sergeant to talk to, getting into the city with any cargo is an easy task."

Roo said, "Would you be willing to mention the time and gate?"

"What's in it for me?" asked the driver, and suddenly Roo was laughing.

"Your loyalty to the Jacobys is unmatched."

The driver shrugged, then jumped into the wagon to grab the last box. "Do you know Tim?"

Roo nodded. "Well enough."

"Then you know he's a swine. His father, Frederick, when he was in charge, well, he's a tough old boot, but he was mostly fair.

If you did something well, there was a little extra in it for you. Randolph's a decent enough fellow.

"But Tim," said the driver, carrying the box over to Roo's wagon, "now there's a piece of work. He's the sort that if you do a perfect job, why, that's what he's paying you for, but if you make the tiniest mistake, you're as likely to get a knife between your ribs as a pat on the back. He has these two bashers who are with him all the time. He's a rough customer."

Roo glanced at Duncan. "At least he thinks he is." He asked the driver, "What's your name?"

"Jeffrey," answered the driver.

"Well, Jeffrey," said Roo, "you've been very helpful." He reached into his purse and pulled out a gold coin. "The gate and time?"

"Just before you get to the city, turn off along the sea trail and come to the small gate that leads to the fishing harbor to the north of the city. That's the gate. During the day watch. It's a sergeant named Diggs. He's taking Jacoby gold."

"Are you known to him?"

The driver nodded. "But Jacoby uses a lot of different teamsters to cover his tracks. He sometimes hires sailors or farmers if he thinks he might be caught smuggling." Roo nodded, remembering the drunken sailor who had run his wagon into Barrett's front door. "So when you see the gate guard, ask for Diggs by name. Tell him you've got netting from Sarth."

"Netting from Sarth?"

"Anything else and he'll be on you like lice on a beggar, but if you say, 'Netting from Sarth,' he'll wave you through. Don't mention Jacoby or say anything else. Just say, 'Netting from Sarth,' and you're in."

Roo took out another coin and flipped it to the driver, who suddenly seemed far less troubled by this hijacking. Jeffrey said, "You'd better mark me up some so Tim Jacoby doesn't kill me."

Roo nodded, and Duncan struck the man hard across the face with the back of his hand. Jeffrey spun around and fell to the ground, and Roo could see a red welt appearing on his cheek. Jeffrey shook his head and stood up. "Better close one of my eyes," he said as he tore his own tunic. Duncan glanced at Roo, who nodded again, and this time Duncan doubled up his fist, drew back, and drove it straight into the man's left eye. He staggered backward and fell hard against the side of Jacoby's wagon, striking the back of his head. He sat heavily on the ground, and for a moment Roo thought he might lose consciousness, but instead he fell over on his side and started rolling in the dirt. Then, with wobbling knees, he stood up. "One more ought to do it," he said in hoarse tones.

Roo raised his hand and Duncan held his blow. "When you're discharged by Jacoby, come see me about a position."

Squinting with his good eye, the driver said, "Who are you?"

"Rupert Avery."

The man laughed a strangled laugh. "Oh, this is rich. Just the mention of your name makes Tim crap in his trousers. No one knows what it was you done to him, but he's got some major hate for you, Mr. Avery."

Roo said, "The feeling is mutual. He killed my partner."

Jeffrey said, "Well, I'd heard rumors, but that was all. Now, if we could get this over with, I'll be along after I lay low a bit, and then I'll be talking to you about that job."

Roo nodded and Duncan unleashed a heavy blow, striking Jeffrey hard enough to lift him off his heels. The man turned in the air as he fell again, this time not rising. Duncan leaned over and looked at the unconscious man. "He knows how to take it, that's for certain. He'll live."

"He's tough enough," said Roo. "And even if I don't hire him, I want to know as much as he does about how the Jacobys operate."

Duncan said, "Well, we'd better be along before a patrol rides by. Might be difficult to explain all this."

Roo nodded. Both men mounted up and Roo headed the wagon down the highway.

The return to Krondor went uneventfully. The only tense moment was when they reached the indicated gate and the soldier inquired about their cargo. Roo asked for Sergeant Diggs by name, and after Roo told him the cargo, the sergeant hesitated a moment before waving them through.

Roo had taken a circuitous route through the city in case they were being followed, and finally reached his own shop. Luis was overseeing the dispatch of four wagons that were to meet with a caravan outside the city and carry goods into the palace. Roo quickly unloaded the goods they had taken from Jacoby's wagon and opened each box for inspection.

As he had suspected, the items involved were all high-tariff. A couple of small boxes contained what appeared to be drugs. Duncan said, "I'm no expert, but I think those are Dream and Joy. I'm not a user, but I've caught a whiff of them in some of the places I've visited."

Dream was a drug that induced hallucinations and Joy caused euphoria. Both were dangerous, illegal, and highly profitable. "What do you think boxes like that would be worth?" asked Roo.

Duncan replied, "As I said, I'm no expert, but I think our friend Jeffrey may end up floating in the harbor for letting us boost it from Jacoby. Maybe ten thousand gold. I don't know. I don't even know who you'd sell it to."

Roo calculated. "Find out, will you. Start with that girl over at the Inn of the Broken Shield, Katherine. She's a former Mocker and would know if there's an apothecary in the city who would be a discreet buyer." The other boxes contained some jewelry, probably stolen, as the rubies were.

After Duncan departed, Roo called Jason over from his work desk. "How much gold can we get our hands on in a hurry?"

Jason said, "You want an exact figure or rough?"

"Rough for now."

"Thirteen, fourteen thousand gold, plus whatever you can raise selling this stuff."

Roo rubbed his chin as he thought. Prudence dictated he sell the jewelry as far from Queg as possible, lest he run the risk of finding some angry Quegan lord's hired assassin in his bedchamber one night.

Luis came into the room from seeing the wagons leave for the caravanserai, and Roo asked, "Has Erik left yet?"

"Saw him last night at the inn. Why?"

Roo said, "I'll tell you when I get back." He hurried out of the office, running after Duncan.

Roo glanced around the room and saw that Erik was nowhere in sight. He and Duncan crossed to where the girl Katherine worked, and Roo said, "Has Erik left yet?"

The girl shrugged. "Saw him here last night. Why?"

"I need to talk to him." To Duncan he said, "See if she can help us, and I'm off to the palace. I'll come back here when I'm done."

"Good," said Duncan, slapping his hand on the bar and winking at the girl. "I've a throat full of road dust and haven't seen a pretty face in weeks."

Katherine threw him a withering look, but said, "What'll you have to drink?"

"Ale, my lovely," said Duncan as Roo hurried out of the inn.

It took a few minutes to convince the gate guard to send for Erik. The guard didn't realize whom he was speaking to, as Roo always showed up on a wagon early in the morning, not on foot late in the day.

Erik arrived ten minutes later and said, "What is it?"

"I need to talk to you a minute."

Erik waved him through the gate and they walked to where they were out of earshot of the other soldiers. "How much gold do you have?" asked Roo.

Erik blinked. "Gold? Why?"

"I need a loan."

Erik laughed. "For what?"

"I've got this information," Roo said. "I don't have a lot of time. I need twenty thousand gold pieces. I have maybe fourteen, and can raise another three or four. I just thought I'd see if you wanted to get in on this investment."

Erik considered. "Well, it's not like I'm going to need a lot of gold where I'm going."

Roo blinked as realization came to him that he and Erik had already bidden each other good-bye. "When do you leave?"

Erik said, "We sail day after tomorrow, but that's not to be shared with anyone."

Roo said, "I'm sorry, Erik. I wasn't thinking. You have a great deal on your mind and a lot to do."

"Things are pretty much under control, actually." He stared at Roo a moment. "Important?"

"Very," said Roo. "I haven't even been home yet."

"Well, come along."

He led Roo through the palace to the office of the Chancellor. Duke James's secretary said, "Sir?"

"It occurs to me that I haven't drawn my pay in a while. Could you tell me how much I have on accounts?"

The secretary said, "A moment, sir." He opened up a larger leather-bound ledger and consulted it.

The inner door opened and Lord James exited his private office suite. "Von Darkmoor," he said with a nod, then he caught sight of Roo. "Avery? What brings you here? Thinking of enlisting again?"

Roo smiled, despite finding no humor in the remark. But the man was Duke of Krondor, after all. "My lord," he said in greeting. "No, I was asking my friend for a loan for a business investment."

James stopped, and his eyes narrowed. "You're seeking investors?"

"Yes," answered Roo.

The old Duke studied Roo's face a moment, then waved him to follow. "Come in, both of you."

Once inside, James signaled to Erik to close the door and, when they were alone, sat down. Looking at Roo, he said, "What's the scam?"

Roo blinked. "It's no scam, m'lord. I've come into some information which may give me a position that will bring great profit."

James sat back in his chair. "Care to share that information with me?"

"With all due respect, no, m'lord."

Duke James laughed. "You're direct enough. Let me rephrase this: tell me."

Roo looked first at James, then at Erik, and finally said, "Very well, but only if you promise not to interfere with my investments, m'lord."

Erik looked scandalized at Roo's affront to the Duke's dignity, but the Duke only looked amused. "I make no promises, young Rupert, but trust me when I say that the kinds of sums of money you're thinking about interest me very little. My concerns have more to do with the safety and well-being of the realm."

"Well then," said Roo, "it's about the wheat crop in the Free Cities."

"What about them?" asked James, now keenly interested.

"Locusts."

James sat, blinked, and then broke into laughter. "And where did you get this tidbit?"

Roo explained about the chain of news, without going into detail about what brought a Quegan trader to Sarth, and when he was finished, James said, "So what do you propose to do, buy up all the wheat in the West, then hold the Free Cities' trading representatives hostage?"

Roo blushed. "Not quite. I mean to underwrite as many grain ships as I can. I mean to form a syndicate. That takes time, and I need to find someone at Barret's who can vouch for me, and time is moving quickly."

"Now, that's an ambitious plan," said James. He picked up a small bell and rang it. Within a heartbeat, the door opened and the Duke's secretary said, "My lord?"

"How much gold is young von Darkmoor owed by the Kingdom?"

"He has nearly a thousand gold sovereigns in back pay coming, my lord."

James rubbed his chin. "Pay him a thousand, and"—he narrowed his gaze—"advance him another two thousand against what we're going to be paying him over the next year."

If the secretary was curious why, he said nothing, only bowing slightly and closing the door. Before it was completely shut, Duke James said, "And send for my grandson Dash."

"Yes, my lord," came the reply as the door shut.

The Duke stood and said, "My two grandsons have come from the court in Rillanon to serve with me. Their parents are still in the capital, as my son must tidy up a few things before joining us." He circled around his desk and said, "James, the eldest, has a strong appetite for the army, like his Great-Uncle William." James smiled. "But Dashel is . . . well, let's say I'm looking for the proper undertaking to engage his . . . unusual talents."

He put his hand on Roo's shoulder. "Do you think you could use a clever lad in this soon-to-be-booming enterprise you're building, Mr. Avery?"

Roo wanted to hire a noble's grandchild as much as he wanted a boil on his backside, but sensing the way this conversation was heading, he said, "My lord, I would be more than happy to have a bright and talented lad join my concern . . . as an apprentice, you understand. I can't show favoritism because he's of high station."

James laughed at that. "Rupert, if you had any idea of my history—never mind. I think you'll find the boy a quick study, and he's getting a bit underfoot around here."

A knock came from the door and James said, "Come in."

The door opened and a young man stepped through. Roo glanced back and forth between the Duke and his grandson. The resemblance was striking. They were of equal height, though the boy might be a finger's width taller. Save for the age, they could have been brothers, not grandfather and grandson. But where the Duke had a beard, the lad was clean-shaven, and where the Duke had nearly white hair, the youth had curly brown locks.

"How would you like to try your hand at commerce?" asked the Duke.

"What do you have up your sleeve, Grandfather?" responded the youngster.

"Something that will keep you out of the gambling halls and taverns, Dash. Meet your new employer, Mr. Avery."

Roo nodded. The young man seemed wryly amused at the news that he was now an employee of Avery and Sons, but he merely nodded. "Sir" was all he said.

"Now, go with Mr. Avery, and when you get to Barret's, ask to see Jerome Masterson. Introduce yourselves and say this, that I would count it a great personal favor if he could facilitate whatever Mr. Avery needs done to establish his little syndicate."

To Roo he said, "Good luck, and I hope you don't go broke too quickly." To Erik he said, "I hope you can find a day when you can enjoy all this immense wealth Rupert is going to put aside for you until you return."

Erik nodded, "I'll say yea to that, sir."

To Dash the Duke said, "Come by and visit us from time to time, you rogue."

The young man said, "That means you're throwing me out of the palace again?"

James laughed. "Something like that. You're Mr. Avery's apprentice until he fires you, so you'll be living wherever he puts you."

Roo thought of the already cramped quarters shared by Luis,

Duncan, and Jason, but said nothing. The three men left the Duke's office, and Roo found he could hardly breathe, he was so excited by the prospects of the coming opportunity.

He barely heard Erik's good-bye as he left the city gate, the grandson of the most powerful noble in the Kingdom at his side, his new apprentice.

Thirteen

Gamble

R OO CLEARED HIS THROAT.

The door waiter turned and Roo winced as he saw it was Kurt. His old nemesis narrowed his gaze and said, "What do you want?"

"I would like to speak with Jerome Masterson," said Roo evenly, ignoring Kurt's lack of civility.

Kurt raised one eyebrow but said nothing. He turned and whispered something to another waiter, a new boy unknown to Roo, who nodded and hurried off. "Wait here," said Kurt, walking away.

"Surly bugger, isn't he?" said Dash.

"You don't know the half of it," said Roo.

The second waiter and Kurt returned a few minutes later, and Kurt said, "Mr. Masterson regrets that his schedule at this time doesn't present an opportunity to speak with you. Perhaps some other time."

Roo's temper began to flare. "Let me guess, Kurt. You neglected to specify who was asking to see him." Roo pushed through the swinging railing and Kurt backed away a step.

"Don't make me send for the City Watch, Avery!" warned Kurt.

Kurt motioned for the young waiter to come closer, and with some hesitancy, he did. "What did you say to Mr. Masterson?"

The boy glanced at Kurt, then Roo. "I told him what Kurt said to tell him: a former waiter wished a word with him."

"That's what I thought," said Roo. He instructed the boy, "Return and say to Mr. Masterson that Rupert Avery of Avery and Son and the grandson of the Duke of Krondor would appreciate a moment of his time."

At mention of the Duke, Dash made a theatrical half-bow, with a wicked grin, and Kurt's face drained of color. He glanced at the now totally confused waiter and said, "Do it!"

Two men returned with the waiter a few moments later. To Rupert's surprise and pleasure, one of them was Sebastian Lender. "Young Avery," said Lender, holding out his hand. They shook.

"Gentlemen, may I present Dashel, grandson of the Duke of Krondor and the newest member of my company."

"And may I present Jerome Masterson," said Lender, referring to the stocky man at his side. Masterson wore a short-cut black beard shot with grey, and his hair was cut straight at his collar. His clothing was finely made but of plain design, and he wore a minimum of jewelry.

"Please, come with me," said Masterson, leading them into the main room of the coffee house.

As they left a gaping Kurt behind, Roo turned and said, "My cousin Duncan will be along sometime soon. Please show him to our table the moment he arrives."

The order for coffee was put in as they settled around a large table in the corner, and Masterson said, "Your grandfather and I are old friends, Dash. Boyhood friends."

Dash grinned. "I think I understand."

Roo did as well. Given what he overheard that night outside the headquarters of the leader of the Mockers, he guessed that the Duke wasn't the only former thief to have migrated to a lawful existence. Then there was always the chance that despite his proper appearance, he was still a thief.

Masterson said, "You look enough like him . . . it's uncanny. Do you take after him in other ways?" he asked with a wink.

Dash laughed. "I've climbed a wall or two in my time, but I've never picked up the knack for cutting purses. My mother frowned on that sort of thing."

They all laughed, and the coffee was served. As each man fixed his cup the way he liked it, Lender said, "So, Mr. Avery. I was conducting some routine business with one of my clients when your message came to us. What is this about?"

Roo glanced at Masterson, who nodded. "Lender is my litigator and solicitor, so he would be here even if you didn't know him. I am right in assuming this isn't a social call, am I not?"

"You are indeed, sir," said Roo. Clearing his throat, he said, "I am looking to form a syndicate."

Lender glanced at Masterson, and then asked, "You mean join a syndicate?"

"No, I mean to form one specifically for an investment."

Masterson said, "I am a partner in several. It might be far easier to propose you as a member of one than to build one from scratch."

Roo said, "I only worked here a short time, but as I understand the workings of such, if I join a syndicate and propose a venture and the partners vote it down, then I'm out of luck."

"Yes, that's true," said Masterson.

"But if I propose the creation of one for the specific purpose of the venture, then only those who wish to participate will accept partnership, and we go forward."

"That is also true," said Lender.

"Well, before we rush down that avenue," said Masterson, "let's hear something about your venture so I can judge the wisdom of starting from scratch."

Roo hesitated, but it was Dash who spoke. "You're going to have to tell someone sooner or later, Mr. Avery."

Roo sighed. His biggest fear was of telling someone in a position to take advantage of the news without benefiting himself. He knew it unlikely from anyone who was recommended by the Duke and a client of Lender's, but he still hesitated.

"Go on," said Lender.

"I mean to underwrite shipping."

"There are dozens of such syndicates already," said Masterson. "Why do we need a new one?"

"I want to specialize in grain shipments to the Free Cities."

Masterson and Lender looked at each other. Masterson said, "That's usually a fairly short-gain, low-risk venture, young man— unless the Quegans are in a raiding mood. But as they've been quiet of late, one must suspect you've a different reason to wish to specialize in a relatively dull enterprise."

Roo colored a bit. "I have reason to believe that the demand for such transport is likely to go up soon and that there will be a very heavy increase in shipping to the Free Cities, so I thought I would be in a position to set up some multiple-voyage underwriting."

Masterson looked at Lender. "The lad knows something." Leaning forward, he lowered his voice. "Out with it, Rupert. I give you my word that whatever it is, you shall be entitled to a full share based on both your participation and your news."

Roo glanced at the other three faces and quietly said, "Locusts."

"I knew it!" said Masterson, slapping the table.

Lender said, "You knew there were locusts in the Free Cities?"

"No," answered Masterson. "I knew there was something that gave him an edge." Again lowering his voice, he said, "There's a type of insect called the twenty-year locust that breeds out there. They're due next year, but sometimes they come a year early and sometimes they come a year late. Any news they are in fact on their way . . ." Masterson looked up and signaled to a waiter, who hurried over. Masterson said, "Would you see if Mr. Crowley and Mr. Hume are upstairs, please? If they are, ask them to please join us."

Turning to Roo, Masterson said, "How reliable is your source?"

Roo was loath to tell him the news was from a fugitive sea trader dealing in stolen gems. "I'd say it's fairly reliable."

Masterson stroked his beard. "There are several ways to play this. Each matches risk to reward."

Two men approached and Masterson indicated they should sit. He introduced everyone. Hume and Crowley were a pair of investors who had participated in several different syndicates with Masterson.

"Our young friend here"—he indicated Roo—"brings us word of a shortage of grain in the Free Cities. How do you react to that news?"

"How much of a shortage?" asked Crowley, a thin, suspicious-looking fellow.

Roo lowered his voice and once again said, "Locusts."

"Who is your source?" asked Hume, a soft-looking man with a wheezing in his chest.

"A Quegan trader put in at Sarth two weeks ago and mentioned in passing to a business associate of mine that they had been found on a farm outside Margrave's Port."

Masterson said, "That would be the logical place for them to first show up."

"If it's as bad as when I was a boy," said Hume, "they could

spread up to Ylith and into Yabon. There would be serious short-
ages in the West."

"And if they go over the mountains into the Far Coast region,
even more," said Crowley.

Masterson turned to face Roo. "There are three basic ways we
can approach this news, my young friend." He held up a finger.
"We can attempt to buy grain now, storing it away in warehouses,
and wait for the demand to increase." He held up a second finger.
"We can do as you suggest and underwrite the cost of shipping
the grain to the Far Coast, making our profit irrespective of the
profit potential in each shipment of grain." He held up the third
finger. "Or we can try to control the grain without purchasing it."

"Options?" said Crowley.

Nodding, Masterson said to Roo. "Do you know about options?"

Roo decided trying to appear more clever than he was would
work against him in this situation. "Not really."

"We agree to buy grain at a price from a group of growers here
in the area. But rather than buy it, we purchase the right to buy
it, for a small part of the costs. If we fail to purchase it, we lose
the option money.

"The benefit is that we can control a huge amount of grain for
a relatively small amount of gold."

"But the risk is you lose everything if the price goes down,"
said Dash.

"Yes," said Crowley. "You do understand."

Masterson said, "I propose we hedge our positions by buying
some grain at market, options on the rest."

"What about the underwriting?" said Roo.

Masterson said, "I've never been keen on underwriting. Ships
sink. If what you say turns out to be true, we'll be sending grain
out on anything that floats, and some of the craft will likely sink.
Let someone else assume the risk and we'll pay a tiny premium."
Masterson was quiet a moment, then said, "I think we option the
entire amount. What hedge we have with grain purchase is trivial
if the price doesn't rise. We diminish our risk by little, but we
diminish our profit potential a great deal."

Hume sighed. "You always win at cards, too." He thought a
moment. "But you make sense. If we are to gamble, then let us
gamble."

Crowley said, "Agreed."

This was all going too quickly for Roo, and he said, "How much will this cost?"

"How much gold do you have?" asked Crowley.

Roo tried to remain calm as he said, "I can put about twenty thousand sovereigns on the table this week."

Masterson said, "A tidy sum. Between us we can raise a hundred thousand. That should prove sufficient for our needs."

"What's our potential gain?" asked Dash, ignoring the fact he was considered Roo's assistant.

Hume laughed and coughed. "If there is a massive grain short-age in the Free Cities, a five-to-one return is not out of the question. If it spreads to Yabon and Crydee, ten-to-one is not outside possibility."

Masterson added, "If all goes as we hope, young Mr. Avery, your twenty thousand golden sovereigns could be two hundred thousand within the next three months."

Roo was almost speechless, but then Lender said, "Or it could be nothing."

Roo felt a cold chill run up his back.

Masterson said, "I propose a new syndicate, gentlemen. We shall be the Krondor Grain Traders Association. Would you draw up the papers, Mr. Lender?"

Then he turned to Roo and stuck out his hand. "Welcome to our syndicate, Mr. Avery."

Roo stood and solemnly shook hands with his three new business partners. As the other men moved away from the table, Masterson said, "We'll post your name as a member, and you'll be able to join us up there." He pointed to the private upper gallery, restricted to members only. Roo had served coffee up there, but would never have been allowed to set foot there otherwise. "I'll see you to the door."

Lender left as well, and Masterson put his hand on Roo's shoulder as they walked toward the main entrance. "When can you have your gold here, Rupert?"

"Within the next two days, Mr. Masterson."

"Call me Jerome."

"Call me Roo; everyone does."

"Very well, Roo. Get it here as soon as possible, and Lender will send word to your office when the papers are ready to be signed."

As they reached the door, Roo saw Duncan entering through one door. Through the other came an older man, whom Roo recognized as Jacob Esterbrook. But next to him walked a young woman so beautiful that Roo almost stumbled. He saw Duncan's mouth open at the sight of her.

She was perfect, thought Roo. Her hair was done up in a current fashion that framed her face in curls, and ringlets hung down the back of her head, a halo of gold. Her eyes were enormous and the blue of late winter skies, and her cheeks held a hint of blush. Her figure was slender and she carried herself like royalty.

"Ah, Esterbrook!" said Masterson. "There's someone here I want you to meet."

Esterbrook nodded as Masterson opened the swinging gate at the rail, ignoring the flustered-looking waiter who had tried to get there first after opening the door of the carriage from which the Esterbrooks had descended.

"Sylvia," said Masterson, nodding in greeting.

"Good day, Mr. Masterson," said the girl with a smile that made Roo's blood pound.

"Jacob Esterbrook," said Masterson, "one of our most important members, may I present to you our newest member, Mr. Rupert Avery."

Esterbook's expression remained unchanged. But something about his eyes bothered Roo. Esterbrook said, "Grindle and Avery?"

Roo said, "It's now Avery and Son, sir." He held out his hand.

Esterbrook regarded the proffered hand a moment, then shook, a quick grip and release that made it clear this was no more than a formality. Something in his manner communicated to Roo that Mr. Esterbrook didn't think much of Barret's newest member.

Then Roo caught himself being regarded coolly by Sylvia, and now he was certain: the Esterbrooks of Krondor didn't particularly care for the company of one Rupert Avery. Roo slowly turned toward Dash, while finding himself unable to take his eyes off Sylvia. "Ah . . ." he began. "May I present my new assistant?"

Sylvia leaned forward ever so slightly, as if to hear better. "Yes?" she asked quietly.

Dash took control. "Dashel," he said with a smile and deep bow. "I believe you know my grandfather."

Esterbrook said, "Indeed?"

"Duke James," said Dash with feigned innocence.

Instantly Esterbrook's and his daughter's manner changed. He smiled and she beamed, and as her smile broadened, Rupert felt his pulse pound even more furiously. "Of course," said Esterbrook, taking Dash's hand and gripping it warmly. "Please remember me to your grandfather when next you speak with him."

Sylvia turned her radiant smile on Roo. "You must come to dinner soon, Mr. Avery. I insist."

Roo could barely speak as he nodded. "I would love to."

Dash turned to Masterson with a grin. "We must be going, sir. We'll be back tomorrow."

"Good day, then," said Masterson, the farewell echoed by Esterbrook and his daughter.

Dash gently propelled Roo out the door and reached out to take Duncan's arm and turn him around as they stepped through the portal into the street. To the gaping cousins he said, "You'd think you two had never seen a pretty face before."

Roo reached home late that night. It had taken half the day to deal with the news that Duncan had returned with, that it would be both possible and dangerous to dispose of the drugs but that the profit potential was very high. Katherine had also been unable to provide the name of anyone who might consider such a purchase.

Then there was the matter of housing Dash. Roo promised that he would secure quarters for Luis and Duncan in a few days, allowing Jason and Dash to share the apartment, but for the time being the newest addition to their company's roster would have to sleep in a makeshift loft above the wagons in the warehouse. If the grandson of the most powerful noble in the Kingdom was discomfited by this revelation, he hid it in good humor. Roo suspected he had seen rougher quarters during his relatively short life. He thought in passing about his asking if he was being tossed out of the palace *again*.

Jason and Roo had sat up for a couple of hours plotting the quick disposal of the gems gained in Sarth. A message was prepared for a gem broker in Salador who had been an old trading companion of Helmut Grindel's, outlining in detail what Roo had to offer, and by the time that had been disposed of, it was after dark.

Roo made it home and used his key to unlock the door. He saw that everyone was already in bed and quietly made his way up-stairs. In the gloom he saw Karli asleep in the bed. There was a tiny shape next to her, and he leaned close. Then he saw the baby.

In the murk of the unlit room the child was little more than a featureless, blanket-wrapped lump, and Roo could barely make out the little bump of her nose. He waited for some strong emotion to come sweeping up out of a natural paternal well, but nothing came. Then he looked at his sleeping wife and again felt close to nothing. Standing back upright, he sighed. It was the fatigue, he told himself. And his mind rushed with concern over the coming investments. If he was being a fool, he would lose everything he had built over the last two years. While he was young and could start over again, he knew that a failure now would rob him of any future chance for greatness and riches.

As he removed his boots, a soft voice said, "Roo?"

He grunted as he dropped one boot upon the floor. "Yes," he whispered. "I'm back."

"How . . . are you?" she asked.

"Tired," he said. "I have a lot to tell you, but in the morning."

The baby stirred, then suddenly it was crying, and Roo asked, "What is wrong?"

Karli sat up in the dark and said, "Nothing. She's hungry. That's all. She needs to eat during the night, two or three times."

Roo sat upon a small chair, one boot on, the other off, and said, "How long does this go on?"

Karli said, "For the next four months, maybe longer."

Roo stood, picked up his boot, and said, "I'm going to sleep in your old room. There's no reason for both of us to be exhausted tomorrow and I have a great deal to do. I'll tell you about it when I get up."

He closed the door behind him and moved to Karli's old bed-room. Stripping off his clothing, he fell into the bed where he and Karli had created their baby, and in the dark his mind raced: first exultation at the prospect of ten years' profits in a few months, then terror that he would be destitute instead. Next he plotted how he would expand once the profits were his, and then he felt fear creep up as he thought how best to recover from the coming disaster. But more and more as sleep approached, he found his mind's eye returning to the image of a wonderful face, with large blue eyes and golden hair, and a laugh that made his stomach knot. Sleep finally came with the dawn.

Roo came downstairs, his head as fuzzy as if he had been drinking the night before. He found Karli in the kitchen, nursing Abigail, and he kissed her dutifully upon the cheek. "We've missed you," said Karli.

"It's good to be back," he said as Rendel, the cook, poured him a steaming cup of coffee. He had developed the habit of starting the day with a cup while working at Barret's, and had purchased beans for grinding when he first came to live in the house.

He studied the baby. The tiny figure lay in her mother's arms, her hands moving in random directions, her tiny eyes opening and closing. From time to time she would look in his direction, and he would wonder what was going on behind those slate-blue orbs. "I've never seen eyes that color," he said.

Karli laughed. "Most babies have eyes like this. They'll turn brown or blue when she's older."

"Oh" was all he said.

"You had a good journey?" she asked.

"Very," he answered. "I came across some information." He fell silent for a few moments, then blurted, "I'm forming a trading syndicate."

Karli said, "Father was always cautious in tying up his future with others."

Roo was in no mood to be compared to his dead father-in-law, whom Karli almost worshipped, but he took the comment as if it were merely an observation. "That discounts risk," he agreed. "But I have ambitions beyond your father's, Karli, and if I'm to realize a rich future for you and the child, I must take some risks."

"Is this venture risky?" she asked. She didn't seem overly concerned but rather interested.

Roo couldn't convincingly shrug it off, so he just said, "Yes."

"You think this will work out?"

Roo nodded. "I think we're going to be richer than you can imagine in a few months."

She managed a small smile. "I always thought we were rich; I know the house isn't much to look at, but Father always liked to keep a modest appearance, lest it attract undue notice. But we always had good food, wine, new clothing. If I wanted anything, I only had to ask."

Roo's fatigue and nerves made this conversation irritating. He finished his coffee and stood. "I have to get to the shop." He again kissed her dutifully on the cheek and glanced down at the now sleeping baby. It appeared so alien to Roo he wondered if he would ever feel anything for the child.

"Will you be home for supper?" Karli asked.

"Certainly," he said. "Why wouldn't I be?"

He didn't wait for a reply as he hurried out the door.

Duncan hailed Roo as he walked into the shop. "Where have you been?"

Roo looked irritated. "Sleeping. You know, when you close your eyes and don't move for a long time?"

Duncan grinned and said, "Oh, you mean dead. Look, your new business partners would like you to come to Barret's at once."

"Jason!" Roo yelled as he turned away from his cousin. "Where are you?"

Jason and Dash came out of the small office and Jason said, "Yes?"

"Where's our gold? In the strongbox?"

"Yes."

"How much do we have?"

"We have accounts due in later this week, but right now you have twenty-one thousand, six hundred, and forty-seven gold pieces, and a few silver coins."

Roo told Dash and Duncan, "Put the box in a wagon and bring it to the coffee house. I'm leaving now."

He hurried out through the front of the shop and down the street. Moving through the crowd was as trying an ordeal as Roo had ever known, so impatient was he to get this business done.

He reached the coffee house and walked straight past the door waiter, who blinked as Roo admitted himself to the main floor.

McKeller, the headwaiter, was moving toward him, and as Roo moved toward the stairs to the second floor, he said, "Welcome, Mr. Avery."

Roo couldn't help but grin. He was a member! He mounted the stairs two at a time and reached the top landing, where before he had always come carrying a large serving tray. He glanced around and saw Masterson's table, and his three new partners and Lender sitting there.

"Glad you could join us," said Masterson dryly.

"I hope you gentlemen haven't been waiting too long," said Roo as he sat. "I have a new baby in the house and things are a bit confused. I didn't get much sleep last night."

All four men made understanding noises and brief comments about their own children, then Masterson said, "Here we have it, gentlemen: the document forming our new trading syndicate." He handed copies around and Roo looked at the neatly executed script.

Roo read it twice, and he thought he understood it, but he wasn't sure. He pointed to a paragraph and said, "Mr. Lender, would you explain this to me, please?"

Lender looked at the indicated paragraph. "That simply pledges your goods and other chattels against any losses beyond those secured by whatever gold you bring to this accounting."

Roo blinked. "How could we go into debt beyond what we agree to?"

Masterson said, "We usually don't, but there are instances when circumstances require a decision on the basis of the partnership, and sometimes we must establish lines of credit. If we need cash and don't have it, a moneylender or admitting new partners are the only alternatives. If we take loans, we often must pledge our personal businesses, even our homes and family heirlooms as security. It's normal."

Roo frowned but said nothing. Then he asked, "But no one can do this without our agreement?"

Masterson smiled. "There are four of us. It would take a three-to-one majority to do so."

Roo was uncertain, but he nodded. Lender said, "If each of you will sign the document before him and pass it to your right, then sign again, we'll have all these copies executed."

A waiter appeared and Roo ordered coffee without looking up. He signed his name four times, and when he was done, he held his admission to the high-risk financial community of the city.

"Now," said Crowley, "to the sums."

Hume said, "I am comfortable with a position of fifteen thousand sovereigns."

Crowley said, "Fifteen is fine with me."

Masterson said, "Mr. Avery?"

"Twenty-one thousand. But I may have more by the end of the week."

Masterson raised an eyebrow. "Very well. So far that means fifty-one thousand." He drummed his fingers on the table a moment. "I have heard this morning of some cautious inquiries about grain shipments to the Free Cities, so I'm beginning to think our young friend is on to something. I will occupy a position that will take the syndicate to one hundred thousand golden sovereigns." He looked at his three partners. "If any of you would care to underwrite more, I will surrender up to a third of my position for a premium, depending on the price of wheat at the time."

Lender said, "Gentlemen, your letters of credit?"

The three men reached into their coats and withdrew letters. Roo looked confused. "I'm having the gold brought here. It will arrive in a few minutes."

The three men laughed. "Mr. Avery," said Lender, "it is usual to keep one's gold in an account at one of the countinghouses in the city, and to draw upon the funds with letters of credit." He lowered his voice. "You'll discover that here at Barret's we deal in sums that would require several wagons of gold to carry if we were to require the gold actually to be present."

Roo looked unsure but said, "I have no such account."

Lender said, "I will help you establish one at one of the more reputable moneylending firms in the city. I will note that you intend to participate to the amount of twenty-one thousand golden sovereigns."

Roo nodded. "Though if more arrives later this week, I may wish to purchase some of Mr. Masterson's . . . position."

Lender nodded and noted that.

"Then we are ready?" said Masterson.

Roo sat back. He had witnessed what was to come next on several occasions as he waited tables, not quite certain about the details of what was occurring, but never before had he had such a keen interest in what was happening.

Lender stood and walked to the rail overlooking the center floor and raised his voice. "Gentlemen, we have a request for an option on wheat. A new syndicate has formed, the Krondor Grain Traders Association. We close our books at the end of the week, best price position to a sum of one hundred thousand sovereigns, subject to revision."

There was a slight buzz at the price, but then the noise in the room returned to normal. The five men sat, and after a half hour passed, a waiter arrived bearing a note. He handed it to Lender, who handed it to Masterson, who read it. He said, "We have an offer of fifty thousand bushels at two silvers per bushel delivered to the docks of Krondor in sixty days."

Roo did the calculations in his head. That was ten thousand gold pieces. Hume asked, "What position?"

"Fifteen percent."

Crowley laughed. "Let me guess. That was from Amested."

Masterson laughed in return. "Yes."

"He's fishing," said Crowley. "He thinks we're onto something and wants to know what it is."

He took the paper from Masterson and scribbled a note on it. "I'm telling him we'll pay three percent for fifty thousand at four coppers per bushel, with a five-percent-per-week penalty for late delivery after sixty days."

Masterson almost snorted his coffee. He laughed. "You're going to make him very curious."

"Let him wonder."

Hume looked at Roo. "You'll meet Amested and the others below in time. He's always trying to find out who is doing what, without taking risks himself. If he thinks there's a killing, he'll try to buy the wheat now, at what we call future prices, and then hold it for us at an inflated price, after we've exhausted our options. He offered us a price he knew we'd say no to, and we just made a counteroffer that we know he'll say no to."

Roo said, "But why not offer him a price he'll say yes to?"

Masterson said, "Your meaning?"

"I mean his coins are gold, as much as any man's, and we don't care if he makes or loses money in this as long as we make ours. If we can use this man to set a price and he comments upon it, and the word gets out . . ." Roo shrugged.

Crowley's leathery old face split in a wide grin. "You're a shrewd young one, aren't you, Avery?"

Masterson held out his hand, and Crowley handed back the note. Masterson balled it up and threw it away and indicated the young waiter should bring him new parchment and pen. When that was delivered, he wrote a note. "I'm telling him what we'll pay, straight out. Ten percent against a price of one silver per bushel delivered at the docks in sixty days. We guarantee up to one million gold sovereigns with a security of one hundred thousand."

Old Hume was now almost splitting his sides trying to control his laughter. "This is priceless. It's exactly what we're doing, but now old Amested will be certain we're lying to him and be trying to figure out what it is we're really up to."

The waiter was given the note and instructed to carry it back to the sender of the earlier note. A few minutes later, Duncan and Dash appeared, carrying the chest of gold. They required the help of two waiters and Lender stood up at once, saying, "We'd better get that treasure to a countinghouse before raiders come looking for us."

The gold was deposited and accounted, and a letter of credit in the amount of twenty-one thousand golden sovereigns was provided to Roo, who turned it over to Lender. Then they returned to the coffee house.

Over the course of the day, notes would appear and Masterson would read them, comment on them, and occasionally write a reply. Once in a while he would simply say, "No," and hand the note back to the waiter.

At the end of the day, he stood and said, "This has been a good start, gentlemen. I shall see you tomorrow."

Roo rose and discovered that Dash and Duncan had spent the entire day downstairs, waiting for him. He cursed himself for a fool. His own anxiety over this investment had completely occupied his mind and made him forget he had a freight business to conduct.

"Head back to the office and tell Jason I'm on my way," he said to Dash. When the young nobleman was gone, Roo said to Duncan, "Why don't you go looking for a nice pair of rooms for you and Luis. Our accounts are settled and I can pay to get you into more comfortable quarters at once."

Duncan grinned. "About time." Then he said, "If we're to be spending time with people of quality, cousin, we need to do something about our wardrobes."

Suddenly Roo felt shabby for the first time in his life. He said, "In the morning."

As Duncan ran off, Roo looked around Barret's, drinking in the fact that he was now an investor. As he made to leave, a voice sounded out of the shadows of a table back under the overhang. "Mr. Avery, a word with you, sir."

Avery recognized the voice of Jacob Esterbrook and moved toward the table. At the table he saw two figures, and his pulse began to race as he recognized the other man as Tim Jacoby.

Jacoby looked at Roo and said nothing as Esterbrook said, "I believe you know my business associate, Mr. Jacoby?"

Roo said, "We've met."

Esterbrook said, "I hope that in the future you gentlemen will put aside your differences." He made no pretense of not knowing there was bad blood between Roo and Tim. "It would be my most sincere wish to see such differences vanish in the future."

Jacoby stood and looked at Roo, saying nothing to him. To Esterbrook he said, "I'll pay my respects tomorrow, Jacob."

After he left, Esterbrook said, "Sit down, please."

Roo did, and after signaling for some more coffee, Esterbrook said, "Mr. Jacoby's father and I are old business associates, and more, friends. Frederick and I started out together, here in Krondor. We began as teamsters."

Roo said, "My father was a teamster."

For the first time since Roo met the man, Jacob Esterbrook looked at him with genuine interest. He asked, "Is that so?"

Roo nodded.

"Can you drive a team, Mr. Avery?"

Roo smiled and said, "I can drive a team, Mr. Esterbrook. Six horses without breaking a sweat, eight if I keep my mind on things."

The man laughed, a genuine sound of amusement and perhaps

even with a hint of affection. "A teamster. Imagine that." He sighed. "Perhaps that's why my daughter finds you so interesting."

At mention of Esterbrook's daughter, Roo found his heart pounding. He forced himself to remain as calm as possible. "Oh?" he said, trying to sound only mildly interested.

"Sylvia is a . . . difficult child," said Esterbrook. "A young woman with a mind of her own. I have little understanding of what captures her fancy. Which brings me to my reason for asking you to join me. She requests you join us for supper at the end of this week. Will you?"

Roo didn't hesitate. "Certainly."

"Good," said Esterbrook, sipping his coffee. "Then we can discuss what we shall do if you find you must kill Mr. Jacoby."

Roo felt as if a cold bucket of water had been thrown on him. Calmly he said, "Oh, I shall someday kill him, have no doubt. He murdered my partner."

Esterbrook shrugged, as if that were of little importance. "Well, if we can find a way to avoid that, my lot in life would be easier." He put down the cup. "And be warned, while you are presently well connected at the palace, you are not the only one. My friend Frederick Jacoby also counts powerful men as friends." Leaning over, he whispered, "If you must kill his sons, be discrete about it, will you, now? And if you can manage, some advance warning so I may distance myself from the Jacobys would be appreciated also." Patting Roo on the shoulder, he made his way around the table. "My coach is now outside. I will see you for supper on Fifthday."

Roo sat alone for a minute, wondering at this new world of intrigue he found himself in. The polite manner in which Esterbrook discussed murder bothered him as much as anything he had witnessed during the war.

Then he thought of seeing Sylvia on Fifthday and his heart almost beat out of his chest. Forcing himself to calmness, he realized he must do as Duncan suggested and improve his wardrobe.

He stood up and left, and until he reached his shop and Jason brought matters of trade to his attention, he couldn't stop thinking about Sylvia Esterbrook.

During the week, Roo fell into a routine. He left home at first light, stopped by the shop and went over the day's shipments with

Luis, Duncan, Jason, and Dash, then went on to Barret's. Sometimes Duncan or Dash would accompany him, depending on what else needed to be done at the shop. Other times he went alone.

Duncan had found a small house to rent not too far from the office, with two bedrooms. Roo told him to hire a cook. Jason and Dash spruced up their own quarters at the shop and seemed to be becoming fast friends. While Jason was a few years older than Dash, it was clear from his manner and comments that Dash was old beyond his years and far more worldly than Jason.

Roo followed Duncan's suggestion and visited a tailor recommended to him by Lender. He supplied Roo with clothing fit for both Barret's and social functions. Duncan went for far more colorful clothing, looking nothing so much like a court dandy as a former mercenary.

Jason came to him on the third day after the syndicate was formed and said, "Can I ask you something without causing offense, Mr. Avery?"

Roo said, "Certainly, Jason. You were the only one at Barret's who tried to set me right when Kurt and the others were trying to trip me up; I consider us friends. What is it?"

"What is it exactly that your cousin is doing?"

"What do you mean?"

"I mean Luis is overseeing the shipping schedule, seeing to rates, and making runs, I'm doing all the accounts and paying the workers, and Dash is helping Luis and me when either of us need him. But Duncan, well . . . well, he's just sort of . . . around."

Thinking of the encounter on the road with the driver from Jacoby's and how Duncan could stand at his back with his sword, Roo said, "I understand your concern. Let's just say he helps me. Is there anything else?"

Jason said, "No. I just . . . well, anyway. Are you heading for the coffee house?"

Roo nodded. "I'll be there if you need me for anything."

Roo reached Barret's less than a half hour later only to discover the upper room in quite a minor frenzy. Masterson waved him over to the table and said, "Something is going on."

Several waiters were hovering nearby, taking pieces of paper that were being scribbled upon by Hume and Crowley. "What is it?" asked Roo.

"We're getting offers. Many of them."

Roo's forehead furrowed. "Where are they coming from?"

Masterson said, "Why, from other members."

"No, I mean where is the grain coming from?"

Masterson blinked. "I don't know."

Suddenly Roo felt certain he knew the answer. He took a waiter by the arm and said, "Send a message to my office. I want my cousin Duncan or my assistant Dash here as soon as possible."

To the others he said, "Have we taken any positions?"

"Not yet," said Crowley, "but the price is dropping and I'm inclined to think it's not going to go lower."

"How low?"

"It's down to two silvers for three bushels, at eight percent secured."

Roo lowered his voice. "I'm willing to bet one of the other brokers has sent someone east to the Vale of Dreams. Would you think that price reasonable if someone is bringing Keshian wheat north through the Vale?"

"What makes you think that?" asked Masterson.

Roo said, "Because I'm a sneaky bastard whose father drove a wagon to all parts of the Kingdom, including the border near the Vale."

Soon Duncan showed up and Roo said, "I need you to start hitting inns near the traders' gates. Listen for Valemen. I need to know if anyone has been buying grain in Kesh, who, and how much."

After Duncan hurried off, Crowley said, "Are you using some magic power we're ignorant of, or is this a guess?"

"It's a guess. But before sundown I think we're going to find that as much wheat as we need, twice over, is on it its way west from the Vale."

"Why?" said Hume. "Why do you think that?"

Grimly Roo said, "Because it's what I would do if I wanted to ruin this syndicate." He then asked, "What sort of surety do we get regarding delivery?"

"The options are secured, so if the person offering the option defaults, he is liable under Kingdom law for the entire price, and more, for the gold we'd lose by not being able to ship the grain. To offer a contract and not make delivery would be terribly damaging ... unless ..."

"Unless what?" asked Roo.

"Unless the association that might bring a claim in the King's Court was already out of business and suffering suit for its own failure to meet contracts."

Roo said, "Now I know someone is trying to ruin us." He was silent a moment. "Do we have grounds to refuse the wheat for poor quality?"

Masterson said, "We don't. We can refuse the contract delivery only if the grain is rotten or otherwise damaged. Why?"

"Because they're paying the lowest prices, so they are going to be bringing in the cheapest grain out there." Roo pointed at his three partners. "Who's offering these contracts?"

"Various groups," answered Crowley.

"Who's behind them?"

Masterson's eyes focused on the pile of notes as if trying to discern a pattern. After a moment he said, "Jacob."

Roo felt his chest constrict in panic. "Esterbrook?"

Hume and Crowley said, "Why would he meddle in this?"

Roo said, "My fault, I fear. He might find things more convenient down the road if I were reduced to poverty quickly. Your ruination would be only an unfortunate consequence, nothing personal, I'm certain."

"What do we do?" asked Crowley.

"Well, we can't be buying wheat that even the most venal millers won't buy." Roo considered things for a few minutes in silence, then suddenly he said, "I have it!"

"What?"

"I'll tell you when Duncan returns. Until then, do nothing, buy nothing."

Roo rose and left, determined to sniff out some information on his own. Near sundown he discovered Duncan in an inn, in a corner, sitting quietly at a table with two oddly dressed men, mercenaries by their arms and armor. Duncan waved him over.

"Roo, these friends of mine have an interesting story." Roo noticed that several tankards of ale had been consumed but that Duncan was as sober as the day he was born, and his ale was hardly touched.

Roo sat and introductions were made. The two mercenaries told Roo how they had been hired to guard a fast post rider who carried a message from the city of Shamata to a trader in Krondor regarding the purchase of a huge shipment of grain from down in Kesh. When he was finished, Roo rose. He threw a small pouch of gold on the table and said, "Gentlemen, pay for your room, drinks, and dinner on me. Duncan, come along."

He hurried back to Barret's and found his three partners almost alone in the upper gallery. He sat down and told them, "Someone is bringing a huge shipment of poor-quality grain to Krondor."

"Are you certain?"

Crowley repeated his question of earlier that day. "Why buy grain you can't sell?"

Roo said, "Someone knows we're writing contracts on options. Someone also knows that we must either pay the full price or forfeit the option price. So they bring grain into the city, enough to meet the contract demand, that we refuse to buy. They keep the contract money and dump the grain."

"But they'll lose money!" said Crowley.

"Not that much. But more than offset by the contract price. And if their purpose is to break us, not make a profit, they won't care if they lose a small amount."

Hume said, "That's predatory."

"Very predatory," said Masterson, "and brilliant."

"What do we do?" asked Hume.

Roo said, "Gentlemen, I have been a soldier, and now it's time to test your resolve. Either we can stop buying, and count what we've contracted for so far as a loss, or we can seek to turn this to our advantage. But it will take more gold than we have so far pledged to make this work for us."

"What do you propose?" said Masterson.

"We stop taking contracts. From this moment on, we say no and our counteroffers must be a margin of what is being offered—so low that no one will take our offers, but enough to let them know we are still in business."

"Why?" said Crowley.

"Because each day a huge shipment of grain, sixty wagons being provided by Jacoby and Sons, is working its way to Krondor." He glanced at one of the offer sheets still on the table. "To be delivered at the docks in forty-nine days. Each day that passes, each day that goes without the buyer of that wheat having someone to sell it to, his concern will rise, for if that grain reaches Krondor before all of it is optioned, then that seller will have to dump it in the harbor. Eventually he will sell at our price, assuming that he will still break us."

"How do we counter this?" said Hume.

"We buy every contract in Krondor, gentlemen. If by the time the wheat reaches the city we own every kernel of wheat between here and Ylith, then we can ship the high-quality grain to the Free Cities and the Far Coast, recoup our investment, and make our profit."

"What do we do with the grain from Kesh?" said Masterson.

"We sell it to farmers for their stock, the army, whoever, as fodder. If we can merely break even on that grain, then the rest will make us wealthy beyond our ambition. Twenty-to-one, thirty-to-one—a hundred-to-one return on our investment."

Masterson grabbed a pen and started scribbling. He worked in silence for nearly ten minutes. "Given what we've seen so far, we need at least another two hundred thousand sovereigns. Gentlemen, we need to attract more partners. See to it."

Crowley and Hume hurriedly left the table and Masterson said, "Roo, I hope you're correct."

"What price do we need to reach to make this a can't-fail proposition?"

Jerome Masterson laughed. "If the grain was free, I wouldn't say it was 'can't fail.' We need to store this grain, and if the shortage in the Free Cities doesn't materialize, we may all be driving wagons for Jacoby and Sons before we're done."

"I'll sail back to hell before that," said Roo.

Masterson signaled a waiter and said, "Bring me my special cache of brandy and two glasses." To Roo he said, "Now we wait."

Roo drank the brandy when it appeared and found it excellent.

Masterson looked at some of the pile of notes before him, and frowned.

"What is it?" asked Roo.

"This doesn't make much sense. I think it's a mistake. We're being offered the same contract, basically, twice by the same group." Then he nodded. "Ah, there it is. It's easy to see why I made the mistake. It's not the same group. It just looks like it."

Roo turned his head, as if listening to something. "What did you just say?"

"I said this group looks like that group," he said, pointing to the two notes.

"Why?"

"Because, save for one investor, they're identical."

"Why would they do that?"

"Because they're greedy?" suggested Masterson. He sighed. "Sometimes people offer contracts they have no intention of fulfilling, if they suspect the other party is going to go broke. If they take our money now, and we go under, they'll just shrug when the contract is due. Whom do they deliver to? they'll say." He shrugged. "It may be word is spreading we're in trouble."

"Trouble," repeated Roo. Then a thought occurred to him. After a while a plan formed in his mind. Suddenly he said, "Jerome, I have it!"

"What?" said Masterson.

"I know how we can not only turn this to our profit, but ruin those who are trying to ruin us." He realized he was speaking over the top, and said, "Well, if not ruin them, certainly cause them pain." Then he grinned. "But I do know how we're going to make an obscene profit on this wheat business." He looked Masterson in the eye. "Even if there is no shortage in the Free Cities."

Masterson was suddenly very attentive. Roo said, "I guarantee it."

Fourteen

Surprise

THE RIDER REINED IN.

The farmers walking home from a long day tending their wheat were surprised as he turned his mount in their direction and approached. Without word they spread out and waited, for while it was peaceful times, the rider was obviously armed and one never knew what to expect of strangers.

The rider removed a large-brimmed hat, revealing himself to be a young man with curly brown hair. He smiled and it was also clear he was little more than a boy. "Greetings," he called.

The farmers responded with salutations of their own, little more than grunts. They resumed walking, for these tired workingmen didn't have time to spend in idle chatter with some bored noble's son out for an evening ride.

"How goes the harvest?" asked the youth.

"Well," answered one of the farmers.

"Have you set a price?" asked the rider.

At this all the farmers stopped walking again. The boy was talking about the two things that interested these men most in the world: wheat and money.

"Not yet," said the farmer. "The brokers from Krondor and Ylith won't be here for another two or three weeks."

"How much do you want for your wheat?" asked the boy.

Suddenly the farmers were silent, looking from one to another. Then one asked, "You look like no broker I've met. Are you a miller's son?"

The young man laughed. "Hardly. My grandfather was a thief,

if truth be told. My father . . . is in service to the Duke of Krondor."

"What's your interest?" asked another farmer.

"I represent a man who is seeking to buy wheat, but who is anxious to set a price now."

That set the farmers to talking low among themselves. After a minute, the farmer who had first spoken said, "This is unusual. We're not even sure of the yields yet."

The boy looked from face to face. Finally he pointed to one man and said, "How long have you farmed this land?"

The man said, "My entire life. It was my father's field before me."

"Do you mean to say you don't know to within a bushel how much grain that field will produce in a year like this?"

The man blushed and grinned. "Well, truth to tell, I can."

"So can you all," said the young man. "Here's my offer: set us a price now, and you'll be paid *now*. We'll take delivery at harvest."

The farmers looked amazed. "Get paid now?" asked one.

"Yes."

Suddenly prices were being shouted so fast the rider couldn't understand any. He said, "Enough!" and held up his hand. He dismounted, held out his reins for a farmer, then pulled some writing instruments from his saddlebags.

The first farmer set a price for a thousand bushels of wheat and the rider nodded. He countered and the dickering was on. When they were done, he wrote down names on the parchment he had taken from his saddlebags. Next to each agreed-upon price and amount he had them make their marks, and then began to count out pieces of gold.

As the rider left, the farmers could not believe their luck. While the price wasn't the best possible, it was fair, and they had the money now.

As Dash rode north, he felt sore in his back and shoulders. He had been to a dozen villages like this one over the last three days and knew that Duncan, Roo, and Luis were doing as he was. But he knew if he rode hard he could make the last village before Sarth just after sundown, which meant that after some dickering with the locals over wheat prices, he could pass along some messages to John Vinci for Roo, sleep a sound night in an inn, then return to Krondor in the morning.

He put heels to the flank of his mount and took her to a tired trot as the sun sank in the west.

As the week ended, four tired riders returned to Krondor and met at Roo's warehouse. Dash grinned as he said, "If there's a grain of wheat between here and Sarth we don't own, it's in some horse's nosebag."

Luis said, "The same for here to Land's End."

Duncan said, "I don't know if I bought all the wheat between here and the Vale route, but I spent all the gold you gave me." He handed his cousin his list of farms and prices.

Roo said, "I did the same from here to the foothills." He looked at the accounts and said, "If this doesn't work, we may want to reconsider joining the King's Army."

Dash said, "I have other options." With a grin, he added, "I hope."

Roo said, "I have to get home and change. I'm dining with Jacob Esterbrook tonight."

Dash and Duncan exchanged glances. Duncan's face turned unreadable, while Dash just continued to grin. Jason asked, "Do you think Sylvia will be there?"

Roo smiled. "I'm counting on it."

Luis's brow furrowed at that, but he said nothing.

Roo left the shop and hurried home. He found Karli in the sitting room, rocking the baby and singing a tune to her. Roo halted and walked quietly into the room, seeing that the baby was sleeping.

Karli whispered, "She's been fussy." Roo kissed his wife on the cheek. "Did your plan go well?"

"We'll know within a week."

"I would love to hear about it over supper. She should sleep awhile."

Roo blushed. "In all the frenzy, I neglected to tell you I'm dining out tonight. I am sorry."

Karli said, "You just got home."

"I know, but it's important. More business."

Karli said, "Business, tonight?"

Roo's exhaustion, his anxiety, and his impatience to see Sylvia Esterbrook again came together and caused him to speak more harshly than he had intended. "Yes! Business tonight! I'm having supper with one of the most important investors in the Kingdom!"

Abigail started awake and began to cry at her father's loud voice. Karli's eyes flashed anger, but her voice was a controlled hiss as she said, "Shush. You've woken your daughter."

Roo wave his hand. "I'm sorry. Deal with her. I've got to clean up and change." Turning his back, he shouted, "Mary! I need a tub of hot water!"

His shout caused his daughter to cry even louder. Karli's face was a mask of control, but her eyes never left her husband's back as he vanished up the stairs to clean up for his dinner engagement.

Roo hurried, and despite having bathed he felt hot and sweaty under his new clothing. He paused before the gate to the Esterbrook house. He should have driven out in a hired carriage instead of riding out, he thought. Instead of showing up at the Esterbrook door calm and relaxed, he was nearly breathless.

He knocked and almost instantly the postern door in the gate opened and a groom stepped through. "Yes?"

"I am Rupert Avery. I'm to dine with Mr. Esterbrook," answered Roo.

"Yes, sir," said the groom, and he disappeared through the small door. A moment later the gate swung wide.

Roo rode into the grounds of the Esterbrook estate and he was dutifully impressed. The house was located on a hillside on the eastern edge of the city, high enough above the next estate that it felt almost rural, though it had taken Roo only a half hour to ride there. The high stone wall had masked the house from his view as he had ridden up the narrow road, except for a small tower of some sort.

Now Roo could see that the tower was actually a constructed observation platform, with a small peaked roof, but with windows looking in four directions. Roo wondered why it was there, then considered it was a perfect place from which to observe the comings and goings at both the caravansarais to the southeast and ships in the harbor. Two moons had risen, and Roo saw a glint of metal and smiled to himself as he dismounted and handed the reins of his horse to the groom. Esterbrook must have one of those clever viewing glasses up there.

The house otherwise was what he had expected. Two stories in height, it was large, but not palatial by any measure. There were gardens, as Roo could smell blooms in the evening. Lights appeared at several windows and there were sounds of activity from within.

Roo knocked on the door and it opened a moment later. Expecting a servant, Roo was rendered nearly breathless by the sight of Sylvia Esterbrook herself answering his knock.

"Mr. Avery," she said with a smile that made his stomach hurt. She wore a deep-plunging gown that revealed she wasn't quite as slender as Roo had thought. It was a pale blue designed to highlight her eyes.

She wore a necklace of diamonds and no other jewelry. Roo barely got "hello" out as he stepped inside.

"May I take your cloak?" she asked.

Roo fumbled with the tie at his neck and then finally got the new cloak unfastened. "Father is waiting for you in his private room. Down the hall and to the left," she said, pointing out the way. "I'll hang this up and see to supper."

Roo watched as she vanished through a door to the right, and he forced himself to take a deep breath. Totally intoxicated by the sight of the girl, he knew that dealing with her father was as dangerous as going into combat.

Roo made his way along the hall, glancing through two open doors to see modest rooms with single beds, tables, and nightstands. Servant's quarters? he wondered.

He reached the large door at the end of the hall, barely seen in the dim hallway—only a single candle on a table halfway along the hall's length illuminated the way. From inside, a voice said, "Enter, please."

Roo opened the large door and stepped inside. Jacob Esterbrook was rising from behind a large desk in the middle of what Roo could only consider a library. He had seen a room in the Prince's palace once when he was training there that had as many books, and was astonished to discover that someone who wasn't royalty had this many in his possession. The room was lit by a pair of candles, one on Esterbrook's desk and another on a reading stand set against the wall opposite the door, two pools of light in the otherwise dark library.

As he approached the desk, in the dim light Roo saw another

figure standing near the wall. Then Roo saw there were two men in the darkness. They stepped forward and Roo's hand reflexively went to his side, where his knife usually hung.

"Now, now," said Esterbrook as if reassuring a pair of children. Into the light came Tim Jacoby, and a younger man, one who looked enough like him that he could only be his brother.

"Mr. Avery, I believe you've already met Timothy Jacoby. This other gentleman is his brother, Randolph." He glanced toward the door and said, "They were just leaving."

Roo stood stiffly as if ready to defend himself. Tim Jacoby said nothing, but his brother said, "Mr. Avery?" with a nod of his head.

"Mr. Jacoby," Roo responded, nodding back. Neither man offered to shake the other's hand.

Tim turned as they walked toward the door and said, "I will be in touch, Jacob."

"I expect you will, Timothy," said Esterbrook. "Give my regards to your father."

"I will," answered Tim.

Esterbrook said, "We took a bit longer to finish our business than I had anticipated. I'm sorry if their presence here caused you any alarm."

Roo said, "It was unexpected."

"Sit," said Esterbrook, motioning Roo to a chair at the other side of his large desk. "We have a bit of time before Sylvia fetches us for supper."

Esterbrook said, "I have made inquiries about you, young Avery." He sat back in his chair and folded his hands over his stomach. Roo had never seen him without his hat and saw the man was bald above his ears, but he let the rest of his grey hair hang to his collar in back. He affected long muttonchop sideburns, but otherwise was clean-shaven. A look of wry amusement passed over his face.

"Your notion of importing bulk wine from Darkmoor had merit. I think it an enterprise worth pursuing. It's too bad you ran afoul of the Mockers. Had I known about you, I could have saved you some loss and saved Sam Tannerson his life."

Roo said, "I'm impressed at your knowledge of the details."

Esterbrook made a gesture of dismissal with his right hand. "Information is valuable, but easy to come by if you have resources."

He leaned forward and said, "Remember this: of all the commodities men trade in, information is the most valuable by far."

Roo nodded. He wasn't sure he fully understood what Esterbrook was saying, or if he agreed. He decided this wasn't a debate or even a discussion but most likely a lecture.

"Now, I hope that in the future you and Timothy Jacoby can put aside your differences, however deep the animosity runs, because I might find it difficult to do business with two men who are at any moment likely to kill each other."

Roo said, "I wasn't aware that we are doing business."

Esterbrook smiled and there was nothing friendly or warm in it. "I think fate has touched you, young Avery. Certainly you have advanced to a station of some notice in a rapid fashion. Marrying Helmut Grindle's daughter gave you some resources that most men your age would envy, but you've prospered far beyond that. Obviously you are well thought of in the palace. Mr. Jacoby's father was very upset that your company received the contract to transport goods to the palace; he thought he was the logical choice.

"You've cut him badly, twice, I believe, in areas of less reputable trading."

Roo was forced to laugh. "One thing I've learned, despite my youth, Mr. Esterbrook, is not to admit anything."

Esterbrook laughed, and this time there was genuine amusement in his reaction. "Very well said." He sighed. "Well then, whatever occurs, I hope we can all manage to work in harmony."

Roo said, "I have a debt to pay, Mr. Esterbrook, but you are not part of that."

"Well, at this point, no," said Esterbrook.

A knock came from the door and Roo was out of his chair as the door opened and Sylvia peeked through. "Supper is served."

Esterbrook said, "We mustn't keep the lady of the manor waiting."

Roo shook his head but said nothing. He followed his host through the doorway, and Esterbrook motioned he should precede him. Roo followed Sylvia down the hall, and as they came into the well-lit antechamber at the entrance to the house, he found himself again captivated by how the candlelight played off her golden hair.

He followed her into the dining hall, his heart beating far too fast for the tiny bit of exertion walking to dinner entailed. He hardly noticed as he moved to a chair at a long table, with his host on his left at the head of the table, and Sylvia across from him. There was room for another seven people to sit at this table.

Roo said, "I have never seen a room like this."

Esterbrook said, "It's an idea I found in a description of a dining hall in a distant court, in one of the kingdoms down in the Keshian Confederacy. That king preferred intimate dining to the usual court chaos, and instead of sitting in the middle of the table, which would be to your right by two chairs, with everyone arrayed to his right and left, he decided to turn the table sideways, sit at one end, and be able to talk to everyone."

Sylvia said, "We used to have this very large round table, and you'd have to shout across it to be heard by whoever sat opposite you."

Roo smiled. "I like it." To himself he vowed to have one made just like this. Then he realized there was no room for a table this large in his small home. Suddenly he remembered the gamble he and his partners were taking, and realized that if they won, he would be able to build a house to match this one. He put aside his worry over what would happen should the gamble fail.

Conversation passed quickly, and Roo couldn't remember half of what was said. Throughout the night he found himself working hard not to stare at Sylvia, but he couldn't avoid it. She drew his eyes. By supper's end he had memorized her features as if they were a map home. He knew every curve of her neck, the set of her lips, the slight imperfection of one tooth in front that was slightly turned and overlapped the one next to it, the only flaw in her beauty he could ascertain.

Without knowing how, he found himself at the door, bidding his host and hostess good night. Sylvia took his hand and held it tightly, moving up close to him so that his knuckles brushed lightly against the top of her breasts. "It's been wonderful, Mr. Avery. I hope you'll visit us again, and very soon."

Roo almost stammered as he promised he would call again. He turned and mounted his horse and rode slowly to the gate. He could only wonder at this magic thing that he felt, and from every indication he was amazed to discover that Sylvia Esterbrook was apparently pleased with his company.

As the gate closed behind him, Roo wondered at that improbable fact.

Sylvia waited until the door was closed and then moved to a window beside the door, watching as Roo rode off. Turning to her father, she said, "What do you think?"

Jacob Esterbrook replied, "A young man with unlikely promise."

"He's certainly unattractive, though there's a wit about him that's charming enough, in a rat-faced sort of way," she said dryly. "But his hand was surprisingly strong." She tapped her teeth with her fingernail. "Those wry lads, they tend to have . . . great stamina."

"Sylvia," scolded her father, "you know I don't like that sort of talk."

Sweeping past her father as she made to climb the stairs to her bedroom, she said, "Father, you know what I am. You made me this way." She smiled at him over her shoulder. "Are you going to kill him?"

Esterbrook said, "I hope not to; he has wit, and from some of the things I've heard of his soldiering days, he has the ability to survive. He would make a better ally than foe, I think."

Sylvia started to climb the stairs, "But that still doesn't keep you from trying to ruin him."

Esterbrook waved away the comment as he turned toward his library. "Ruining a man is far different from killing him. If he's ruined in this wheat speculation, I may even offer him a position with one of my companies. Then I would not have to worry about a rising competitor, and he might be made a valuable asset."

Sylvia vanished at the top of the stairs and Jacob walked back toward the library. To himself he said, "Besides, if I need to, I'll have Tim Jacoby kill him."

Roo sipped at his coffee. It was his fifth or sixth cup of the day and he was drinking from habit, not any enjoyment of the drink.

Dash hurried up the stairs to the table where Roo sat with his partners. "Message for you."

He handed a note to Roo. The gem buyer in Salador had offered a price lower than Roo hoped for, but not too low to make Roo consider shopping for a better deal. He quickly calculated and said, "Reply by fast rider. Forward the gold at once."

Dash said, "And Duncan says there's starting to be some rumblings around the inn. A miller was overheard last night, while he was getting drunk, saying that he has no wheat to grind because the farmers aren't bringing it into the city."

Roo nodded. "Keep me informed."

Dash hurried away and Roo said, "It's starting."

Masterson nodded and signaled for a waiter to come to the table. The young man did and Masterson wrote out a note and handed it to the waiter. "Take this down to the floor, please. It's for Mr. Amested."

Roo sighed. "How are we doing?"

Masterson said, "We are now in debt, or have paid out six hundred thousand golden sovereigns' worth of wheat options. You have created the largest single seizure of wheat in the history . . . of the world!" He ran his hand over his face. "I doubt there's a grain of wheat between Malac's Cross and the Far Coast that's not going to show up at the city gates in the next two weeks with our name on it. We'd better have guessed right, Roo."

Roo smiled. "None of you would have gone along with my plan if you didn't realize it would work." He hiked his thumb toward the floor below. "It all turns on one fact, Jerome. Everyone here, including you and me, is a greedy bastard."

Masterson laughed. "There's more truth in that than not, Roo." He leaned forward. "Truth to tell, when I was a boy I cut purses for a living. Got a chance to go straight and I did, in the army, during the Great Uprising. I was little more than a kid, but like every man serving, I got the King's pardon. I decided to turn my hand to honest business, and found that the biggest difference between honest business and dishonest is in how you approach your mark." He leaned back. "Oh, it's not like I'm taking everything a fellow has, and if we work well together, we both end up making money, but often it's just as vicious as if I cut his purse and ran through the market."

Roo said, "Where are we with price?"

"We're steady at three silver pieces for ten bushels against a six percent guarantee."

Roo said, "I'm too tired to calculate the numbers. How much do we stand to make?"

Masterson said, "I have no idea. We still need grain buyers from the Free Cities to show up and start running up the price."

"Not for a few more days, I hope," said Roo. "We still need to buy a few more cheap options." He lowered his voice. "Duncan reports word is starting to spread that wheat from the outlying farms isn't coming in. In a few days no one will be making offers. We need to finish this today, by tomorrow at the latest."

"I'm out of gold, and I've put up everything I own as security to the moneylenders," said Masterson. He laughed. "I should be scared to death, but the truth is I haven't felt this happy since I was a boy running through the city with the City Watch hot on my tail!"

Roo said, "I know what you mean. It's . . . like putting your life on the line for one toss of the knucklebones."

"Never cared for dice," said Masterson. "Always preferred cards. Lin-lan or pokiir. You against the other fellows."

Roo said, "I've got gold coming from Salador. Another ten thousand, if we need it."

"We're going to need it," said Hume, who had just walked up. "We're so overbought now we don't have the coppers to pay for our coffee." He leaned over. "Keep it on you, in case we all need to make a quick escape."

Roo laughed. "I don't think that's going to happen. Any minute I expect we'll see what we've all been waiting for, and when that happens . . ." He grinned. He held out his hand, palm up, then suddenly closed it, saying, "We have them!"

A few minutes later a waiter appeared with two notes. Masterson opened the first one and said, "Amested's agreed and he's in for ten thousand. He is just about popping to know what we're doing, gentlemen."

Crowley walked over and sat down. "What's that? Amested's?"

"Yes, he's in," said Masterson.

"What's the other note?" asked Roo.

Masterson opened it and read it, then grinned. "Here it is."

"What does it say?" demanded Crowley impatiently.

"A syndicate is offering us thirty thousand bushels at two silver for three bushels secured by a ten percent option."

Roo slammed his hand on the table. "It's them. It has to be. The greedy bastards couldn't resist. They're ours."

Masterson did some calculations. "Not quite." He sat back,

blowing out his breath, his cheeks puffing out. "We don't have enough gold."

Roo groaned. "How short are we?"

Masterson calculated. "We could use that ten thousand gold pieces you have coming from Salador."

"Is that enough?"

"Almost," said Masterson. "But we'd still be two thousand gold short."

Roo groaned. "I need to get out of here." He stood up. "I'll think of something."

He left his companions and walked down the stairs through the heart of the coffee house. He stepped outside and found the streets relatively uncrowded. Catching sight of the house where he had hidden the silk that launched his career, he crossed the street, avoiding puddles. It had rained hard the night before, which was partially responsible for the light traffic in the city.

Reaching the porch of the abandoned house, Roo saw that no one had replaced the broken hasp on the lock he had forced. Whoever owned the place had merely stuck the screws back into the stripped-out holes as if the sight of the lock on the door would keep the curious out. As there was nothing inside worth stealing, thought Roo as he pushed open the door, it was probably a safe bet.

He wandered through the house, again finding some sense of place there. He hadn't said anything to Karli, but when he was rich he intended to buy this house. Having quarters close to Barret's was appealing to him, for he had already decided that while the freight company would be the heart of his business empire, it would be only one of many ventures he would embark on.

Trading at Barret's was like nothing he had ever encountered before; it was gambling on a scale undreamed of by any soldier losing his pay in an alehouse. It was intoxicating, and Roo was drunk with possibilities.

He sat there a long time, listening to the rain when it came, and the sounds of the city, as the light faded and the day trailed off. When at last he decided he needed to return, it was near sundown.

He left the house and crossed the street to find Dash waiting for him. Dash said, "Luis says the first load of wheat has shown up. One of the villages outside of Land's End harvested early."

Roo swore. "Do we have room for it in our warehouse?"

"Barely, if we push everything else outside into the yard and street."

Roo said, "This could turn ugly. We don't have the gold to rent storage at the docks and there's no ship in from the Free Cities."

"There is," said Dash.

"What?" asked Roo.

"We've got word of a Free Cities trader docking at noon. I've been looking for you for hours to tell you."

Roo's eyes widened and he said, "Then come with me!"

He hurried to the docks on foot, breaking out into a trot when traffic opened, and Dash kept up with him. As they reached the docks, Roo said, "Where's the ship?"

Dash said, "Out at anchor. There." He pointed.

Roo said, "The master must be at customs. Come on."

They hurried to the customs shed and found a busy clerk going over documents, while two very impatient men waited nearby. Roo said over the counter, "Has the master of the Free Cities ship been in?"

The clerk looked up and said, "What?"

One of the two waiting men said, "Aye, he has, and he's still waiting for that stone-headed clerk to sign off on his paperwork so he can turn his cargo over to his buyer," and he pointed to the man next to him.

Roo said, "I have cargo for the Free Cities, if you're unbooked."

The Captain said, "Sorry, lad, but I am booked. I have letters of credit and authorizations to secure cargo. My employer was most emphatic about this." He lowered his voice. "If it's a tiny bit of cargo, I might be able to squeeze it in, but otherwise I'm instructed to fill my ship with grain and hurry back as fast as possible."

Roo grinned. "Grain?"

"Aye, lad. Wheat. I'm to purchase high-quality wheat at a fair market price, then leave as quickly as possible." He glowered at the clerk. "Which is why I'd like this business done as soon as possible so I can let my lads go ashore. They've been at sea three weeks, and we'll be here but a day or two."

"Who have you contacted for your wheat?" asked Roo.

"No one yet, though I fail to see how that is any business of yours."

Rupert stood and said, "Captain, I forgot my manners. I am very sorry. May I be allowed to introduce myself and my companion." He turned to Dash and said, "This is my associate, Dashel Jameson, grandson to the Duke of Krondor." He put his hand on his chest as the Captain and his buyer both rose at the mention of the Duke. "And I am Rupert Avery, of the Krondor Grain Traders Association." Almost unable to contain himself, he said, "How much grain do you need?"

"Enough to fill a ship, Mr. Avery."

Roo turned to Dash. "Is what arrived today enough to fill his ship?"

Dash said, "I think so."

Roo said, "Good. To price: what do you offer?"

The Captain said, "You have the wheat here, in Krondor?"

"Yes, I can have it at the docks at first light."

The Captain got a calculating look on his face. Roo knew what he was thinking: if he could grab the wheat before word got around about the shortage, he might make enough of a profit for the ship's owner to make it worth having his crew forgo any shore leave. At last he said, "I'm prepared to offer two silver pieces of common weight"—the agreed-upon size of the coins used to trade between the Free Cities—"for three bushels of wheat at dockside tomorrow."

Roo said, "I'll take a silver per bushel."

"Three silvers per four bushels," said the Captain.

Roo said, "I'll take a silver and a copper per bushel."

"Wait a minute!" exploded the Captain. "You just set a price of a silver per. Now you raise it?"

"Yes," said Roo, "and in a minute it will be a silver and two coppers." Then he leaned forward and said very quietly, "Locusts."

The Captain's face flushed and he looked as if someone had just lit a fire in his trousers, but after glaring at Roo a long moment, he stuck out his hand and said, "Done! A silver and copper per bushel at dockside at first light."

Roo turned and put his hand on Dash's shoulder and steered him out of the customs house. "It's going to work," he said when they had cleared the street.

The next morning the wagons paraded to the docks, unloading the grain onto barges that carried it out to the ship. The Captain and Roo both stood by comparing tallies, while stevedores hauled the large sacks of grain off the wagons and carried them down the gangplanks to the barges.

By midday the tally was done and the two men compared figures. Roo knew the Captain was intentionally counting light and showed six less bushels than Roo. For slightly more than a half-piece in gold, Roo thought he'd let the Captain have his little triumph. "I'll accept your figure, Captain."

The Captain motioned to his mate, who produced a chest, out of which the Captain counted sacks of gold. He let Roo inspect the contents of each bag, and when the transaction was done, Roo handed the contents to Duncan, who stood nearby with a chest that would be taken to the countinghouse where Roo now had his accounts established.

As they led the now empty wagons from the dock, Roo rode next to Duncan on the lead wagon. He felt an elation unlike anything he had known in his life. "It's going to work," he said to no one.

"What?" asked Duncan.

Roo couldn't contain himself any longer. He laughed long and hard, then whooped. He said, "I'm going to be a very wealthy man, cousin."

"How very nice for you," said Duncan dryly. Roo didn't notice his cousin's lack of enthusiasm.

The floor of the coffee house was in chaos. Grown men screamed at one another and several fights had to be broken up by waiters. McKeller could be heard saying, "Gentlemen, gentlemen, please, remember yourselves!" several times.

Roo had one man hurl himself across a table at him, and his battle training served him well as the man found only air where Roo had stood a moment before. The man knocked himself nearly senseless when he struck his chin on a chair.

Taking the steps two at a time, Roo found a pair of waiters protecting the upper floor from those not authorized to mount the steps. Not that the upstairs was much quieter than down below, but at least there was no brawling. Grown men seemed on the verge of breaking down in tears or screaming in frustration. Roo pushed past two angry men to find several more at tableside, confronting an equally angry-looking Masterson.

"I don't care what you say," screamed Masterson at a pair of men who leaned over the table, their hands pressing hard into the wood. "You signed the note, you provide the wheat, or pay the market price. You have three days!"

One of the men looked enraged, but the other looked ready to beg. "I can't. Please. I'll have to sell everything I've ever acquired. I'll be penniless."

Masterson's temper seemed on the verge of getting the best of him. "You should have thought of that before you sold me wheat you didn't have title to!"

Roo took him by the arm and over his shoulder said, "Excuse me, gentlemen, we'll be back in a moment."

"What?" asked Jerome, still angry.

Roo tried to keep a straight face and, failing, turned his back to the others around the table so they wouldn't see him grinning. "How much?"

Masterson said, "They owe us two hundred thousand bushels of wheat, and they don't own any!" Then he suddenly realized whom he was talking to, and started to snicker. Covering his face with the back of his hand, he feigned coughing. "I don't care much for Meany over there, and his cousin Meaks isn't much better. Thought I'd let them sweat a bit."

"Are they involved with Jacoby?" asked Roo, keeping his voice down.

"No," answered Jerome. "Not as far as I can tell. I did what you requested and ferreted out every syndicate or association that I thought had Jacoby participation, and they're not among them."

Roo said, "I've been thinking. We can't ruin every investor in Krondor, else we'll have no one to do business with. What do these two do?"

Masterson suddenly grinned. "Meany has a lovely little mill he manages badly, and Meaks a bakeshop that does a tidy business not far from here. Mostly they speculate, and only on a modest scale." He whispered. "Someone must have put the word out there was going to be a bloodletting. I've got notes here from people two or three times over, far more than they're worth if they default."

Roo nodded. "Well, if we take Krondor Grain Traders and turn it into a permanent syndicate, it wouldn't hurt our position in future to have a few businesses we own to constantly generate gold. Would you like to own a share in a bakery and mill?"

Masterson rubbed his chin. "Not a bad notion. You and I with Crowley and Hume need to sit and discuss this. We can bully out those other partners who came late, but Brandon Crowley and Stanley Hume were with us from the start."

"Agreed," said Roo. He turned and went back to the table. "Mr. Meany?" he asked.

The angrier of the two men said, "Yes?"

"As I understand it, you don't have the wheat you contracted to deliver to us at the agreed-upon price?"

"You know I don't!" shouted Meany. "Someone went out and bought up every grain from here to Great Kesh! I've word from every grain buyer in the Principality there is no wheat for sale anywhere! How can we meet these contracts if we can't buy grain?"

Roo said, "An unfortunate circumstance to find yourself in."

The other man, Meaks, said, "Please. If we're forced to account on the due date, we'll be ruined. I have a family!"

Roo pretended to think upon it, then said, "We'll consider taking your note."

No sooner were those words out of his mouth than Meaks was saying, "Oh, thank you, sir!" His relief brought him to the edge of tears.

Meany said, "You will?"

"At a reasonable rate of interest, and we may require property as ..." Roo glanced at Masterson and whispered, "What's the word?"

Masterson said, "Collateral."

"... collateral. Prepare a list of your holdings and return here on the due date, and we'll work something out. Can't have your family out on the streets now, can we?" said Roo pointedly to Meaks.

The two men left and Roo began dealing with the men who were coming in before the due date to plead for more time because there was no grain to buy. He noticed the notes Masterson had set aside for him to peruse, and made a mental list of the names on them. Not one of those men came to see him.

At the end of the day, Roo and his three partners, along with Sebastian Lender, sat down. Roo said, "Gentlemen, I propose we form a standing company."

Crowley said, "Say on."

"We have, according to Jerome, managed to achieve the single most stunning manipulation of any market in the Western Realm in the history of Barret's."

Lender said, "I think that is a safe assessment."

Jerome said, "Well, none of us would have expected it to turn out the way it had."

Roo said, "My point is that we've done as well as we did because you gentlemen were steadfast. Lesser men would have broken and run."

Crowley looked unconvinced, but Hume appeared pleased at the remark.

"I was a soldier for two terrible years," said Roo, "and I understand the incalculable benefit of having men at your back you can trust." He looked from face to face. "I trust you four men."

Crowley looked genuinely moved at that.

Roo said, "I propose we keep our newfound wealth pooled, and form a new company, one as diverse and widespread as any seen before." In his mind he knew he was proposing the formation, overnight, of a company to rival Jacob Esterbrook's far-flung holdings.

Crowley said, "And you will preside over that company?" There was a note of suspicion in his voice.

"No," said Roo. "I'm still new at this, and while I think I have a knack for this sort of business, I also know that we got lucky." He started to laugh. "I doubt anyone will sell a grain contract in the Kingdom for a long time without having purchased the grain in advance."

The others laughed in return.

"No," said Roo, "I was thinking you should preside, Brandon." It was the first time he had used Crowley's first name.

"Me?" asked Crowley, obviously surprised.

"Well," said Roo, turning to Jerome, "Mr. Masterson and I have, shall we say, less than pristine histories." Masterson laughed at that. "And while I respect Mr. Hume, it seems to me you're the senior member here. Your age and experience would serve us well.

I propose that you preside, and Mr. Hume could act as the company's second officer. I will be content to be but one of four partners. I will conduct a fair bit of business on my own, outside the company. Running Avery and Sons will take some of my time. And I expect we'll all have undertakings we will wish to pursue outside the company. But we're about to be confronted with many, many men who will not be able to meet the notes they sold us." He outlined his discussion with Masterson and his offer to Meaks and Meany. "We could end up with shared interests in dozens of businesses scattered around the Bitter Sea. For that reason, gentlemen," he said to them all, "I propose that this day we found the Bitter Sea Trading and Holding Company."

Masterson slammed his hand down on the table. "Damn me if you're not a shooting star, Roo Avery! I'll ride with you."

Hume spoke next. "I will join with you; yes, I will."

After a moment Brandon Crowley said, "Presiding Officer?" He nodded. "Very well, I will join with you also."

Roo said, "Mr. Lender, would you be so kind as to execute an agreement to this effect?"

"I would be pleased, Mr. Avery."

Masterson rubbed his hands together. "I think, gentlemen, it is time for a drink." He turned his head and shouted to a nearby waiter to bring his private brandy and five glasses.

When the drinks were poured and each man held one, Masterson said, "To Mr. Rupert Avery, without whose tenacity and conviction not only would we not soon be very wealthy men, we'd probably be begging in the street."

Roo said, "No. Please. Each of us here is due some credit. I would rather we toast"—he held up his glass—"the Bitter Sea Trading and Holding Company!"

Each man in turn said the name of the new company, and as one, they drank a toast.

Fifteen

Consolidation

THE INN WAS CROWDED.

In a dark corner five men sat, keeping their voices low despite the din of the common room. One nearly spat as he spoke, so intense was his anger. "The bloody bastard strangled the market and we're going to be ruined. You said this was going to be easy pickings. I took multiple positions in three different syndicates, all secured with the same collateral! If I default on more than one of them, I will have to flee Krondor or go to prison! You said there would be no trouble!" He pointed an accusing finger at the man across the table from him.

Timothy Jacoby leaned forward. "I promised you nothing, deWitt. I said you'd have an opportunity to make a killing." His own anger matched that of his companions. "But I never *guaranteed* you anything."

A third man said, "This is pointless. The question is, what do we do?"

"I'm going to see Esterbrook," answered Jacoby, standing abruptly, so that his chair fell backward, striking a drunk who lay facedown at the next table. The drunk barely stirred. Jacoby glanced at the nearly comatose man. "Meet me back here in two hours. I'll have some sort of answer."

The five men rose and left and after a minute, the drunk stood up. He was a young man of average height, and the only thing remarkable about him was his hair, which was a very pale blond, nearly white when seen in sunlight. He kept a wool sailor's cap tight on his head, so that this unusual feature was hidden. Moving with purpose, he left the room and followed the five men out the door.

Once outside the inn, the blond man glanced around until he saw a figure appear from deep within a nearby doorway. He waited until the second figure closed to him. "Well?" asked Dash of the false drunk.

"Go back and tell your employer that he's stirred up a hornet's nest. Tell him Tim Jacoby is rushing to get some answers from Jacob Esterbrook. I'm going to follow Jacoby and see if I can overhear what he and Esterbrook are going to plan."

Dash said, "Well, at least you don't have to try to climb to the rooftops and hang upside down outside windows. You never were very good at that."

Jimmy smiled at his younger brother. "Well, you weren't much for picking pockets, either." He gripped his brother by the arm. "You are certain Father believes I'm out dining with you?"

Dash shrugged. "That's what I told him. Don't worry. Unless you get yourself killed, Grandfather will sort things out with Father should we run into trouble. He always does."

"Well, hurry along. They're due to meet back here in two hours. You would do well to have someone else inside before then, in case I can't get back ahead of Jacoby." He patted his brother's arm. "See you later tonight."

Dash hurried off into the darkness, and Jimmy moved to where his horse had been hidden. He mounted and rode out toward the eastern gate, looking about to ensure no one spotted him or was following him.

As he left the city gate, he caught sight of Jacoby on the road ahead, his figure outlined against the darkness by the light from the large moon, which was directly overhead. Jimmy slowed his own horse, lest he ride upon the heels of his prey.

By the time Jimmy reached the outer wall of the Esterbrook estate, he was certain getting inside would prove easy. Getting out, he thought to himself, might prove more difficult.

Like his brother, Jimmy had grown up in the palace at Rillanon, where their father, Arutha, had served with their grandfather, then Duke of Rillanon. Arutha—named for the late Prince of Krondor—had been raised in a far more genteel fashion than his father, who had been a notorious boy thief until Prince Arutha had taken him into service.

But the grandsons had listened to their grandfather James's stories, and by the ages of seven and five the palace was constantly troubled by two boys climbing walls, skipping along rooftops, picking locks, eavesdropping on state meetings, and otherwise creating difficulties far beyond what one would expect from two children of their size or experience.

By the time they were eleven and nine, the boys' father had decided that the hearty life along the frontier would teach them a thing or two. So Jimmy and Dash had been packed off to the frontier court at Crydee, home of Duke Marcus, the King's cousin.

Their visit had lasted two years, and by the time the two brothers returned to Rillanon, they were sunburned, tougher, more self-reliant, fair trackers, better hunters, and now thoroughly incorrigible. In the subsequent five years, both sons had been thrown out of the palace by their father and grandfather several times in the hope they would discover just how lucky they were to be among the elite of the Kingdom.

Each time the boys managed rather well, living by their wits and guile, and frequently using the skills developed driving the palace staff to distraction to provide sustenance. They had even run afoul of the Thieves' Guild in Rillanon on two occasions and survived to tell the tale.

The last time they had been banished from the palace, their father had relented after three weeks and had gone looking for them, only to find they now had a controlling interest in one of the seedier bordellos along the docks. They had won it playing cards.

Jimmy tied his horse out of sight down the road, where he would likely not be seen if Jacoby came riding past before Jimmy could recover the mount. He hurried up to the gate and quickly looked it over. Two easy footholds and a handhold later and he was peeking over the top of the gate. A servant was leading Jacoby's horse toward the stable and there was no one else in sight. He heard the door to the main house close, and assumed Jacoby had just entered.

Jimmy jumped down from the wall and hurried toward the house, keeping off the pathway and stooping low beside a line of decorative shrubbery. Reaching the house, he glanced about. He didn't know where Jacob's library was, save it was on the ground floor, and he knew that only because Dash had mentioned it.

Silently he cursed himself for not thinking of asking Dash if he knew. Ah well, he thought, preparation had never been his strong suit. Dash had the more devious mind.

He glanced into a few windows and saw no one moving. He at last found himself staring at a dim room in which only a pair of candles burned, but he could hear voices raised.

"Don't come in here and demand anything of me, Timothy!"

Dash risked a better look and was rewarded by the sight of Timothy Jacoby leaning over a desk, knuckles hard against the surface, as he yelled at Jacob Esterbrook.

"I need gold!" shouted Jacoby. "Lots of it!"

Esterbrook waved his hand as if wafting away a bad smell. "And I'm supposed to give it to you?"

"A loan, then, damn it!"

"How much?" asked Esterbrook.

"I hold option orders for sixty thousand sovereigns, Jacob. If I can't meet the order, I'm going to forfeit everything we own unless some grain comes on the market in the next three days."

"You're worth more than sixty thousand, Timothy, a great deal more."

"It's not the price!" Jacoby nearly shouted again. "It's the penalty for the grain not delivered. By the gods, wheat is up to three silvers a bushel and rising! There is none to be had. Every miller in the Kingdom is in Krondor howling at the grain brokers. Someone has bought up all the contracts and there is none to be had."

"What about all that cheap grain you have coming in from Kesh?" asked Esterbrook.

"We're delivering that tomorrow, but that's less than half the contracts we took. When I secured that grain, how was I to know that little insect and his partners would order up five times that amount? Instead of choking him on it, we're making him wealthy. The market price has doubled over the option we've secured."

Jacob pointed at Timothy. "You got greedy, which is bad. But you were stupid, which is worse. You let your distaste for Roo Avery color your judgment. And what's more, you killed a completely innocent man for merely being his business partner. You're the only man in Krondor who won't be given a chance to negotiate his way out of this."

"Innocent!" said Jacoby. "Ask my father about Helmut Grindle. He knew a man's throat was below his chin and which side of a dagger had the edge. He just happened to be in the way. Avery has a knack of taking goods from me that are difficult to replace, and my customers for those goods are less than forgiving."

"Running drugs for the Mockers, again, Tim?" The disgust in Esterbrook's tone could not be hidden. "You made that bed, so lie in it alone."

"Are you going to loan me the gold or not?" demanded Jacoby.

"How much?"

"If grain comes onto the market in the next two days, I can survive with sixty thousand gold sovereigns. That will bail out deWitt and the others who came along because I told them. If it doesn't, you don't have enough to save my company. DeWitt won't be the only one fleeing the city to avoid prison." He lowered his voice, and Jimmy could barely hear him as he warned, "But if I'm taken, Jacob, there are things I can tell the magistrate that might buy me a lighter sentence. I can take a few years in prison, Jacob, but you're not a young man. Think on that."

Esterbrook considered it. He looked out the window and Jimmy ducked out of sight. He heard footsteps approach and crouched as low into the shadows as he could, holding motionless. "I thought I saw something," he heard Esterbrook say.

"You're imagining things," said Jacoby.

Jimmy heard the sound of a quill on parchment. "Here's a letter to my accounts keeper," said Esterbrook. "He will honor the letter. But be warned, I am going to hold your father responsible if you default, our old friendship not withstanding."

"Thank you, Jacob," said Timothy, and his tone was icy.

Jimmy heard the door slam and was judging how best to time his move to the wall: Jacoby's horse was in the stable and if he hurried, he might get to his own horse before Jacoby cleared the gate.

He was about to move when he heard someone enter the library. "Father?"

He chanced a peek and saw a stunning-looking young woman enter the room. He conceded that for once Dash hadn't exaggerated a woman's loveliness. He could see why Avery was smitten, as were Roo's cousin and young Jason, from what Dash had reported. Dash and Jimmy had grown up near the center of power in the Kingdom, and many beautiful women had paid attention to the grandsons of the Duke of Rillanon as soon as they were old enough to appreciate it. They had enjoyed the benefits of such attention, and had an education regarding women and their pleasures far beyond their years, but they also had something of an askance view of them as well. Jimmy, like his brother before him, marked Sylvia Esterbrook as a very dangerous creature, one able to find powerful allies.

She said, "What was all that bellowing about? Was Tim being a bully again?"

"Trying to," answered his father. "It seems young Avery not only has managed to survive Jacoby's attempts to bury him, but is turning the tables, as they say. I had to loan Jacoby the gold to keep him from being ruined."

"Then Timothy will try to kill Rupert?"

"Almost certainly."

"Will you let him?" asked Sylvia.

Jacob rose and came around the desk toward his daughter. "I think I shall absent myself from the conflict. I think it opportune for us to visit our country home for a few weeks. By the time we return, the matter will be settled."

"Well, if you must have someone killed, please do it soon, Father. Being out of the city is such a bore."

Jimmy had met some calculating women in the eastern courts, but Sylvia Esterbrook was easily the most cold-blooded he had encountered. As much as he wished to hear more of this conversation, he knew he couldn't afford to let Jacoby get too far ahead of him. He started back toward the wall, wondering if it would do Avery any good to warn him. Then he considered how beautiful Sylvia Esterbrook was, and how unlikely it was that Avery was used to the attention of such a woman, and discarded the idea as worthless.

In the dark he could hear Tim Jacoby's horse moving down the road as the gate closed. Jimmy dropped to the ground while the servant returned to the house, and when he heard the door to the house shut, he rose, ran to the wall, and quickly climbed over.

A few minutes later he was upon his horse, heading back toward Krondor. He fervently hoped Dash was already at the inn, because there was no possibility he could overtake Jacoby and resume his posture of being the drunk at the next table.

Inside the house, Jacob Esterbrook closed the door to his library behind him, and said, "Old Frederick's health isn't what it used to be, and I suspect that soon Timothy will be totally out of control. It would be better for us if either he or Rupert were to be removed from the landscape quickly. Either a very dangerous young man, who might rise to a dangerous level of power someday, or an unstable ally—potentially more dangerous than the opponent—will be removed. Either way, we profit."

"If Roo kills Tim, how does that profit you? He's not one of your partners, and given he's going to see your hand in much of what has been going on around the city the last few months, do you think he will be inclined to do business with you?"

"If Tim kills him, that question is academic. If he kills Tim, he will be a young man of great influence, and I will groom him to help our cause. I count on your charms to make him wish to do business with me."

"Do you want me to marry him?"

"No, he's already married."

She laughed, a sound both lovely and chilling. "The little rogue. He never mentioned a wife. Well then, I shall just have to seduce the ugly twit and become his mistress."

"But only if Tim doesn't kill him, daughter."

"Yes, Father. Now, would you care for supper?"

Roo sat motionless as Tim Jacoby stalked forward and threw papers down upon the table. Masterson was the one to pick them up, and he said, "You have the grain, then?"

"Yes," said Jacoby, his fury turned to dark, cold anger. "A broker came into town this morning and I secured what I needed to meet the contract."

Roo forced himself not to smile. He had had Luis pretend to be the broker, and had sold grain to Jacoby for more money than Jacoby was being paid for it now. He had conspired not only to sell the grain twice, but to make a profit both times.

Jacoby turned to look at Roo. "Avery," he said calmly, "I don't know how you managed this, but I smell something here that stinks like week-dead cats. And when I find out what it is you did, and how you did it, we'll have a score to settle."

Roo rose slowly, so that a fight wouldn't erupt in the balcony at Barret's. He came around the table and looked at his taller foe. "I told you once before, when I took your knife out of your hand, that you weren't the first enemy I've made. But you went too far when you punished an old man because you were angry with me, Jacoby. If you're ready to die, we can step into the street right now."

Jacoby blinked and his jaw tightened, but he did nothing for a moment; then he turned and stalked off, pushing past others come to settle their debts with the Krondor Grain Traders Association.

Roo returned to his chair and Masterson said, "Selling him our grain so that he could meet his contract may have made us a bit more gold, Roo, but we all might have slept better if we had put Jacoby and Sons out of business outright."

"If we had done that, we'd be spilling blood right now." Looking at Masterson, he added, "I've seen the inside of the death cell; I have no desire ever to see it again." Then he smiled. "Can you imagine Jacoby's reaction when he discovers that we were the ones selling him grain so he could deliver it back to us? At a loss?"

Masterson nodded with a smile. "He might burst at that discovery."

More men came, some with the grain, now being delivered for a fraction of the price it was commanding on the open market. The others came to plead for time or to offer compromise offers.

As they had agreed to do, the partners heard every offer of compromise, and in most instances took part or all of a company in settlement. By the end of the day the Bitter Sea Trading and Holding Company controlled a pair of mills, sixteen ships, a half-dozen shops in the city, and other holdings as far away as the cities of Ylith, Carse, and Malac's Cross.

As day came to an end, Roo rubbed his hand over his face. "How have we done?"

Masterson looked at Lender, who consulted with a scribe employed to keep accounts. "In the last four days, you've captured assets that are, conservatively, worth in excess of one million four hundred thousand golden sovereigns, gentlemen. I would set the Bitter Sea Trading and Holding Company's current net worth in excess of two million gold. When we deliver the grain we're shipping ourselves to Bordon and Port Natal, that will rise to something in excess of three million gold."

Roo couldn't help but grin despite his bone-numbing fatigue. "Damn me," he said quietly.

"When's the party?" said Masterson.

"What?" asked Roo.

"It's traditional around here for the newest member of a syndicate to host a party for his partners and those doing business with him. Given you're presently doing business with just about every trading concern in the Kingdom and half of those in Kesh and Queg, I hope you have a large house."

"A party?" said Roo. Then he thought of the house across the street. "Soon, I think."

He turned and leaned across to whisper to Lender. "Can you find out who holds title to that house across the street and how much they require to purchase it?"

Lender rose. "I'll find out at once."

Roo also stood. "I must for home, gentlemen. My wife has seen less of me since we started this mess than you four have, by half. I must reacquaint myself with her and my daughter."

He left word at the door that should anyone need to reach him they could do so at the office of Avery and Sons. Then he walked home.

Karli looked up as Roo entered the dining room. He smiled and said, "I have something to tell you."

The baby rested in Karli's arms as she nursed. Karli said, "Yes?"

Roo pulled out a chair and sat down. Putting his arm around his wife's shoulders he said, "You are married to one of the richest men in the Kingdom." He couldn't repress a giggle.

Karli pulled back. "Are you drunk?"

Roo looked injured. "Woman! I am not drunk." He stood. "What I am is very tired and very hungry. I'm going to take a bath, and if you would tell Rendel, I would like supper as soon as she can manage."

Karli said, "Don't you want to say hello to your daughter?"

Roo looked confused. "She's a baby! How is she going to know if I say hello or not?"

Karli looked stricken. "She needs to know her father, Roo." She held up the baby and put her over her shoulder. "She smiled at me today."

Roo shook his head. "I don't know what it is you're talking about. I need a bath." As he began to leave the room, he said, "Did I tell you I plan on buying a new house?"

"Why?"

Roo turned on his wife and his face hardened into a mask of outrage. "Why!" he shouted. The baby began to cry at the loud noise. "Do you think I intend to live the rest of my life in this tiny hovel your father was satisfied with? I'm going to buy us a town house across from Barret's! It's three stories tall and has room for a large garden. . . ." He shook his head and took a deep breath. "I'm going to buy a country house as well. I'm going to own horses and dogs and hunt with the nobility."

As he spoke, his anger faded and a strange dizziness overtook him. He reached out and gripped the doorjamb. "I need to eat something."

He turned and mounted the stairs while Karli tried to quiet the crying Abigail. "Mary!" shouted Roo. "I need a tub of hot water, now!"

As Roo vanished up the stairs, Karli ignored the tear running down her cheek as she said, "Hush, my love. Your father loves you."

The music filled the night. Roo stood at the door, wearing the finest clothing he could buy. He greeted each guest as they arrived and he was the man of the hour.

Every merchant of worth and importance was in attendance, and many nobles who had come as friends of friends. The new house was turned out and decorated and filled with the finest furniture that money could buy. It was clear to anyone who paused to consider, a man of consequence had taken up residence across the street from Barret's Coffee House.

Karli stood next to her husband, wearing a gown that had cost more gold than she could believe, but trying to look as if she wore such raiment every day. She glanced at the stairway, wondering how her daughter fared, for she was upstairs in a very noisy house and she was teething. Mary was nearby, but Karli didn't trust anyone to look after her daughter.

It had taken months to find the owner of the house, negotiate a price, fit it up, and move in. Karli had insisted they keep the old house she had grown up in, and Roo hadn't been willing to argue with her. After the dust had settled on his manipulation of the grain trade in the city, he turned out to be worth far more than even he had dreamed possible. When the last ship had returned from the Free Cities, the net worth of the Bitter Sea Trading and Holding Company wasn't in excess of three million gold pieces, it was closer to seven million—for the locusts had spread to the Far Coast and Yabon, and grain prices were at a record high. Additionally, several of the businesses they had acquired had proven quite lucrative, showing a quick profit as soon as Roo and his partners had taken control.

Now Roo knew he was a man of importance, as the great and near-great of the city came to his home to pay their respects. Roo felt as if his chest would burst when a cadre of horsemen rode up before a carriage and from the vehicle Dash, his brother Jimmy, and their father and mother emerged. Behind it came another carriage, bearing the crest of Krondor, and coming to visit his house were the Duke and Duchess of the city. Even those who attended out of curiosity, those cynical souls who judged Roo the current favorite, a man likely to be forgotten in a year, were impressed as the most powerful lord after the king came to call.

Dash entered and smiled at Roo as he took his hand, shook it, then kissed Karli's. Turning, he said, "May I present my brother, James? We call him Jimmy so as not to confuse him with Grandfather."

Roo grinned as he shook hands with Dash's older brother. They were attempting to keep secret the fact they had, indeed, met before, and that Jimmy was helping his brother to make Roo a very powerful man. Behind them came a man who could be no one else but their father, the resemblance was so strong. Dash said, "This is my father, Arutha, Lord Vencar, Earl of the Court."

Roo bowed slightly and said, "My lord, it is an honor to welcome you to my home. May I present my wife?" He introduced Karli and then was introduced in turn to Elena, Dash and Jimmy's mother. The handsome woman said, "We are pleased you asked us to attend, Mr. Avery. We are pleased our son has discovered a legitimate interest"—she glanced at Dash—"for a change." Her slight accent betrayed her Roldem origins.

Behind them came Duke James and the Duchess Gamina, whom Roo welcomed warmly. Gamina said, "I am more pleased than you can imagine to see you in such surroundings, Mr. Avery, given the grim circumstances of our last meeting."

Roo said, "That makes two of us, my lady."

James leaned over and said in Roo's ear, "Remember, thou art but mortal, Roo."

Roo's eyes narrowed and he looked slightly confused, but the Duke swept past and entered the large room off the stairway; other guests waited outside in the garden. Everything there was in bloom, as Roo had paid a great sum to bring in fully mature plants and for a short time Karli had rejoiced in the size of her new garden. But Roo couldn't escape the notion she didn't like the new house.

Jerome Masterson came from the large room and, from behind, whispered in Roo's ear. "The Duke of Krondor himself! You're a success, lad." He patted Roo on the shoulders. "You're about to find more invitations to dinner arriving than you could answer in a year. Accept the best only, and be polite to the rest. He patted Roo's shoulder again and wandered back into the crowd.

Karli said, "I should go check on Abigail."

Roo took her hand and patted it. "She's fine. Mary's up there, and if there's any problem, she'll come fetch you."

Karli didn't looked reassured, but she stayed.

The clatter of horses announced the arrival of Jadow Shati and several soldiers from the garrison. Roo greeted them and shook hands. "How's the leg?"

Jadow grinned, his broad smile revealing remarkably white teeth. "Fine, though I now know when rain's coming." He patted his left leg. "Almost have all my strength back."

Roo introduced his former companion to his wife, and Jadow led the soldiers with him inside. Roo didn't know any of them, and laughed to himself; these were obviously new barrack companions of Jadow's who had come along on the promise of free food and drink.

The evening wore on, and at last Karli had persuaded Roo that she needed to check on their daughter. While she was gone a large carriage rolled up and Roo's heart began to pound when he saw who was inside.

Jacob Esterbrook and his daughter arrived and Roo felt his heart beat hard in his chest. Sylvia let the doorman take her cloak, and Roo saw she was dressed in the newest fashion, a gown cut so low as to be close to scandalous by more conservative court standards. Her father wore expensive but conservative dress, a short-cut jacket over a tunic with a single row of ruffles in front, black hose, and black leather shoes with silver buckles. He went hatless and carried a simple cane with an ivory hilt.

Roo took Sylvia's hand and was loath to release it and greet her father. "Roo," said Jacob, shaking hands firmly, "I must confess you've done remarkable things, young man. We must meet soon and discuss some ventures I have in mind."

He moved along, and Sylvia lingered. "We've just returned from the country and I would love it if you would come for supper again, soon, Roo." Her eyes never left his and the way she said his name made his knees week.

Then she leaned forward and whispered in his ear, "Very soon."

Then she was moving past him and he felt her breast brush against his arm. He turned to watch her as she vanished into the now crowded house.

"And who was that?" came Karli's voice.

He turned and discovered his wife standing before him, returned from upstairs. Roo blinked, then said, "Ah, that was Jacob Ester-brook and his daughter, Sylvia."

Karli made a disapproving noise under her breath. "The shame of the woman, coming out in public half-naked like that. And look at those men fawning over her."

Roo narrowed his gaze, for one of the men fawning over her was Duncan, who was quickly cutting off every other young man in the room as they sought to get close to Sylvia. Roo turned to greet his next guest, and said, "Well, she's pretty and her father is one of the richest men in the Kingdom and has no sons. She's quite a catch for any single lad."

Karli said, "I noticed that didn't keep you and the other married men from drooling down her dress." She took Roo's arm in a possessive fashion and stood there until it was clear no more guests were to arrive.

The party lasted well past midnight and Roo couldn't remember a tiny fraction of most of the conversations he had held. He had

been pointedly vague when pressed on matters of business, referring people to Jerome or telling them to stop by at Barret's the
next business day.

He mixed as best he could, trying to keep track of who spoke
to him on which matter, but the truth was he was drunk on wine
and success. He was one of four partners in the Bitter Sea Trading
and Holding Company, but he was rumored to be the driving force
behind the sudden emergence of this powerful new company.
Women flirted with him and men sought to engage him in conversation, but throughout the night he was only concerned with
two things: basking in the glow of triumph and keeping track of
Sylvia Esterbrook.

Each time he caught sight of her across the room, his breath
caught in his throat, and when he saw another man hovering over
her, he felt anger building inside. Karli kept him moving among
the guests, only pausing to speak with the Duke and his family,
forgetting for the time she socialized with nobility that moments
before she was furious with Roo for his behavior around Sylvia.
Twice she left to nurse Abigail, and when she returned she found
her husband watching Esterbrook's daughter.

At some point the crowd began to depart and bade their hosts
good-bye. While Roo and Karli were standing at the door, Jacob
came and took Roo's hand. "My thanks for inviting us to the celebration of your new company, Rupert." He smiled at Karli. "Mrs.
Avery, it's been a pleasure to meet you."

Karli smiled but glanced around and said, "Where is your daughter, Mr. Esterbrook?"

Jacob smiled. "Oh, she's somewhere in there." He took his
cloak when the doorman presented it to him, folding it over his
arm while waiting for his coach to be brought up from where it
was waiting. "I have no doubt at least a half dozen of those young
lads have agreed to escort her home. I am not able to keep late
hours any more."

"Indeed," said Karli coolly. The coach arrived and Esterbrook
departed. A little while later, Duke James and his wife and their
son and his wife left, again setting Karli nearly glowing with pride.
While many rich and powerful men had visited her father in his
modest home, no noble had ever passed through their portal. And
in the first evening of entertaining in the new house, the most

powerful man in the Kingdom after the royal family had come calling.

Seeing that neither Jimmy nor Dash had accompanied their parents, Roo said, "Excuse me a moment, please," to his wife and left.

He found Jimmy talking to the very pretty daughter of a miller who now worked for the Bitter Sea Company and took him by the elbow, moving him away without even an apology. "Where's Dash?"

Jimmy glanced over his shoulder and made an expression of regret to the young woman, mouthing that he would be back in a moment. "He's over there." Jimmy pointed across the room.

Sylvia Esterbrook commanded a portion of the main salon, with a circle of admirers around her. At her side stood Duncan, his most charming smile on display as he told some story of his adventures, to Sylvia's amusement and the irritation of the other young men. Dash stood a short way beyond, watching in a very observant fashion. "It's his turn," said Jimmy.

"His turn for what?" said Roo.

Jimmy whispered, "We're taking turns to make sure no one gets fingermarks on your young Miss Esterbrook." He glanced back at the young woman he had been speaking with and said, "That particular young lady is . . . very interesting, and as I am really not in your employ and Dashel is, he thought it the brotherly thing to do to watch over your friend for you, while I . . . take advantage of the opportunity to become . . . better acquainted with that sweet girl there."

" '*Your* young Miss Esterbrook'? 'Watch over *your* friend'?" repeated Roo, his expression darkening.

Jimmy whispered, "It wouldn't do if one of these young gentlemen got a little too much to drink and made a fool of himself over such an unusually pretty woman, would it? Given Mr. Esterbrook's importance in the community, I mean?"

Roo said, "I guess not. Is Dash seeing her home?"

"Either he or Duncan," said Jimmy.

Roo nodded and said, "Get back to your young lady." He moved through the party until he found Luis, who was sitting as if at home, his bad hand kept in a large pocket on the side of his new jacket.

Luis raised his good hand, holding a drink. "*Señor,*" he greeted Roo in his native Rodezian dialect. "You are a man of consequence, to all appearances."

"Thank you," said Roo. "Who's at the shop?"

"Bruno, Jack, and I believe Manuel. Why?"

"Just thinking." He glanced around. "I would like you and Duncan to stop by there on your way back to your house. Just to check up on things."

Luis glanced past Roo and caught sight of Roo's cousin and Sylvia. After a second, he said, "I understand." He stood. "But that leads me to another matter."

"What?" asked Roo, still distracted.

"I would like to find other quarters."

"Why?" asked Roo, his attention suddenly focused upon Luis.

Luis shrugged. "I am a man of simple needs, and your cousin, well . . . Duncan has many friends calling. I enjoy my work, and find little time to rest given his . . . late hours."

Roo thought of it a moment and realized that with the money he was now paying Duncan, he was probably bringing a different barmaid or whore home every night. The house he and Luis shared was tiny, and it had to be difficult for the solitary Rodezian. "Find yourself new quarters tomorrow. I'll raise your pay to whatever is necessary to cover the extra expense. Make it a nice, quiet place."

"Thank you," said Luis with one of his rare smiles. "Now I will explain to Duncan we need to check up on the shop on our way home."

Roo nodded and returned to the door, where Karli was bidding guests good night. "There you are," she said with a dark look. "Where have you been?"

"With Luis." He came to stand beside her, bade good night to another departing guest, and then said to Karli, "He wants his own quarters, so I gave him leave to find a place away from Duncan."

"That I can understand," said Karli.

Roo sighed. He knew she and Duncan had never gotten along on the few occasions he had come to the house. There was something about him that simply put her off, and the harder Duncan tried to win her over with his charming nonsense, the more distasteful she found his company. She had tried to keep her dislike to herself, but Roo saw it, and after he asked her about it, she had admitted as much.

A little while later, Luis and Duncan came to the door, and while Luis bid Karli good night, Duncan leaned over and whispered into his cousin's ear, "I would really like to stay a while longer, Roo."

Roo said, "I'd sleep better if you checked out the shop and made sure everything was in order."

Duncan's features clouded. "I'm sure you would."

Roo took him by the elbow and steered him a few steps away. "I've also told Luis to move out of your house."

This caught Duncan completely off guard. "What?" he said.

"Well," said Roo in a conspiratorial tone, "you're rising in the world along with me, and . . ." Letting his gaze wander to where Sylvia and the daughters of several other wealthy men stood in conversation with a number of young men, he added, "And I thought you might do with a little more privacy for your . . . en-tertaining. I told Luis to find himself new quarters."

Duncan didn't know what to make of this for a moment, but then he smiled and said, "Thank you, cousin. Most generous of you."

Roo hurried Duncan back to the door, where he bade Karli good night. A little while later, Dash came and said, "I'm going to escort Miss Esterbrook back to her father's house."

Roo nodded and attempted to look uninterested. He turned to find Karli's eyes fixed upon him. Smiling, he said, "This is going on longer than I wanted. Why don't you check up on Abigail while I shoo out the last of the guests? I'll be up in a while."

Karli looked unconvinced, but she nodded, lifted the hem of her dress, and walked to the stairway and quickly climbed to the second floor.

Roo made a brisk tour of the room, politely making it clear to those still there that the party was drawing to a close. He found Jerome Masterson asleep in a large chair in a small room off the main parlor, his arms wrapped around a now empty bottle of very expensive Keshian brandy. Lifting his partner by the arm, Roo carried him to the main salon, where he saw his bookkeeper deep in conversation with another young man. He motioned for Jason to come over and gave Masterson's care over to him, instructing him to see his partner got home safely.

As he reached the door, the last of the guests were leaving, including Sylvia and Dash. As the last visitor departed, Dash's hired carriage pulled up to the door. Sylvia turned to bid Roo good night and feigned a stumble, falling against him. He caught her and felt her body hard against his. She whispered, "My goodness! I must have had too much wine." Her face was mere inches from his as she looked into his eyes and said, "What must you think of me?"

Then, as if by impulse, she kissed his cheek and whispered, "Please come soon." Stepping back, she turned and said, "Thank you again, Rupert. And again forgive my . . . clumsiness."

She moved quickly down the steps and entered the carriage as Dash held the door open for her. He glanced back at his employer, then climbed in after her, and the carriage headed off down the street.

Roo watched until it disappeared and then returned to the door. He walked inside and found the three hired servants waiting. He thanked them for their good work, paid them with a bonus, and sent them on their way. He knew Mary would already be asleep, as would Rendel, for they would both be up at dawn the next day. He pulled off his coat and tossed it on the end of the banister, too tired to hang it in the wardrobe his wife had purchased for his clothing.

His mind was afire with images of Sylvia Esterbrook and he could not be rid of her feel, her scent in his nostrils, her warmth, and her lips upon his cheek. His body ached for her as he entered the darkened bedroom he shared with Karli. He glanced over and found Abigail asleep in her crib and was relieved. If the baby had been in bed with his wife he would have retired to one of the guest rooms rather than risk awakening her.

He quickly undressed and got under the covers. In the darkness, he heard Karli say, "Did everyone finally go?"

Still slightly intoxicated, he laughed. "No, I left a few of them in the garden; I'll set them loose in the morning."

Karli sighed. "Was the party a success?"

He rolled over and said, "You were there; what did you think?"

"I think you enjoyed being with those powerful men . . . and beautiful women."

Roo reached out and felt his wife's shoulder through the thin cotton of her nightshirt. "I like looking," he tried to say lightly. "What man wouldn't? But I know where home is."

"Really, Roo?" she asked, rolling on her side to face him. "Do you mean that?"

He said, "Of course I do." He pulled her toward him and kissed her. A moment later he was fully aroused and pulling her nightshirt over her head.

He took her fast and hard and at no time was he thinking of her. For those passion-filled minutes, his mind was completely engulfed with images of another woman. As he panted to a conclusion, he could only think of Sylvia's scent and touch. After he had spent himself, he rolled over and lay on his back, staring at the ceiling and wondering if Sylvia's carriage had reached her home yet.

They had ridden in silence. Dash had waited for her to speak first and she had said nothing until halfway to the estate. At last she said, "I'm sorry, but I've forgotten your name."

"Dashel," he said with a grin. "Jameson. You met my father and brother."

She frowned. "Your father?"

"Arutha, Lord Vencar."

She gasped as if completely embarrassed. "Oh my! Then your grandfather is . . ."

"The Duke of Krondor," he finished. "I'm that one."

She regarded him in a new light. "I had you confused with that other fellow, who doesn't speak much when I'm around."

"That would be Jason," said Dash. "He's completely awestruck by you, miss."

"And you're not?" she asked, a playful tone in her voice.

Dash's grin widened. "Not particularly."

"I bet I could change your mind," she said, leaning forward so her face was inches from his and her gown provided an ample expanse of bosom for his inspection.

He leaned forward also, until his nose was almost touching hers. Whispering in a conspiratorial tone, he said, "I bet you could, too."

Then he sat back. "But I am, unfortunately, pledged to another."

She leaned back, resting against the seat. Tapping her chin, she laughed. "Who is the lucky woman?"

"I don't know," he said. "But she's the daughter of some noble house, no doubt. My grandfather will inform me when the time comes."

She feigned a pout. "That's a disappointment."

Dash shrugged, as if bored by the discussion. "It seems to have worked out for my mother and father. They are, by all outward appearance, rather fond of one another."

They rode on in silence for the rest of the journey. When they entered the estate, the gateman ran alongside the carriage so he could open the door for Sylvia. Dash got out and presented her with his hand and she stepped down. He escorted her to the door and she opened it, turned, and said, "Are you sure I can't convince you to come inside?" She moved close to him and slid her hand down his chest until it was below his belt.

Dash endured the fondling a moment, then stepped back. "I'm very sorry, miss."

He turned and hurried to the carriage and climbed inside, while Sylvia went inside the house displaying a wicked smile and sounding a poorly concealed laugh.

The carriage rolled through the gate and toward the city as Dash considered that his employer was in for a great deal of trouble. He now regretted he had been so generous with Jimmy, allowing him to pursue the miller's daughter. After a minute, Dash stuck his head out the window and shouted, "Driver!"

"Yes, sir?"

"Take me to the Sign of the White Wing!"

"Yes, sir!" came the reply.

Dash sat back and sighed. After a long moment of reflection, he muttered, "Bitch."

Sixteen

Friends

KARLI FROWNED.

Roo was dressing hurriedly for his supper appointment and did not seem to pay attention to what she was saying. Catching sight of her expression, he said, "I'm sorry, dear. What was that?"

"I said I was hoping you would be dining in tonight. I have something to talk to you about."

Smoothing back his hair with a brush, he glanced in the mirror at his reflection and frowned slightly. No matter how rich the clothing, how expensive the barber, he still didn't care much for how he looked.

A tiny sound of delight caused him to look down and he saw his daughter crawling in the doorway. Then she shrieked with joy as she gripped the doorjamb and stood. She couldn't quite walk yet, though she was trying, but she could manage to stand now, if she had something to hold on to. Karli turned, impatience on her face. "Mary!" she shouted.

"Yes, ma'am?" came the reply from the next room.

"You let Abigail out of your sight and she was crawling here on the landing," scolded Karli. Mary seemed to have some strange notion that she could set the baby down and leave and return to find the child in the same place. That hadn't been true for nearly three months now. "What if she fell down the stairs?" said Karli.

Roo saw his daughter grinning at him, drool dribbling down her chin. Little teeth were emerging, and she often fussed through the night, but he had to admit he was becoming fond of her.

He bent down and picked up the child, who viewed him with a skeptical eye. The baby put out her hand, trying to stick as many fingers as possible into his mouth, when Roo was suddenly greeted by a very strong odor.

"Oh no," he said, holding the child at arm's length, while he looked for any sign of a diaper leak on his new coat. Not seeing one, he carried the baby—still at arm's length—into the next room, where he said, "Dearest, the baby has filled her diapers . . . again."

Karli took the girl and sniffed delicately, saying, "I believe you're right."

Roo pecked her on the cheek. "I'll try not to be too late, but if talks go on into the night . . . don't wait up for me."

Before she could say anything, he was out the door. His carriage had been brought around from the storage yard behind the house. He had purchased it the month before and occasionally rode around the city in it, just to be seen.

The Bitter Sea Company, as it was known, was rapidly consolidating its power base, and the name Roo Avery was on its way to becoming famous throughout Krondor and the Western Realm. As Roo climbed into the carriage, he considered what he might do to further expand his reach financially. The Blue Star Shipping Company was reportedly in financial difficulty, and Roo thought the Bitter Sea Company would be needing more ships soon. Perhaps he should have Duncan sniff around the waterfront for further rumors, while he had Dash and Jason talk to their contacts. Roo wished he could convince Dash's brother, Jimmy, to come to work for him as well, considering how useful he had proven during the grain manipulation. But while Dash was working with Roo with his grandfather's blessing, the Duke seem determined to keep his other grandson working at the palace.

Roo settled back into the carriage and used a gold-topped walking stick to knock on the roof, signaling the driver he was ready to leave. The other thing that passed through Roo's mind as he rode through Krondor was how he might exact revenge on Timothy Jacoby. Hurting him in the grain swindle hadn't been enough. Twice since then Jacoby and Sons had pulled trades to the disadvantage of the Bitter Sea Company. It was also attracting other firms into loose alliance, due in the main to fear of the Bitter Sea's growing power. But merely being more successful than Jacoby and Sons wasn't enough for Roo. Until Tim lay dead before him, he wouldn't count the debt for Helmut squared.

He considered a half-dozen plans and discarded them all. When a confrontation finally occurred, events had to appear as if Roo had nothing to do with inciting it; otherwise he might find himself back in the death cell, and now he had far too much to lose.

As if wealth was a lodestone, attracting more wealth, so his success in forming the Bitter Sea Company had caused more opportunities to appear. He now controlled most of the freight between Krondor and the north, and a very serious percentage of it between Krondor and the Eastern Realm. Only between Kesh and the Kingdom did he fail to gain any significant presence. Much of that trade had been secured by Jacoby and Sons, and those contracts appeared unbreakable. In fact, if anything, they appeared to be growing, as caravans from the south seemed on the rise.

Thoughts of business and trade vanished as the carriage approached the gates of the Esterbrook estate. The servant inside the gate inquired who was seeking admission and Roo's driver called out his master's name. The gate quickly opened. This was the fourth time since his grand party that Roo had visited the Esterbrook house. The first time, Sylvia had been flirtatious and charming. The second she had lingered after her father had bid Roo good evening, and she had again kissed his cheek, pressing her body against his, and again she blushed and claimed it was the effect of the wine. The last time she had again lingered, only this time the kiss had been passionate and not on the cheek, and she had said nothing about wine, only that he should return soon. The dinner invitation had arrived two weeks later.

Despite his impatience to see Sylvia again, Roo waited for another servant to open the door once the carriage came to a stop. He dismounted and said to the driver, "Return to the city and get supper. Then return here later. Wait here until I appear. I do not know how late I may be."

The driver saluted and drove off, while Roo mounted the steps to the door. When the servant opened the door for him and he stepped inside, he was greeted by Sylvia, who smiled broadly at him. "Rupert!" she exclaimed as if she weren't expecting him. The sound of his name on her lips sent a shiver through him, and sight of her in another of those scandalously low-cut gowns caused him to flush in excitement. She slipped her arm through his and kissed him on the cheek, pressing her bosom hard against him. "You look very handsome tonight," she said softly in his ear. He swore she almost purred when she spoke.

She led him to the dining room and he saw only two places set. "Where's your father?" he asked, suddenly alarmed and excited at the same time.

She smiled. "He's out of the city on business. I thought you knew. I could have sworn I wrote something to that effect on the invitation. Didn't I?"

Roo sat after she had taken her seat and said, "No, I thought the invitation was from Jacob."

"It was from me. I hope you don't mind."

Roo felt his face flush. "No," he said quietly, "I certainly don't mind."

He could hardly eat and found himself reaching for his wine-glass repeatedly. By the time Sylvia announced supper was over, he was fairly down the road to being drunk. He rose and escorted her toward the entryway. He couldn't remember one word in ten they had spoken. As they left the dining room, Sylvia turned to the servants and said, "That will be all. We will not be needing you further tonight."

Instead of leading Roo toward the front door, she instead guided him up the stairs. He was afraid to speak, lest he wake her from some dream. Down a long corridor they walked and then she opened the door. She stepped across the threshold and gently pulled him through. Reaching around him, she pushed the door closed while he stood motionless, staring at the gigantic canopied bed that occupied the room.

Then she wrapped her arms around his neck and kissed him. Whatever shreds of rational thought Roo still possessed vanished at that moment.

In the darkness, Roo stared up at the canopy above. He could hear Sylvia breathing slowly and evenly and assumed she was asleep. He was exhausted, but also too keyed up to sleep. She was the most incredible women he had known. She was the most beautiful woman he had ever seen, but for the well-bred daughter of a rich merchant, she was an astonishing mix of playful childishness and wanton sensuality. She made love like a veteran of the Sign of the White Wing and was willing—no, eager—to perform acts that would have appalled Karli.

Thinking of his wife, he pushed aside a twinge of guilt. He knew now that he didn't love her; he had married her from pity. He looked at where Sylvia lay, and sighed. This is the woman he should have upon his arm, he thought, not the dowdy little woman who was now at home, asleep in the belief he was discussing business with some shipping magnate. It was Sylvia whom he should be presenting to nobility, and it was Sylvia who should be bearing him children.

His heart pounded in his chest and his love for Sylvia became a bittersweet pang. He lay upon his side, staring at the barely seen outline of her in the darkness. In his boyhood dreams he had never imagined he would be the man he was at this moment, nor would he have dreamed that a woman of Sylvia Esterbrook's stunning beauty and charm would be sharing her bed with him.

Rolling on his back, he stared at the dark cloth above him and wondered at the miracle of change he had experienced since the night he and Erik had fled from the hounds in Ravensburg.

Thinking of Erik made Roo wonder where his friend might be and what he was doing. He knew Erik was across the sea somewhere with Calis, de Loungville, and some men he didn't know. And he had no idea what they were doing, but he suspected it was something dire. And he knew exactly why they were doing it.

Feeling no peace at such thoughts, he gently reached out and ran his hand down the amazingly soft skin of the woman at his side. She instantly stirred and moved in a languid fashion. Without words she rolled over and came to him, engulfing him in her arms. Amazed at how she knew instantly what he wished, he left all thoughts of Erik behind.

Erik pointed at the rocks. "To port! To port!"

The storm raged as the steersman fought to pull the tiller hard, turning the ship to port and away from crashing death. Erik had stood at the prow of the dragon ship for hours, looking through the dim murk of the early morning light, swirling snow, and fog, trying to avoid running the ship aground.

They had shot past the southern tip of Great Kesh, catching the current that they had been told would carry them swiftly across the sea to Novindus. Days had passed and the dragon boat with its sixty-four passengers—Calis, de Loungville, Erik, Miranda, and sixty soldiers of Calis's Eagles—sped across the ocean.

The rowers pulled in shifts all day and all night, adding their muscle to the current, and the boat raced across a seemingly empty expanse of ocean. Miranda used her magical ability from time to time to judge their position and claimed they were where they should be.

The weather had grown bitter cold and occasionally they would sight an iceberg floating northward. Miranda had told Erik one night that the southern pole of the world was captured by ice year round, a mass so large the mind couldn't imagine, and from that massive shelf of ice pieces the size of cities would fall into the ocean, drifting northward to melt in the warm air of the Blue or Green Sea.

Erik had remained dubious until one day he had seen what he had thought to be a sail on the horizon, only to find later in the day it was one of those huge pieces of ice Miranda had warned about. From that point forward they had kept extra watches and set the rowers to shifts around the clock to keep moving.

They had found a peninsula of that ice-covered land, and unfortunately came upon it too quickly. They were now trying desperately to keep the ship from crashing against it. Calis had warned that if they were stranded there, they would die a cold, hungry death, and there was nothing that could be done to save them.

"Row, damn you!" shouted Bobby de Loungville over the roar of surf, wind, and the groaning of wood as the ship heaved and turned against every demand of nature.

Erik could feel them moving sideways, as the powerful current took them into the tug of the surf. "More to port!" he shouted, and the two men on the tiller pushed to obey. Calis stood at the rear of the ship and added his superhuman strength, and the tiller creaked alarmingly. They had been warned that the long tillers of these Brijaner dragon ships could snap off, and then the only possible way to steer would be by controlling the stroke of the rowers. They had also been warned that even an experienced crew of

Brijaners could do this only with difficulty, and no man on this boat was either experienced or a Brijaner.

Miranda appeared upon the deck and with a large motion of both arms shouted a word that was nearly unheard at the bow where Erik watched. Suddenly a force pulled hard against the ship from the rear, and Erik had to grab at the rail to keep from going over into the water. The boat hesitated in its dash to destruction, and then stopped a moment in the water.

Then the ship obeyed the rowers and tiller, turning to break free of the pull of the tide, and started to move on a course parallel to the coastline. Miranda let her hands drop and took a deep breath. She made her way to the bow of the boat and Erik watched her with interest. She shared the tiny cabin in the rear with the Captain, and Erik had some idea that this was more than mere courtesy on Calis's part. There was something between them, though Erik couldn't begin to guess what it might be. De Loungville acted like the Captain's personal guard dog when Calis and Miranda were inside, and only an event of the gravest consequence would cause a crewman to dare to try to get past him.

Miranda was certainly attractive enough, thought Erik, as she came near, but there was something about her that still disturbed him in a way that made any notion of being intimate almost impossible to imagine. Almost, because like the other men on the boat, Erik hadn't been with a woman in months.

As she came to his side, she pointed dead ahead into the murk. "I dare not use another spell, certainly not one that powerful, for a few days, lest we call undue attention to ourselves. So pay heed: if you could see through this mess," she said, "you would see a tiny grouping of three stars, almost a perfect equal triangle, two hands' spans above the horizon, one hour after sundown. If you point toward that, you'll eventually come to the coast of Novindus less than a day's rowing from Ispar. Steer along the coastline, bearing to the northeast, and you'll find the mouth of the river Dee. We need to use nonmagical means to find our destination."

Miranda was obviously tired from the magic she had employed to keep the boat off the rocks, and more talkative in five minutes than she had been the entire trip. Erik wondered if it was just because of the magic she used, or from some other reason, but was reluctant to ask if everything was all right. Then he considered that nothing associated with the voyage was right. Miranda was far closer to the truth of this mission than Erik, and Erik knew enough to expect they might not be coming back. He imagined she must be even more worried than he was. Finally he said, "Are you all right?"

She looked at him in open surprise, her expression frozen for a long moment, then laughed. Erik was unsure of the cause of that laughter, but finally she gripped his arm, through the heavy fur cloak he wore, and said, "Yes, I'm all right." She sighed. "The sighting spells I was using along the way were a whisper in the noise of a market at noon. The spell I just cast to keep us from the rocks was a shriek in the night. If someone is looking for us, or if wards have been set to detect magic . . ." Shaking her head, she turned away.

"Miranda?" asked Erik.

She halted and looked over her shoulder. "Yes, Erik?"

"Are we going to get home, do you think?"

Whatever amusement she had revealed a moment before vanished. She paused only briefly when she said, "Probably not."

Erik resumed his position, watching the murk for sudden danger. After another few hours, Alfred, the corporal from Darkmoor, came and said, "I'm relieving you, Sergeant."

Erik said, "Very well," and returned to the rowing oars. Once he had broken Alfred down, stripped him of the rank and attitude that had made him a bully and brawler back home, the man had turned into a first-rate soldier. Erik considered it likely that he would be one of the first to be promoted to corporal when they returned to Krondor . . . then amended the thought to *if* they returned to Krondor.

Other than the tiny cabin where the Captain and Miranda slept, the only place to sleep was either leaning over the extra oars behind the last rowers' bench, like a galley slave, or lying on the deck between the rowers. They slept in shifts. Lesser-trained men might have come to blows, given the cramped quarters, the months at sea, and the coming danger, but de Loungville and Calis had picked the sixty most disciplined men in the company. Any temper was deferred, and any discomfort was kept to oneself.

Erik lay down and almost instantly dropped off to sleep. Fatigue was a constant companion, and after years of soldiering and grabbing sleep when he could, little could stir his mind enough to keep him awake. But as he fell into slumber, he did wonder in passing how his friends back home were doing. He wondered if Roo was making any progress toward being a rich man, and how Jadow's leg had healed, and how the other men in the command were training. He wished he had Greylock to talk to, and then he thought of Nakor. That funny little man, and Sho Pi, had not returned from Stardock with the Captain, and Erik pondered what they must be up to as sleep overtook him.

A dozen young men and women laughed, while twice that number scowled, muttered, or jeered.

"It's true!" insisted Nakor.

Sho Pi stood beside the man he had claimed as his master, looking to defend him should any of the angry students decide it was time to take matters into their own hands. He wasn't concerned over Nakor's ability to defend himself against up to a half dozen of them—he knew exactly how adept Nakor was at open-handed fighting, the Isalani style taught at the temple of Dala—but against a full dozen or more he would need help.

"Sit down," cried one of those who had been laughing at one of those nearby who was jeering.

"Why don't you make me?" demanded the object of the instruction.

Nakor said, "Wait a minute." He crossed to where the two young men were standing opposite one another and grabbed each by the ear.

It was a beautiful dawn at Stardock, and Nakor had gotten into a discussion with a student at the predawn breakfast. As the sun began to rise in the east, Nakor had decided to conduct a class outside, away from the musty dark halls that usually served for places of instruction. As he led the two howling young men into the center of the large circle, all three factions of students began to laugh.

Sho Pi glanced up at the high window overlooking the lawn upon which the lesson was being conducted, and saw the faces at that window. Since being left in charge of the Academy, Nakor had left most of the daily operation as he had found it, though from time to time he had taken it upon himself to teach a lesson on one thing or another.

Most of his time was spent with the nameless, mindless beggar who was now a fixture of the island. Each morning, two students were delegated to throwing the beggar into the lake, a marginal effort toward keeping the man clean. Once in a while one or another of the more ambitious students would try to apply soap to the man, often resulting in a bloody nose or black eye.

When not soaking wet, the man scampered from place to place, watching what everyone else did, or he slept, or he haunted the kitchen area, trying to steal food unless it was given to him. When presented with meals, he knocked the plates over, as a child might, and proceeded to squat and eat with his fingers from the floor.

The rest of Nakor's time was spent in the library, reading and making notes. Sho Pi was occasionally given the opportunity to ask a question or request instruction in something that he wished to understand better. Nakor often obliged him by sending him on some strange quest or asked him a seemingly incomprehensible riddle. When he accomplished the quest or admitted failure, or when he guessed the answer of the riddle, Nakor's reaction was one of universal indifference.

The two howling students were released and Nakor said, "Thank you for volunteering to aid me in demonstrating the truth of my claim."

To the student who belonged to the faction known as the Blue Riders, after Nakor's previous tenure at the Academy, he said, "You believe I am being honest when I say that the energies we call magic can be manipulated without resorting to all the mumbo-jumbo most of you think is required, is that not so?"

"Of course, Master," said the student.

Nakor sighed. All the Blue Riders called him master, despite his objections, a legacy of Sho Pi's doing.

To the other student, a member of the faction calling themselves the Wand of Watoom, he said, "And you don't think it's possible, correct?"

"Of course it's not possible. Sleight-of-hand, street mummery, certainly, but not true manipulation of the forces of magic."

Holding up a finger, Nakor said. "Then observe." As he moved to position himself behind his student, the nameless beggar came pushing through the circle of students. Once in a while the man whom everyone but Nakor counted mad showed an interest in what was going on. He squatted a few feet away and watched.

Nakor asked the student behind whom he stood, "Did you take any training in the reiki I taught last month?"

"Of course," said the student.

"Very well," said Nakor. "This is much the same thing. Make a fist." He took the arm of the student and bent it back, then positioned the young man's feet in a fighter's stance. To the other student he said, "Just stand there, if you don't mind."

Nakor said, "Pull back your arm and feel the energy that is in you. Close your eyes if it will help."

The student did so. "Now," said Nakor, "feel the energy in you, coursing through you and around you. Feel it flow. When you are ready, I want you to strike a blow at that young man's stomach, but more than just a blow, I want you to release the energy through the knuckles of your hand.

"Get ready," he said to the student who was about to be struck. "Tighten your stomach or something. This might hurt."

The doubting student smirked, but braced himself in case. The first student struck the blow and it thudded into the second student's stomach, causing him barely to flinch.

"Need to work on this," said Nakor. "You're not feeling the energy."

Suddenly the beggar jumped to his feet and pushed the first student aside. He balanced himself perfectly on the balls of his feet, and closed his eyes, and Nakor stepped away as he felt a fey energy crackle through the air around him. Then the beggar whipped back his hand, shot it forward, exhaling his breath as he said something that sounded like "shut." When the blow struck, the doubting student seemed to fly backward off his feet, with an audible explosion of breath from his lungs. He sailed a half-dozen feet through the air to land atop two other students, who barely had time to react and catch him.

The struck student doubled up, holding his stomach and obviously choking. Nakor rushed over, rolled the boy on his back, and picked him up around the waist, forcing him to breathe. With a ragged inhale, and tears running down his face, the student looked at Nakor with eyes wide. Barely able to speak, he said, "I was wrong."

"Yes, you were," agreed Nakor. He told two other students, "Take him inside and have the healer check him over for injury. Something inside may be damaged."

He turned to find the beggar was back on his haunches, watching with vacant eyes. Sho Pi came over and said, "Master, what was that?"

Softly Nakor said, "I wish I knew."

Then he turned to the other students. "You see? Even that poor creature knows enough to utilize the power that is already there, around you, everywhere." Seeing that most faces were only showing astonished confusion, Nakor waved his hand toward the main building and said, "Very well. This lesson is over. Go back to whatever it is you do at this time."

As the students departed, Nakor came over to where the beggar squatted, and hunkered down to gaze at the man's eyes. Where, for a brief instant, something powerful and wise had been glimpsed, now only a vacant pair of orbs were seen. Nakor sighed. "My friend," he said, "just what are you?"

After a moment he stood and turned, to find Sho Pi, as he had expected. "I wish I were a smarter man," he told his self-appointed student. "I wish I knew more."

"Master?" was all Sho Pi said.

Nakor shrugged. "Wish I knew what's happened to Calis, too. I'm getting bored here, and besides," he said, looking into the blue western sky as the sun cleared the horizon behind him, "something's going on. We're going to have to leave soon, whether or not someone from Krondor comes to run things here."

"When, Master?" asked Sho Pi.

Nakor shrugged. "I don't know. Soon. Maybe this week. Maybe next month. We'll know when it's time. Come on. Let's get some food."

At the mention of food the mindless beggar jumped up and with grunting and hooting sounds started shambling toward the dining hall. Nakor pointed after him. "See, our very basic friend there understands the relative importance of things."

Then to Sho Pi, in the Isalani tongue, he said, "And he hits like a Grand Master of the Order of Dala."

Sho Pi answered in the same language, "No, Master. Harder. Whatever else, that man has more *cha*"—he used an ancient word for personal power—"than any priest I ever saw when I was a monk in the temple." Lowering his voice, he said, "He could have killed that boy, I think."

Nakor said, "Had he wanted to, no doubt."

As they entered the dining hall, both men considered what they had just witnessed.

Roo awoke to a grey, predawn light showing in the window. He realized that he would barely be able to return home before Karli awoke. He knew it possible the baby had slept through the night and Karli might be convinced he had returned earlier, but he would have to move quickly.

He left the bed as quietly as he could, regretting the need. The memory of Sylvia's body and her urgent demands throughout the night aroused him despite his fatigue. He dressed and quietly left the room, moving down the stairs and out the door. He approached his coach, where his driver was dozing, and woke the man, instructing him to head for home at once.

Inside the house Sylvia lay awake, smiling to herself. In the darkness, she thought, the little troll wasn't too difficult to take. He was young, enthusiastic, and a lot stronger than he looked. She knew that while he thought himself in love with her, he had barely begun to experience the depth of obsession she would bring him to. Within a month he would be willing to compromise some minor business matter for her. Within a year, he'd betray his business partners.

She yawned and stretched in satisfaction. Her father wouldn't be returning for a few days and she knew she'd receive a note from Roo before midday. She'd ignore him for a day or two, then invite him back to the house. For a sleepy moment she wondered how long she should wait before her contrition scene, when she announced to Roo that she couldn't continue to see a married man, no matter how much she loved him. As she started to drift off to slumber, she considered there were a couple of young men in the city she should invite to the house before her father returned.

Roo tiptoed upstairs and slipped into the bedroom. The dawn was now breaking, and in the half-lighted room she could see Karli was asleep. He slipped out of his clothing and into bed next to her.

Less than a half hour later she awoke, and Roo pretended to be asleep. She arose and dressed, then went to where the baby was quietly singing to herself. After waiting awhile, Roo arose and went down to the dining room.

"Good morning," said Karli, feeding the baby.

Abigail giggled and said, "Da!" at sight of Roo.

Roo yawned.

"Did you get much sleep?" asked Karli, looking at him with a neutral expression on her face.

Roo pulled out a chair and sat, while Mary came from the kitchen with a large mug of coffee for him. "I feel like I slept for five minutes," he said.

Karli asked, "Late night?"

"Very. I don't even know what time we finished."

Karli made a noncommittal sound as she spooned mashed vegetables into the mouth of the hungry child.

After a few minutes, Karli said, "I have something to tell you."

Roo felt his chest tighten. He wondered for a panic-stricken moment if somehow she knew he had betrayed her, and then forced the thought aside. She hadn't suspected anything when he returned from Ravensburg after having tumbled Gwen, and he decided she had no reason to suspect anything now. Calmly he said, "What is it?"

She said, "I wanted to tell you last night, but you were in such a rush..."

"What is it?" Roo repeated.

"We're going to have another baby."

Roo looked at Karli and saw her eyes were searching his face, looking for a reaction. And he sensed she was fearful of what that reaction would be.

"Wonderful!" He forced himself to sound pleased. He stood, came around the table, and said, "This time a boy." He kissed her cheek.

"Maybe," Karli said softly.

Trying to sound jovial, Roo said, "It has to be a boy. Otherwise I'm going to have to have all the signs changed to 'Avery and Daughters,' and wouldn't that be something to see?"

She smiled weakly. "If a son will make you happy, I hope it's a boy."

He said, "If it's as wonderful a child as this one, then I'll be happy."

Karli didn't look convinced, and as Roo started to leave the room, laying his half-drunk cup of coffee on the table, she said, "Aren't you going to eat?"

"No," he said as he took down his coat from the peg on the wall next to the outer door, "I have to make straight for the office. I have an important letter to write, then I have to come back over here for a meeting at Barret's."

Without waiting for her to say anything else, he left the house and Karli heard the door slam. She sighed as she attempted to keep most of the food going into the baby's mouth and not onto the floor.

Time passed and life took on a strange but steady tempo. Roo conspired to steal away to Sylvia once or twice a week, while spending a like number of nights each week with his business associates. There had been a horrible scene when she had claimed remorse because he was married, and he had to beg for weeks to get her to agree to see him again. She had at last relented when he had sent her a diamond and emerald necklace that had cost him more gold than he could have imagined only two years before. Sylvia finally admitted she loved him, and Roo had fallen into a routine of illicit love and lying to his wife.

His strengths as a businessman emerged quickly, and rarely did he enter into a bad bargain, and those few he did become enmeshed in created little financial hardship. Over the course of months the Bitter Sea Company grew and prospered.

Roo also learned how best to deploy the skills of those working for him. Duncan was most valuable at ferreting out rumors and keys to trading opportunities among the inns and taverns of the caravansaries and docks. Jason was proving adept at the single most confounding element of business to Roo, the management of funds. There was far more to being a merchant prince than merely buying and selling. Such odd concepts as cross-collateralization and mutually shared risk among non-members of the company, where best to invest gold not being used for purchases, and when to seek safety by simply letting the gold sit—all these were areas of knowledge where Jason showed an uncanny knack, while Roo could barely follow along. Six months after he first bedded Sylvia, Roo's company took control of a countinghouse and began its own banking.

Luis was proving to be a treasure to Roo. He could be as gentle with an angry woman customer as he could be merciless with the toughest teamster. Twice he had to prove to one of the more belligerent that even with one crippled hand he was more than able to enforce his orders.

Dash was the mystery to Roo. He seemed indifferent to any personal gain, but was pleased by the growth of the Bitter Sea Company as much as Roo was. It was as if he was serving the company for the sheer pleasure of seeing it thrive rather than to benefit himself. And upon occasion, he even contrived to involve his brother in some scheme or another. Between the two of them, Jimmy and Dash could be a formidable pair against whom Roo wouldn't wish to find himself pitted.

As Karli grew with what he hoped was his son, Roo felt life could hardly be better save for two sour notes: the continued existence of Tim Jacoby and the absence of his friends from the old days.

Seventeen

Disasters

ROO SIGHED.

The baby squirmed in his arms as the priest droned through his incantations and poured scented oil on the baby's forehead. While he was thrilled at having a son, Roo decided that nothing would ever make the naming ceremony any more bearable.

"I name you Helmut Avery," said the priest at last.

Roo handed the child to Karli and kissed her upon the cheek. Then he kissed little Abigail, who was squirming in Mary's arms, and said, "I must rush to the office for a while, but I'll be home in two hours at the latest."

Karli looked dubious, knowing as she did that her husband often worked impossibly long hours, sometimes throughout the night and the next day, before returning home. "We have guests coming," she reminded him.

"I remember," he said as his family left the temple. Walking down the steps, he left Karli behind, saying, "You take the carriage. I'll walk from here."

Roo made his way along the streets until he was clear of Temple Square, when he found a public carriage and hired it. Within minutes he was leaving the city, on the road for the Esterbrook estate. He wondered at his foul mood. Sylvia had become such a source of wonder for him that any anger or frustration was left behind. And for reasons he hadn't pursued, her father never seemed to be at home these days, so within minutes of his arrival for supper—or like today, a surprise midday visit—Sylvia would welcome him with open arms and quickly lead him upstairs. Roo was astonished and delighted to discover her appetites matched his own. Occasionally he wondered who had first taught a well-bred young lady like Sylvia so many inventive lovemaking tricks, but she had never volunteered anything of her past before meeting Roo, nor had she asked about his previous experiences.

As the carriage rolled into the Esterbook estate, Roo realized the cause of his foul mood. Of those who attended Helmut's naming ceremony this day or who would attend the celebration that evening, the one Roo most wished could be there wasn't.

Erik signaled and the column of riders halted. By hand signs, the order to dismount was passed. Erik rode at the head of the column next to Miranda and Bobby de Loungville, while Calis and a man named Renaldo scouted ahead.

The boat had been beached at the location Calis had planned on, and the Captain had been visibly relieved when agents from the distant City of the Serpent River had appeared within days. News from the front was grim.

A great fleet was nearly half completed, and the armies of the Emerald Queen now held total control of the continent, save the small region south of the Ratn'gary Mountains and some of the western coast. Otherwise, the reports were uniformly dreadful. The Emerald Queen's host was ravaging the entire continent. They were stripping the land of every resource as they sought to create the great fleet they needed to cross the ocean and invade the Kingdom. The deaths of thousands of slaves captured during the war were ignored.

Several minor rebellions among the host of former mercenaries had been crushed mercilessly, with the rebels publicly crucified or impaled before elements of the army. As further punishment, one man in a thousand had been selected by lot to die by being burned alive before his comrades, a further warning that any sign of disobedience would bring only utter destruction.

Erik had thought about the time every man in his squad was held accountable for the other five. Each member of the squad had effectively seen that no one failed, because it would have returned every one of them to the gallows.

The only good news in all of this for Calis's company was that the Emerald Queen's whole attention was turned to the immediate area around the City of the Serpent River, the city of Maharta, and the Riverlands. The area in which Calis and his company were to operate was almost devoid of any sign of her army.

Calis observed that that would probably cease to be the case as they neared their destination. Horses had been secured and brought to the boat. Local clothing had been exchanged for their Brijaner gear, and six of Calis's agents took the Brijaner longship and moved it down the coast to a fishing village where they had made arrangements to hide it in a large drying shed until the time to escape came.

No one mentioned that few felt that possibility likely.

Now they were in the mountains, having moved through the foothills for a week, and had yet to encounter anything remotely dangerous. Erik had been one of those to flee the Saaur through the tunnels occupied by the Pantathians, and knew some of what they were likely to find, for once it had been determined that Calis's Eagles—whom the Pantathians thought to be only a rebel company of mercenaries—had entered the mountains, a full-scale Saaur occupation of the area had resulted. Erik knew only the bold deception in pretending to be one of the human companies replaced by the Saaur, and moving directly to the front, in the opposite direction from that which logic dictated they take, had saved them on that prior journey.

Renaldo ran up, and between pants reported to de Loungville. "The Captain's found a safe campsite and says we're done for the day."

Erik glanced around and saw several hours of daylight were left. De Loungville saw the same thing and said, "We're close?"

Renaldo nodded. He pointed through the trees. "There's a ridge there, and from there you can see both the river gorge and the bridge. I take the Captain's word for the latter."

Erik understood. Calis's vision was far more acute than any human's. But if they could see the gorge, they were but a day's ride from the bridge and from there to the entrance to the mines, another day's ride. If they decided to abandon the horses, it would be an extra two-day march from the bridge to the caves.

Erik dismounted, feeling mixed emotions; if they rode, things would be easier on the men, but to abandon the horses near the mines was a death sentence for the mounts. They were unlikely to cross the bridge by themselves and on the other side there was no fodder. Some might even fall to their deaths. Erik considered for a moment the irony of worrying more about the horses' survival than his own.

He shrugged off the thought as orders were passed to make camp. The men fell to with the discipline beaten into, taught to, and expected from them. Alfred had been recently promoted to corporal and was reminding Erik more each day of Charlie Foster, the corporal who first made Erik's every day a living hell at Bobby de Loungville's whim. Now, years later, Erik understood that making these men obey without hesitation or thought ensured the best chance for each man's survival and, more important, the achievement of the mission's goals.

When camp was readied, a rotation of guards was established and each man went to eat—trail rations and a cold camp, so as not to risk anyone seeing a fire. Winter was rapidly approaching, so it would be an uncomfortable night for everyone.

While everyone else was eating, Erik inspected the horses and made sure every mount was sound. He also saw that every man was where he was expected to be, then moved to where de Loungville, Calis, and Miranda sat.

Calis indicated Erik should sit. "Horses are fine," Erik said.

Calis said, "Good. We're going to have to find a place around here to leave them."

Miranda said, "Why bother?"

Calis shrugged. "I don't discount the chance we may get out of this and need a quick route out of the mountains. If there's a canyon around here with enough grazing for a week or two, I'd like to put the horses there. The heavy snows are not yet upon us, and the horses may prove useful."

Erik said, "When we passed around the peak at midday, I saw a small valley below us." He indicated the general direction. "I can't be sure, but I think there is a route down from the trail. A goat path, at least."

Calis said, "We're going to rest here for a couple of days, so investigate it tomorrow. If there's a way in, put the horses down there."

Erik was still not comfortable with the Captain, though he had spent enough time with Bobby to speak his mind when he felt the need. Still, if anything, the Captain appreciated direct talk when it concerned the mission. "Captain, why are we waiting? We run the risk of discovery each day we delay."

Calis said, "We're waiting for someone."

Miranda said, "I have an agent, and he's trying to find some local men we need to talk to."

Erik waited and no more was said, so he resigned himself to having to wait to find out who this mysterious agent of Miranda's might be, and who those local men were. He excused himself and rose to go see how the men were doing.

Erik was not surprised to find each man was doing exactly what he was supposed to do and that he needed to instruct none of them. This was the finest group of soldiers in the history of the Kingdom, according to Lord William and de Loungville, and Erik felt a fierce pride at being included in that number. He downplayed his own role in the creation of this unity, but took credit for his own evolution as a soldier.

He had spent hours reading every book on warfare and tactics and had taken the opportunity to speak with everyone in the palace he could on various military topics. He had even had occasion to discuss such issues with visiting nobles who came to call at the palace. Sometimes they'd chat over supper in the soldiers' commons, sometimes at a state dinner at the Prince's palace, and occasionally in the marshalling yard as some Border Baron or Eastern Duke had observed the training of Calis's Crimson Eagles.

Erik didn't think of himself as being particularly gifted in strategy, supply, or deployment, but he felt he had a knack for leading men, or at least getting them to do what needed to be done without having to resort to bullying and threats the way some officers did. He really enjoyed the feeling that if he led, other men would follow, and he couldn't quite put his finger on why he felt good about that; he just did.

Finishing his inspection, he sat and pulled a ration pack out of his saddlebags. He unwrapped the wax-dipped cloth, ensuring that the flaking pieces of wax fell onto another cloth; he knew that if he didn't inspect the site when they broke camp and make sure than not one flake of wax lingered to betray their passing, de

Loungville would. As much as his relationship had changed with
Bobby since the fateful day when Bobby had ordered Erik hung,
he still was not exempted from a public dressing-down if the Sergeant Major felt Erik wasn't discharging his duty.

Calis and Miranda approached and Erik said, "Captain?"

"We're going to walk a bit," said Calis. "Set your sentries and tell
them the call sign is two finger snaps and 'magpie.' Is that clear?"

Erik nodded. "Clear."

Whoever might blunder into this camp would be warned with
two finger snaps by the sentry. If he didn't respond instantly with
the word "magpie," he would be greeted with deadly force. Erik
hoped that no itinerant traders or mendicant friars came wandering
down that trail for the next few days.

As Calis began to depart, Erik said, "Captain?"

Calis halted. "Yes?"

"Why 'magpie'?"

Calis indicated Miranda with a nod of his head.

Miranda said, "Because it's the word my agent has, and besides,
magpies don't exist on this continent, so no lucky guesses."

Erik shrugged and returned to eating his supper.

Calis said, "We need to speak of a few things."

Miranda sat on a fallen tree bole. "Such as?"

Calis sat beside her. "If we survive, do we have a future? You
and I, I mean?"

Miranda took his hand in hers. "That is difficult to say." She
sighed. "No, that's impossible even to think about." She leaned
over and kissed him. "We have been special to each other since
we met, Calis." He said nothing. "We have found feelings for each
other that few people know." After another moment of silence she
said, "But the future? I don't know if we'll be alive next week."

Calis said, "Think on it. I plan on surviving."

Miranda studied his face in the golden light of the late afternoon
sun as it streamed through the trees. She laughed.

"What is so funny?" he asked, his lips turning up in a guarded
smile.

"I am," she said, standing and reaching behind her to unfasten
the ties of her dress. "I was always a fool for a pretty blond boy.
Now come, warm me up. It's a cold day."

As her dress fell to her ankles, he rose and wrapped his arms around her, his hands upon her buttocks; he picked her up in his arms, as easily as he would a child. Kissing her between her breasts, he playfully spun her around in a circle, then laid her gently down on the ground and said, "Boy? I'm past a half century of age, woman."

Miranda laughed. "My mother always said that younger men made enthusiastic lovers but often took themselves far too seriously."

Calis paused a moment, studying Miranda's face. "You never speak of your mother," he said softly.

Miranda said nothing for a long time, then laughed. "Get out of your clothes, boy!" she said in mock-command. "The ground is cold!"

Calis smiled broadly. "My father told me always to show respect to my elders."

Quickly they coupled, losing their fear of what tomorrow might bring in one of the most basic and life-affirming acts possible. For brief moments, their experience was one of shared joy and a denial of death, fear, and misery.

Two finger snaps were quickly followed by the word "magpie," spoken with a slightly odd accent. Erik was at the sentry point only moments before de Loungville and Calis.

They had waited three days, and Calis had decided that if Miranda's agent didn't show, he would move ahead, regardless. The horses had been moved to a lush valley that would keep them grazing for weeks. Erik also knew that if no one survived to return, the horses would find their way out of the valley and down into the lower meadows as winter approached. That made him feel better for a reason he couldn't articulate. While the mountains of Darkmoor were less impressive than those they now approached, Erik recognized the change in the weather. The nights would quickly fall below freezing and snow would come with the next storm. Winter was almost upon them.

The man who came into view in the lead was oddly dressed, in whitish armor that Erik instantly marked as not being any metal with which he was familiar. For one thing, it should have clanked loudly, but it didn't; for another, it should have made the man wearing it plod along, but he moved lightly upon his feet. His head was completely enclosed in a helm with two narrow eye slits, and upon his back he wore what appeared to be a crossbow of some alien design. Otherwise he fairly bristled with swords, daggers, and knives.

The two men who followed were familiar figures to Erik, who greeted them softly when they were close. "Praji! Vaja! It's good to see you again."

The two old fighters returned the greeting. "We'd heard you were among those who got away from Maharta, von Darkmoor," said Praji.

The two old men were armed as mercenaries, but Erik wondered how well they could still fight, given their advancing age. Still, he had seen firsthand two years previously Praji and Vaja's toughness, and nothing he saw now indicated they were any less skilled—just tired.

Prajichitas was as ugly a man as Erik had ever encountered, but smart and likable. Vajasia was a fading peacock of a man, still vain despite advancing years, and the two dissimilar men were as loyal to each other as brothers.

Miranda said, "Boldar, any trouble?"

The walking arsenal removed his helm, revealing a youthful face, freckled and pale, with red-brown hair and blue eyes. A slight sheen of perspiration was the only sign of exertion, while Praji and Vaja both came into camp and sat with open displays of fatigue.

The man named Boldar said, "None. It took me a while to track down your two friends, Calis."

Calis glanced at Miranda, who said, "I described you. He was to come here and find you even if I had gone."

Calis didn't look pleased at the "if I had gone" part. He asked Praji, "How goes it in the east?"

"Badly. Worse than we've ever imagined. This Emerald Queen bitch is far worse than we remembered at Hamsa and the other places we've run across her." He pulled off his boots and wiggled his toes. "Do you remember General Gapi? From the mercenaries' rendezvous before the assault on Lanada? He was sent against the Jeshandi in the northern steppe—a big mistake, from my experience with those horsemen—and they beat him to a bloody stump. One man in ten sent into the grasslands got back. Anyway, the

Emerald Queen took it personally; she had Gapi staked out over an anthill and smeared honey on his balls. Made all her generals watch until he stopped screaming."

Vaja shook his head. "You don't fail in her army." The old fighter smiled. "Gives a whole new meaning to 'do or die.' "

Calis said, "So the Jeshandi still hold?"

"No more," answered Praji, a sad note in his voice. "After Gapi's failure, they unleashed five thousand Saaur into the grasslands. The Jeshandi handled themselves well enough—they made the lizardmen bleed more than anyone else so far—but they were finally crushed."

Erik nodded in silence. He had faced the Saaur and their monstrous horses only once, but he knew that despite their size the Saaur were as good horsemen as he had ever seen. No human force could face them one to one; it took three or four human riders to neutralize one Saaur. In his idle moments, Erik had wrestled with plans to defeat the Saaur in open combat, and had yet to devise one that seemed remotely plausible.

Praji said, "There are some stragglers still riding in the foothills, raiding a camp here and there for food, but as a force, the Free People are no more."

Calis was silent a moment. Of all the cultures in this remote continent, the Jeshandi counted the largest number of elven people. Each elf who was killed was a loss no human could understand. His mother's people would be mourning this news for decades. Shaking off his reflective mood, he asked, "What of the Clans to the south?"

Praji said, "That's where he"—he pointed at Boldar—"found us. We were in a camp with Hatonis last night—"

Erik blurted, "You were in the Eastlands this morning?"

Praji nodded. "This lad has the means of getting us around in a hurry."

Boldar held out a device, turning it slightly in his hands. It was an orb with a series of small protruding switches. "We got here in the blink of an eye," continued Praji. "We spent most of the day trekking around these bleeding mountains trying to find you."

Turning back to Calis, Praji said, "We are pretty helpless, old friend. The Emerald Queen's fairly got her army lining the banks of the river on both sides these days. We hardly get a bowshot at her lumber barges. Best we can do sometimes is attack from ambush and try to run a barge aground on the banks, that sort of thing. The last time we tried to raid into the City of the Serpent River we lost half our force and did no damage to speak of." He sighed. Looking directly at Calis, he said, "The war here is over, Calis. Whatever you propose to do here in the Westlands, it had better be something special, because that fleet she's building is going to be ready to sail next year, year after at the latest. We thought we were buying ten years for you, but it's more like three or four."

Calis nodded. "And two of those are gone." Looking at the two tired old men, he said, "Get something to eat."

As Praji and Vaja were handed cold rations, Miranda turned to Boldar. "Did you bring it?"

Boldar unshouldered his bag and reached inside. He pulled out a small amulet. "Cost a fair bit, but not as much as I thought it would. I'll add the cost to what you owe me."

"What is it?" asked Calis.

Miranda handed it to him and Erik observed it as Calis held it up. It seemed nothing more than a simple gold neck decoration. Miranda said, "It's a ward against scrying magic. As of this moment, no magician can find you and anyone within a dozen paces of you. This may save our lives when it's time to get out of here."

Calis nodded. He handed it back to Miranda, but she put up her hand. "I don't need it." She reached out and pushed his hand back toward him. "You do."

Calis hesitated, then nodded and put the amulet around his neck. Turning to where Bobby de Loungville stood, he said, "We leave at first light."

Erik stood and started his rounds. De Loungville didn't need to tell him what to do or that now was the time to do it.

Jason came running into Barret's, gripping a sheaf of paper and parchment, and looked around the room. Spying Roo on the stairs, he called his name and raced past a pair of startled waiters.

"What is it?" asked Roo. His eyes had dark circles under them, as he had missed sleeping for the better part of two days. He had promised himself he would stay away from Sylvia for a few days. He intended to spend time with his wife and children, getting some needed sleep in the master suite while Karli slept with the baby in the nursery, but each of the last two nights, as if he had no volition, he had told his driver to take him to the Esterbrook estate.

Jason lowered his voice. "Someone's convinced Jurgens to call our note."

Roo instantly lost his fatigue. He took Jason by the arm and led him to the table that was now thought of as the Bitter Sea Company table, where Masterson, Hume, and Crowley sat. Roo came, sat, and said, "Jurgens has called our note."

"What?" said Masterson. "He agreed to the extension." Looking at Jason, he asked, "What happened?"

Jason sat down and spread out the paper work before him. "This is far worse than an untimely debt call, gentlemen." He pointed at a ledger sheet. "Someone at our countinghouse has been . . . for lack of a better term, embezzling funds."

At that both Hume and Crowley sat upright. "What?" demanded Crowley.

Jason politely and patiently began to explain, despite several interruptions. The short explanation was that not only had someone cleverly buried tens of thousands of golden sovereigns through clever transfers from account to account, they had also managed to avoid detection for months. Now there was almost a quarter-million sovereigns unaccounted for. The only reason Jason had been able to uncover the deceit was because of the note being called. "The worst of it, gentlemen," said Jason, "is that one way or another, the call comes at the most critical moment for the Bitter Sea Company since it was founded. If we can't meet this demand note from Jurgens, we lose the options on Blue Star Shipping, and without those ships, we can't make a half-dozen critical contracts."

"What's the worst?" asked Roo.

"The worst? If this note is not met, you can lose it all."

Suddenly Crowley was saying, "This is your doing, Avery! I told you we were moving too fast. We needed time to consolidate, to build capital reserves, but you insisted we keep taking positions. Luck turns, Rupert! And it has just turned on us!"

Masterson said, "What's the note?"

Jason said, "Six hundred thousand golden sovereigns."

"How light are we?"

Jason laughed bitterly. "Exactly what was embezzled. We can

liquidate a few holdings quickly and maybe come to four hundred thousand. But there's easily two hundred thousand less than we need."

"Who did this?" demanded Hume.

Jason said, "More than one scribe had to be involved." He sat back and scratched his chin. "I hate to say this, but it's as if the entire firm was being employed to ruin the Bitter Sea Company."

Roo was silent a moment, then said, "That's exactly what happened. That countinghouse was just too ripe a plum for any of us to pass up." He pointed a finger at Crowley. "That includes you, too, Brandon."

Crowley reluctantly said, "That is true."

"Someone set us up, gentlemen. Who?"

"Esterbrook," said Masterson. "At least, he's one of the few with the resources."

"But he hurts himself," said Roo. "He's involved in a half-dozen deals with the Bitter Sea Company."

"But we're big enough to be causing him some concern," said Hume.

Masterson said, "There are others. Wendel Brothers, Jalanki Traders, hell, the big trading houses in the Free Cities, Kilraine and the others, all of them have reasons to be wary of us."

Roo said, "Jason, go to the office and get Luis, Duncan, and any of the other men who can be trusted and know how to hold a sword. Then go to the countinghouse and put everyone there under guard. We're going to get to the bottom of this before whoever is working against us there catches wind that we know."

Jason stood up. "I'll leave at once."

Masterson said, "If this was an arranged betrayal, he'll find the countinghouse office empty, I'll bet."

Roo pushed back the chair and shook his head. "I won't take that bet." The dark feeling inside was threatening to rise up and sweep over him. He could feel a deep dread building that he might be reduced to a penniless freebooter as quickly as he had risen to prominence. He took a deep breath. "Well, worry won't feed the team, as my father used to say. I suggest we put our minds to how we raise a quick quarter-million golden sovereigns of capital in"— he glanced at the demand note Jason had left on the table—"the next two days."

The others were silent.

* * *

Duncan glanced around the inn, then indicated with a quick nod the man he had located. Roo went over to sit next across from the man while Luis and Duncan came to stand on either side.

"What . . . ?" began the man as he started to rise.

Duncan and Luis each placed a hand on his shoulders, forcing him back into his chair. "You're Rob McCraken?" asked Roo.

"Who wants to know?" responded the man, obviously feeling less brave than he tried to sound. His face had gone pale and he kept glancing around for a route of escape.

"You have a cousin named Herbert McCraken?"

The man tried again to rise, but found that the two men held him tightly. "Maybe."

Suddenly Luis had a knife lying alongside the man's neck, and he said, "You were asked a question that requires a more certain answer, my friend. It is either 'Yes, he is my cousin,' or 'No, he is not my cousin.' And be sure that the wrong answer will be very painful."

Softly the man said, "Yes, Herbert is my cousin."

"When did you last see him?" asked Roo.

"A few days ago. He dined with my family. He's a bachelor, so he comes by every two or three weeks for a meal."

"Did he say anything about leaving for a journey?"

"No," said Rob McCraken. "But he did say good-bye in a funny sort of way."

"What do you mean?"

The man glanced around. "He lingered at the door and . . . well, he hugged me hard, and we haven't done that since we were kids. It could have been a longer good-bye than I thought."

"Most likely. If he were to decide to leave Krondor and live elsewhere, where would he go?" asked Roo.

McCraken said, "I don't know. Hadn't thought that way. We have kin in the East, but they're distant. A cousin in Salador. Haven't seen him in ten years."

Roo paused, drumming his fingers on the table. "If your cousin was to come into a lot of gold unexpectedly, where then do you think he might go?"

The man's eyes narrowed. "Enough to purchase a Quegan title?"

Roo glanced at Luis, who said, "I think a minor title if he took it all."

Roo stood up. "Sarth." To Duncan he said, "Get as good a description as you can of this Herbert McCraken, then send a dozen riders to Sarth. If they take extra horses, they should be able to overtake him within ten hours."

Roo said to Luis, "Head for the docks and start asking questions. No ships in from or bound for Queg are registered, but you never know if one has slipped in claiming to be from the Free Cities or Durbin. Sniff around and double-check that no one matching McCraken's description is trying to slip aboard a ship bound out of the city. We have enough eyes and ears down there working for us that we should be able to find him."

To both men he said, "I have something to do, but I will be in the office at first light. If we haven't found this man by noon tomorrow, we're ruined."

Duncan sat in the chair Roo had just vacated. "Paint me a picture with words, Rob, and spare no detail. What does Herbert look like?"

"Well, he's a plain-looking fellow, about my height."

Without waiting for another answer, Roo departed, walking to where he had left his carriage. Once inside, he ordered the driver to take him to the Esterbrook estate.

Calis signaled in the murk, and Erik turned, relaying the gestures. They were traveling in near blindness, sixty-seven of them spread out in a long line, walking in pairs. Calis led, as he had the ability to see in the dimmest light, while Boldar Blood brought up the rear, claiming to have the power to see in the dark, which seemed highly improbable to Erik, but so far the strange mercenary hadn't made a single misstep. It was some magic property of his helm, Erik judged.

Miranda kept close to Calis's side, since she had the ability to see that came close to Calis's. The rest of the party were forced to move as best they could, using the light of a single torch carried at the center of the column. Erik knew from experience that those closest to the middle of the line were nearly blind when looking away from the torch, while those at either end stood a chance of seeing something beyond the faint fall of illumination.

The signal word was passed that something or someone dangerous was ahead. Each man in line quietly readied his weapons, while Bobby de Loungville came forward from his position half the distance between the torch and Boldar. A step behind him came Praji and Vaja. Erik wished the old mercenaries had not come along, but two old men on horseback alone in the mountains would have stood little chance of getting back to what passed for civilization in this harsh land.

Erik moved forward and felt a slight breeze against his cheek. As he reached the Captain's position, Calis whispered, "Something's moving down there."

"Down there" was the deep circular well that served as the vertical "highway" from this, the topmost level, down into the bowels of the mountain. Erik and the survivors of Calis's company had trudged up the spiral ramp that hugged the inside of this vast well over two years before, and now they were getting ready to descend into it. Erik listened, but as was often the case, the Captain's hearing was far more sensitive than Erik's.

Then faintly, a sound.

It resembled nothing so much as a hand brushing stone. A few seconds later, it repeated. Then silence.

They stood motionless for a full five minutes before Calis signaled for the first five men to accompany him. Erik glanced around and selected the four soldiers at the head of the column, and pulled his own sword.

A covered lantern was lit, and the shutters closed so that only a faint single line of light showed, allowing the men to see slightly, while, it was hoped, not being seen in return.

The six moved out and Erik carried the lantern. They moved down the tunnel, which was heading slightly downward, as it had been for miles, and then found themselves stepping into the vast well. As was the case at most tunnel intersections, the lip of the road that spiraled inside the well flared out, providing extra room for those entering and leaving the roadway to negotiate around one another. They paused and listened, and again they heard the faint scraping, coming from below.

They moved slowly down the ramp, pausing at each quarter turn of the road around the well, until they again heard the sound. Finally the sound ceased, and they continued on.

Erik judged that each full revolution around the well dropped them about twenty feet. They were three full turns around from where they had entered the well when they found the corpse.

Calis signaled to be alert, and the four men accompanying Erik and Calis turned their backs to the light, two facing uptrail and two facing down. By not looking at the light they wouldn't blind themselves to anything approaching out of the darkness.

The figure was covered in a robe, and when Calis pulled back its hood, Erik couldn't help but audibly gasp. It was a Pantathian.

Erik had never been this close to the enemy. He had seen them once from a distance, in these very tunnels, and another time from a ridge at the great rendezvous when one had come by inspecting troops.

"Turn him over," whispered Calis, and Erik reached down and moved the body so that it was on its back. A great gaping wound had half-eviscerated the creature and a large portion of intestine protruded through its shredded robes.

Calis pointed toward an object in the creature's hands, and said, "Remove that."

Erik did so and as soon as he touched the object, he wished he hadn't. An odd energy swept up his arms and made his skin crawl. He suddenly wished he could strip off his clothing and scrub himself until his skin bled and his hair fell out.

Calis seemed to react strongly to the object, even though Erik was the one touching it. Erik turned the thing in his hands and realized it was a helm. It was halfway toward his head when Calis said, "Don't."

Erik stopped, realizing that he had been about to don the helm, and said, "What do I do?"

"Put it down," said Calis. Turning to another soldier, he ordered, "Bring the others here."

The soldier took the lamp and vanished, leaving Erik to endure a very strange few moments in the darkness. While he stood there, strange images came to him of dark men in alien armor, women of incredible beauty, but none were human. He shook his head, and by the time he'd rid himself of these images, the column arrived.

Miranda came and said, "What is it?"

Calis pointed. Miranda knelt and examined both the corpse and the helm. She picked it up, and if she was affected by it, she gave no outward sign. Finally she said, "I need a bag."

One of the soldiers nearby produced a cloth bag and she put the helm inside. To Boldar she said, "You carry this. Of everyone here, this should give you the least amount of discomfort."

The odd mercenary shrugged, took the bag, and stuck it inside a large rucksack he carried on his hip.

Miranda looked at the corpse and after a moment said, "There seems to be an unexpected turn of events here."

Calis said, "This one looked to be fleeing, to be protecting this artifact."

Miranda said, "Or he was stealing it." She shook her head in frustration. "Speculation gets us nowhere. Let's continue."

Calis nodded and signaled, ordering the column downward.

They moved through gallery and plateau, around and around as they descended into the heart of the well. At an otherwise non-descript tunnel, Calis signaled them to turn.

The column entered the tunnel, which led downward at a steep angle. As they moved deeper into the tunnel, the temperature quickly rose. It had been getting bitter at night in the mountains, and the tunnels had been just as cold, but as they moved downward, each step seemed to take them toward heat. And as it grew hotter, an odor also grew. It stank of sulfur, and the sweet sick smell of rotten meat.

They entered a broadening tunnel, and Calis signaled; every man drew his weapon. They had discussed this part of the mission until each member of the company could repeat orders in his sleep.

This was the first of the Pantathian galleries, and inside they would find serpent priests, and breeding females. Eggs and young would be housed in some sort of crèche, and the orders were simple: enter and kill every living thing.

Calis signaled and the charge began.

It ended almost as quickly as it began.

The stench in the gallery was far more oppressive than it had been in the tunnels. The overwhelming odor caused more than one man to double over and retch. Everywhere they looked, bodies lay scattered. Most were Pantathians, some infants of that race, while others were alien, the Saaur. But not one was intact. The lone Pantathian they had encountered in the tunnel was almost undamaged compared to those within this hall. The body parts had been strewn around the hall and everywhere the rot of death filled the air with an almost unbearable stink.

Calis pointed to a throne. A figure lay at the foot that had once sat upon it. It was a Pantathian corpse, and it was mummified, and it lay in pieces.

"There," Calis choked, trying to keep his composure while lesser men retched and vomited.

Miranda and Boldar both seemed immune to the smell, and they moved to the corpse. Miranda waved her hands and spent a full minute inspecting the mummy, then turned and said, "Artifacts?"

"Armor, sword, shield, all of what you'd expect," answered Calis.

"Well," said Miranda, "someone got to those items before we did." She looked around the cavern, inspecting the carnage as one of the soldiers lit a lantern, illuminating the large hall. "Those died defending and paid a price. The one we found must have been days in dying."

Erik took two men and looked around in neighboring galleries. In one large pool of hot water a half-dozen smashed eggs lay, some with half-formed Pantathians floating in scummy pools. In another gallery they found a dozen tiny figures, babies from their size, and among them lay the bones of many creatures, some of them human.

After they inspected the entire area, Erik reported back. "Captain, it's the same as here." He lowered his voice and said, "I don't see a single wound that looks like it was made by a weapon." He pointed to a dead Saaur warrior's upper torso. "He wasn't cut in two, Captain. He looks like something tore him in half."

Boldar Blood said, "I've seen a few creatures that could do that." He glanced at Erik and Calis, his face masked by the alien helmet he wore, his eyes not visible in the black eye slits. "But very few, and not on this world."

Calis and Miranda looked around and Calis said, "Something came through here like a fire through summer grass and killed everyone."

De Loungville said, "Well, someone saved us some butchery."

Calis looked disturbed for the first time since Erik had met him.

He said, "Bobby, someone has walked off with items of power unlike any seen on this world since my father donned the white-and-gold armor."

De Loungville said, "There's a third player, then?"

Miranda said, "By all appearances, there is a third player."

"What now?" asked de Loungville.

"We move downward," said Calis without hesitation. "We must find who it was that raided this warren and if other warrens have also been destroyed." To the assembled company he said, "The orders are changed." Instantly every man there gave full attention to Calis. "We have another mystery. We will continue to move into the mountains, and if we find living Panthathians, we slay them, to the last living being." He paused. "But if we find who also is killing them, that enemy of our enemy may be no friend of ours; we need to find out who this other foe is." He lowered his voice. "They are powerful and now possess some of the most powerful artifacts of the Valheru—the Dragon Lords. They should be feared."

He turned and signaled and the party moved back up the tunnel, returning to the well. When they reached it, Calis called a halt to the march, letting the men rest and eat. When at last it was time, he signaled, re-formed the column, and ordered them downward, deeper into the well.

Eighteen

Discovery

ROO NODDED.

Duncan drew back his fist and struck the man in the chair. The man's head snapped back and blood began running down his nose. "Wrong answer," said Duncan.

Herbert McCraken said, "I don't know."

Duncan hit him again.

Roo said, "It's very simple, McCraken. You tell me who arranged for you to embezzle my gold and who has it, and we'll let you go."

"They'll kill me if I do," he answered.

"We'll kill you if you don't," said Roo.

McCraken said, "If I tell you, I've got no bargaining power. What's to keep you from cutting my throat once I talk?"

"No profit in it," said Roo. "The gold is mine; it's not as if we're trying to break the King's law in getting it back. If I take you to the City Watch office and file charges with the Duke's constable, once we get a magistrate who can understand that puzzle of accounts you created, you'll be working on the harbor gang for the next fifteen years."

"If I tell you?"

"We'll let you leave the city . . . alive."

He thought a minute, then said, "Newton Briggs is the man's name. He arranged for the transfer of funds."

Roo glanced at Jason, who stood in the shadows behind McCraken, where he couldn't see him. Softly Jason said, "He was a partner in the countinghouse before we bought it."

McCraken said, "He wasn't happy to lose control. I think someone paid him to steal from you. All I know is he promised me enough gold to buy a Quegan title, and a villa, and set up my own business."

"Why Quegan?" asked Duncan.

Luis, who stood behind the man, keeping him in the chair, said, "Many in the Kingdom dream of being a rich Quegan noble, living in a villa with a dozen young slave girls"—then he shrugged—"or boys."

Roo laughed. "You're an idiot. You were played for a fool. You set foot on the docks of the city of Queg and within minutes you'd be on your way to the galleys. Whatever gold you had would be forfeit to the state. Unless you have powerful allies there, noncitizens of Queg have no rights."

McCraken blinked. "But I was promised. . . ."

Roo said, "Let him loose."

"Just let him go?" asked Duncan.

"Where's he going?"

Luis had found McCraken waiting at a warehouse for a rendezvous with someone—now they knew it to be Briggs—less than four hours earlier. Duncan had already sent a rider to bring back those men heading for Sarth; if all went according to plan, they should be back at Roo's headquarters within the hour.

The man stood up and said, "What am I to do now?"

"Go to Queg and try to buy a patent of nobility," said Roo. "But use someone else's money. If you're in the city by sundown tomorrow, it won't be just your confederates who will be trying to kill you."

The man wiped his bloody lip with the back of his hand and stumbled out the door. Roo said, "Wait a minute, Duncan, then follow him. He's too scared to try to get away on his own. If there's another player in this, he may lead us to him. And don't let him really get away; we may need him to give testimony to the Royal Courts. He may be the only thing that stands between us and a charge of robbery."

Duncan nodded. "Where will you be?"

"At the docks," said Roo. "Just against the possibility there is a ship that might be Queg-bound on the morning tide. Send for us there."

Duncan nodded and left.

Roo said, "Jason, return to the office and wait there. Luis and I will send word if we need you somewhere else."

Jason departed. Luis said, "We have a ship ready to sail as soon as you give word."

"Good," said Roo. "If we find our gold thief is making a break from the city, I want to catch him out beyond the breakwater. By the time any royal warship comes to investigate, I want the matter settled. I want the gold in our possession should some revenue cutter board us. It will be much easier to explain then."

Luis shook his head. "Why move the gold? Why not just stick it somewhere in a back room and wait for the Bitter Sea Company to fold?"

Roo said, "Because that's both smart and risky. If you knew these boys were going to get out of the city and not talk, it would be the smart thing to do. But if you thought they might be caught and forced to talk, well, eventually this trail will lead back to whoever is the brains behind this fraud, and at that point"—he snapped his fingers—"we come with every sword we can hire, and it's a free-for-all." He sighed. "But if the gold is safely gone, on its way to some port or in a wagon heading over the mountains . . ." He shrugged.

"Whoever planned this certainly timed things correctly," said Luis.

Roo said, "That's what has me worried. Not only did those bastards at the countinghouse have to be in on this, they had to know something more about the Bitter Sea Company and its finances than they could from people like McCraken and Briggs." He held up one finger. "They had to know that Jason or someone else would be close to discovering the fraud. It's just been going on too long." He held up a second finger. "And they had to know that we're a few weeks from being able to cover such a loss." He shook his head in frustration. "We've got caravans coming in from the East, and a grain shipment putting into Ylith today. Our Far Coast fleet should be at Carse or putting out for the return leg home. Any of those will be bringing enough gold to cover that shortfall"—he struck his fist into his hand—"but not today!"

"A spy?"

"An agent of some sort," said Roo. He moved toward the door. "Besides Duncan, you are the only person I fully trust, Luis. You were with me in the death cell and you swam the Vedra River with me. We've looked death in the face together, and except for Jadow and Greylock, there's not a man left in Krondor I'd want at my back besides you."

Luis's expression was one of mild amusement. "Even with one hand?"

Roo opened the door. "You're better with a knife in one hand than most men are with a sword and two hands. Come along, let's start combing the docks."

Luis slapped his employer on the back as he followed him through the door and shut it behind him. The shed was one of many the Bitter Sea Company owned in the Merchants' Quarter, and from there the pair moved quickly toward the docks.

After they had left, a figure rose from the roof of the shed. Lightly jumping to the cobbles, the shadowy observer watched Luis and Roo as they vanished into the darkness, then turned and whistled lightly, pointing after them. Two more figures emerged from a block farther down the street and rapidly approached the first. The three figures conferred for a moment, then one of the two returned the way he had come. The others followed Roo and Luis toward the dock.

"Ambush!" shouted Renaldo.

"Wedge!" shouted Calis and instantly every man was deploying. The column was in a large gallery, easily two hundred feet across, with six entrances. As they had trained, forty of the men formed a shield-to-shield wedge, with their swords poised to strike down any attacker. The other twenty men unshouldered shortbows and calmly set arrows to bowstrings as an inhuman snarling and shrieking filled the gallery.

From three tunnels ahead streams of Pantathians rushed forward to attack Calis's Crimson Eagles. Erik attempted a rough estimation of the opposing forces, but quickly stopped trying to count as the first wave of attackers began to fall to the bowmen. Then they struck the shield wall.

Erik laid about him with powerful strokes of his blade. Twice he heard steel break under his strikes as Pantathian soldiers tried to block with their swords. He discovered little skill in their opponents. Without waiting for instructions from Calis, he shouted, "Second rank! Swords, and follow me!"

The twenty bowmen dropped their bows and drew swords. Erik circled around the right end of his line and hit the Pantathians in the flank. As he had suspected, they quickly collapsed in confusion.

But rather than flee, they simply hurled themselves at the Kingdom soldiers, until suddenly the last two went down before Calis's men and the gallery fell silent. Boldar Blood said, "Like hacking firewood."

Erik glanced at the strange mercenary and noticed that the blood that was splattered on his armor was running off, as if unable to cling to the strange white surface. Catching his breath, Erik said, "They were brave, but these weren't warriors." He signaled two men toward each tunnel mouth, to stand alert in case other Pantathians might be heading this way.

"Not brave," said Boldar. "Fanatics."

Calis looked to Miranda, who said, "We've never heard of anyone fighting them hand to hand. They prefer to use stealth and cunning to make war."

Erik used the toe of his boot to turn one over and said, "It's small."

"They are all small," said Calis. "Smaller than the one we found yesterday."

Erik glanced at de Loungville. "Are they sending youngsters against us?"

"Maybe," said the Sergeant Major. "If they're as beat up in other parts of this warren as that crèche we found yesterday was, they may be desperate to keep what's left intact."

Erik quickly inspected his own men, while Calis and Miranda inspected the Pantathian dead. No man of Calis's command had suffered a significant injury. "Only cuts and bruises," Erik reported.

"A few minutes' rest, then we move on," said de Loungville.

Erik nodded. "Which tunnel?"

De Loungville repeated the question to Calis.

"The center, I think. If we need to, we can double back," said the Captain.

Erik hoped that was so, but he kept his thoughts to himself.

* * *

Roo crouched behind a bale as a strong contingency of armed men moved warily through the darkness. Fog had rolled in, and in the early morning gloom a man could barely see his hand at arm's length from his face.

Roo and Luis had scouted the docks when one of Roo's men reported a large company of guards and a wagon heading for the docks. Roo had followed while sending Luis to fetch more men.

Suddenly Roo spun, reacting to the soft sound of movement behind him. As Roo had his sword ready, Duncan held up his hand and whispered, "It's me!" Roo dropped the point of his sword and turned to look at the wagon as he came up the quay. Duncan knelt next to his cousin. "McCraken's headed here. I lost him for a moment in the fog, saw someone—you—duck down that alley"— he pointed behind Roo—"and followed. I expect we'll see Herbert show any moment."

Roo nodded. "It's our gold in that wagon, no doubt."

"Are we going to hit them on the docks?"

Roo counted. "Not unless Luis gets back with our men before they get that boat launched," he whispered. "All our men are either on the *Bitter Sea Queen* or at the warehouse, waiting for orders."

The wagon came to a halt and a voice cut through the darkness. "Down to that longboat." A single shuttered lantern was uncovered and the wagon and the men around it were now clearly seen, as silhouettes outlined by the faint light.

Men unlatched the tailgate and began unloading several small chests. Suddenly another figure stumbled out of the dark into the small pool of lantern light around the wagon. Swords were drawn, as an alarmed voice said, "It's me! McCraken!"

A man jumped off the wagon seat and grabbed the lantern as two guards gripped Herbert's arms. The man with the lantern held it up and stepped foward.

Roo sucked breath hard. It was Tim Jacoby. Then at his shoulder he could see Tim's brother, Randolph. Tim said, "What are you doing here?"

"Briggs never showed," said McCraken.

"Fool," said Tim Jacoby. "You were told to wait until he showed up, no matter how long it took. He's probably at the warehouse looking for you right now."

Randolph said, "What happened to your face?"

Herbert raised his hand to his face, then said, "I fell in the dark and hit my lip on a crate."

"Looks like someone hit you," said Tim Jacoby.

"No one hit me," said McCraken, too loud for Tim Jacoby's liking. "I swear it!"

"Keep your voice down," Tim ordered. "Did anyone follow you?"

"In this fog?" said McCraken. He took a breath. "You've got to take me with you. Briggs was supposed to show up at sundown with my gold. I waited and he never got there. I was promised fifty thousand gold for my part in this. You've got to make good on this."

"Or what?" asked Tim.

Suddenly McCraken was afraid. "I . . ."

Roo noticed that none of the men around the wagon had moved since McCraken's arrival. The longboat at the bottom of the quay's steps rocked gently against the stones. "Keep talking," urged Roo silently, knowing that each passing minute brought Luis and his own men that much closer. Taking them here would be so much easier than a sea battle. He had only until sundown to pay the note, and if he couldn't take Jacoby's men on the docks, he would be forced to try a sea chase and taking Tim's ship before noon.

Whispering to Duncan, he said, "If I need to, I plan to keep them here until Luis comes. Can you circle around behind them?"

"What?" whispered Duncan. "You want just the two of us to try to stop them?"

"Slow them down, that's all. Get behind them and follow my play."

Duncan rolled his eyes and whispered, "I hope to the gods you're not going to get us killed, cousin." Then he turned and disappeared into the fog.

McCraken said, "If you don't make good on this, I'll testify before the Duke's constable. I'll claim you and Briggs forced me to falsify the accounts."

Tim shook his head. "You're a very stupid man, McCraken. We were supposed to have no contact. That was Briggs's job."

"Briggs never showed!" said McCraken, his voice nearly hysterical.

Tim nodded, and suddenly the two guards gripping McCraken's arms tightened their grip, holding him motionless. Jacoby swiftly drew a poniard from his belt and drove it into McCraken's stomach. "You should have stayed in the warehouse, McCraken. Briggs is dead, and now"—the accountant slumped in the grip of the two guards—"so are you." With a motion of his head he indicated they should dispose of the body in the harbor. The two guards took two steps down the stairs beside the longboat and threw the body into the water a few feet in front of the bow. Another body found floating in the harbor would hardly be worth mention in Krondor.

Roo waited until he calculated almost all the gold was loaded on the boat, then he stepped out and with as much authority as he could muster shouted, "Don't move! You're surrounded."

As he hoped, those near the wagon and the boat couldn't see who was out there in the fog, and that hesitation gave Roo the advantage he had hoped for; had they instantly charged him, as good a swordsman as he was, he would have been overwhelmed.

A strangled cry sounded from the back of the wagon and a man fell to the cobbles. Roo wondered at this, until he heard Duncan's voice shout, "We told you not to move!"

One man near the body glanced down and said, "It's a dagger! This ain't the City Watch!"

He took a step and was brought down by another dagger, and a different voice said, "We never said we were the City Watch." Moving slowly forward from beyond the other side of the building that had sheltered Roo, a figure could be dimly seen. Roo thought he recognized the voice, and then he made out some familiar features. Dashel Jameson walked casually forward until he was visible to both sides.

In the distance, hooves striking cobbles could be heard and Dash said, "And we also have reinforcements on their way. Put down your weapons."

Some of the men hesitated, when a third dagger sped out of the darkness from where Dashel had emerged and thudded into the side of the wagon. "He said put down your weapons!" shouted a different, odd-sounding voice.

Roo prayed to Ruthia, Goddess of Luck, that it was Luis and his men whose hooves clattered through the early morning, approaching rapidly. Jacoby's guards slowly knelt, placing weapons on the cobbles.

Roo waited another moment, then came forward. "Good morning, Timothy, Randolph." He tried to sound casual.

Jacoby said, "You!"

Just then Luis rode into view and a dozen horsemen came after, fanning out to surround those men already on the ground. Several carried crossbows, which they leveled at the wagons and at the boat.

"Did you think I'd let you flee with my gold?"

Jacoby nearly spat, he was so angry. "What do you mean, *your* gold?"

Roo said, "Come along, Tim. McCraken and Briggs told us everything."

Jacoby said, "Briggs? How could he? We—"

"Shut up, you fool!" commanded Randolph.

Roo glanced to where McCraken floated in the bay. "So you sent Herbert to join Briggs, did you?"

"I'll send you to join them in hell!" snapped Timothy Jacoby, pulling his sword from his belt, despite the crossbows pointed his way.

"No!" shouted Randolph, pushing his brother aside as three bolts were unleased.

Two bolts took Randolph in the chest and another in the neck, and blood exploded across the men standing behind him. He hit the ground like a fly swatted out of the air by a human hand.

Tim Jacoby rose up from the ground, holding his sword in one hand and a poniard in the other, and there was only madness and rage in his eyes. Luis started to draw back his dagger to throw, but Roo said, "No! Let him come. It's time to finish this."

"You've been a thorn in my side since the day we met," said Tim Jacoby. "You've killed my brother!"

Roo leveled his sword and said, "And Helmut died at your hands." He motioned for Jacoby to come toward him. "Come on! What are you waiting for?"

The men stepped back and Jacoby rushed Roo. Roo was the experienced soldier, while Jacoby was nothing more than a murdering bully, but now he was a murdering bully inflamed by hatred and the desire for revenge.

He closed on Roo faster than he'd anticipated, and Roo was forced to defend and retreat against the lethal two-handed attack.

"Light!" commanded Duncan, and quickly men opened the shutters on the one lamp, throwing an eerie glow through the fog as the two men struggled. One of the horsemen jumped down, opened a saddlebag, and pulled out a bundle of short torches. He struck steel and flint while Roo and Jacoby slashed and parried, and brought a light to life. He quickly lit and distributed flaming brands to Luis's men, and a circle of light surrounded the two combantants.

Luis had his men pick up the weapons Jacoby's men had put down and moved the guards toward the wagon. Roo fought for his life.

Back and forth the attacks and defenses moved the two men, each waiting for the other to make a mistake. The fury was finally flowing out of Jacoby as he tired, while Roo vowed he would never go so long without practicing his weapons again. Clashing steel echoed across the harbor. Upon distant ships at their moorings, guards lit lanterns and called questions.

A watchman came out between two buildings, saw Randolph lying in a spreading pool of blood, the two fighters, and the two bands of men, and retreated hastily. When he was safely out of harm's way, he produced a tin whistle and began blowing it fiercely. A squad of three constables appeared a short while later, and the watchman explained what he had seen. The senior constable sent one of his men to headquarters for more men, and then accompanied the other man back toward the dock.

Roo felt his arms begin to ache. What Jacoby lacked in skill he gained back by using two weapons, a style of fighting difficult to defend with a single blade.

Jacoby had a tricky move, an advance with his sword extended, followed by a slash with his left hand. It was designed to cut across the chest of any opponent who tried to engage his sword and riposte. The first time he tried it, Roo barely escaped with a tear in his tunic.

Roo wiped perspiration from his brow with his left hand, keeping the point of his sword directed at Jacoby. Jacoby's right boot heel tapped, and then he extended and advanced, following with the left-hand slash. Roo leaped backward. He chanced a glance over his shoulder and saw that he was being driven toward a large pile of crates, and once his back was against them, he would have no room to escape.

The tap of Jacoby's boot heel against the cobbles saved Roo's life, for he leaped backward before he turned to look again at Jacoby, and barely missed the poniard slashing through the air. Roo crouched.

As he expected, he heard the boot heel tap again, and without hesitation Roo leaned foward. He beat aside Jacoby's extended blade, but rather than come straight in, Roo dropped his own blade, extended his left hand downward to touch the stones, and ducked under the vicious slash of the poniard. For a moment he was completely vulnerable, but Jacoby's blades were in no position to take advantage. Roo knew that any experienced fighter might kick with his boot, sending Roo to the stones, but he doubted Jacoby had ever seen this move. With his right hand, Roo thrust upward, catching Jacoby in his right side, just below the ribs. As the sword traveled upward, it pierced lung and heart.

Jacoby's eyes widened and a strange, childlike sound issued from his lips, and his fingers ceased to possess any strength. Sword and poniard fell from his hands. Then his knees wobbled and he collapsed upon the ground as Roo yanked his blade free.

"Don't anyone move," said a voice.

Roo glanced over his shoulder and saw the senior constable approaching with riot club in one hand, absently slapping the palm of the other. Gasping for breath, Roo felt a giddy admiration for the officer of the Prince's City Watch, willing to confront two dozen armed men with nothing more than his badge of office and a billy.

Roo said, "Wouldn't think of it."

More horsemen could be heard approaching as the constable said, "Now then, what have we here?"

Roo said, "It's simple. These two dead men are thieves. Those men over there"—he pointed to the disarmed guards by the wagon—"are hired thugs. And that wagon and that boat are loaded with my stolen gold."

Seeing no one was attempting to cause trouble, the constable put his billy under his arm and rubbed his chin. "And who might that wet fellow floating in the harbor be?"

Roo blew out and took a deep breath. "By name, Herbert McCraken. He was an accountant at my countinghouse. He helped those two steal my gold."

"Hmmm," said the constable, obviously not convinced. "And who might you be, sir, to be having countinghouses, accounts, and large shipments of gold?" He glanced down at the Jacoby brothers, and added, "And a surplus of corpses."

Roo smiled. "I'm Rupert Avery. I'm a partner in the Bitter Sea Company."

The constable nodded. As horsemen rounded the corner and approached the group, he said, "That's a name few haven't heard in Krondor in the last year or so. Is there someone here likely to vouch for you?"

Dash stepped forward. "I will. He's my boss."

"And who might you be?" asked the constable.

"He's my grandson," said the lead rider.

Trying to see the figure on horseback through the gloom, the constable said, "And then who might you be?"

Lord James rode forward into the circle of torches and lanterns and said, "My name is James. And in a manner of speaking, I'm your boss."

Then the other newly arrived riders appeared, soldiers in the garb of the Prince's personal guards, and Knight-Marshal William said, "Why don't you take these men"—he pointed to the Jacoby guards—"into custody, Constable. We'll deal with these other gentlemen."

The constable was nearly speechless at being in the presence of the Duke of Krondor and the Knight-Marshal, and hesitated a long moment before he said, "Yes, sir! Titus!"

From out of the shadows came a young constable, barely twenty years of age by his appearance. He carried a crossbow. "Yes, Sergeant?"

"Arrest that lot over there."

"Yes, sir!" said the young constable and he pointed his crossbow at them in menacing fashion. "Come along, and no funny business."

Other constables appeared and the sergeant moved them to positions surrounding the dozen captives, escorting them away.

Roo turned to Lord James and said, "I don't suppose you just happened to be out for a very early morning ride, m'lord?"

James said, "No. We had you followed."

Out of the shadows came the girl Katherine and Jimmy.

"Followed?" asked Roo. "Why?"

"We need to talk," said James. Turning his horse, he said, "Get cleaned up and get your gold to safety, then come to the palace for breakfast."

Roo nodded. "Straight away, m'lord." To Luis and Duncan he said, "Get the gold off the boat and back to our offices." Then he turned to Dash and said, "And tell me: whose employee are you? Mine or your grandfather's?"

Dash grinned and shrugged. "In a manner of speaking, both of yours."

Roo said nothing for a moment, then said, "You're discharged."

Dash said, "Ah, I don't think you can do that."

"Why not?" demanded Roo.

"Grandfather will explain."

Roo shrugged. Suddenly too tired to think, he said, "I could use some food and coffee." He sighed. "A lot of coffee."

The men began loading the gold back into the Jacoby's wagon, and two men took the Jacoby brothers' bodies to load into the wagon beside the gold. Roo put his sword away, wondering what was coming next. At least, he reasoned, he could meet the demand note and keep his company alive. Never, he vowed silently, would he let his company become that vulnerable again.

Roo sipped at the coffee and sighed. "This is excellent."

James nodded. "Jimmy buys it at Barret's for me."

Roo smiled. "Best coffee in the city."

The Duke of Krondor said, "What am I to do with you?"

"I'm not sure I take your meaning, m'lord."

They all sat around a large table in the Duke's private quarters. Knight-Marshal William sat beside the Duke, while Jimmy, Dash, and Katherine filled out the company. Owen Greylock entered the room and sat.

"Good morning, m'lord, Marshal, Roo," he said with a smile.

"As I was explaining to your old friend here, Captain Greylock, I'm at something of a loss as what to do with him," said James.

Greylock looked confused. "Do with him?"

"Well, there are several dead bodies down at the docks and a lot of gold with little explanation as to how it got there."

Roo said, "M'lord, with all due respect, I've explained this all to you."

"So you say," replied James. He leaned forward and pointed a finger at Roo. "But you're a convicted murderer, and several of your business dealings in the recent past have bordered on the criminal."

Roo's fatigue made him prickly. "Bordering on the criminal isn't the same as being criminal . . . m'lord."

"Well, we could impound the gold and hold a hearing," said Marshal William.

Roo sat straight. "You can't! If I don't get that gold to my creditors by the end of the day, I'll be ruined. That was the entire thrust of Jacoby's plans."

James said, "Will everyone but Mr. Avery please leave us for a while. Breakfast is now finished."

Greylock looked at the food still on the table with regret, but he rose and departed with the others, leaving Roo alone with Lord James.

James stood and came to the empty chair next to Roo and sat. "This is how it is," he said. "You've done very well. Remarkable doesn't begin to cover how well you've done in your rise, young Avery. At one point I thought we might have to take a hand in seeing you survive the attempts your enemies made upon you, but you didn't need our help. That's to your credit.

"But my threat wasn't hollow; I want you to understand something, and that is, no matter how powerful you become, you are no more above the law than you were when you and Erik killed Stefan von Darkmoor."

Roo said nothing.

"I'll not attempt to impound your gold, Rupert. Pay off your creditors and continue to prosper, but always remember that you can be put away as quickly now as you were when we first tossed you into the death cell."

Roo said, "Why are you telling me this?"

"Because you are not done with our service, young Avery." James stood and paced as he said, "Reports from across the sea are worse than we thought they'd be; far worse. Your friend Erik may already be dead for all we know. Everyone who went with Calis may be." He stopped his pacing and looked at Roo. "But even if they reach those goals they set out to achieve, this much you can bank on: the host of the Emerald Queen is coming, and you know almost as well as I that if she lands on these shores, your hard-won riches mean nothing. You and your wife and children will be nothing more than objects to sweep aside as she marches toward *her* goal: the destruction of every living thing on this world."

Roo said, "What do you want me to do?"

"Do?" said James. "Why do you think I want you to do anything?"

"Because we wouldn't be having this meal if you were only trying to remind me either of your ability to hang me on a whim or about the terrible things I saw when serving with Calis." Roo's voice rose in anger as he said, "I bloody well know both those facts!" He slammed his fist on the table, causing dishes to jump and clatter. Then he added, "M'lord."

"I'll tell you what I want," said Lord James. He leaned over, hands on the back of one chair and the table, and put his face before Roo's, eye to eye. "I need gold."

Roo blinked. "Gold?"

"More gold than even a greedly little bastard like you can imagine, Rupert." He stood up. "We've the biggest war in the history of this world about to be unleashed on these shores." He walked to a window that overlooked the harbor and made a sweeping motion with his hand. "Unless someone with a great deal more power and intelligence than are possessed by every ruling lord in this Kingdom comes up with an unexpected solution, we will see the biggest fleet in history come sailing into that harbor in less than three years' time. And on that fleet will be the biggest army ever seen."

He turned to look at Roo. "And everything you see from this window will be ashes. That includes your house, your business, Barret's Coffee House, your docks, your warehouses, your ships, your wife, your children, your mistress."

At the last, Roo felt his throat almost close. He thought no one knew about his relationship with Sylvia. James spoke calmly, but his manner betrayed a tightly controlled anger. "You will never understand the love I feel for this city, Rupert." He motioned around the hall. "You will never understand why I hold this palace dear above all other places on this world. A very special man saw something in me that no one else would ever have seen, and he put out his hand and elevated me to a station that no one of my birth could ever have imagined." Roo saw a slight sheen of moisture in Lord James's eyes. "I gave my own son that man's name, to honor him." The Duke turned his back to Roo, to look out the window again. "And you have no idea how much I wish we could have that man with us here, now. Of all men, he would be the one I would wish to tell us what to do next as this terrible day approaches."

Taking a deep breath, the old Duke composed himself. "But he is not here. He is dead, and he would be the first to tell me that dreaming of things that cannot be is a waste of time." He looked again into Roo's eyes. "And time is something we have far less of than we had thought. I said that fleet would be here in less than three years. It may be here in less than two. I won't know until a ship from Novindus appears."

Roo said, "Two, three years?"

"Yes," said James. "This is why I need gold. I need to finance the biggest war in the history of the Kingdom, a war that dwarfs any we've fought. We have a standing army of fewer than five thousand men in the Principality. When we raise the banners of the Kingdom, both Eastern and Western Realms, we can put perhaps forty thousand men in the field, trained veterans and levies. How many men does the Emerald Queen bring against us?"

Roo sat back, remembering just those forces at the mercenaries' rendezvous. "Two hundred, two hundred fifty thousand if she can get them all across the sea."

James said, "She has six hundred ships as of our last report. She is producing two new ships a week. She's destroying the entire continent to keep production that high, but she's got her heel on the throat of the entire population down there and the work continues."

Roo calculated. "Fifty weeks, minimum. She needs at least one hundred more ships to carry provisions for that many men. If she's prudent, she'll build for another one hundred weeks."

"Have you seen anything to indicate prudence?"

"No," said Roo, "but on the other hand even someone willing to kill every man in her service must have some idea of what she needs to accomplish her goals."

James nodded. "Two or three years from now, they will be in that harbor."

Roo said, "What part do I play?"

James said, "I could tax you until you bleed to finance this war, but even if I sent out the army to grab every coin from the Teeth of the World to Kesh, from the Sunset Islands to Roldem, it wouldn't be enough." James again leaned over and spoke softly, as if he feared someone might be listening. "But in that two or three years, with the proper help, you might be able to finance that war."

Roo looked as if he didn't understand. "M'lord?"

James said, "You need to make enough profit in the next two years so that you can loan the Crown what we're going to need to finance this coming war."

Roo let out a long breath. "Well, that's unexpected. You want me to get rich beyond dreaming, so I can lend it to the Crown, to fight a war that we may not win."

James said, "Essentially."

"From what you said, I suspect the Crown may not be in a position to repay me in a timely fashion if we survive this coming ordeal."

James said, "Consider the alternatives."

Roo nodded. "There is that." He rose. "Well, if I'm to become the richest man sitting atop the ash heap in three years, I'd better set about gathering more wealth. To do that, I need to pay off my creditors by sundown."

"There is one other thing," said James.

"What, m'lord?"

"The matter with the Jacobys. There is the father."

"Do I need fear more attacks?"

"Possibly," said James. "The judicious thing to do would be go see him at once, before he learns that you killed his sons. Forge a peace, Rupert, because you need allies, not enemies, for the coming years, and I cannot help you in all things; even my reach has limits."

Roo said, "After I settle with Frederick Jacoby, I'll need to tell all this to my partners."

"I suggest you buy them out," said James. "Or at least gain control of the Bitter Sea Trading and Holding Company." Then James grinned, and Roo could see both a reflection of the boy thief who had once run the streets of Krondor and the echo of his grandsons in his face. "You were planning on that eventually, anyway, weren't you?"

Roo laughed. "Eventually."

"Better sooner than later. If you need a small amount of gold to accomplish that, the Crown can lend it to you; we're certainly going to take that back and a great deal more besides."

Roo said he would let the Duke know, and he departed. As he left the palace he considered how his fate was once again linked to that of the Crown, and how no matter how he tried, he could not free himself of the fate dictated for him the moment he and Erik had killed Stefan.

As he reached the gate, he realized he had neither horse nor carriage waiting for him. Then he decided the walk to the office would help set his mind to what he would need to say to Frederick Jacoby when he told him his sons were dead.

Erik directed the scouts to check the gallery ahead. They had been hearing faint sounds for nearly ten minutes, but the origin of them was unclear. There were side passages and galleries in profusion, and noises echoed in strange and disorienting fashion.

A few minutes later they returned. "It's filled with lizards," whispered one of the scouts. Erik signaled the man to follow him to where Calis and the others waited and the man quickly diagramed how the gallery was laid out.

It was an almost perfect half circle, with a long ramp down from the entrance, running to the right, and a flat ridge running to the left. The swordsmen would charge down the ramp, while the archers would follow, deploying to the left, to rain arrows down upon the serpents.

Calis gave orders, and Erik and de Loungville relayed them. Erik heard Calis tell Boldar to stay with Miranda and guard her, then Calis was moving past, insisting on taking the lead personally.

As was the case before, each man did exactly as he was bidden to do, without hesitation or confusion, but once into the gallery, the battle was joined. And as Erik had learned firsthand, and had read in every book William had given him to read, once the battle was joined, plans were so much chaff on the wind.

These Pantathians were full-sized adults, half again as big as those young warriors they had fought earlier in the day. The tallest

measured just short of Erik's chin, and their best warrior was no
match for Calis's meanest, but they had numbers on their side.

Two hundred or more had gathered in the gallery, and Erik
noted in passing that some showed recent wounds. But he hadn't
time to dwell on where else the Pantathians were battling. He
assumed it was with that third player Calis referred to.

Every man in the company knew that surprise only gained them
a slight advantage, and that they must quickly press that advantage, killing as many Pantathians as possible. Orders were passed
on the other side of the hall, the hissing language of the serpent
priests impossible to understand. Erik laid about him with as much
efficiency as he could muster; in the first two minutes of battle, a
snake man died for each blow he delivered.

Then the defense got organized and began to push the attackers
back. Just as the tide of battle seemed to tip, the twenty bowmen
took up position on the ridge overlooking the gallery and began
to rain arrows down upon the Pantathians.

Erik shouted, "Advance!" and waded into the dying foemen,
and could hear others repeat his order. As before, the Pantathians
refused to yield and stood their ground, dying either by arrow or
by sword blow.

Then it was silent.

Erik glanced around and could see twitching bodies all around.
A few were his own men, but most were green-skinned. He
glanced around, taking mental inventory, then after looking twice,
turned to find de Loungville, gasping for breath, standing a short
distance away. "We have seven down, Sergeant Major."

De Loungville nodded. Erik directed others to get the wounded
and move them back up to the ridge where the archers waited.
Erik then joined de Loungville, Calis, and Miranda in inspecting
the hall. Scouts were sent into nearby galleries, barely visible in
the light.

The air was humid and hot. Breathing was difficult. A crack in
the floor along the far wall bled steam in a steady flow. Several of
the Pantathians were still alive, and Calis's men quickly executed
them. The orders had been defined: if it was a Pantathian, kill it.
No serpent man, woman, or child was to be spared. Erik had felt
little concern for the order, but the men had discussed it.

After a battle in which comrades had fallen, carrying out the orders was easy enough. Then a scout called out, "Sergeant! Over here!"

Erik turned and trotted over. "What is it?"

"Look, sir."

Erik looked at a gallery and saw a bubbling pool of hot water in the center of the room. It had obviously been hollowed out by the serpent priests, as the marks of tools were visible in the rocks. More than a dozen large eggs were arrayed around the pool, close enough to incubate, but not so close as to cook the young.

One of the eggs was moving.

Erik approached the egg as a fracture appeared along one side, and then with a loud crack, it split. The tiny body that tumbled out was little larger than a dog. It blinked as if confused and cried in a sound that was eerily like that of a human baby.

Erik raised his sword and hesitated as the tiny creature made its inquisitive crying sounds. Then the baby Pantathian turned its gaze upon Erik.

The baby's eyes narrowed, and Erik saw hatred in those newborn orbs. With animosity bordering on rage, the tiny creature hissed and hurled itself at Erik.

Reflexively Erik brought his blade down, severing the tiny creature's head from its shoulders.

Erik felt his gorge rise, and swallowing hard, shouted, "Break them!"

The scout joined him and they smashed the remaining eggs. Tiny bodies spilled from the eggs and Erik found himself wishing he could have been anywhere else. The stench that quickly rose from the creatures was noxious beyond anything he had endured.

Leaving the chamber after the grisly work was over, Erik saw others repeating his actions in other galleries close by. More than one man left the galleries retching at what they had seen.

After a few minutes, Miranda said, "There is something. . . ."

"What?" said Calis.

"I don't know . . . but it's close."

Calis stood motionless, then said, "I think I know what it is." He moved to a tunnel leading downward. "This way."

De Loungville said, "Two dead, five wounded, only one too badly to keep up."

Only the briefest flickering of the muscles along Calis's jaw betrayed his pain at hearing that report. Calis was starting toward the ramp leading to where the wounded were being cared for when de Loungville said, "I'll ask him."

Erik knew that Bobby was going to ask the man if he preferred a quick death at the hands of his comrades, or if he wished to risk being left alone to whatever fate brought him, hoping that Calis's company would return this way and be able to pick him up. Erik knew which choice he would have made, or at least he thought he did, and wondered how de Loungville could volunteer for such a task.

Then, as the other wounded and the archers descended the ramp, Erik realized that he knew exactly why Bobby could do it. He had seen the horrors of the Pantathians and their allies first-hand, and a well-thrust knife blade and a single moment of hot pain was far better for one of your companions than the lingering agony you would suffer if captured.

A strangled grunt of pain told Erik how the man had chosen. De Loungville returned, his face set in an unreadable mask, and he said, "Form up the column."

Erik gave the order and the men got ready to move on.

Nineteen

Revelations

ROO SIGHED.

He had left the palace and walked home, thinking the entire way about the best manner to approach Frederick Jacoby. If the old man was more like the quiet Randolph, an accommodation might be reached. If he was like the volatile Timothy, the feud would almost certainly continue until one house or the other was destroyed.

Roo entered his home. The only noise came from the kitchen, where Rendel and Mary readied food for the day. The upstairs hallway was still, and he knew he'd find his wife and children still sleeping. He wondered at the hour, and realized he had no idea what time it was. From the light, no later than eight of the clock.

He pushed open the door to the room Karli slept in with the baby, and found her asleep. He now considered waking her, but decided to wait until the baby demanded feeding. Roo walked softly to the bedside and studied his wife and son in the dim light coming through the curtains.

In the shadows, Karli looked very young. Roo suddenly felt terribly old and sat down in the rocking chair Karli used to soothe the baby when he was fussy. He didn't sleep as well as his sister had, and cried more often.

Roo ran his hand over his face, feeling fatigue in his bones. His eyes were gritty and his mouth had a bitter taste in it: too much coffee and a hint of bile from killing men.

Roo closed his eyes.

Some time later the baby's cry woke him. Karli sat up and said, "What is it?" She saw her husband in the chair. "Roo?"

"I must have fallen asleep."

"Why didn't you go to bed?" she asked.

"I have something to tell you," he answered as she began to nurse the hungry child.

"What?"

"The men who killed your father are dead."

She didn't react.

After a moment he said, "They attempted to ruin me, and I found out in time. We fought . . . and they're dead. I just came from the palace and a long discussion of these events with the Duke."

"Then it's over," she said.

"Not quite," said Roo.

Karli stared at him a moment. "Why not?"

"The two men have a father." He took a deep breath. "Your father had an old rival, Frederick Jacoby."

She nodded. "They were boys together, in the Advarian community up in Tannerus." Her voice softened. "I think they were friends once. Why? Did he have Father killed?"

"No, his son Timothy ordered it. I think his brother Randolph may have helped, or at least he knew about it and didn't do anything to prevent it."

"So those men are dead?"

"Yes."

"But Frederick is still alive," observed Karli. She looked sad, as if on the verge of weeping. "So you have to kill him, too?"

Roo said, "I don't know. I need to make some sort of peace with him if I can." He stood up. "And I should go do it now. The Duke insists."

Roo started around the bed, then paused and turned. He leaned over and kissed the back of the baby's head, then kissed Karli on the cheek. "I probably won't get home until supper. And what I really need is sleep."

She reached out with her left hand and gripped his right. "Be careful."

He squeezed her hand in reply and left the room.

He called down to Mary to have his coach brought around, went to his room, quickly washed up and changed his tunic. Then he went downstairs and out the door. His coach was there, and as he entered, he saw another figure waiting inside for him.

Dash nodded in greeting. "Feeling better?"

"Tired," said Roo. "What brings you here?"

"Grandfather thought it prudent if I tagged along. Mr. Jacoby might have servants or other members of his household who are going to take the news of the brothers' death badly." He pointed to the sword that lay across his knees.

Roo nodded. "You know how to use that?"

"Better than most," Dash said without boasting.

They rode along in silence until the coach pulled up before the Jacoby residence. Dash followed Roo out of the carriage and to the door. Roo hesitated a moment, then knocked. A young woman opened the door a few moments later. She was pretty in an unspectacular way—dark hair and eyes, strong chin and straight nose. "Yes? May I help you?" she asked.

Roo found he could barely bring himself to speak. He didn't know what to say. After a moment's hesitation, he said, "My name is Rupert Avery."

The woman's eyes narrowed. "I know your name, Mr. Avery. It is not one spoken with affection in this house."

"I can imagine," Roo said. He took a deep breath. "I suspect it will be even less so when you discover what brings me here. I would like to speak to Frederick Jacoby."

"I'm afraid that's impossible," said the young woman. "He doesn't see visitors."

Roo's expression betrayed something, for after a moment the woman said, "What is it?"

Dash said, "Pardon me, ma'am. Who are you?"

"I'm Helen. Randolph's wife."

Roo closed his eyes and then took a deep breath. "I fear I have grave tidings for you and for your father-in-law."

The woman's knuckles where she gripped the door whitened. "Randy's dead, isn't he?"

Roo nodded. "May I come in, please?"

The woman stepped back and it was clear she was close to fainting. Dash moved and took her by the elbow, keeping her upright. Just then two children ran into the entry hall, complaining over a childish inequity. She separated the two of them, a boy and girl, looking to Roo to be about four and six. "Children," she said, "go to your room and play quietly."

"But, Mother," said the boy, irritated at his complaint being ignored.

"Go to your room!" she said sharply.

The boy looked injured by the command, but the girl just skipped away, counting their mother's deafness to the boy's grievance a victory in the eternal sibling war.

When the children were gone, she looked at Roo and said, "How did Randy die?"

Roo said, "We had cornered Randolph and Timothy at the docks—they were trying to make off with gold they had taken from me—and Timothy tried to attack me. Randolph pushed him aside, and was killed by a crossbow bolt fired at Timothy." Trying to think of anything that might lessen the sting the woman felt, he said, "It was over quickly. He was acting to save his brother."

Helen's eyes filled with tears, but her tone was one of anger. "He was always trying to save his brother! Is Tim alive?"

"No," said Roo softly. He took a deep breath. "I killed him."

As the woman turned, Dash said, "It was a fair duel, ma'am. Timothy died with weapons in his hand, tryng to kill Mr. Avery."

"Why are you here?" said the woman. "Are you here to gloat over the fall of the house of Jacoby?"

"No," said Roo. "I'm here because Duke James asked me to come." He sighed, feeling more tired than he had ever felt in his life. "I had nothing against your husband, or you or your father, ma'am. It was only Tim I had issue with. Tim arranged to have my partner—my father-in-law—killed. Tim was trying to ruin me."

Helen turned her back on them. "I have no doubt of that, Mr. Avery. Please follow me."

She led them through a large hallway, and Roo saw that the house was much larger than one might think from the street, being very deep in its plan. Then they entered a garden at the rear of the house, surrounded by a large stone wall. An old man sat alone in a chair, bundled in heavy robes, with a large quilt over his knees. As they approached, Roo saw his eyes were blinded by cataracts, and then that part of his face was motionless. "Yes? Who's there?" he said, his speech slurred and his voice weak.

Helen raised her voice. "It's me, Father!" To Roo she said, "He's hard of hearing. He had a seizure two years ago. He's been like this ever since."

She turned to face Roo. "It's your chance, Mr. Avery. All that's left of the once-great trading house of Jacoby is a blind, half-deaf crazy old man, a woman, and two children. You can kill us all now and put an end to this feud."

Roo put up his hand and his expression was one of total helplessness. "Please. I . . . I have no wish to see any more suffering for either of our families."

"No suffering?" she said, as again tears came. "How am I to make do? Who's to run the business? Who will care for us? It would be far kinder for you to pull your sword and put us all out of our misery." She began to cry in earnest, and Dash stepped forward and let her lean against his shoulder as she sobbed.

"Helen?" said the old man, his speech slurred by the affliction of his seizure. "Is something amiss?"

Roo went and knelt by the old man. "Mr. Jacoby?"

"Who is this?" he said, reaching out with his left arm. Roo saw that his right lay motionless in his lap. Roo took the left hand and said, "My name is Rupert Avery." He spoke loudly.

"Avery? Do I know you, sir?" asked the old man. "Knew a Klaus Avery when . . . no, that was Klaus Klamer. What was the Avery boy's name?"

Roo said, "No, I don't think I've had the honor of meeting you before. But I . . . knew an old friend of yours. Helmut Grindel."

"Helmut!" said the old man with a grin. Saliva dribbled from the side of his mouth.

Helen composed herself, and with a thank-you pat to Dash's shoulders, she came and used a handkerchief to wipe the old man's chin.

"He and I grew up in the same town, did you know that?" said the old man. "How is he?"

Roo said, "He died recently."

"Oh," said the old man. "That's too bad. I haven't seen him for a while. Did I tell you we grew up in the same town?"

"Yes, you did," said Roo.

With delight, the old man said, "Do you by chance know my boys? Tim and Randy?"

Roo said, "I do, sir."

The old man picked up Roo's hand slightly, as if for emphasis. "If you're one of those rascals who is always stealing apples from our tree, don't admit it!" he said with a laugh. "I've told Tim to keep the other boys out of that tree! We need those apples for pie! My Eva bakes pies every fall!"

Roo looked at Helen, and she whispered. "He gets confused. Sometimes he thinks his sons are still children. Eva was his wife; she's been dead thirteen years."

Roo shook his head and released the old man's hand. He said, "I can't."

"Tell him?" asked Helen.

Roo shook his head no.

"Randy?" said the old man, motioning to Roo. Roo leaned over to put his head next to the old man's. Whispering, the old man said, "Randy, you're a good lad. Look out for Tim; he's got such a temper. But don't let the other boys steal the apples!" He reached out with his good hand and patted Roo on the shoulder.

Roo straightened up and spent a few moments watching the old man, who was again lost in whatever dreams or memories he spent his days within. Roo stepped away and said to Helen, "What purpose? Let him think his sons still live, for the gods' mercy."

He thought of the coming fleet and the destruction that would be upon Krondor within a few years, and said, "Let us all have a few years of pleasant dreams."

Helen led them away from the garden and said, "I thank you for that small gesture, sir."

"What will you do?" said Roo.

"Sell the house and business." She started to weep again. "I have family in Tannerus. I'll go to them. It will be hard, but we'll endure."

Roo said, "No." He thought about the boy and girl and his own two children, then said, "I do not think the children need suffer for the . . . mistakes of their fathers."

"What do you propose?" asked Helen.

"Let me take charge of Jacoby and Sons. I will not take a copper of profit from the company. I will operate it as if it were my own, but when your son is old enough, it will be his to control." Roo glanced around the house as they walked toward the entrance. "I never spoke more than a word to Randolph, but it seems to me your husband's only flaw was to love a brother too well. It was only Tim with whom I had dispute." Taking the woman's hand, he said, "Let it end here, now."

The woman said, "You are generous."

Roo said, "No. I am sorry. More than you will ever know. I'll have my solicitor draw up a contract between you as surviving widow of Randolph Jacoby and the Bitter Sea Company to operate Jacoby and Sons until such time as either you wish to dispose of the property or your son is ready to take control.

"If you need anything, anything at all, you only have to ask." He pointed to Dash. "My associate will come fetch you this afternoon and take you to the temple. Have you other relatives who should come with you?"

"No. They live out of the city."

"I would bid you a good day, Mrs. Jacoby, but that would seem an empty sentiment. Let me depart by saying I wish we had met under different circumstances."

Holding back more tears, Helen Jacoby said, "So do I, Mr. Avery. I even suspect had circumstances been otherwise, you and Randolph could have been friends."

They left and entered the carriage. Dash said nothing and Roo put his right hand over his face. After a moment, he began to weep.

Calis signaled and the column came to a halt. They had encountered small commands of the Pantathians over the last three days. Calis judged they had moved twenty miles north of where they had encountered the large well in the heart of the mountain. Several times they had found more signs of struggle and destruction. Occasionally they encountered Saaur corpses, but as of yet they hadn't seen a single living lizard man. Having faced them once, Erik was grateful for that small boon.

Erik fought against a growing sense of futility. The galleries seemed to wander under the mountains forever; he remembered maps back at the palace that suggested this range might be as much as a thousand miles long. If the Pantathian home realm wasn't as closely confined as Calis's theory proposed, they would be dead long before destroying the snake men's nest.

Men were tense; the other specter that haunted their imaginations was who this mysterious third player might be. No fallen were seen who were not Pantathians or Saaur. The only human remains were those belonging to pitiful prisoners, dragged under the mountain to feed the Pantathian young. Whoever or whatever was warring on the Pantathians seemed intent on the same mission as Calis and his men: three breeding crèches had been found with infant Pantathians littering the rooms, all torn to pieces.

The more evidence he observed, the more Erik was convinced they weren't looking for anything remotely like another invading force. Several bodies appeared to have been torn asunder, literally ripped limb from limb. Some of the young Pantathians looked as if they had been bitten in two. Erik couldn't put aside images of some monstrous creature from an ancient fable, materialized here by a magician to destroy his enemies.

But when he had wondered aloud on this, Miranda's only answer was "Where are the Pantathian magicians, then?"

Erik had heard some of Miranda's speculations as they marched: the entire population of Pantathian serpent priests was out in the field serving the Emerald Queen. Even when she said it, Miranda didn't sound convinced.

A scout returned and said, "Nothing ahead, but there are some odd echoes, Sergeant."

Erik nodded and asked, "What do you mean by odd?"

"Nothing I can put a name to, but there's something ahead, perhaps at a great distance, but it's making enough noise we should be able to get very close without being heard."

Calis was told and said, "We're close to being ready to drop."

Miranda wiped her forehead. "The heat down here is as bad as in the Green Reaches of Kesh."

Erik couldn't argue. The men were wearing the lightest clothing possible under their armor, and it had taken a lot of attention to keep them from throwing away the heavy fur cloaks, which were now rolled and stowed in the heavy backpacks they lugged. Erik took time to remind each man that once they were back out of the mountains, winter would be upon them and it would be as cold as it was now hot.

Calis ordered a break and rest, and Erik assigned men to keep watch, while others grabbed what sleep they could. As he reviewed every detail he could remember, de Loungville motioned for him to come to a distant part of the cavern.

"Some stench?" he offered.

Erik nodded. "Sometimes the sulfur makes my eyes burn."

"What do you think?"

Erik looked confused. "About what?"

"About all this?" Bobby waved his hand around.

Erik shrugged. "I'm not paid to think."

Bobby grinned. "Right." Then the grin vanished. "Now, what do you *really* think?"

Erik shrugged. "I don't know. Sometimes it seems to me we've got no chance of ever seeing daylight again, but the rest of the time I just keep moving, one foot ahead of the other, go where I'm told, keep the men alive, and don't dwell on tomorrow."

De Loungville nodded. "Understood. But here's the hard part. That one-foot-at-a-time attitude is fine for the soldiers in the trenches, but you've got responsibilities."

"I know."

"No, I don't think you do," said de Loungville. He looked around to make sure no one else was listening. "Miranda has the means to get herself and one other out of here in a hurry. Special means."

Erik nodded. He had long ago accommodated to the idea of Miranda's being a sorceress in some fashion, so this didn't surprise him.

"If anything happens to me, your job is to get the Captain out with Miranda, understand?"

"Maybe I don't."

"He's special," said de Loungville. "The Kingdom needs him more than a couple of sorry sods like me and you. If you have to, hit him over the head and toss his limp body at Miranda, but don't let her leave without him."

Erik tried not to laugh. The only member of this company stronger than Erik was the Captain, and from what Erik had seen over the last few years, Calis was significantly stronger than Erik. Erik had a pretty good notion that if he hit Calis over the head, it probably wouldn't slow him a beat.

"I'll see what I can do," he said noncommittally.

They moved out two hours later and Erik kept what de Loungville said in mind. He discounted the admonition because he didn't want to imagine a situation where de Loungville wasn't around to tell him what to do, and he didn't think he could tell the Captain to do anything.

They moved along a long, narrow tunnel that seemed to slope gently downward. The heat continued unabated, but didn't seem to get worse.

Twice they took breaks and scouts were sent ahead. Both times they returned to report the distant sounds they couldn't identify.

Two hours later, Erik could hear the sounds they mentioned. Rumblings, the thunder faintly heard, with high-pitched keening, echoed from a great distance, or at least that's how it seemed to Erik.

They reached a gallery and again found the signs of battle. But unlike the ones found earlier in the day or on the previous day, these were relatively fresh. "This struggle took place yesterday," observed Calis. He pointed to places where deep pools of blood were still congealing. A soldier called Calis over to a breeding pool, and Erik followed.

"Gods!" said Erik looking at the carnage. It was the biggest hatching pool found so far. Eggs were smashed and yolk and albumen floated in the water. The stench of rotten eggs was nearly overpowering, then Erik noticed something. "Where are the bodies of the young?"

A single arm lay floating in a bubbling pool of pinkish water, and around the verge splatters of blood were evident. At last Calis said, "Something feasted here."

The image of something ripping open the eggs and devouring the Pantathian young was one Erik didn't wish to dwell on, so he turned around and left. "We should keep moving," said Calis at last.

Erik formed up the men and moved them out.

The ceremony was as brief as the one that had been conducted for Helmut. Roo stood with Karli beside him. The children were home with Mary.

Helen and her two children stood silently while the priest of

Lims-Kragma intoned the benediction for the dead and lit the pyre. The girl played absently with her doll while the boy looked on with his face set in an expression of confusion.

When the ceremony was over, Karli said, "It is over?"

Roo patted her hand. "Yes. The widow is a woman of remarkable strength but no bitterness. She also cares most for her children."

Karli looked at the children. "Poor babies." She went over to Helen and said, "I find no pleasure in this; if I can help, don't be ashamed to ask."

Helen nodded. Her face was drawn and pale, but whatever tears she might have had remaining were held in check for later that night, when she was again alone.

Karli returned to Roo's side. "Are we going home?"

Roo shook his head. "As much as I would like to, I have business I must oversee." He glanced at the distant afternoon sun. "I must discharge a debt before sundown. After that . . . I don't know."

Karli nodded. "I must return to the children."

Roo kissed her dutifully upon the cheek. "I'll be home when I can."

As Karli departed, Roo crossed to Helen. He studied the widow and thought what a fine and brave woman she was. Nothing like the beauty that Sylvia was, but nevertheless a woman who drew him.

She turned to find him staring at her, and he lowered his eyes. "I just wanted to repeat what I said today. Whatever you need, it is yours."

Calmly she said, "Thank you."

Without knowing why, he said, "You never have to thank me." Then he impulsively took her hand in his and held it briefly, saying, "Never."

Without waiting for her to say anything, he turned and left.

He rode without clear thought from the temple to Barret's. Fatigue and emotions new to him made him unable to focus his mind. He thought of the struggle and the death, then he saw the face of Helen Jacoby. The children, he would think, and then he would think of his own children.

His driver had to alert him to the fact he was outside of Barret's, and he wearily made his way to his usual place of business. His three partners were waiting for him and he sat heavily, signaling to the waiter for a large cup of coffee.

Masterson said, "How did it go?"

"I got the gold," answered Roo. He had intentionally not let his partners know about the recovery until now. His conversation with Duke James stuck in his mind, and he knew he needed to talk to his three partners while they were still frantic from worry.

"Praise be!" called Hume, while Crowley just sighed deeply.

Masterson said, "Where's the gold?"

"On its way to pay off the note."

"Good, good," said Crowley.

Roo paused a moment, then said, "I want you to buy me out."

Masterson said, "What?"

Roo said, "This is all going too fast. We're very vulnerable, and I find I spend most of my time on the Bitter Sea Company and not enough time on Avery and Son's business."

Crowley said, "Why should we buy you out?"

"Because I've earned the right to quit," said Roo. For emphasis he slammed his hand upon the table. "I'm the one who fought a duel this morning to save our collective backsides. I don't mind saving my own, but I didn't see any of you gentlemen down there in the dark with a sword in your hand, fighting for your lives!"

Hume said, "Well, I mean, had we known . . ."

Crowley said, "I don't think I'm persuaded we owe you any sort of quick exit, Mr. Avery."

Masterson had been quiet, then he said, "So you think this partnership should be dissolved?"

Roo said, "Or at least reorganized."

Masterson smiled slightly. "How?"

"Let me buy controlling interest," said Roo, "if you won't buy me out. Either way, I don't care, but if I'm going to be putting my life on the line, it will be for my own interests."

Masterson said, "You're a fast one, Roo Avery. I think you'll do fine with or without us. If you're avid for a break, I'll sell to you."

Hume said, "This is all too much for me. I'm confused."

Crowley said, "Bah! This is just a trick to get me to step down as Presiding Officer of the Bitter Sea Company."

"Sell me half your interests, gentlemen," said Roo, "and I'll make you rich. But I won't put myself again in the position where I'm risking my life and my family's future to protect *your* gold."

Masterson laughed. "That's right, Avery. I'll tell you what: I'll sell you just enough, if the others will, to give you control, but I won't give you it all. It may have been your knack for a deal and your bloody damn luck that won us this wealth, but it was a lot of our gold at risk."

Hume said, "I'll do the same. I spend too much time here on Bitter Sea Company business and not enough on my other concerns."

Crowley said, "Well, I won't do it. Buy me out or sell to me, one or the other."

Roo looked at Crowley and said, "What price?"

"To buy or to sell?"

The other three men laughed, and after a moment, Crowley did as well. "Very well," said Crowley. "I'll set you a price." He picked up a quill and scribbled a total on it, then pushed it across to Roo.

Roo picked up the parchment, saw the figure was ridiculously high, and shook his head. He picked up the quill, drew a line through the total, wrote another one, and passed the parchment back to Brandon Crowley.

Crowley looked at the total. "That's robbery!"

"Then I'll take the first number as your offer to buy me out?" said Roo.

Masterson laughed. "He's got you, Brandon."

Crowley said, "I'll take the difference between the two."

Which was as Roo knew he would, so Roo said, "Done!" To Hume and Masterson he said, "You gentlemen bear witness."

They quickly agreed on the transfer of ownership, and before he knew it, Masterson was breaking out his special brandy again. After the events of the last two days, Roo was emotionally and physically drained. The single brandy got him close to as drunk as he could remember being.

He struggled down to find Duncan waiting for him at the door. "Luis says to tell you the gold got to where it needed to go, and all is well." He smiled.

Roo smiled in return. "You're a good friend as well as my cousin, Duncan." He gave his cousin a very unexpected hug. "I neglect to tell you that."

Duncan laughed. "Been drinking?"

Roo nodded. "Yes. And you are now talking to the owner of the Bitter Sea Trading and Holding Company." He signaled for his carriage. "I believe that makes me one of the richest men in Krondor, Duncan."

Laughing, Duncan said, "Well, if you say so."

The carriage rolled up and Duncan opened the door, then helped to get Roo inside. "Where to, sir?" asked the driver.

Roo leaned out the still-open door and said, "Duncan, I need a favor. I was to dine this night with Sylvia Esterbrook and I simply am too exhausted. Would you be a friend and carry my regrets to her?"

Duncan grinned. "I think I can manage it."

"You're a good friend, Duncan. Have I told you that?"

"Yes," said Duncan with a laugh. He closed the door and said, "Get home with you!"

The carriage rolled away and Duncan went to where his horse was tethered. He mounted and started to ride out toward the Esterbrook estate. After a block, he turned his horse and headed back toward the small house he now shared with a prostitute he had met at the docks after Luis had left.

He found the woman sleeping through the day and unceremoniously yanked the covers from her. She snorted and awoke, saying, "What?"

He stared at her nude body a moment, then reached down and pulled her dress off the floor. "Get your things and get out!" he commanded as he threw it at her.

"What?" asked the still-confused woman again, sitting up. "I said, *get out*!" he shouted. For emphasis, he slapped her hard across the face. "I need to bathe. Be gone by the time I'm done."

He left the shocked and crying woman in the bedroom and moved down to the end of the hall, where a tub sat next to a small stove. He heated water and inspected his face in a polished metal mirror. Rubbing his hand over his chin, he decided he needed to shave. Stropping a razor, he hummed a nameless tune while in the next room the whore whose name he couldn't recall gathered up her belongings and cursed him under her breath.

The screams echoed down the tunnels and Erik, Calis, and the rest of the company moved as cautiously as possible. A bright light shone ahead, from where a battle appeared to be taking place. Occasionally the sound of struggle paused, and then the clash of steel and shouts resumed. The hissing scream of Pantathians was punctuated by what Erik recognized as Saaur war cries and something else, something that raised the hair on the back of his neck.

Erik used hand signals, despite the din sounding ahead, against the faint possibility that someone might hear them coming. Renaldo moved to where Erik stood, at the van, and both of them stepped forward far enough to see what was ahead.

A vast cavern, as big as any they had encountered opened before them, a circular well similar to the one when they had used to enter the mountains. It rose so high overhead that Erik had no idea where it stopped, but they had arrived near the bottom.

Below them, one revolution down the circular ramp that hugged the inside of the well, a scene of desperate horror greeted them. The largest cache of Pantathian eggs they had seen so far lay in a vast pool of bubbling water. Erik quickly apprehended details. A stream of water ran down a wall into the pool, and Erik presumed it was cold, for the eggs would be cooked otherwise. The ice melt from above and the hot water from below must be mixed to keep the eggs incubated.

The pool was easily sixty feet across, and crouched in the middle was a creature so alien Erik couldn't define it. He waved to those behind him and stared while the rest of the company filed out of the tunnel and spread out along the lip of the ramp. Erik felt pain in his shoulder and found Calis's hand gripping him tightly. Erik whispered, "Captain?"

Calis blinked and said, "Sorry," as he removed his hand.

Erik knew he was startled but was surprised at how much.

The creature in the pool stood seventeen or eighteen feet tall, with large leathery wings on its back. It was a pearlescent black in color, with emerald green eyes. It divided its attention between savaging the remaining eggs in the pool—picking them apart and pulling the tiny Pantathians from within, devouring them with a gulp—and fighting a battle with the surviving defenders. The creature's head was horselike, but it had wide-set curved horns, like a goat, and each arm ended with human-looking hands, five fingers with long sharp talons where nails should be.

"What is that thing?" asked de Loungville.

"Mantrecoe," said Boldar. "You'd call it a demon, I guess. It's a being from a different plane of reality. I've never seen one, but I know about them." He turned to Miranda and said, "Did you know?"

She shook her head and said, "No. I thought we faced something else entirely."

"How did it get here?" asked Boldar. "The seals between this realm and the Fifth Circle have been intact for centuries. If one of those things had come through the Hall, we would have known."

"It didn't come through the Hall of Worlds, obviously," said Miranda, straining to watch. Then she said, "Now we know where the Pantathian magic users are."

Suddenly a keening howl filled the room as the creature screamed in pain. It turned to face a group of serpent men who were incanting a spell against it.

Calis said, "Over there!"

He pointed and Erik saw a tunnel, about twenty feet beyond the other side of the struggle. "What?"

"That's where we need to go."

"Are you mad?" asked Erik, before he could remember who he was speaking to.

"Unfortunately, no," said Calis. To Bobby he said, "Start walking the men around the ramp to just above that door and then drop a rope. Try not to call attention to yourself. I don't want to have to deal with either side of this struggle if we can avoid it."

De Loungville signaled and Erik took the lead, moving as close to the wall as he could, so that at times as he circled the well, following the ramp's rise, he saw only the head of the creature as it ducked, weaved, and tried to get past magic wards and blasts of energy. Twice waves of searing heat rose off the battle below, and once he was almost blinded by a flash of light so bright it left him blinking for a moment.

He reached the position above the tunnel entrance Calis wanted, and turned so the man behind him could pull a rope out of Erik's backpack. Erik saw nothing to which he could tie the rope, so he braced himself and nodded for the next soldier to shinny down the rope and head up the tunnel.

Each man followed orders without thought or hesitation. Two archers waited nearby, ready to fire at either the Pantathian magicians or the demon, but both sides seemed intent on their struggle.

After the tenth man descended, Calis approached and said, "How are you doing?"

"My arms ache, but I'm all right," said Erik.

Calis said, "I'll hold this for a bit." He took the rope with one hand, and Erik was again impressed with just how much more powerful the Captain was than he appeared to be.

More men climbed down, ducking into the tunnel. Erik couldn't judge, but it seemed to him the contest was slowly turning the demon's way. Each time the Pantathian magicians launched an assault, the creature returned even more viciously. The magicians appeared to be tiring, if Erik could judge these alien creatures.

Suddenly it was Miranda climbing down and Calis said, "Erik, you next."

Erik complied, and was followed by de Loungville; then the rope fell. Calis leaped the twenty and more feet to the stone floor, landing as lightly as if he had jumped only a few. He found his company spread out down the tunnel, backs against the wall. Calis moved past and said, "Follow me," when he reached the other end of the line.

The men fell in, and Erik took up a position at the rear, glancing back at the struggle. A strange hissing scream cut through the air and Erik judged one of the magicians had been taken by the demon.

They came to a small chamber, barely large enough to hold the company. Calis said, "Listen, everyone. Something has changed the balance of forces we find opposing us and we need to discover what this new agent is." He glanced about, "Boldar?"

"Yes?" asked the mercenary.

"You put a name to that thing. What do you know about it?"

Boldar's helm turned in Miranda's direction and she nodded once. "Tell him."

Boldar removed his helm. "It's a *mantrecoe*, in the language of the priests of Ast'hap'ut, a world I've visited. I've never seen one, but I've seen temple paintings."

Boldar paused, as if considering his words. "Other worlds live by other rules," he began. "On Ast'hap'ut, they've had . . . dealings with these creatures. Ritual sacrifices and invocations, and a sort of worship.

"On other worlds they're considered creatures from a different energy plane."

"Energy plane?" said Calis.

Miranda spoke. "A lot of beings exist out there in the universe in places that follow different rules than this world does, Calis. You've heard your father speak of the Dread?"

He nodded and no small number of the men made signs of protection against evil. "He defeated a Dread Master once." The Dread were the stuff of legends, along with the Dragon Lords. The Dread were considered the mightiest of the creatures of the void, the soul-suckers and life-drainers. The tread of their foot withered the grass, and only the mightiest magic could defeat them.

"Well," continued Miranda, "that creature out there, that demon, is similar; the universe it lives in is governed by different laws from our own." She glanced back down the tunnel and said, "It's not as alien to our sense of how things work as the Dread may be, but it is different enough that its presence means some very difficult days are ahead."

"How did it come here?" asked Calis.

"I don't know," Miranda answered. "Perhaps we'll find out ahead." She pointed at the tunnel leading away from the struggle.

Calis nodded. "Let's go."

He led the way, with Erik, Boldar, de Loungville, and the others trailing behind. "At least we understand why we found some untouched pockets of young here and there," said de Loungville.

Erik nodded. "That thing is too big for some of the chambers."

Boldar said, "It might not always have been that way."

"What do you mean?" asked Calis, not stopping as he moved through the dark tunnel. They had returned to their single torch in the center of the line and Erik found it odd hearing his voice in the gloom.

"It may be that this creature slipped through a dimensional scission."

"Scission?" said Calis.

"Rift," supplied Miranda. "That might make sense. If a tiny demon came through unnoticed and spent some time gathering its strength, preying upon the unwary in these tunnels until it could raid the outlying crèches . . ."

"But that doesn't answer how it got here, or why," said Calis.

They moved quickly down the tunnel until it suddenly emptied into a large chamber. A half-dozen other tunnels also entered, and before them rose up gigantic double doors of ancient wood.

The doors were open and they moved through the doorway into the biggest hall encountered so far. Erik's eyes had difficulty understanding what he saw. It was a temple, but unlike any human temple he had ever encountered. "Mother of all gods!" said one of the men coming into the hall behind Erik.

A full hundred yards of floor stretched out before them, and everywhere they looked, torn and mutilated bodies were strewn. The stench was nearly overwhelming, even to men who had been smelling the stink of dead for days now.

A thousand torches had once lit the room to what must have been brilliance, but presently only one torch in ten still burned. The hall was rendered into gloomy darkness and flickering shadows that danced on every surface, giving the room an even more terrifying aspect than it would have held.

And that aspect would have been frightening at the light of noon.

The rear wall was cut to form a statue of heroic proportion. A regal-looking woman sat atop a throne, a figure measuring over one hundred feet from toe to crown. Her robes flowed down from her shoulders, leaving her breasts bare. In two arms she held life-size creatures, one obviously Pantathian, the other resembling the Saaur, though of smaller stature than any Saaur Erik had seen. The entire statue was green, as if cut from the largest single piece of jade in the universe.

Before her a huge pit yawned, and Erik picked his way through the litter of bodies to glance downward. "Gods!" he whispered.

He couldn't begin to estimate the number of humans who must have gone into that pit to fill it, because he had no concept of the depth. But just from what he could see, it had been a staggering population. Then he realized the dark railing wasn't that color from paint or stain but from generations of human blood.

Boldar came forward and said, "This begs repayment. I thought you a rather cold-blooded crew when Miranda told me where we were headed and why, but now I understand why you must destroy these creatures."

"This is only a part of it," said Calis from behind. He pointed to cases used to display artifacts arrayed on both sides of the huge statue. "There. That is where we must go."

Erik looked around. He didn't much like the idea of attempting to walk across the mountain of bones. Then he spied an entrance near the base of the pit. "Maybe that way?"

Calis nodded. "You, Boldar, and Miranda, with me." To de Loungville he said, "Spread out the men and search. Anything that looks as if it might be remotely important is to be carried back here."

Miranda said, "But carefully. Do not let alien devices or objects come into contact with one another."

Boldar echoed that. "There can be nasty consequences if the wrong sorts of magic come into contact."

De Loungville ordered the men to spread out, and torches were distributed so the men could have more light to inspect the ruins of this temple. Calis led the others to the small door Erik had seen, and it was indeed an access to the altar, so that they could get to the huge idol without crossing the pit.

As they reached the large dais upon which the idol sat, Calis motioned for Boldar and Erik to stand back while he and Miranda cautiously approached the nearest case. Looking like nothing so much as bookcases, thought Erik, these were fashioned of stone, blackened by what he knew now to be centuries of human blood. He saw Miranda and Calis were indifferent to the cases. They studied the items displayed within them.

Erik didn't see anything remarkable about any of them; they mostly consisted of jewelry, a few weapons, and some other nondescript items. But Calis and Miranda approached them as if they were repositories of evil.

Quietly they looked, moving toward the cases and away, then barely touching them. Suddenly Calis said, "They are wrong!"

Miranda said, "Are you certain?"

"As I know my own heritage!" He picked up a dagger and said, "The helm that we carry brings sounds, tastes, ancient visions. There is nothing of that here."

Miranda took another weapon, and examined it, then she tossed the shortsword to Erik, hilt first, and said, "Von Darkmoor: strike something."

Erik glanced around, and saw nothing close by that looked a

likely target. He moved to the other side of the huge idol and struck the edge of one of the large stone cases. The sword shattered as if it had been fashioned of base metal.

"Not very well made," said Erik inspecting the hilt still in his hand. Having been a smith for years, he said, "The blade wasn't even steel."

Calis knelt and picked up a piece of shattered metal. "It wasn't supposed to be steel. It was supposed to have been something . . . far more deadly."

Erik tossed away the hilt.

Calis moved around the statue, inspecting it. "This is supposed to be the Green Mother of All," he said quietly. "In a strange fashion, she would be my aunt."

Erik's eyes widened slightly, and he glanced at Miranda and Boldar. Miranda watched Calis's face closely, as if she were anxious about something. Boldar returned Erik's questioning glance with a shrug.

Miranda said, "These are . . . stage properties." She waved her hand at the artifacts in the cases. "It's as if a company of actors were staging this." She looked around the vast hall. "This is a theater more than a temple."

Boldar looked at the carnage on the floor and the bones in the pit. "The murder is real enough."

Calis said, "Look here."

Erik came over and saw a faint crack along the back of the huge idol. He put his hand over it and felt a draft of air. "There's an entrance behind here."

Calis put his shoulder to the idol and Erik pushed as well. Rather than the enormous resistance they expected from an idol this massive, it rolled away a few feet, being hinged on the opposite side from where they stood. A man-sized opening was visible in the wall behind the idol, an entrance to a flight of stairs leading downward.

Miranda knelt and examined the base of the idol from behind. "This is marvelous engineering," she observed.

Boldar looked at the metalwork. "Nothing like this was forged on Midkemia."

Erik also looked at the marvelous wheels, pulleys, and hinges and was forced to agree. He wished for enough time to linger over these items—he was still fascinated by the smith's arts—but Calis was already moving down the stairs.

Erik gripped his torch tightly in his left hand, his sword in his right, and called over his shoulder, "Sergeant!"

De Loungville shouted back, "What?"

"There's a passage down here. The Captain's heading down it."

"Understood!" said de Loungville as he continued to have the men look over the corpses for anything that might shed light on what had happened in this strange underground city of serpent men.

Erik stepped on the top step and followed the others downward.

Duncan knocked on the gate and was quickly answered by a servant; he assumed the gateman had been waiting for Roo to arrive.

"Yes?" asked the servant.

"I bear a message for Lady Sylvia from Rupert Avery."

Seeing the rider was dressed in fine clothing, the servant opened the gate, asking, "And who might you be, sir?"

"I am Duncan Avery."

"Very well, sir," said the servant, closing the gate behind Duncan as he rode up to the front of the house.

Duncan dismounted and gave the reins to another servant, and walked to the door. He knocked loudly.

A few moments later the door opened, and Sylvia stood regarding Duncan. She wore another of the stunning evening gowns only the boldest young women of Krondor would dare to display themselves in; she was one of the few who could do justice to it.

Duncan smiled his most charming smile.

She said, "I was expecting Rupert."

"He sends his regrets. I thought it far more civil to bring word in person, rather than letting an impersonal note serve."

She stepped aside and said, "Do come in."

He entered and said, "He regrets that the press of business and family matters conspire to keep him away this evening. He is devastated."

Sylvia allowed herself a slight smile. "I somehow find it difficult to imagine that Roo said it in quite that fashion."

Duncan shrugged. "I thought perhaps if you had no objection,

I might offer you my poor company as an alternative."

She laughed. Taking his arm in hers, she pressed her bosom hard against him as she walked him to the dining hall. "I doubt women find your company poor, dear . . . Duncan, is it not?"

"It is indeed, Sylvia. If I may presume?"

Reaching the dining room, she said, "You may presume a great deal, I think." She led him to the chair at the end of the table and motioned for him to sit, as a servant pulled out her chair. "We met that night at the party; now I remember."

Duncan smiled and she studied his face a while.

"Let us eat," said Sylvia. "And drink. Yes, I find I'm in the mood for a great deal of wine." Motioning to Duncan's goblet, she told the servant, "Some of Father's best."

As the servant disappeared to fetch a bottle of wine, Sylvia fixed Duncan with as penetrating a gaze as she could. "Good cousin Duncan. Yes, Roo has spoken of you." She smiled again. "Let us drink a great deal, dear Duncan. Let us get drunk together. And then, later, we'll think of some other things we might do."

Duncan's smile broadened. "Whatever your pleasure, I am at your service."

She reached over and scratched the back of his hand with her nails. "Pleasure and service; my, what a treasure you are!"

The servant arrived and poured wine, and supper commenced.

Twenty

Discovery

ROO SMILED.

He had slept a long night, and had awakened to a house full of noise. But rather than irritating him, the noise delighted him. The baby squealed and made cooing noises, while Abigail talked her baby talk.

Karli seemed her usual subdued self, but smiled at whatever small comment he made. He lingered over breakfast, and finally, when he left for the office, she walked with him to the door, where he paused.

"Would you like to live in the country?" he asked.

"I hadn't given it any thought," answered Karli.

He looked out the door across the street to Barret's and said, "When I was a child I used to run for hours, or at least it seemed like hours, without seeing another person. The air is clean and there's a silence at night. I think I'd like to build us a house outside the city—a place where the little ones can run and play and grow strong."

She smiled at his reference to the children, for he rarely spoke of them. "Will you be able to conduct your business from so distant a home?"

He laughed. "I now control the company. I think I can delegate more day-to-day business to Dash, Jason, and Luis."

"And Duncan?"

"Of course," he said. "He's my cousin."

She nodded.

"I would have to come in from time to time, and you and the

children would come with me for holidays, and we'd stay in the city during winter, but when the weather's warm, a place a day's ride from the city wouldn't be much of a hardship."

"Whatever you think best," she answered, lowering her eyes.

He reached out to touch her chin, gently lifting it. "I want you happy, Karli. If you don't wish to live away from the city, we'll stay here. If you think it would be nice, we'll build another house. You decide."

She seemed genuinely surprised. "Me?"

"Yes," he said, smiling. "Think on it. I'll be across the street if you need me."

He crossed and entered the building. Kurt practically fell over himself opening the gate for him as he said, "Good morning, Mr. Avery."

Roo almost tripped, he was so surprised by the usually surly waiter's politeness. He turned to discover men who had barely glanced at him since he had become a member rising to greet him. "Good morning, Mr. Avery," was repeated by men whose names he could barely recall.

When he mounted the stairs, he discovered a new railing had been put across the last third of the upper balcony, and on the other side sat Luis, Jason, and Dash. Dash nimbly jumped up and with a dramatic flourish opened the swinging gate in the rail.

"What is this?"

Dash grinned. "I arranged with Mr. McKeller for us to take a permanent position here, with an option for the rest of this side of the balcony area in the future."

"Really?" said Roo, fixing Dash with a baleful look. "And what was all this business below?"

Dash attempted to look innocent. "I merely let it be known yesterday afternoon, after you left for the day, that you were now controlling owner of the Bitter Sea Company." Lowering his voice, he added, "You're probably the richest man in Krondor this morning, Rupert."

Dash held out his hand, and Jason produced a fist full of papers. He handed them to Dash, who passed them along to Roo. "The trading fleet from the Free Cities returned on the evening tide last night!"

Roo grabbed the sheets and looked them over. "This is fantastic!" Not only had they sold the last shipments of grain at far above the projected market value—the locust plague had crossed the Grey Towers and struck hard at the Far Coast—the ships had returned carrying cargo brilliantly selected at prices sure to realize a profit. They had projected the ships returning empty, so indeed Rupert was far more wealthy than he had imagined.

"There you are!" said Crowley, hurrying up the stairs.

Roo said, "Good morning, Brandon."

"Don't you good-morning me, you thief."

"What?" said Roo, his good humor vanishing.

"You knew that fleet was coming in, yet you sat there and cozened us with babble about risk and—"

"Cozened!" exclaimed Roo. He stood up. "Brandon, I offered to *sell* you my share of the Bitter Sea Company!"

"Part of a clever plot to cheat us all, obviously."

"Oh, mercy," said Roo, turning toward Dash.

"Don't deny it," challenged Crowley.

Roo turned. "Brandon, I have no patience for making denials." He looked at his former partner. "Here's what I will do. You have a choice. I will tell Jason to account the profits on the fleet and give you what would have been your share of the profits from this voyage had you not sold me your share in the Bitter Sea Company last night.

"If I do this, do not ever again expect me to invite you into any business with the Bitter Sea Company. The gold we account you today will be the last you will ever see from us. In fact, should fate put us at odds, I will ensure you're crushed." He smiled as he said this. "Or you can simply accept that you bet the wrong way on the turn of the card and leave with some attempt at good grace. If you can manage that, I will be sure to invite you to join with the Bitter Sea Company on other ventures in the future when I seek partners. Those are your choices; what do you prefer?"

Crowley stood there for a long moment, then said, "Bah! You're giving me a fool's choice. But I wasn't here to beg favors. I want no part of your ill-gotten profits, Roo Avery. A bargain's a bargain, and you'll not hear otherwise from Brandon Crowley." He turned and left, muttering under his breath.

After he'd gone, Dash laughed. Jason said, "If he'd taken but a day to think on your offer, he'd have been a far wealthier man."

Roo nodded emphatically. "That's the whole point of his complaint. He's mad at himself."

"Do you think you've made an enemy?" asked Luis.

Roo said, "No. Brandon just enjoys complaining. He'll be back the second I invite him, to make sure he's involved in any rich deals, but he'll keep complaining."

The other partners showed up later that morning, but unlike Crowley they simply congratulated Roo on his good fortune, and themselves on their increased profits on the portion of the company they still owned.

Roo spent the next hour exchanging pleasantries with other men of note in the coffee house. About midmorning, the last social visitor departed, and Roo asked, "Where is Duncan?"

"I haven't seen him since yesterday," said Dash.

Roo shrugged. "I asked him to run an errand for me after leaving here. Knowing Duncan, I'd wager he went out after that and found some woman to tumble." Roo then glanced about to ensure no one else was close by, then motioned to his three companions to come closer so he could speak softly. "Someone has betrayed us."

Jason looked at Luis and Dash. "How do you know?"

"Someone knew more about this company than would be possible without inside communications; that party sent word to the Jacobys."

He explained how he had agreed to run Jacoby and Sons for Helen and her children. "Jason, go over to their office and introduce yourself to anyone who might still be there; most of Tim's hired men are in prison today, so there may not be anyone around but a clerk or two. If they need convincing, have someone go to Helen Jacoby's home and get confirmation as to our arrangement.

"Go over the books and see what is due and what is needed, but also keep an eye out for any hint of who our betrayer might be."

Jason nodded. "I'll go at once."

After he left, Roo said, "Very well, gentlemen, what else concerns us today?" He sat and began attending to the duties of being the richest man in Krondor.

Duncan stood at the door while Sylvia gave him a long kiss. "Stop that," he said, "or we'll be back upstairs."

She smiled, and closed the sheer night-robe she wore, which had fallen open. "No, sorry to say. I must get some sleep and the morning is half-over. Now go."

She closed the door behind him as he walked down to where a groom brought his horse, and waited until she heard the horse moving away. She walked to the left hall and continued down to the office. Opening the door, she stepped through.

Jacob Esterbrook looked up and, seeing the open robe, said, "Cover yourself, Sylvia. What would the servants say?"

"Whatever they say," said Sylvia, ignoring his instruction and letting the robe stay open. She enjoyed outraging her father. She sat down on the other side of the desk. "There's not one of them who hasn't seen me undressed from time to time." She neglected to mention that several of them had shared her bed over the years as well. Both she and Jacob pretended he didn't know of her indulgences.

"Was that young Avery?"

She grinned. "That was the other young Avery. Duncan came in his cousin's stead. So I decided he might as well fulfill all of Roo's duties."

Jacob sighed. "You create potential difficulties, Sylvia."

She laughed, leaning back, allowing the robe to fall even farther open. "I always create difficulties; it's my nature. But this Duncan is as venal as any man I've met, I'll wager, be the price gold or flesh. I think we can use him, especially if we offer him both gold and flesh."

"Really?" said Jacob, ignoring his daughter's brazen attempt to embarrass him.

"He could prove a useful weapon," she said with a smile.

Jacob nodded. "Well, having an ally inside the Bitter Sea Company is very useful. Having two would be even better. But considering the situation, I'd like to remind you what disaster might befall us should you blunder and let the two discover each other."

She stood, stretching and arching her back, like a cat. "Have I ever made a mistake where men are concerned, Father?"

He sat back in his chair. "Not so far, daughter, but you are young."

"I don't feel young," she said, turning and leaving his office.

Jacob considered for a moment the creature who was his daughter, then dismissed such musing. He had never understood women, not Sylvia, not her dead mother, not the occasional wench he tumbled down at the Sign of the White Wing. To him women were to be either used or ignored. Then he thought again of his daughter and realized that ignoring such a one as she could prove deadly. Sighing at what he saw her to be, he refused to assign blame to himself; he had never intended for her to turn out as she had and, besides, she served the needs of Jacob Esterbrook and Company admirably.

Erik pointed. "What is that?"

They had found a long tunnel leading away from the bottom of the flight of stairs behind the idol. De Loungville reported finding nothing of interest among the slain above, and Calis ordered the rest of his company down to the tunnel.

Seeing how tired the men were, Calis had ordered a halt. They slept for what Erik judged to be several hours on the landing at the bottom of the stairs, before moving along the large tunnel that led away into the gloom.

While waiting, Erik had noticed what appeared to be a large pipe leading along the ceiling of the hall. "Drainpipe?" offered Praji.

Erik tried to inspect it, and finally said, "Hand me a lantern."

Vaja obliged and Erik looked closely. Erik held the lantern close and said, "It's no pipe. I think it's solid." He took out his sword and gently tapped the blade against it.

A shriek loud enough to cause those awake to cover their ears and to jolt every sleeping man to alertness echoed down the tunnel while an angry green flash nearly blinded Erik.

Praji, who had been standing next to Erik, said, "Don't do that again," while Miranda waved her hand, her mouth moving as she softly spoke an incantation.

Erik felt his arm sting to the shoulder and said, "Don't worry, I won't."

Miranda said, "It's a conduit."

"For what?" asked Calis.

"Life."

Erik frowned and looked to Boldar, who stood next to his employer. The alien mercenary shrugged. "I have no idea what she's talking about."

Calis said, "We move out, now!"

The men formed up and they moved down the tunnel. Erik heard Alfred mutter, "Given that shriek, no one's going to be surprised when we show up."

Erik said, "Given what we've seen, anyone who's surprised by anything down here is an idiot."

"There is that," agreed the former corporal from Darkmoor.

Erik said, "Take the rear, Alfred. I need someone with a steady nerve back there."

With a faint smile at the praise, the one-time brawler stepped aside to let the other men pass.

They followed the tunnel until they came to a large wooden door. They carefully inspected the door, listening for noise, and when they heard nothing, Calis put his hand against the wood. He pushed and the door swung inward.

Calis and Erik stepped into a large chamber, and Erik's hair bristled, even down to the hair on his arms. The room was filled with strange power, energies that swept through him, filling him with a giddy feeling.

Everything was illuminated by a series of lanterns in the ceiling, recessed so the source of the light couldn't be seen unless one stood directly underneath. The soft glow was tinged with green, and Erik suspected that the green flash of light he had seen when his blade had touched what Miranda called a "conduit" and the alien light in this room were related.

Five figures turned as they entered, and instantly Calis's sword was out and he was charging. Erik, Praji, and Vaja didn't wait for orders, duplicating the captain's attack.

Miranda shouted, "Back!" to those behind her while she began casting a spell.

Five Pantathian serpent priests began casting spells. A sixth priest, in ornate robes, sat motionless atop a large throne, observing without any change of expression. Erik dove under the outstretched arm of a priest as a blinding blast of energy exploded off the creature's hand. Erik rolled over on his back, just catching a glimpse of Miranda using some type of mystic shield to deflect the blast down toward the floor.

Calis, Praji, and Vaja were standing together when another ball of energy exploded in their direction. Praji and Vaja took the blast full in the face, and both men fell backward, their bodies erupting into flames. Erik judged them dead before they hit the stone floor.

Calis turned and took part of the blast on his left side, stumbling and howling in pain as the energies flamed around him. For a tortured moment he seemed a living candle, alight and being consumed. Then the magic fire vanished, but the entire left side of Calis's body was smoking char and weeping wounds.

"Calis!" shouted Miranda, while Erik continued to roll, right into the first serpent priest. He knocked the creature over and slashed past it as he stood, killing another priest. Without hesitation he slammed his boot heel into the throat of the creature he had knocked over, leaving the serpent priest thrashing in pain as it suffocated, trying to breathe with a crushed windpipe.

A third priest turned to face Erik, attempting to conjure, but it died before any spell was realized as Erik severed its head from its shoulders.

Suddenly a shout from the other end of the tunnel alerted Erik that more trouble was likely to descend upon them. He turned toward the remaining three priests. One also was about to conjure a spell when a thin stream of light, a blinding white and purple pulse, slammed into its head as Miranda attacked.

The creature hissed in agony, then its head erupted in mystic flame; a brief flash, and the head was gone. The decapitated body slumped to the ground.

Calis pulled himself upright by force of will to kill the fifth priest before Erik could reach him. Even injured, Calis was powerful enough to drive his sword completely through the priest.

Erik spun to face the door as de Loungville cried out, "Saaur! They're coming!"

Erik turned to face the seated priest. Miranda also came forward, first to grip Calis and help him to keep standing, and second to protect him. She spared the smoking corpses of Praji and Vaja only a momentary glance, as it was obvious they were far beyond mortal help. Then she joined Calis in turning to confront the last Pantathian, preparing to defend Calis should the High Priest launch an attack.

But the seated Pantathian only blinked as he regarded the carnage before him.

Erik slowly approached and saw that the five priests had been protecting something, an object that sat in a stone well in front of and a few feet below the base of the throne. Erik moved slowly toward it, shifting his gaze back and forth between the object and the figure on the throne.

The object looked like a large green emerald, but one aglow with a fey light. "Gods!" said Miranda in a voice hoarse with fear.

"Your gods have nothing to do with this, human," said the figure upon the throne, what Erik took to be a High Priest. Its speech was sibilant but otherwise understandable. "They are newcomers to this world, trespassers, and pretenders."

Erik glanced up and saw a faint shimmer of green energy pouring from a metal rod, falling in a faint cascade upon the stone. He followed the rod back to the wall above the door and surmised it was the same one he had struck. The sounds of battle rang out in the hallway.

Erik glanced at Calis, who weakly said, "Get that door closed and block it off somehow."

Erik ran to where de Loungville stood. "Captain says to get this door closed and blocked off," said Erik.

De Loungville shouted out, "Fall back!" He turned to Erik and said, "We've got one advantage. They're so damn big they can't come through the tunnel but one at a time, and we're hacking them down as they show their ugly faces."

The men fell back and Erik saw that most were covered in blood. He imagined it must have been grim work at the end of the line. The last man through was Alfred, who thrust and parried at an unseen opponent. Then Erik saw a huge green head as a Saaur warrior, attempting to fight while half hunched over, pushed forward. Erik didn't wait but took out his dagger and threw it with all his strength at the creature over the shoulder of the retreating Alfred. The blade took the Saaur in the neck, and it clawed with one hand at the blade as it fell forward, half blocking the door. A shout from behind the creature told Erik the creature's allies had seen him fall.

De Loungville didn't hesitate but shouted, "Drag him inside!" Three men on each side grabbed the creature, nearly twelve feet tall, and pulled it through the portal, while another soldier duplicated Erik's action and threw his dagger at the next Saaur. It had the desired result, causing the creature to retreat long enough for them to get the door closed. There was a large wooden bar, and Erik motioned for other soldiers to set it across the door, into two huge iron supports. A moment later came the sound of a large body hitting the door followed by an angry exclamation Erik assumed to be a Saaur oath.

"Block the door!" shouted Erik.

Four of the men dragged the dying Saaur away from the door, while others took some idols of stone, lizard figures crouching as if guarding something, and pushed them before the door. Erik turned to see Miranda and Calis slowly approaching the green gem.

"What is this thing?" Miranda asked.

The seated figure said, "Your lowly intellect is incapable of understanding, human."

Calis hobbled with Miranda's help to stand next to the object, letting the green light bathe him. The burns he had received from the magician's blast must have been causing him incredible pain, but he showed no sign of it. He said, "It is a key."

The serpent said, "You are more intelligent than you look, elf."

Calis shook off Miranda's support and reached over the edge of the pool in which the emerald rested and the Pantathian stood up slowly, as if infirmity or age were weighing heavily upon him. "No!" he commanded. "Do not touch this! It is nearly finished!"

"It is finished," said Calis as he put his hand upon the gem and closed his eyes. Green pulsing light seemed to crawl slowly up his arm. Calis's wounds were still terrible, raw flesh and singed hair, but the green light seemed to strengthen him. He removed his hand from the gem's surface and walked toward the creature, who now stood upright, looking at Calis with amazement upon its face.

"You should be dead," said the priest. "This is decades of work, the life force of thousands of slaughtered creatures, and it is the key that will bring back our Mistress."

"Your mistress is a fraud!" shouted Calis. He came up to the Pantathian, weaving slightly, and said, "You are snakes lifted up and given arms, legs, speech, and cunning, but you are snakes!" He leaned forward until he was nearly nose-to-snout with the creature. "Look into my eyes, snake! See what you face!"

The old priest blinked and stared into Calis's eyes. Mystic communication passed between them, because suddenly the priest fell to its knees, turning away, holding up its arms as if shielding itself from Calis's gaze. "No! It cannot be!"

"I carry that blood within me!" shouted Calis. Erik wondered where the strength to hold himself that way came from; a lesser man would be dead from the burns.

"It is a lie!" screamed the lizard man, turning away.

"Your Green Mother is the lie!" shouted Calis. "She is no goddess! She is one of the Valheru!"

"No! They were lesser kin. None were as great as She Who Birthed Us! We labor to bring her back so that in death we will be born again to rule at her feet!"

"Fools!" said Calis, and Erik could sense the strength leaving him again. Miranda took careful hold of his right side, helping him stay erect. "Murderous fools, you are nothing but what she made you, bent creatures of no natural root, the makings of a vain thing who knew only her own pleasures. You were dust under her feet, and when she rose with her brethren during the Chaos Wars you were forgotten!" Calis stumbled, and de Loungville came to help hold him. "If there was any possible way to redeem you and your kind, we would not be here."

Then Calis took a deep breath. "You are a pawn and have always been a pawn. It is no fault of your own that you must be destroyed, but you must be obliterated, root and branch."

"You are here to do this?" said the High Priest.

"I am," said Calis. "I am the son of he who imprisoned your Alma-Lodaka!"

"No!" shrieked the High Priest. "None may speak the most holy of names!" The old serpent rose, pulling a dagger from its robes. Erik didn't hesitate, but ran two steps up the dais and hacked as hard as he could at the High Priest. The old creature's head sailed from its shoulders, landing a short distance away, while the body collapsed.

Erik looked at Calis who said, "You did well."

"What now?" asked de Loungville, as the thudding against the door became more rhythmic. "They've gotten themselves a ram. That's a heavy bar on the door, but it won't hold forever. Those Saaur are strong."

Calis said, "Find us another way out, or we have to fight back the way we came."

De Loungville turned and ordered the men to start searching for another exit. "Here is what their temple was about," said Calis, as Miranda helped him sit upon the steps. "Tens of thousands of lives given up over the last fifty years in vile sacrifice so they could create that." He pointed weakly at the green stone. "It is a thing of captured life."

Miranda said, "Your father spoke once of the false Murmandamus using the captured lives of those who died in his service to shift into the same realm as the Lifestone. We should have suspected they would again use such means." She pointed at the stone. "This is a far more powerful tool than that simple deception."

"What do we do with it?" asked Erik.

Calis groaned in pain. "You," he said to Miranda, "take it. You must take it to my father. He and Pug are the only two men on this world who might understand how to utilize it." The pounding on the door served to underscore the urgency of his words. "If the Emerald Queen gets this key to Sethanon, joins it with the Lifestone . . ."

Miranda nodded. "I think I understand. I can get a few of us out of here. . . ."

"No," said Calis. "I'm staying. I'm the only one who might begin to understand what else we might find here. Take the Valheru helm we found, and this key. Try for the surface." He looked at Boldar and said, "Take the mercenary with you. He'll keep you alive until you find a place you can use your arts to get home."

Miranda smiled. "You bastard. You told me you don't know anything about magic."

Calis said, "There is no magic, remember?"

"I wish Nakor were here," said Erik.

Calis said, "If Pug couldn't find the Pantathians after looking for them for fifty years, it follows this place is very secure, and I suspect that using magic to get in *or out* is equally impossible."

"Damn you," she said, a tear running down her face. "We do need to climb up to the surface, or near it."

"Well, then we'd better hope there's another way out."

A few minutes later, de Loungville reported they had found a stairway at the rear of the hall leading upward. "There you go," said Calis, trying to smile. "I need to rest a bit. And the men need to look around."

Miranda took his hand and gripped it. "What do I say to your father?"

"That I love him, and say the same to my mother," said Calis. "Then tell him that a demon is loose and there's a third player in this. I think when he looks at this gem he will find it is not what it seems to be."

"What do you mean?"

"Let the Spellweavers examine this thing without my theories coloring their opinions."

Miranda approached the object with caution and gently touched it. She muttered and cast about with her hands, then picked up the object. "I don't like leaving you."

Calis managed a brave smile. "I don't like it much either. Now, if you can manage to give me a kiss without touching my injured side, do so, and get out of here."

Miranda knelt and kissed the right side of his face, then whispered, "I'll come back for you."

"Don't," said Calis. "We won't be here. We'll find our own way out. I'll get to that Brijaner ship, somehow. Get Duke William to send someone our way, just in case, but don't you dare come back here for me. There are still other priests in these mountains, almost certainly, and even if we've killed their inner circle, they will be powerful enough to find you when you use your magic to return."

Then he fingered the magic ward she gave him. "Besides, how will you find me?" His question was punctuated by another assault on the door.

She gripped his good hand with her left, while holding the glowing gem with her right. "Stay alive, damn it!"

"I will," he promised. "Bobby!"

De Loungville said, "Captain?"

"Take a dozen men and go with them."

De Loungville turned and shouted, "Squad two and squad three, come here!"

Twelve men left their searching of the hall and reported. "Go with the lady," he instructed.

Calis said, "You too, Bobby."

De Loungville turned and with an evil grin said, "Make me." To the twelve men who waited, he pointed to the door and said,

"Take the lady and the mercenary and get the hell out of here!"

The twelve men glanced at Miranda and Boldar. Boldar nodded once and set off in the van, and six men followed, while the other six waited until Miranda gave Calis's hand one more squeeze and set off. Then they followed her.

Erik turned to Calis. "What do we do now, Captain?"

"How many men do we have left?" asked Calis.

Erik didn't have to count. "Now that two squads are gone, we're down to thirty-seven, including you."

"Wounded?"

"Five, but they can still fight."

"Help me up," said Calis.

Erik gave him a hand up, then slipped his arm around his waist—keeping his hand on Calis's belt, avoiding his burned flesh. Calis leaned his good side heavily upon Erik and said, "I need to see anything that may be an artifact of the Ancient Ones, the Dragon Lords."

Erik had no idea how he would know if he stepped on such an artifact, but Calis said, "Remember how that helm felt when you touched it?"

Erik said, "I can't forget that."

"That's what we're looking for."

For a tense fifteen minutes they combed the hall. A door with a large bar on it was discovered behind a tapestry. Once it was open, Calis said, "Stand back." He forced Erik to let go and hobbled to the entrance. Inside sat a suit of armor. It glowed with a green light, and Erik felt the hair on his arms rise up once again.

Calis said, "This is the true repository of her power."

Erik assumed he meant the goddess or lady Dragon Lord, or whatever she might be, but he was distracted by the creaking sounds of wood and groaning hinges as the Saaur continued to pound methodically at the heavy door.

Bobby said, "What do we do with it?"

"We destroy it," said Calis.

He took a staggering step forward, and both Erik and de Loungville hurried to help him walk. Erik felt his skin tingle and fought back the urge to scratch as he came nearer the artifacts. Besides the armor, a set of emerald jewelry was displayed: a tiara, a necklace that was a full choker of huge stones, matching bracelets, and rings. Calis gently reached out and touched the breastplate. Then he snatched his hand back, as if his fingers had been burned.

"No!" he said.

"What?" asked de Loungville.

"It's . . . wrong." He quickly touched each item in the room and said, "It's all contaminated. Something has . . . changed this."

Suddenly, and for the first time since Erik had known him, Calis revealed fear in his expression. "I'm a fool! Almost as big a fool as the Pantathians."

To Bobby he said, "We must destroy this as quickly as we can, but most of all, we must escape."

De Loungville said, "You'll get no argument from me, Captain."

Calis said, "Erik, you were a smith. How best to destroy this armor?"

Erik picked up the breastplate, a shimmering thing of green metal with a serpent depicted in bas-relief upon it. As he touched it, strange images, haunting music, and an alien rage flooded through him. He dropped it to the floor. It rang as it struck the stone. "I don't know if it can be destroyed, at least by normal means," said Erik. "To forge metal, great heat is needed; great heat can also rob steel of its temper. If we could build a hot enough fire . . ."

Looking around, Calis said, "What can we burn . . . ?" Then he collapsed, and Bobby lowered him to the floor.

Looking at Erik, he shouted for Alfred. When the corporal reached them, de Loungville said, "To my distress, I find myself suddenly in command. At this moment, I would appreciate any suggestions either of you might have."

Alfred said, "We should get the hell out of here, Sergeant Major. That door won't hold much longer."

"What about these damned things?" Bobby asked Erik.

Erik tried to think as quickly as he could. "I know nothing of this magic business. I know armor, horses, and fighting." Then he continued, "All I know about these things is Miranda's warning not to let them come into contact with one another. If each man wrapped a single item, we might bring them with us. At least that would keep them out of their hands." He indicated the thudding door.

"Do it."

Erik gave orders and the men grabbed tapestries and wrapped the armor, jewelry, and other objects in cloth. Erik said, "Each man is to watch those around him. If any other man looks . . . different—lost, confused, or distracted—tell me at once!"

He distributed the items among different men, no one man carrying anything, no matter how small, without another standing next to him. De Loungville said, "You start. I'll follow. If they don't break in the door, I'll leave in ten minutes."

"See if you can jam this other door after you get through it," suggested Erik.

"Get out of here," said de Loungville with a mocking smile.

Erik lit a torch and hurriedly led the men carrying the artifacts through the second door. A flight of stairs led up into the gloom and he began climbing.

Nakor lay under a tree dozing when he suddenly sat up. Glancing around, he saw Sho Pi sitting a short distance away, watching him. The mad beggar also sat watching him.

"What is it?" asked Nakor.

"I didn't wish to disturb you, Master, so I waited; Lord Vencar has arrived. The Prince has sent him to take control here."

"Not that," said Nakor, standing. "Didn't you feel it?"

"Feel what, master?"

Nakor said, "Never mind. We're leaving."

Sho Pi also stood. "Where are we going?"

"I don't know. Krondor, I think. Maybe up to Elvandar. It depends."

Sho Pi followed Nakor as he hurried toward the large building that dominated the island. Near the building, the mad beggar hurried off toward the kitchen. The bandy-legged Isalani gambler entered the building and headed straight to the central hall, where he found a well-dressed man sitting at the head of the table, Kalied, Chalmes, and the other magicians sitting there as well.

The Earl of the Court said, "And you must be Nakor."

Nakor said, "I must be. I have to tell you a couple of things. To begin with, these here are all liars."

The other magicians gasped or objected, but Nakor simply kept talking. "They don't mean to be, but they've become so used to doing things in secret they can't help themselves. Don't believe anything they say. But otherwise they mean well."

Arutha, Lord Vencar, began to laugh. "Father said you were remarkable."

"I think Lord James is pretty unusual, too," said Nakor. "Hell of a card player." He winked. "Only man I've ever met who could cheat me at cards. I admire that."

Arutha said, "Well, we can talk about this over supper."

"No we can't," said Nakor. "I've got to leave."

Arutha, who looked something like his father but with lighter hair, said, "This minute?"

"Yes." Nakor turned toward the door. "Tell these stubborn dolts that something really bad is going to happen soon and they'd better stop fooling around and get serious about helping the Kingdom or there won't be any point to anything anymore. I'll be back in a while."

If the Prince of Krondor's representative had anything more to say, Nakor didn't hear it as he turned down a hallway and almost ran, he was walking so fast.

Sho Pi said, "Master, I thought you said we were leaving."

"We are," replied Nakor as he started to climb a flight of stairs.

"But this isn't the way to the docks. This is the way to—"

"Pug's tower. I know."

Sho Pi followed Nakor as he climbed the circular stairs that led to the top of the tower. When they reached the top floor, they were confronted by a wooden door with no apparent lock. Nakor pounded on it. "Pug!"

A strange shimmer covered the surface of the door, and the wood flowed and twisted, forming a face. "Begone!" said the face. "This room shall not be entered."

Nakor ignored the admonition and pounded upon the door even louder. "Pug!" he shouted.

Sho Pi said, "Master, he's not been here—" He stopped speaking when the door opened.

Pug looked out. "You felt it too."

"How could I not?" said Nakor.

Sho Pi said, "But they said you weren't here."

Nakor narrowed his gaze as he looked at Sho Pi. "Sometimes I despair, boy. Are you stupid or just too trusting?"

"How long have you known?" asked Pug, motioning for them to come inside.

They moved inside and the door closed behind them. "First day I got here. You make a lot of noise coming and going." Then he grinned. "One day I came up the stairs, really quietly, and I heard you and your lady friend." His eyes grew wide and he shook his hand as if touching something hot. "You two!" He laughed.

Pug looked heavenward. "Thank you for not disturbing us."

"No reason to. But we've got to go."

Pug nodded. "We risk attack."

Nakor said, "I don't think so. Whatever we feel is making enough noise out there that even if anyone is looking for you, they won't notice you moving the three of us. Where are we going? Krondor?"

Pug shook his head. "No. We're going to Elvandar. I need to speak with Tomas."

Nakor motioned for Sho Pi to stand close and took his student's hand. Pug linked hands with the two of them and the room shifted and shimmered; then they found themselves in a forest glade.

Pug said, "Follow me," and led them a short distance to a shallow river. "This is the river Crydee," said Pug. Then he called out in a loud voice. "I am Pug of Stardock. I seek counsel with Lord Tomas!"

A few minutes later two elves appeared on the other side of the bank. One called out, "You are bidden enter Elvandar!"

They waded across the stream and Pug said to Sho Pi, "None may enter Elvandar unbidden."

Once they were on the other bank, Pug said, "I hope you don't mind if I hurry along."

The elf said, "Not in the least."

Pug smiled. "Galain, isn't it?"

"You remember," said the elf.

Pug said, "I wish I had the time to be social."

The elf nodded. "I and my patrol will return to the court in a few days' time. Perhaps then we may visit."

Pug smiled. He took Sho Pi's and Nakor's hands again and moved them to another location in the forest.

Sho Pi's eyes widened, and Pug remembered his first reaction to seeing the heart of the elven forest. Giant trees, dwarfing the most ancient oaks, rose to form an almost impenetrable canopy.

Some of the trees showed leaves of the deepest green, while others had leaves golden, red, or silver in color, a few white as snow; a strange soft light bathed the area. Giant boles rose with steps cut into the living wood, and branches broad enough to serve as walk-ways spread in all directions.

"It's a city of trees," said Sho Pi.

"Yes," said an old man who stood nearby, leaning on a long bow. His hair was pure white, and his skin showed years of aging, but his body was still erect, and he wore the green leathers of a hunter.

"Martin!" said Pug, stepping forward.

The old man took Pug's extended hand and shook. "It's been a long time."

"You look well." Nakor grinned.

"You old card cheat!" said Martin, gripping Nakor's hand. "You don't look a day older."

Nakor shrugged. "For one not gifted with long life, Martin, you look remarkable."

The old man smiled. "For a man my age, you mean." He glanced around. "Here I linger. Elvandar has been kind to me. I think the gods decided to let my final years be peaceful."

Pug said, "You deserve some peace in your time."

Martin Longbow, once Duke of Krondor, brother to King Lyam and uncle to King Borric, said, "Seems that once more peace is at risk."

Pug nodded. "I need to speak to Tomas and Aglaranna. Is Calis here?"

Martin picked up his bow. "I was sent to wait for you. Miranda arrived an hour ago, with the strangest young man." He began walking. "Tomas said you'd be here shortly. Calis is . . . well, he may not return."

"Ill news," said Nakor.

"Who is this?" Martin motioned to Sho Pi.

Nakor said, "Sho Pi. A disciple."

Martin laughed as he moved through the trees. "Seriously, or are you doing the mendicant holy man act again?"

"Seriously," said Nakor, looking injured. "I never should have told Borric about that scam. He's told every one in his family about it."

Martin's brown eyes narrowed. "There was a reason." Then he laughed. "It's good to see you again."

"Are you coming?" asked Pug.

"No, I rarely sit in the Queen's Council anymore. I am content to be a guest here, waiting out my time."

Pug smiled. "I understand. We'll talk this evening, after supper." He gripped Sho Pi's and Nakor's hands, and closed his eyes, and again the air shimmered and they were someplace else.

They stood in the center of a large platform set high in the trees. A voice said, "Welcome, Pug of Crydee."

Pug couldn't help but laugh. "Thank you, old friend."

A large man, easily six inches over six feet in height, approached and took Pug's hand, then hugged him. "It is good to see you again, Pug." His features were youthful, but his eyes were ancient. His features were a blend of human and elf, with high cheekbones, pointed ears, and blond hair. To any who had seen Calis, there was no doubt this was his father.

Pug slapped his friend on the back. "Too many years, Tomas," he said with genuine regret.

Sho Pi and Nakor were introduced to Tomas, Warleader of the Elven Host of Elvandar. Then they were presented to a stunning woman of regal bearing, Aglaranna, Queen of Elvandar. Nakor smiled and said, "Nice to meet you, Lady," while Sho Pi knelt in greeting. The Elf Queen was a young-looking woman, despite her centuries of age. Her hair was a fine red-gold, her eyes a deep blue, and her beauty breathtaking, despite being alien.

An elf who looked young by human standards came to stand next to Tomas. "This is Calin," said Tomas, "heir to the throne of Elvandar and brother to my son."

Prince Calin greeted the two newcomers, then said to Pug, "Miranda arrived an hour ago."

"Where is she?" asked Pug.

"Over there." Tomas indicated a second platform, off to the side of the first.

Sho Pi followed in awe. The trees themselves were alive with lights and magic. There was a profound sense of peace and rightness here that he had not imagined possible.

They came to the indicated place, where Miranda was inspecting a strange glowing gem, as well as a helm. None of the elves gathered near her touched anything, but they peered closely at the objects.

Pug hurried over. "Miranda!"

She turned and, upon seeing him, nearly flew to him, throwing her arms around his neck. "It's so good to see you again."

"Calis?" asked Pug.

"He's been injured."

"How badly?"

"Badly."

Pug held her a moment, then said, "Tell me where to find him."

"I can't. He wears a ward that protects him from magic sight. It shields him from the Pantathians, but it shields him from us as well."

"Tell me about it," said Pug.

Miranda reconstructed the events of the journey, the discovery, and the escape. "I left six men, those who survived the fights on the way out, in a frigid cave in the peaks," she finished. "I pray they've gotten down from the mountains, but I fear they are all dead."

Pug said, "Every one of us knew the risks."

Miranda nodded, clutching his hand, but her face was drawn. "There is this," she said, "and Calis judged it critical I bring it here."

Pug looked at the key. "What is it?"

"A Pantathian thing. A key to free the Green Lady from the Lifestone," said Miranda.

Pug looked dubious. He looked at the object for long minutes, placing his hand over it, but not quite touching it. He closed his eyes several times, and his lips moved. Once a tiny spark of energy leaped from the palm of his hand to the stone. At last he stood upright and said, "It's a key of some sort, that's certain, but to free the Valheru. . . ."

He looked at the assembled Spellweavers of Elvandar and addressed the eldest. "Tathar, what do you see?"

"This is something of those whose name may not be spoken," said the senior adviser to the Queen. "But there is an alien presence here as well, one of which I have no knowledge."

Pug said, "The demon you spoke of, Miranda?"

"No. It was a nearly mindless thing, a killing device, pure and simple. I witnessed it at work, and while it was powerful and able to hold a dozen serpent priests at bay, it had cunning but no intelligence—at least not enough to have conceived this device. Whatever fashioned this thing was more than that simple being. Someone sent it through a rift into the heart of the Pantathian home to wreak havoc and destroy them, the same intention as ours."

Pug said, "Once before, we dealt with duplicity; why not now?"

Tomas stood next to his friend and said, "What do you think?"

Pug stroked his beard. "As Murmandamus was but a false icon, to manipulate the moredhel to rise up and capture Sethanon, a Pantathian ruse, so might not this be a demon ruse to use the Pantathians to capture the Lifestone?"

"Toward what end?" asked Aglaranna.

Pug sighed. "Power. It's a powerful tool, no matter who wields it."

"Weapon," said Nakor. "Not a tool."

"What of the Valheru?" asked Tomas. "Can some other force imagine they can do anything with the Lifestone, use it somehow, without having to deal with those trapped within the stone?"

Pug said, "The problem is that the only source of lore we have is what you remember, from the memory of Ashen-Shugar." Tomas possessed the memories of the ages-dead Dragon Lord whose armor he had donned during the Riftwar. "But he alone of the Valheru had nothing to do with the creation of the Lifestone. He knew something of its nature, something of its purpose, that it was to be a weapon to destroy the new gods, but beyond that he was ignorant of its nature."

"So you suspect that someone else, whoever is behind this demon's entering our world, may have a purpose for the Lifestone that hasn't occurred to us?" said Miranda. "Could they simply grab the Lifestone and use it as a weapon, the way a man might use a sword or crossbow?"

"That," said Pug, "I do not know. It's clear, though, that someone is prepared to try."

"What do we do?" asked Miranda.

Pug said, "We wait and study this thing, and see what they do next."

Miranda said, "What about Calis?"

Tomas said, "We wait."

Miranda said, "I want to return to look for him and the others."

Pug said, "I know you do, but it would be foolish. They will have moved on, and whoever we face, whoever is left alive there will be on guard and looking for him as well. The second you pop into existence there, whatever magic is left will fall on you like a burning house."

Nakor said, "I'll go."

Pug turned and said, "What?"

"I will go," he said slowly. "Get me to Krondor and I will get a ship and I will sail down to that place he left his boat and I will get him back."

Pug said, "You're serious?"

Nakor said, "I told this one"—he motioned to Sho Pi—"we had to go on a trip. This is just a bit farther than I thought."

He grinned a moment, then the smile faded. In the most serious tones anyone had heard Nakor use, he said, "A great and terrible storm is coming, Pug. It is black and deadly and we don't understand yet what is behind it. Everyone here has a duty. I do, too: to find Calis and the others and bring back whatever they've learned after Miranda left."

Aglaranna said, "Take from us whatever we can give if it will help you find our son."

Nakor said, "Just get me to Krondor."

Pug said, "Any particular place?"

Nakor thought a moment. "The court of the Prince will do."

Pug nodded, then to Sho Pi he said, "You too?"

"I follow my master."

Pug said, "Very well; join hands."

They did, and Pug wove a spell, and suddenly they were gone.

Calis was unconscious and Erik carried him as he would a child. Bobby was barely conscious, and leaned on Alfred's shoulder. Of the thirty-seven men who had left the deep temple of the Pantathians, nine were alive. Three times they had encountered hostile forces and had to fight. At Calis's insistence, they had continued on. Despite his demand they leave him, they carried him.

Erik had found a deep fissure in the mountain, from which heat rose in shimmering waves. He had ordered the armor and other items thrown into the fissure, certain that even if the heat wasn't sufficient to destroy the Valheru artifacts, no mortal would be able to retrieve them.

A few minutes after he had done this, the mountain shook with a terrible quake, and rocks fell, killing one man, injuring another. A howling wind shot through the tunnel they were in, knocking them down and deafening them for nearly an hour afterward, and a crackle of angry energy shot along the ceiling of the tunnel, as if mad lightning were seeking a way upward, back into the sky.

Erik judged that even when they attempted to destroy those magic items, it was wise not to let them come into contact. He hoped the violence heralded the destruction of the Valheru artifacts.

Then they had been attacked, first by a ragged band of Pantathians, who appeared to have been survivors of the demon's raid on one of the crèches, and twice they had been forced to confront the Saaur. The only reason they were alive was that those other forces were trying to get out of the mountains as desperately as Calis's company, and didn't pursue once combat was broken off.

But the attacks had forced them upward, higher into the mountains. Alfred came from the head of the line and said, "There's a cave ahead."

They entered the cave and Erik looked out its mouth. Arrayed at his feet were the snow-covered peaks of the mountains as the late afternoon sun struck rose and golden highlights across the ridges. For a brief moment he thought that despite his pain and fear, beauty endured, but he was just too tired, hungry, and cold to enjoy it.

"Make camp," he ordered and wondered how long they could survive. Men broke torches out of a backpack and used them to make a small fire. Erik took inventory and judged they had enough food and things they could burn to keep them alive for five or six days. After that, no matter how damaged the men, they would have to start down from the snow line, trying to avoid detection from whatever Pantathians had escaped the destruction of the Dragon Lord artifacts, and find forage enough to keep them going.

He wondered if the horses were still in the valley, and if he could even find that valley. With both Calis and de Loungville hurt, Erik was now leading the survivors.

"Sergeant," said Alfred. "Better come here."

Erik worked past the men struggling to light a fire and knelt next to Alfred. De Loungville's eyes were open.

"Sergeant Major," said Erik.

"How's the Captain?" asked de Loungville.

"Alive," said Erik. He marveled at that simple fact. "Any lesser man would have been dead this morning. He's asleep." Erik looked at the pale complexion of his immediate superior and said, "How are you?"

De Loungville coughed and Erik could see blood fleck the saliva running from his mouth. "I'm dying," said de Loungville in the same matter-of-fact tone in which he would have asked for another helping of supper. "Each breath is . . . harder." He pointed to his side. "I think I have a piece of rib sticking me in the lung." Then he closed his eyes in pain. "I know I have a piece of rib sticking me in the lung."

Erik closed his eyes and fought back regret. If the man had been allowed to rest and if the bone fragments had been discovered, something might have been done, but a fragment sticking him while he was being half carried, dragged, forced to walk . . . it must have been sawing into that lung for half the day. The pain must have been incredible. No wonder de Loungville had been unconscious most of the time.

"No regrets," said de Loungville as if reading Erik's thoughts. He reached out and took Erik's tunic in his hand. Pulling him close, he said, "Keep him alive."

Erik nodded. He didn't need to be told whom de Loungville spoke of. "I will."

"If you don't, I'll come back and haunt you, I swear it." He coughed and the pain was enough to cause his body to spasm, and his eyes filled with tears.

When he could speak again, he whispered, "You don't know, but I was the first. I was a soldier, and he saved me at Hamsa. He carried me for two days. He raised me up!" Tears gathered in Bobby's eyes; Erik couldn't tell if it was from pain or emotion. "He made me important." De Loungville's voice grew even weaker. "I have no family, Erik. He is my father and brother. He is my son. Keep him—" De Loungville's body contorted in spasm, and he spewed blood across his chest. A great racking attempt to breathe brought only tears to his eyes and he pulled himself upright.

Erik wrapped his arms around Bobby de Loungville, holding him close, tightly so he wouldn't flop on the stones, but as gently as he would a child, and listened with tears running down his own cheeks as de Loungville tried to take a breath that would not come. Only a gurgling sound of lungs filling with blood was heard, and then de Loungville went limp.

Erik held him closely for a long minute, letting the tears fall without shame. Then he gently lowered him to the stone. Alfred reached out and closed the now vacant eyes. Erik sat unable to think, until Alfred said, "I'll find a place where the scavengers won't get him, Sergeant."

Erik nodded, and looked back to where Calis lay. Feeling the bitter cold, he began pulling Bobby's heavy cloak off his body. He said to a soldier near by, "Help me. It's what he would have done."

They stripped the Sergeant Major's body and piled the clothing upon the unconscious half-elf. Erik looked at his color and wondered. If he survived the blast in the Pantathian hall, he might survive this cold, provided he could rest and heal.

Erik knew that the only possibility would be to rest a few days, and then cold and hunger would force them out of the cave and down the mountain. He turned as Alfred and another man picked up de Loungville's body and carried it out into the snow, and he returned his gaze to Calis's face.

"I promise, Bobby," Erik said softly. "I'll keep him alive."

A short time later, Alfred and the other soldier returned, and Alfred said, "There's a small ice cave over there." He pointed slightly to the west. "We put him in there and piled some rocks over the entrance." Sitting as close to the fire as he could, he said, "I don't think it ever thaws out up here. He'll be safe there, Sergeant."

Erik nodded. His mind pleaded to fall into black despair, and he felt as if he needed nothing more than to lie down and sleep. Instead he knew he had to plan and to work, for there were six other men, and one very special being who was more than a man, who were now dependent upon him to survive, and he had made a promise, a promise he would honor. He took a deep breath, pushed aside fatigue and failure, and turned his mind to getting everyone out of these mountains.

* * *

Roo looked up as a commotion broke out downstairs. Several voices were raised in protest. "What . . . ?"

"Nakor!" he said as the Isalani gambler hurried up the stairs, a step before three waiters trying to halt him.

"You can't go up there!" shouted Kurt, trying to overtake Nakor.

Roo stood up and said, "It's all right, Kurt. He's an old . . . business associate."

"I tried to tell him," said Nakor. He grinned at Kurt as the now disgruntled waiter turned and descended the stairs.

Roo said, "What brings you here?"

"You do. I just came from the palace, and Lord James tells me he can't give me a ship. I need a ship. He said you have ships, so I came here to get a ship from you."

Roo laughed. "You want me to give you a ship? What for?"

Nakor said, "Calis, Erik, Bobby, the others, they're stuck down in Novindus. Someone has to go get them."

Roo said, "What do you mean, 'stuck'?"

Nakor said, "They went down to find and destroy the Pantathians. I don't know if they destroyed them, but they hurt them badly. Calis sent Miranda to his father on some important business, and now they are all stuck down there with no way to get home. Lord James says he can't spare the ships and is going to keep them here to defend the city. So I thought I'd get one from you."

Roo didn't hesitate, but turned to Jason and said, "What ships of ours are in the harbor?"

Jason consulted a sheaf of paper. Thumbing though the pages, he said, "Six, of the—"

"Which is the fastest?"

"*Bitter Sea Queen*," answered Jason.

"I want it outfitted for a six-month voyage and I want fifty of the toughest mercenaries we can hire ready to go with us at first light tomorrow."

"With us?" asked Nakor.

Roo shrugged. "Erik is the only brother I've known, and if he's down there with Calis, I'm going."

Nakor sat down and helped himself to a cup of coffee from a pot on the corner of Roo's desk. He sipped the hot brew and said, "You going to be able to do this thing?"

Roo nodded. "I've got people I can trust I can leave in charge." He thought of Sylvia and Karli, and then Helen Jacoby, and said, "I need to say a few good-byes."

"I need to eat," answered Nakor. "Oh, Sho Pi is downstairs. Being more polite than I, he believed them when they said he couldn't come up here."

Roo motioned to Jason to fetch Sho Pi and said, "And then I must go find Luis and Duncan. I need to work out who's in charge of what while I'm gone."

Jason nodded and departed, and Roo said, "We'll get them back."

Nakor smiled, nodded, and drank more coffee.

Epilogue

Rescue

ERIK POINTED.

Calis nodded. "I see it."

The five remaining soldiers sat atop a bluff, overlooking the ocean, before a rude hut they had called home for more than two months. "The fisherman who carried word spotted it on the horizon before sundown yesterday. He said they were sailing far to the south of the Queen's ships' normal patrol. Too close to the iceberg floes for anyone who knows the local waters."

"A Kingdom ship?" asked Renaldo, turning to look at Micha, the other soldier who had accompanied Calis, Erik, and Alfred down from the mountains.

"Perhaps," said Calis, forcing himself upright on a makeshift crutch. He had endured punishing conditions when they had come down from the mountains, three months earlier. After six days in the caves, with nothing more than torches and each other for a source of warmth, they had started downward. Calis had regained a bit of strength during that time, but had to be assisted for the first two days.

They reached a cave below the snow line where Erik started a fire and trapped some hares, and they rested another two days. After that it had been a long walk, for not only could Erik not find the valley with the horses in it again, he almost put them on the wrong side of the river Dee, with no way to ford to the southern side.

But eventually they had reached the coast and found the fishing village. The village had been raided by a Saaur patrol, and the drying shed with the Brijaner ship burned down, and the six men left to guard it killed. The Saaur had left warriors behind for two weeks, but when no one returned they had left to rejoin their compatriots. A black despair had washed over all five of them, but after a day of dejection, Erik had organized the other three healthy men and begun a modest camp some distance from the village.

The villagers had been more than willing to help, in exchange for work, and because these men were obviously enemies of their oppressors. Not one member of the village had suggested they be turned over to the Emerald Queen's army.

As they watched, the ship grew slowly on the horizon. At last Calis said, "It's a Kingdom ship."

Alfred and Renaldo let out a whoop of pleasure, while Micha gave a short prayer of thanks to Tith-Onanka, the God of War. Calis stood, leaning on his crutch.

"We'd better get to the village."

Erik walked near Calis in case he needed help. He had taken more damage than any mortal should have to endure, and still he lived. He was healing. He would carry burn scars on the left side of his face, but his hair was growing back. For the severity of the wounds—which Erik had cleaned daily, and regularly performed reiki on—the scars weren't bad. There was some weakness on his left side and he limped, but Erik was certain once they reached the Kingdom, some help, from the Prince's chirurgean or one of the healing priests at one of the temples, would bring the Captain back to his former vigor.

They didn't speak at all of Bobby de Loungville, alone in his icy tomb high in the mountains above. Erik had some vague sense that the unwillingness to speak of the dead was Calis's elven heritage. He also sensed some deep personal loss: Bobby had been more than just a friend to Calis. He had been the first man recruited to Calis's special cause, and he had endured longer than any man in Calis's command.

As they reached the beach, Erik realized with something close to shock that now only Jadow Shati stood longer in term of service to Calis than he, and he had barely served for three years. He shook his head.

Calis noticed and said, "What?"

Erik shrugged. "I was just thinking that longevity isn't a hallmark of this service."

"That's the truth," said Calis. "And I fear the carnage has only just begun. Of us five here, none may be alive when this is all done."

Erik said nothing. They reached the village, where one of the older fishermen, named Rajis, said, "Do you wish to meet that ship?"

"Yes," said Erik. "It is one of ours. It will take us home."

The villager nodded, and shook Erik's hand, then Calis's and the others'. "We can only say thank you," said Calis.

"If we help you in defeating the Emerald Queen, you need not thank us."

They entered a boat and were pushed out into the surf and two fishermen began to row. As the ship approached, Erik said, "That's not a royal ship."

Calis nodded. "They fly a trading banner."

"What?" said Alfred. "It's a merchantman?"

"So it would seem," answered Calis.

After a few minutes, Erik said, "I don't know. . . ." He stood and began waving. As the ship approached, figures on the deck began waving back, then suddenly Erik recognized one of them. "It's Roo!" he shouted. "It's Roo!" A moment later he said, "And Nakor's with him! And Sho Pi!"

Soon they were alongside the ship and a rope ladder was dropped. Two sailors shinnied down ropes and helped Calis climb aboard. Erik waited to be last, then bade the two fishermen good-bye.

When he got on deck, he found Nakor, Sho Pi, and Roo waiting. Roo came over and the two boyhood friends embraced. After a moment, Erik said, "It's good to see you—more than you can ever know."

Looking at the five men, sunburned, undernourished, ragged, and dirty, Roo shook his head. "Just you five?"

"That we know of," said Calis. "Miranda had a dozen with her."

Nakor said, "If they aren't here by now, they didn't get out. She got to Elvandar with a strange man named Boldar. I saw them there. Then Pug sent me to Roo so I could come get you."

Calis stood. "There is much we must talk of, things I saw under the mountains that I don't yet understand. Perhaps your odd perspective on things might help me sort it out."

"We have a long voyage ahead," said Nakor. "Plenty of time to talk. First you need to eat, then sleep. Then Sho Pi and I will look at your wounds."

The other three men were shown below, and Erik said to Roo, "Why you?"

Roo shrugged. "Duke James was loath to lend Nakor a ship. I've come into some money and had a few ships lying around the harbor, so I thought I'd give him one." Glancing at the retreating Isalani's back, he said, "Then when I considered what a maniac he could be, I thought it best if I came along to make sure I got my ship back."

Erik laughed. Roo said, "De Loungville?"

Erik lost his smile. "Up there," he said with a tilt of his chin toward the distant mountains, their peaks hidden by clouds.

Roo was silent for a long moment before he turned toward the quarterdeck. "Captain!"

"Yes, Mr. Avery?"

"Take us home."

"Aye, aye," said the captain. He gave word to the first officer and the ship came about, slowly turning away from Novindus.

Erik put his arm over Roo's shoulder and asked, "Any trouble getting here?"

Roo laughed. "We had a run-in with one of the Queen's smaller cutters. I'd brought along some of the nastier brawlers I could hire on short notice and we let them come alongside us, then we boarded and sank her. I don't think they have much experience with pirates down here."

Erik laughed. "So are you the richest man in the Kingdom yet?"

Roo said, "Probably. If not, I'm working on it." He laughed. "Let's get you some food."

The two men went below, and the ship came fully around and began the long journey back the way she had come, heading for a distant port that the two men called home.